Deadly Finish

JOHN FRANCOME

Deadly Finish

headline

First published in 2009
by HEADLINE PUBLISHING GROUP

First published in paperback in 2010
by HEADLINE PUBLISHING GROUP

4

Cataloguing in Publication Data is available from the British Library

ISBN 978 0 7553 5749 9 (A-format)
ISBN 978 0 7553 4992 0 (B-format)

Typeset in Veljovic by Avon DataSet Ltd,
Bidford on Avon, Warwickshire

Printed and bound in Great Britain by
Clays Ltd, St Ives plc

Headline's policy is to use papers that are natural, renewable and
recyclable products and made from wood grown in sustainable forests.
The logging and manufacturing processes are expected to conform to the
environmental regulations of the country of origin.

HEADLINE PUBLISHING GROUP
An Hachette UK Company
338 Euston Road
London NW1 3BH

www.headline.co.uk
www. hachette.co.uk

Chapter One

June

The train crossed the river twice on the way into London. Why should that be? Mariana wondered. Then she remembered that Ascot was west of the city and the Thames lay like a wriggling snake across the map, looping and doubling back in a way that confused even English natives, which she wasn't. Seven years' residence in a country didn't make you one of those.

She shook thoughts of rivers and snakes from her head and reached for the hand of the man by her side, a tall Yorkshireman, awkwardly trussed up in a morning suit, a top hat perched on his pinstriped knee. He grinned and eagerly returned the pressure of her fingers. A pang of fierce emotion gripped her. She'd promised herself not to fall in love again – it hurt too much when it went wrong. But love was not ordained by logic and what she felt for this particular man broke all the rules she'd laid down for herself. Not even Emile had ruled her heart the way Simon now did. The idea of soon being married to him would have thrilled her – if she wasn't petrified it would never happen.

There was an air of barely suppressed gaiety in the carriage. Most of the passengers were returning from the first day of the Royal Ascot meeting, early birds who had cut out before the last race of the afternoon in order to beat the rush. Many of them carried winnings in their pocket, a substantial lunch in their bellies and more than enough champagne in their veins to keep laughter ringing out. The fact that all were gussied up to the hilt in tailcoats and extravagant summer dresses, with headgear to match, added to the party atmosphere.

Only the man sitting opposite Mariana looked less than enchanted. And Mariana knew that she was the reason. She smiled at him, playing the one card in her life that never failed – her golden Brazilian beauty. But Simon's uncle stared back at her without sympathy, his flinty grey eyes immune to her charm.

Anger flared within her and she quickly looked away. How had he found out? Had someone come to him with information or was it just his natural suspicion that had led him to investigate her story?

Whatever the reason, the man had her measure and she was running out of options. The one she preferred right now was to smash the carriage window and, like some super-powered action heroine, hurl Simon's beloved Uncle Geoffrey out of the speeding train to his death in the river below.

Simon savoured the journey into London in a tipsy glow of well-being. The sun was shining on a brilliant summer afternoon, he was with the two people he loved most in his life – and he had just witnessed the most important winner of his career.

On the face of it, few casual followers of the Flat racing season would have been surprised to see that Willowdale Stables of North Yorkshire had saddled a winner on the first afternoon of Royal Ascot. Willowdale had been winning high-class races for three decades but for the best part of that time Simon's father had been in charge.

As Aquiline had crossed the line ahead of the other nineteen runners in the six-furlong Coventry Stakes, his uncle had grabbed Simon in a hug that con-certinaed the breath from his lungs. 'Just think what your father would say,' he'd blurted into Simon's ear.

'Did Dad ever win the Coventry?' he'd asked once he'd freed himself from his uncle's grip.

'Never. And he tried often enough. It was about the only decent race he didn't win here, mind.'

It was tough to follow a legend. Philip Waterford had built Willowdale from scratch and turned it into the best training yard for Flat horses in the north-east. For thirty years he had sent out horses in the peak of condition to compete at courses throughout the British Isles and, in the latter stages of his career, all over the world. Phil had saddled runners in the Breeder's Cup, the Melbourne Cup and the Arc de Triomphe – which he won twice. Add to that a Derby win and a plethora of victories in Group 1 races and the task of succeeding his father would have daunted men less prone to intimidation than Simon.

A journalist who pounced on Simon after the presen-tation lost no time in bringing up Phil's name. 'I suppose your thoughts are with your father at this moment.'

'I think of him all the time,' Simon said. 'To be honest, I feel a bit of an impostor.'

By his side, Geoff had raised a quizzical eyebrow. As the journalist turned away, he said, 'Don't do yourself down, son. There's no guarantee even Phil would have got that horse here in the shape you did.'

Simon supposed there might be some truth in that. Aquiline was as temperamental as he was quick over the ground. He had taken special handling in the months leading up to this moment. But, as with anything to do with horses in a yard, it had not been him alone who had put in the time. Though he was the boss, training was a team effort. One member of the team in particular sprang to mind – as she invariably did.

'Where's Mariana?' he asked. He looked around for the distinctive figure of his fiancée. At an inch under six feet in a sunshine-yellow dress and a riot of blond shoulder-length curls that no hat could obscure, Mariana was easy to spot. Since she'd exploded into his life, she'd amazed him in many ways – not least in her knowledge and rapport with horses. She gave Aquiline a daily massage, led him out for picks of grass and sought other ways to calm his erratic nature. If anyone deserved special credit for today's performance, it was her. But she had refused to stand on the dais by his side for the presentation or to pose for the photographs that followed. Her modesty was admirable but Simon thought it misplaced, though in the press of events he'd had no chance to persuade her otherwise.

'She's with Jeremy.' Geoff indicated behind Simon where a group of race-goers was assembled around

Aquiline's owner. Even over the chatter of the excited throng wine-merchant Jeremy Masterton's voice could be heard, flowing in an effortless public school drawl as he held court. He cut a handsome figure, every inch the successful racehorse owner in his tailcoat and top hat, which he wore with the ease of long familiarity. It seemed entirely appropriate to Simon that the best-looking woman in sight should be standing by his side. But Mariana caught his glance and rolled her eyes fractionally. Whenever Simon was inclined to be jealous of the man who had ushered this glorious girl into his life, he remembered what she had once said about him. 'I'd only consider going to bed with Jeremy if I had trouble sleeping.'

She patted Jeremy's arm and disengaged herself from the group. Simon savoured the sight of her gliding through the crowd towards him and noted the way she turned heads. It still seemed improbable that she had chosen him to share her future.

'Here she comes,' he said.

Geoff laid a heavy hand on his arm. 'Look, we've got to have a talk.'

'Sure, what about?'

'Not now – later. But it needs to be in private – all right?'

His uncle had seemed intent, his grip urgent. Why was that? Simon wondered as the train travelled onwards.

Often in his life Geoff had wished he were not such a nosy bugger. Important business relationships had gone sour, not to mention a marriage, because he had not been able to resist turning over stones. But any

5

Yorkshireman worth his salt would prefer to be tagged a suspicious bastard than a fool. And a fool is what he would have been if he had not followed his instincts in the matter of Mariana Hamilton.

The first thing his instincts told him was that, just to look at her, the girl from Brazil was clearly out of Simon's league. Compared to her, the honest local lasses his nephew had courted before were drooping lilies in the shade of a magnificent sunflower. She was a woman who wouldn't look out of place on the arm of a prince or a playboy or, at any rate, a sophisticated city smoothy like Jeremy Masterton.

Jeremy, as it happened, had been responsible for introducing Mariana to Simon; she had accompanied him to Willowdale in the spring to look at Aquiline. According to Simon, Jeremy claimed he'd met her at a charity lunch where she'd been the guest of Meg Russell, a well-preserved widow in her fifties who was spending her late husband's fortune on thoroughbreds and her leisure time with Jeremy. Given Meg's friendly nature, her patronage of Mariana seemed credible enough and Geoff had taken the Brazilian girl at face value, even when she took up residence in March at Meg's house across the valley.

Every time Geoff dropped in at Willowdale at the beginning of the Flat season, he encountered Mariana. He could hardly miss her, for Simon was to be found at her side – 'drooling like a lovesick puppy' as Ken, the head lad, put it. According to Ken, Simon had been squiring her around every evening, taking her to the best restaurants and night spots in the county.

Head lad was a misnomer of a title for Ken, he was

at least Geoff's age and a Willowdale stalwart for thirty years. He could be an invaluable source of information, as on this occasion. 'He took her clubbing in Leeds the other night,' Ken confided.

Clubbing? Judging by past behaviour, Simon was as likely to take to the dance floor as walk through a minefield. On the other hand, Mariana seemed capable of luring a lovesick swain wherever she wanted. Even in a shapeless sweater with her honey-blond curls blowing over her unmade-up face, she looked all set for a Sunday supplement photographer to appear and start snapping away.

Ken had guessed what Geoff was thinking. 'The boss has got it bad,' he said.

'Physical infatuation – she's pretty enough. He'll soon get her out of his system.'

Ken had looked at him shrewdly. 'I wouldn't bank on it. She's got a head on her shoulders that one.'

'Really?'

'And she knows how to handle a horse.'

That had been food for thought.

When it became clear that the romance was not going to blow itself out quickly – after Mariana had made herself a fixture at Willowdale House as well as in the yard – Geoff tried to reconcile himself to her presence. Maybe it was simple jealousy that was driving his opposition. After all, no Brazilian angel had ever warmed his bed, nor was ever likely to at his time of life. It would be churlish, he thought, to hold her good looks against her. After all, this was about Simon's happiness, not his. And Simon could hardly keep the grin off his face from morning till night.

His daughter, Alison, was the next to speak up for

the newcomer. 'I went shopping with Mariana in Leeds. She works for a fashion house – or used to.'

'Used to?'

'Till recently, anyway. She's given me a fabulous Brazilian bikini, though I'm not sure I've got the nerve to wear it. It's one of those dental floss ones – you know.'

Geoff wasn't sure he wanted to have this conversation with his daughter. It made him uncomfortable.

'I'll take it to South Africa next time I go out to see Mum,' Alison said. 'See what she thinks.'

Geoff thought that, knowing his ex, she'd probably steal the bikini for herself. Karen kept herself in shape, a necessary requirement for a husband hunter. She was currently on her third, a steel magnate with a weakness for the bottle, hence Alison's residence in England, for which Geoff was profoundly grateful.

'Do you think it will last with this girl and Simon?' he asked.

'God, I hope so. It's about time Simon took up with someone nice. And don't call her "this girl". You should make an effort to get to know her properly.'

Geoff took the comment to heart and treated Mariana to a swanky lunch to unveil her mysteries. And she'd responded up to a point. She'd talked at length about her father and how he had trained many winners in South America – she'd even brought him newspaper cuttings, not that he could read them, being in Portuguese, but the photos were clear. He'd seen for himself how well she sat in a saddle. Her affection for horses was the part of her story he could buy. But what about the rest of it? Her activities from the age of sixteen to the present. Where were the photos and scrapbooks of her life in Europe? Somehow he didn't believe she'd spent all that time marketing bikinis.

He asked her about previous boyfriends but she'd not been forthcoming. There had been one or two but 'no one special'.

The special man in her life turned out to be Simon for, just as Geoff had reconciled himself to Mariana's place in the yard, his nephew announced his engagement.

'Are you sure?' was the first thing he said. 'You've known her less than a month.'

But there was no budging Simon. 'We won't get hitched till the summer. Give you time to get used to it, Uncle.'

'*This* summer?' At first Geoff had thought his nephew had been joking but it turned out he'd been serious. There was a registry office booked for next month.

Simon was a man of twenty-nine, running his own business and making daily decisions on the welfare of animals worth hundreds of thousands of pounds. Geoff didn't feel he had any option but to clap him on the back and say, 'Congratulations.'

But his misgivings would not be denied. He owed it to Simon's parents – his late sister and brother-in-law – to satisfy himself that Mariana was no more or less than she claimed to be. He'd promised Phil as he waited for the operation to clear the cancer from his throat that, if it came to the worst, he'd look out for Simon as if he were his own son. In truth that's how he felt about the lad. And though Phil had survived the op, the worst had come along just the same three agonising months later.

He was duty bound to investigate the girl's background.

He tried the civilised route, quizzing Mariana about her family, and discovered that all her relatives, barring a half-sister, were – conveniently – no longer living. Then he tried talking to Meg and Jeremy. Meg, it turned out, had only recently become acquainted when Mariana had approached her to recommend a possible distributor for a line of Brazilian beachwear. And Jeremy said that she was a protégée of Meg's, then admitted that he'd known Mariana for 'a year or two' from bumping into her at fund-raising events for the Jockeys Disability Charity, of which he was a trustee. And Geoff had learned no more than that, even when he confided in Jeremy that he was thinking of hiring a private inquiry agent to look into Mariana's past on behalf of his nephew.

Jeremy had been less than impressed. 'Good God, man, Simon's old enough to choose his own wife, isn't he?'

In consequence, Geoff didn't feel he had much option but to put the matter in the hands of a professional. Within days he'd hit paydirt. Dirt, anyway.

To her credit, Mariana didn't deny what he'd discovered though she did try to explain. She'd been a penniless student at the time and escort work paid the bills and left her time for her studies. She'd given it up years ago.

Geoff wasn't unsympathetic. The girl had been on her own in London with rent to pay. In those circumstances a person might well cash in whatever chips they held – and Mariana's assets were undeniably bankable.

It was when Mariana insisted that all she had done was to sell her company to a few lonely men that Geoff felt his heart harden. He didn't take kindly to having the wool pulled over his eyes. He'd seen the prices listed by the escort agency on the internet. Not even millionaires paid that kind of money simply for a dinner companion. All the same, he agreed to allow her to tell Simon herself. He told himself that people were allowed youthful mistakes. If Simon could live with the knowledge that his fiancée had subsidised her studies by selling herself, then that was his business. He had no doubt that Mariana would be persuasive.

But, as he sat on the train opposite his lovesick nephew and the girl who had bewitched him, he guessed that she had not kept her promise. Well, if Mariana wouldn't come clean herself than he would have to do the deed. He regretted that he hadn't done it already.

Simon had been pondering Geoff's request to have a private talk. Despite Aquiline's win and the prevailing party mood, Simon could plainly see that something was eating away at his uncle. Even Mariana, it seemed, couldn't cheer him up. As their journey approached its end – just one more stop remained before Waterloo – Simon reckoned he had worked out what was on Geoff's mind: a horse called Jennifer Eccles.

Aquiline wasn't the only fancied runner from Willowdale taking part in the Royal Ascot meeting. Jennifer Eccles was entered for Friday's big race, the Coronation Stakes, a mile-long contest for three-year-old fillies. Although she was among the fancied runners she hadn't enjoyed the most conventional start to her racing career. Arriving in the yard at the beginning of the previous season, she had picked up an injury before she'd even seen a racecourse. One niggle led to another and throughout the summer she remained on the sick list, to the frustration of one of her owners, Charlie Talbot. Charlie had acquired the horse in partnership with Geoff who had spotted her at the Deauville sales and bought her for £20,000. At the end of the season, without Jenny making one appearance in a race, Charlie had blown his top.

Geoff had brought him to the yard to look the horse over and Simon summarised what the vet had told him about her condition the previous day. It boiled down to the fact that Jennifer Eccles had split a pastern bone and no one had a clue how long it would take to mend – if ever.

'So you're saying she might never race at all?' Charlie was a jumbo-sized Cockney who'd made money developing houses in the south-east property boom. He looked quite capable of putting an apartment block up with his bare hands – or tearing it down.

'I wouldn't bank on it,' Simon said in reply. 'It happens sometimes – a horse doesn't ever get fit enough to run. It's a pity. She's such a pretty thing.'

She was too, a shapely chestnut with a blaze of white running from her brow down to the tip of her nose.

'She'd be a damn sight prettier turned into dog meat,' Charlie snapped. 'At least then I'd have something to sell. She's costing me an arm and a leg just to keep her in this luxury hotel of yours.'

Though Charlie wasn't exactly a charmer, Simon could understand how he felt. Keeping a horse in training wasn't cheap, even if you shared the cost, as Charlie was doing with Geoff. What with regular vet's bills and no outings to the racecourse to look forward to, it was not surprising Charlie was unhappy. Simon had heard from Geoff that the big man was feeling the pinch now the property market had gone sour.

'You can sell out to me, if you like.'

Simon was as surprised by Geoff's words as Charlie obviously was.

'What do you mean?'

'I feel I've landed you with a bad investment so I'll buy you out. I'll give you fifteen thousand for her.'

It was a generous offer as Charlie had only paid £10,000 for his share in the first place, particularly considering that it was unlikely the horse even had a future in racing.

Charlie's big pink face screwed into an expression that plainly said, 'What's the catch?'

'You'll give me fifteen grand for a horse with a wonky leg? What do you know that I don't?'

'Nothing. As I said, I'm the reason you invested in the horse and you haven't even got a run out of her. I feel responsible.' Geoff broke into an unexpected grin. For much of the time he could be mistaken for a caricature of a stony-featured Yorkshireman. His smile was all the more persuasive as a result. 'I'll give you back the ten for your half and another five to make up for what you've laid out in stable costs. Deal?' He held out his hand.

As Simon remembered, the big man almost snapped his uncle's arm off in his eagerness to accept.

The irony was that from the moment Charlie bowed out of the picture, Jennifer Eccles began to pick up. Over the winter, the leg which had bothered her had healed and grown strong. By early spring, Simon was able to give her some serious work and she surprised everyone with her speed. She made her debut at Bath in April and won in a canter by ten clear lengths.

Shortly after her second win in a listed race at Newmarket, Charlie Talbot paid an unannounced visit to the yard. Simon, though pushed for time, proudly showed him a resurgent horse.

'She doesn't look any bloody different to last time.'

'Believe me, she is. The vet said it would take time for her to recover and it did.'

Charlie wasn't impressed. 'As I remember it, there wasn't any guarantee she'd recover at all. Last time I saw her she was only fit for dog food.'

'You said that, Charlie, not me.'

The big man ignored the rebuke.

'So what's she worth now then?'

'I couldn't say exactly.'

'There's a surprise. More than a measly fifteen grand though, eh? Probably ten times that. And if she wins big races and goes on to breed she'll be worth millions.'

'Hang on, don't get carried away.'

'Don't tell me what to do, you long streak of Yorkshire piss. You and your uncle stitched me up like a kipper.' He turned the malevolent glare of his beetroot-red face full on Simon, his small blue eyes like chips of ice. 'Tell dear Uncle Geoff he'll be hearing from my solicitor very shortly.'

But it was Dave, the vet, who received the letter,

demanding past medical reports on the horse's condition. Dave showed it to Simon with some amusement. 'He won't get any joy out of me,' he said. 'I always said she might improve with time and she did. End of story.'

Geoff had been disappointed, as he put it, to hear of these developments. 'I'll give Charlie a call,' he told Simon.

'Well, for God's sake, don't give him any more money. You've been more than fair with him.'

'Don't worry. I'll sort it out.'

But whatever was said on the phone had not smoothed the matter over. Simon learned that Charlie had subsequently turned up at Geoff's west London home with a couple of rough-looking labourers. He claimed they were working on a development just round the corner from Geoff's property and were passing on the off chance.

'He had the nerve to present me with an invoice which valued Jennifer Eccles at a quarter of a millions pounds,' Geoff told him. 'Taking into account the ten grand I'd reimbursed him, he was looking for one hundred and fifteen thousand.'

Simon had laughed – it seemed the only sane response. 'What about the other five you paid him?'

'He said I'd given him that for the training fees, so it didn't go to the value of the horse. On reflection, paying him that extra has caused all this trouble. I only did it because it was the first horse he'd had a part of and I felt bad about the way things had turned out.'

Simon saw the point. It had made the buyout seem too good to be true for a man with a suspicious nature.

'Charlie's not a man who believes in luck,' Geoff had added. 'He's the wrong type to get involved in horseracing.'

Amen to that, Simon had thought.

Since then, he had learned, Charlie's builders had been seen sitting in a van outside Geoff's flat. Geoff didn't have a regular schedule for his London visits but somehow these men seemed to know his movements. When he accosted them, they suggested that they'd leave him alone once he'd settled Mr Talbot's invoice.

Simon wasn't up to date on recent developments in the argument – last time he'd asked, Geoff had said curtly, 'Forget it, it'll blow over soon', but he'd spotted Talbot's familiar figure in the crush at Ascot that afternoon, his bulk uncomfortably encased in a grey morning suit. Geoff had seen him too, Simon knew, and he'd turned away to avoid coming face to face with his adversary just before the running of the Coventry.

Simon wouldn't be at all surprised if this business with Talbot was what was depressing Geoff. That night they were due at a dinner with Jeremy to celebrate Aquiline's victory but he'd make a point of talking to his uncle before they went out. It wasn't fair that he should carry the burden on his own.

Mariana noticed the two men step into the carriage as the train pulled out of Richmond. She knew they hadn't just got on because she'd seen them on the platform at Ascot. They'd stuck out from the crowd because they plainly weren't race-goers. One was short, in jeans and a white vest which showed off muscular arms. The other was tall, maybe as tall as Simon though it was hard to tell because his height was exaggerated by his haircut of tall, greased-up spikes. Surrounded by men in their Ascot racing uniform, the pair were hard to miss. Mariana had been amused at the incongruity and the way that neither the race-goers nor the scruffs appeared to acknowledge the others' presence.

The English were meant to be sober and conservative in their choice of clothes but, in her observation, they could be as flamboyant in their way as any other race on earth – some of the Ascot fashions on show proved that. What set them apart was their ability to walk through the world in a bubble of isolation. Nobody, for example, appeared to notice the man on the train who had spent his entire journey so far knitting. He sat a few rows down the carriage on the other side of the train clicking away with what looked like one long needle bent back on itself, the two ends fencing with a strand of olive-green wool. She watched, diverted from her troublesome thoughts by the clicking of those two points, wondering why no one else appeared to find this behaviour odd. A grown man, dressed like an office worker in suit and tie, was skilfully knitting a sweater. It was weird. But then, given the top hats and tailcoats and the glistening black spikes of the hairdo of the guy walking down the aisle, this train seemed positively surreal.

Spiky hair passed the knitting man without a glance and stopped by Simon. His companion slumped into the empty seat beside Geoffrey and stared insolently into her face.

How typical. They had ignored everyone else but now they had decided to pick on her.

Geoff turned from the window to look at the fellow who'd taken the seat next to him. He registered an unshaven face and bare arms, a silver bracelet on the wrist. The man standing in the aisle next to Simon was more noteworthy. What kind of idiot went round with his hair sticking up like that? He thought that look had gone out with Sid Vicious.

The train began to slow as it approached Clapham Junction and Geoff found himself hoping that these two clowns would get off. The standing guy was openly staring down the front of Mariana's dress. She was undoubtedly the reason the men had invaded their space. Put out the honeypot and the flies will appear.

The spiky-haired fellow said something Geoff didn't catch but his friend sniggered and Simon turned and glared at him.

'What did you just say?' The tone was sharp.

Mariana laid her hand on Simon's arm.

The reply was clear this time. Loud and provocative. 'I said the bitch has nice tits.'

Simon's eyes narrowed with fury. Geoff noticed Mariana's knuckles whiten as she restrained him.

The man spoke again. 'So which of you two ugly bastards is banging her?'

Time froze for a second. Part of Geoff's brain registered that they were pulling into a busy station, the platform teeming.

Simon sprang to his feet and swung a punch. The spike-haired man appeared unsurprised. It's what he wants, thought Geoff as the fellow stepped inside the blow and butted his nephew in the face.

But he was on his feet himself by then, jabbing with a left he knew had the power to lay this scum on his back. He'd boxed as a lad, still trained on a punchbag at the gym twice a week, he'd take this arrogant fool apart with the greatest pleasure.

I'll knock his head off, he thought as he launched himself forward.

Mariana watched in disbelief as the brawl erupted out of nowhere. Blood spattered over her magnificent yellow dress as Simon clutched his wounded face. Geoff threw himself at Simon's assailant but the man in the vest blocked him and held him back.

The train had stopped in the station and there were shouts and yells down the carriage. A woman's screams sounded over the signal that the doors were opening and the two attackers were gone, pushing their way out of the carriage and disappearing into the crowd on the platform. No one, it seemed, tried to stop them but she wasn't looking any longer. She knelt on the floor in front of Simon.

'Let me see, let me see!' she cried.

Other passengers were there now, offering handkerchiefs and strong hands. Simon was helped into a seat.

'He'll be all right,' a voice said in her ear.

She looked for Geoff and realised he was lying next to her on the floor.

Across the aisle the man in the business suit was staring at her with a blank white face. Shock, she thought. At least he'd stopped knitting.

'I can't find a pulse,' said someone.

Her legs were wet. She was kneeling in blood. The dress was ruined.

'I think he's dead,' said the voice. 'He's been stabbed.'

Mariana's heart lurched within her chest but Simon was looking at her now, battered but undeniably alive.

They were talking about Geoff.

Oh God.

Somehow, given her sinful thoughts and all that she had done, she knew it had to be her fault.

Chapter Two

March

Simon wasn't in the yard when Mariana paid her first visit to Willowdale but he heard about it. The latest blonde to emerge from Jeremy Masterton's Jag had apparently stopped half his staff in their tracks – the male half, that is. The girls also conceded, though with more reservation, that the girl had been remarkably pretty.

Simon heard the news with weary resignation. He knew how much Jeremy liked to show off the symbols of success – his car, his racehorse, a glamorous female companion. As Simon was in the business of keeping his owners happy he played his part in making everyone welcome at the yard, though it was not possible to be entirely unstinting in his admiration. For he was aware that the car belonged to Meg's late husband and Jeremy had it on permanent loan; that Aquiline was the first decent animal Jeremy had ever owned; and that the girl was just the latest in a line of attractive young women he tried to impress. Simon had no doubt that, when bedtime came, Jeremy would be laying his head on Meg's pillow. And he didn't imagine that today's blonde visitor would be seen in his yard again.

He was forced to reconsider the next day when the girl returned, this time in Meg Russell's Range Rover. There was no sign of Jeremy, just the two women. This was a turn-up for the books. Meg had never been known to bond with any of Jeremy's young guests.

The woman was a few years younger than Simon, in her early twenties he supposed. Tall and slender, her hair streamed behind her like a banner in the breeze, attracting all eyes as she strode across the courtyard. Up close, her skin was a creamy café au lait of impossible perfection. She wore a brand-new fleece and jodhpurs that appeared sprayed on to her long legs. Her pristine riding boots gleamed. If *Vogue* had dressed her for the occasion, Simon would not have been surprised. She didn't look real to him and, as a Yorkshire trainer with his feet firmly planted on the ground his father had bequeathed him, reality was what mattered.

Mariana was Brazilian, he was told. Or half Brazilian, since her father was English and she'd been brought up in South America; her father, now dead, had been a successful trainer over there. Mariana loved horses and was thrilled to visit a fantastic yard like Willowdale.

This information was mostly conveyed by Meg. The girl only said enough to confirm her mentor's enthusiasm.

Simon filed all of it away under 'bullshit' and, while making the necessary responses, kept a lid on mounting irritation. Maybe it was her cover-girl perfection or his natural suspicion of women who were too pretty – based on painful recent experience – but after he saw her look with disdain at the dirty manger in a horse's stall, he realised he didn't want her at Willowdale. Her presence was a distraction a busy working yard could do without – especially if she was going to criticise the way things were done.

That said, she was right. The manger was a disgrace and he made a note to get Ken on the case. Clean mangers and water buckets didn't make horses run any faster but it was a question of standards and he didn't want to let his slip.

However, when Meg announced that Mariana was her guest for a few days and asked if Simon would mind her coming over in the mornings to ride out, what could Simon say? He'd known Meg all his life – she'd only ceased to be 'Auntie Meg' since his father's death – and he could hardly refuse. Particularly since the girl would be riding one of Meg's horses. So he forced a smile and agreed to the request but he resolved to avoid having anything to do with her. And for the next few days he'd steadfastly turned his gaze away when he'd glimpsed an elegant rider in the distance on the gallops.

Circumstances intervened. When there was a scare about Meg's horse Soft Centre, a fancied contender for the Lincoln handicap, Simon put in a call to Meg and she turned up with Mariana in tow. He led them to the paddock where a deep-chested grey horse with a scarlet rug on his back was being led round by Ken.

'There's my boy,' Meg cried. 'Didn't I tell you he was handsome?'

All owners thought their horses were handsome, in

Simon's experience, and he would never dream of arguing with them. After all, being horses, by definition they were all glorious creatures. But having grown up with the animals, he was well-attuned to their individual peculiarities of looks and personality. To him, Soft Centre was an average-looking fellow with a stubborn disposition and only one real talent – to gallop like the wind when conditions were right. And conditions were far from right at present.

The Brazilian girl was cooing over the horse in predictable fashion, tickling his chin, while Meg looked on indulgently.

'Mind your fingers,' Simon said. 'He'll make a mess of your manicure if he gives you a nip.'

The girl turned her black eyes on him. 'He won't bite me,' she said with a smile, 'but would you prefer I did not touch him?'

He couldn't help noticing that her teeth were small, white and perfect. And that the raw wind that whistled down his neck appeared to have no effect on her. Even Meg, a stylish and always well-presented woman, sported a nose red with cold.

'No, you go ahead,' he said, trying not to sound too grudging, 'just don't say I didn't warn you.'

'So what's the matter with him?' Meg said. 'He looks fine to me.'

'I know but he's got a sore on his belly and we can't put a saddle on him at the moment.'

She looked dismayed. 'You mean he's got some kind of infection?'

'No. It's just a sore spot. The girth has pinched him for some reason and we can't get a saddle on him.'

Meg looked relieved. 'I thought you were going to

tell me something serious. That he couldn't run next week.'

'Well, I'm not sure he can.' This was the awkward part. Even though Simon loomed over Meg by almost a foot he felt like a small boy again as she scrutinised him with a familiar penetrating stare. 'He's a stuffy sod and if we can't get some work into him before Saturday it will be a waste of time going. It would be fine if we could swim him but the only time we put him in the pool he nearly drowned. He's a horse who needs to be exercised if he's got any chance in a race like the Lincoln.'

Meg nodded, absorbing the information. Other owners might have embarked on recriminations – how had some fool managed to over-tighten the girths? – but Meg was a businesswoman, a director of her late husband's retail business, and more concerned with solving the problem.

'What do you normally do when this sort of thing happens?'

'We give the horse a few days to recover. And if he has to work, we put him on a lead rein and exercise him from another animal.'

'But you can't do that with Softy?'

The truth was, they couldn't. 'We tried it this morning and he wasn't having any of it. Just dug his feet in. You know what he's like.'

Meg nodded – she knew. If Soft Centre's lineage had included a mule, no one would have been surprised.

'Why don't you ride him without a saddle?' said the girl.

Simon was astonished she'd even followed the conversation.

'He's hard enough to ride with a saddle,' he snapped.

The force of his words registered on her face. 'I'm sorry, I just thought if the saddle was a problem . . .' Her voice tailed off.

'It's not a bad idea, is it?' said Meg.

Simon took a breath. 'Not in theory, no. But nobody ever rides bareback. There's no one here who's ever had any experience of doing it. Isn't that right, Ken?'

The older man chewed on the thought. 'None of them would have a clue,' he said.

'I can do it,' the girl said. 'That was how my father taught me to ride.'

Simon was rendered almost speechless. He managed one word. 'No.'

'Why not, Simon?' Meg's hand was on his arm. 'She could do us a good turn.'

'Oh yes, please.' The girl's eyes were huge with excitement.

Simon turned to Ken for support but the head lad was a man of his own mind. He ignored Simon's glare and said, 'I don't see why not. Just be careful, lass, eh?'

Simon could have put his foot down, he supposed. His father would have done so but he prided himself on being less of a curmudgeon than his old man. In his father's day, Willowdale had been a dictatorship but Simon had no desire to be a dictator.

He turned to the girl and spoke to her seriously for the first time. 'Do you really know what you are doing?'

She didn't answer directly but looked him in the

eye. 'Don't worry, Mr Waterford, I will look after your horse.'

And she did. Ten minutes later, Simon was watching Mariana ride Soft Centre around the paddock without the benefit of a saddle. There had been a certain amount of fussing around as the horse was tacked up to the girl's satisfaction, with a strap around his neck and a thick pad over his withers. Finally Ken had boosted her on to the animal's back where she had remained with surprising ease and no little form.

'Don't they make a picture,' Meg purred by his side.

Simon made no comment.

Mariana relaxed into the passenger seat of Meg's car. She'd tried to keep up her riding but it hadn't been easy living in London. She'd certainly not ridden without a saddle for some years. It was funny that the body did not forget, however.

'So, what did you think of that?'

Meg's sharp eyes were on her, eager for her impressions.

'It was wonderful.' She spoke from the heart. To be in a real racing yard had been a thrill and she was going back to ride Soft Centre again, Meg had arranged it with the trainer. 'But,' she added, 'I don't think Mr Waterford likes me.'

'Nonsense. You're doing him a favour.'

'Well, he seemed very bad-tempered.'

Meg laughed and started the car. 'Simon's bark is worse than his bite. Don't take any notice of that.'

'OK then – I won't.'

When she'd been told – by Jeremy, back in London – that she'd be visiting Willowdale she had looked the yard up on the web. Naturally she'd been impressed by the extensive grounds, the fine horses and the celebrity owners but she'd been a bit surprised that the business was headed by a man not much older than she was. There was something about his picture on screen that brought to mind old photographs of her father – a tall, skinny man with unruly fair hair and kind eyes.

In the flesh, despite his abrupt manner, those eyes had still held warmth. But he was critical and defensive, wary of a woman like her, she could see that. She didn't mind. A blunt honest man was such a contrast to the many smooth operators in her past. She'd like to make a friend of a man like him, who wasn't impressed by her looks. But first she'd have to prove herself in his eyes. Luckily, with Soft Centre, she might have a way of doing it.

It had been a good night at Hughie's wine bar in north-west London but the party crowd had now rolled home. Hughie was eager to get going himself, particularly since he had someone to roll home with. Carla rarely paid a visit to the bar these days but she had been a guest of the insurance broker who had hired the downstairs room for his fortieth and Hughie had persuaded her to stay on for a nightcap. She stood on the wine bar step, a wrap around her bare shoulders, puffing on a cigarette as Hughie helped the lads load the van with the last of the sound system. She'd spent regular intervals on that step throughout the night. The smoking ban, Hughie reflected, had brought about many converts to fresh air.

He paid off his two boys and threw in a couple of

bottles as an extra thank you. 'No need to open the shop on the dot,' he'd added as they headed off to his music store in Kilburn, where they dossed down in the rooms above.

'You and I have a lot in common,' Carla said as the van drove off. She lit another cigarette and offered Hughie the packet.

'Meaning?' He'd given up years ago, in the first flush of the new century, a decision he was proud of. He took a cigarette anyway – the odd one didn't count.

'I mean you care about the next generation. You want a better life for them than you had.'

He chuckled. 'Because I give them a bit of extra after a hard evening?'

She drew heavily on the white tube in her mouth. Her lips were full and the angles of her face sharp. In the pale light of the night-time street she looked half her age. At twenty-five, he reflected, she must have been a real looker.

'Because,' she said, 'you care for these boys who are scuffling around, trying to survive playing music. It's a tough business.'

'You're not kidding.' He spoke from experience. The wine bar and shop were a middle-aged compromise. It wasn't exactly following his musical dream but it was a realistic means of living a life. Anyway, he couldn't say he had a musical dream these days – maybe he'd never had one. 'I remember what I was like at their age, that's all. You need a bit of a helping hand.'

'Exactly. I do the same for my girls.'

Hughie suppressed a chuckle, though not well enough.

'You think that's funny?' There was a harsh note to her smoky voice. 'Girls shouldn't spend too long in my business. The smart ones get out early, use it as a stepping stone. Those are the ones I like to help.'

Hughie considered the notion of a madam happily losing her best whores. He supposed there were always plenty of fresh faces happy to be represented by Carla's escort agency. At the rates charged by Chrysalis Girls, they would hardly be slumming it. However, he couldn't see much of a comparison between Carla's highly priced protégées and the scruffy guitar-strummers who crashed out at his place in Kilburn. He kept his mouth shut, content to let his companion expand on her generous nature. A long night on the Pinot Grigio had loosened her tongue, for once.

'You'd be surprised where some of my girls end up. Estate agents, car dealers, conference managers. I can lift the phone to government departments and law firms and get help if I need to.'

'Really?' Hughie took the information with a pinch of salt, though Carla undoubtedly knew many influential people who relied on her discretion. 'So where's the best place one of your . . . graduates has ended up?'

She took the last drag from her cigarette and ground the lipstick-stained butt into the pavement. 'The best place?' She considered the matter and shrugged. 'Best for who? I think I might have some success in helping a girl at the moment and it really would be the best thing for her.'

Hughie waited impatiently. He was eager to get her home now but he knew better than to force the pace.

'What does she want to do?' he asked, as was expected.

'To train racehorses. She's passionate about it. Imagine that.'

As a matter of fact, Hughie could do that quite easily. He burst out laughing. The idea of Carla turning one of her little tarts into a trainer was really quite funny.

'You've got no chance,' he said.

The early morning weather was filthy up on the gallops and the damp even seemed to penetrate Simon's rainwear, reviving an old ache in his shoulder. Once the Willowdale horses had returned to the yard, Simon retreated to the office to dry off and make some calls. He was washing down paracetamol with a much-needed mug of tea when Ken stepped in.

The older man raised an eyebrow at the sight of the painkillers and Simon pulled a rueful face. There was no need for explanation. Ken had driven him to A&E the day he'd been dumped off his hunter shortly after he'd taken over from his father. He didn't ride out so much these days.

'You owe me a fiver, boss.' There was a gleam of satisfaction in Ken's eye. 'She showed up like she said.'

'Seriously?' But there was no need to query the older man. Simon shoved his hand in his pocket and handed over a crumpled blue note.

With the sleety rain gusting across the hillside in the grey morning, he'd announced with confidence that Meg's houseguest would not arrive to exercise Soft Centre as she had promised. Ken had disagreed – hence the small wager. Simon might be the governor in the yard but it rarely paid to disagree with the head lad.

The wind rattled the windowpane as a reminder of the elements.

'Where is she?' Simon said.

'I sent her off on her own. No point in getting revved up with the rest of the string. I told her you would meet her at the bottom of the all-weather gallop. She looks great.'

'Huh.' Simon reached for his damp jacket. 'It's not what she looks like that bothers me. They won't get too many gales like this out on the Pampas or wherever she comes from.'

'I believe the Pampas is in Argentina.'

'Clever old sod, aren't you?'

Simon grabbed the keys to the Land Rover. He was more concerned about the horse, he told himself. The Lincoln was just a few days off and it was his responsibility to make sure Soft Centre got there ready to run.

He drove up the track in second gear, his wheels bestriding the muddy stream that inundated the middle of the pathway. He parked under the large oak that marked the lower boundary of the open hillside and peered through the slanting rain for sight of horse and rider. They were about half a mile away, making their way towards him.

It was impossible to tell that Mariana didn't have a saddle. Whoever had taught her to ride had done a good job. Riding was as much to do with confidence as skill and it was plain the girl possessed the inner belief that told her that what she was doing on a horse was right. Not that it was something that Simon had ever felt himself.

He got out of the Land Rover. 'Are you OK?'

'Yes, he's fine,' she said. 'What would you like him to do?'

Mariana had been up the gallop a couple of times so at least she knew where she was going and, more importantly, exactly where the gallop ended. The biggest problem in riding any racehorse was slowing the animal down but Soft Centre had been up on this gallop nearly every day for the last two seasons. He would know himself when it was time to ease off.

'Just go a good strong canter for four furlongs then let him stride along for the last bit. If you can't pull him up at the end, steer him to the left in a big circle so that he doesn't head back home. But he should be fine.'

Simon got back in the vehicle and drove to a spot where he could see the entire gallop. Even at this stage he still had reservations about the girl riding bareback. There weren't many professional jockeys who would do what Mariana was about to do – he certainly wouldn't do it himself.

The rain speared down as Soft Centre set off and got straight into his stride. Simon watched Mariana in admiration. He realised she must possess extraordinary strength and balance because she was somehow able to maintain herself in a jockey's crouch with no irons. She looked in perfect control as she put the horse through his paces.

Mariana had slowed Soft Centre to a walk at the end of the gallop when suddenly a pheasant shot out of the undergrowth and up into the leaden sky with a shriek.

Soft Centre reared upwards in panic, pitching the girl from his back. He began running backwards, dragging the girl across the turf as she hung on to the reins.

Simon swore out loud. This was just the kind of thing he'd been afraid of. Ken should never have let her out on her own. Though if she was hurt it was her own stupid fault.

No, that wasn't true. It was his yard. It would be his fault.

Simon was out of the Land Rover making for Soft Centre, who'd come to a halt, the girl in a heap on the wet ground at his feet. Simon didn't run, fearful of spooking the horse further. He'd barely made ten yards when Mariana rose from the turf and somehow, in a miraculous fluid motion, hopped up on to the horse's back.

He laid a hand upon the horse's bridle and looked up at her.

She was a far different woman to the fashion plate who had been turning heads in the yard. She looked as if she'd been pitched into a puddle of mud, with scarcely an inch of her once pristine riding jacket and caramel-coloured jodhpurs not soaked and stained an earthy brown. Her face was as spattered and grass-stained as if she'd been camouflaged for a commando exercise. There was no blood and bruising, as he had feared, and no sign of tears. Her face was split from side to side in a melon-sized grin – she really did have an enormous mouth, he thought.

He'd raced up here prepared to shout at her, then as he'd watched her tumble he'd been terrified by his own concern. But now, he couldn't help it, he laughed. She'd never feature in the pages of *Vogue* looking like that.

Her eyes – they were freakishly large too – flashed with an emotion he couldn't read. Anger no doubt.

'I'm sorry,' he said eventually. 'You look very funny.'

She ignored the remark and he realised she wasn't angry at all, just exultant.

'Mr Waterford,' she said, leaning her muddy face closer, 'this is a fantastic horse!'

It occurred to him that it wasn't just the horse who was fantastic.

He shut the thought off as quickly as it had occurred and turned for the warmth of his vehicle. In a few days Soft Centre would be in good enough condition to take the field in the Lincoln. Then there would be no need for Mariana to return to Willowdale.

As he drove back down the slippery path his shoulder hurt like buggery.

Hughie was surprised to catch sight of a familiar face on the far side of the bar. From this morning's conversation with Carla – he'd succeeded in persuading her to stay the night – he'd assumed Jeremy Masterton would still be in Yorkshire. His presence in London was surely not good news for that lady's most recent philanthropic scheme.

He approached Jeremy from behind and laid a hand on his arm, interrupting his animated conversation with Susie behind the bar. She shot Hughie a glance of gratitude as Jeremy turned towards him.

'Stop distracting my staff, you old lecher,' Hughie said with a broad grin.

'Just because you want to keep all these beautiful

girls to yourself,' Jeremy replied, turning back to the bar. But Susie had seized her chance and moved swiftly to the other end of the counter.

Jeremy grinned – his air of confident self-satisfaction would be hard to puncture.

'I thought you were up in Yorkshire,' Hughie said.

'God's own country.' Nobody could sound less like a Yorkshireman than Jeremy but Hughie knew that, as a boy, Jeremy had spent many school holidays with a horse-mad uncle and aunt in Leyburn.

'I'm backwards and forwards all the time,' Jeremy added, 'as you know.'

'Keeping the fragrant Meg happy.'

'Of course.' Jeremy raised his glass in a salute, then swallowed its contents. 'And keeping an eye on my horse. Best I've ever owned.'

Hughie tried to keep a straight face but Jeremy divined what he was thinking.

'Yes, I know that wouldn't be hard but Aquiline is special. He's going to win a decent race or two this season. And next year, who knows?'

'A Derby winner at last, eh?'

'Well . . .' he laughed. 'You're trying to get me to say something stupid, aren't you?'

Hughie nodded, he enjoyed winding Jeremy up about his God-awful nags.

'Seriously,' Jeremy continued, 'the trainer thinks this is a horse to go to war with.'

'The trainer would be young Master Waterford, I take it?'

'Simon, yes. He's a bright fellow – I keep telling you.'

'A chip off his miserable old man's block.'

36

'Actually, I think he's his own man and he's certainly not miserable.'

'And is Simon impressed by the little tart you've been flashing around his yard?'

Jeremy stared at Hughie in surprise. 'How do you know about that?'

Hughie intended to milk the moment and let Jeremy stew but his friend drew the obvious conclusion.

'You've been talking to Carla, haven't you?'

'Better than that.'

Jeremy let the remark sink in. 'In that case, I suppose she told you I was doing her a favour. And Willowdale as well, as it happens. Mariana's a decent rider. She's helping to get one of Meg's horses in shape for the Lincoln.'

'Sounds like it's favours all round then,' Hughie said and he signalled to Susie for another bottle.

Simon had been in love properly just once. The affair had started off sweet but soon turned sour. He looked back on it now as one of the worst experiences of his life. Like Mariana, Caroline had been a head-turner, and three months into their affair she'd turned the head of a college friend and gone off to wreak havoc with him instead. Simon was of the opinion that those who compared falling in love with catching a disease were on the right track. And up on the rainy gallops with the muddy Brazilian girl he had felt the onset of familiar symptoms.

When she turned up two days before the Lincoln in her little red car, he waylaid her.

'Soft Centre is fine now,' he said. 'So I've arranged

for you to ride out for another yard down the road.'

Her face fell. 'Have I done something wrong?'

'Not at all. You've been terrific. But I have a roster of staff who earn their living here. We don't need anyone else.'

The light seemed to drain from her golden complexion.

'I've upset somebody?'

'Not at all. It's just that it – you coming along every day – it upsets the apple cart.'

He'd put it badly but the message was clear. She'd nodded and accepted his thanks for all her hard work. Then they'd shaken hands and she'd got into her car. She'd sat for a long time in the driver's seat, staring ahead, then wiping her eyes before driving off. He'd watched from the office window.

That day, one of the girls was off sick and Simon's shoulder hurt like hell from reading in bed half the night because he couldn't sleep.

Ken took him aside. 'A word of advice, Mr Waterford?'

It irritated Simon no end when Ken called him that. Ken had been as much a part of his growing up as his father or his uncle, he'd clipped him round the ear as a boy and taught him to ride and he couldn't run the place without the older man. And he only called Simon 'Mr Waterford' when he thought Simon was ballsing things up.

'OK, Ken, tell me what's wrong.'

'You shouldn't have made that Brazilian girl leave. She's just what's needed round here.'

Simon didn't even attempt to talk himself out of it. He called Meg at once.

'What on earth did you say to the poor girl? She's just packing her things.'

'Don't let her leave before I get there.'

He drove straight over and found Mariana loading her car.

'Just one question,' he said to her as he strode towards her. 'Do you want to come back?'

She considered him sombrely. 'Are you all right, Mr Waterford? You don't look well.'

He wasn't well but he couldn't tell her that she was the reason.

'Will you?'

Her big eyes flashed. 'But you have enough people at your yard. You said so.'

'There's a girl off sick.'

'I have nowhere to stay. Meg has been kind but I really should go.'

Jesus, the bloody woman was going to make him beg. 'There's places at Willowdale. We've a hostel, there's rooms in my house.'

Part of him was aghast at what he'd just said – he'd invited her to come and live with him. What kind of fool was he?

'OK,' she said. 'Let's try it then.'

She moved into Willowdale House that evening, into the big spare bedroom at the opposite end of the corridor to his. He laid down various house rules, about keeping out of each other's way and respecting mutual privacy. They discussed her duties in the yard. They toasted their agreement with a bottle of locally brewed beer which she claimed to like but sipped as if it was cough mixture. Then he made her a rudimentary supper which she polished off with more enthusiasm.

Before they said good night she insisted she massaged the shoulder which was giving him so much trouble. By the morning, remarkably, the pain had gone.

Hughie didn't bet much these days and he made a conscious effort not to interest himself in the landmarks of the racing season. But subconsciously he could never turn his back on it. And at half past three on a Saturday afternoon, with traffic in the bar down to a handful of determined boozers, it was excusable to turn on the TV in the office and put his feet up.

Once, the Lincoln Handicap from Doncaster had loomed large for him on the calendar. As the contest which marked the beginning of the Flat season, it had been a significant betting race in his past and the result a superstitious indicator of his fortune for the year ahead. Which, on mature reflection, only showed what a fool he used to be. Picking the winner from twenty-odd runners in the first big handicap of the season when you had no idea how fit they were had always been a mug's game.

This year his interest was focused as much on the coverage of the race as on the result. Jeremy's girlfriend, Meg Russell, had a fancied runner and Jeremy was on a three-line whip, as he'd put it, to attend – not that Jeremy had ever been known to avoid a racing jolly-up. In between shots of the horses, Hughie picked out the Russell party in the parade ring, He could identify most of them, Jeremy, of course, and the tall trainer, Simon Waterford. He caught a glimpse of a youthful-looking matron laughing with the jockey – Meg, he supposed – and then the camera moved on, leaving him frustrated.

The race itself followed a familiar pattern – what appeared to be a flat-out cavalry charge up the straight-mile section of the course. As often happened, the runners split into two groups on either side of the track, making it deceptively difficult to see which horse was leading the race.

Jeremy had been bullish about the chances of Meg's horse, Soft Centre, who had finished third the previous year. The yard's feeling, Jeremy had stated with confidence, was that the horse was a stronger prospect as a five-year-old and, from the starting prices, it seemed the bookies agreed. Hughie wasn't so sure – the handicapper had given him extra weight this year.

All the same, Soft Centre was leading the group on the far rail as the runners entered the final furlong. He seemed to have an advantage over the horse at the head of the stand side pack. But as the camera angle changed so did Hughie's opinion. It was no surprise to him when the four-year-old closest to the camera crossed the line half a length ahead.

Naturally, the after-race excitement was centred on the winner's connections, a boisterous consortium of Yorkshire office workers trumpeting a local victory. But Hughie spotted Simon in the crowd, shaking hands with the winning trainer, and behind him he caught a glimpse a tall girl whose curly blond hair was not contained by her woollen hat. Hughie looked on, no longer frustrated.

'Well done,' Simon said to Mariana as he guided her out of the crush in the unsaddling enclosure.

She looked at him sharply. 'What do you mean?'

'We wouldn't have had Softy in the race at all if it wasn't for you. The work you put in made all the difference.'

'But he didn't win.'

He realised that the tension in her face was not due to the biting wind. She was unhappy with the result.

'Second is grand, considering he was giving away twelve pounds to the winner,' he pointed out.

'You're trying to make me feel better.'

'It's not just that. It's true. Meg's happy.'

She shrugged. 'I think he should have won. There must have been something we could have done.'

Simon laughed. As he'd said, it had been a heck of a job getting Soft Centre there in the first place. But he recognised the intensity Mariana brought to her involvement. She wanted perfection and she wanted to win. When it came down to it, he felt like that too.

'Cheer up,' he said. 'We'll have plenty of winners this season.'

She stared at him seriously. 'We?'

'Us. The yard. That includes you.'

'You want me to stay?'

Of course he wanted her to stay. He was in love with her – he couldn't fight it any longer. But suppose she only wanted the job? Now he was her boss, how could he tell her how he felt?

But if he didn't, what kind of trouble was he storing up?

He should tell her now, before things got even more complicated.

In the scrum of people milling towards them he saw

Meg and Jeremy. She was clutching his arm, talking merrily. She didn't look too disappointed.

On impulse, he turned Mariana out of the crowd and leant close. 'Listen,' he hissed. 'I've got to tell you – it's only fair. I don't just want you to work for me – do you understand what I'm saying?'

She blinked and something softened in her face. 'Oh,' she said.

'The job's yours,' he continued, 'but I realise you might not want it now.'

He searched her face, waiting for her response

As he did so, a hand descended on his back and Jeremy's voice invaded their small space. 'Here he is! Fantastic job, Simon. Softy couldn't have run better.'

He was forced to turn to Jeremy and hoist a smile on to his face.

Meg stood on tiptoe to kiss him. 'It was a marvellous run in the circumstances.'

Simon realised he was expected to say something but he couldn't.

Another voice answered for him. 'Next time we're going to come first,' Mariana said. 'Aren't we, Simon?'

He felt Mariana's fingers entwine with his. Her hand was cold but the touch flooded him with warmth.

'Yes,' he said. 'If you say so.'

Chapter Three

August

Alison Hall sat on her haunches in the living room of her father's Notting Hill flat. The August sun splashed through the high windows, casting shifting shadows of the plane tree from the road outside across the grand Turkish rug that covered the polished wooden floor. She'd played on this rug as a little girl. Played by herself mostly, for she'd never had playmates when she came to London on holiday. Her school friends had been back in Yorkshire and, later, in South Africa. And there'd been no brothers or sisters to play with anywhere. Not that she cared about being an only child – you don't miss what you don't have. Except at moments like this. Right now she longed for a brother or sister to share the burden of packing up her dead father's belongings.

Piled behind her were cardboard packing cases which she was slowly filling with framed photographs and mementos which Geoff had displayed around the room. Almost every item was freighted with memory for her. Despite the years she'd spent in South Africa living with her mother, she'd been a regular visitor to England and her father had made a point of sharing the significant events of his life. So she recognised the tiny bronze statue of Rough Going, the Coronation Cup winner in whom her father had had a share, and the wooden horseshoe carved from timber salvaged from the old stables in Uncle Phil's yard and a signed photograph of Geoff shaking hands with Lester Piggott at Newmarket. And the items on view were only the tip of the iceberg. What was she going to do with it all?

At least she had help in her difficult task. From down the hall came the sound of music – Mariana had tuned the radio to some Continental channel where pop was interspersed with bursts of Spanish. Or maybe it was Portuguese, which would make more sense for a Brazilian. Whatever it was, it sounded cheerful and refreshingly foreign. Her dad would not have approved but too bad.

Having Mariana with her was almost as good as having a brother or sister. Better, in some ways, because she brought a sense of purpose that Alison was having trouble summoning up. She was usually an energetic, capable person but here she felt weary before she'd even packed one box of her dead father's possessions. Grief, she thought, was like having mud on your wheels, dragging you down and slowing you up. She forced herself to put a silver cigarette box next to a set of commemorative playing cards. This was her reject pile – Geoff was not a smoker or a card-player. Come to think of it, maybe she'd get rid of the lot.

'You want coffee?' Mariana was in the doorway. She wore an apron over jeans and a ragged T-shirt, her hair scrunched into an unruly bun, a picture of perfection. Alison thought that it would be easy to hate her if the Brazilian girl's appearance wasn't so entirely uncalculated. It was Mariana's fierce honesty, she knew, which had persuaded Simon it was safe to love her. And the selflessness which led her to put Alison's affairs ahead of her own. It had been decided, after her father's murder, that Simon and Mariana's wedding should be postponed until the end of the season. Some women might have resented the reversal of their plans but Mariana had agreed – they had all agreed – that to go ahead as arranged would have been inappropriate.

'This is hard.' Alison indicated the piles spread across the floor. 'I could just ask some house-clearance people to take everything away.'

'But you can't!' Mariana protested, scandalised. 'You mustn't throw away all the things your father collected. They meant something to him.'

'Yes, but not to me. Well, not a lot of them, except to make me feel sad.'

Mariana slipped to her knees and put an arm around Alison's shoulder. 'Perhaps this is too soon for you.'

'It'll be a long time before it gets any easier. And the sooner it's done, the sooner I can put this place up for sale.'

'Are you really sure you want to sell?'

This was a universal reaction. When Alison announced her intention to divest herself of a spacious, high-ceilinged flat in super-trendy Notting Hill in the depths of a property downturn, everyone protested. Keep it or let it out, they insisted, at least wait until you can sell it for what it's really worth.

But Alison didn't care about the money. The whole subject of assets and wealth made her uncomfortable. The reason for that was plain enough. Until two months ago she had been working as an equine nurse, living in Yorkshire in her dad's house and keeping an eye on it while he was away in London during the week on business. She earned enough to run a car, enjoy the odd night out and take a sunshine holiday in the summer. Geoff had resisted taking any rent from her until she told him she'd get her own place unless he did. All the same, she was able to ride out at Willowdale every morning on one of her father's horses and he'd given her a credit card in lieu, as he'd put it, of a clothing allowance. If she didn't use it every so often he'd complain it was no fun having a daughter who was even more tight-fisted than he was. Didn't she have any of her mother's genes in her body?

For all the jokes, she'd known her dad was pretty well off and she could have sponged off him merrily, like one or two indulged daughters she knew. The problem was that she thought less of those girls and she would have thought less of herself had she done so. But now, as the extent of her father's estate had come to light, she rather wished she'd allowed her doting dad to splurge on her more often, just for his own pleasure.

The fact was, as she was well aware after several sessions with Clive Silver, her father's solicitor, she now had more money than she could ever have expected. Barring bequests to various charities, it had all been left to her. She owned a house with twenty acres of ground in Yorkshire, this London flat, a boring but dependable portfolio of investments, and a clutch of racehorses. By any standards she was rich.

Her mother had come over for the funeral, though the chances were the reading of the will had been of more interest. She'd left with a couple of modernist paintings that, Alison knew, had been bought in the early years of their marriage. She had the feeling her mother had been hoping for a little more.

'So,' Karen had said as they waited in the Notting Hill flat for the taxi to take her to Heathrow, 'you made the right decision, after all.'

The decision in question was that of the thirteen-year-old Alison who had opted to return to live with her father in England at the time of her mother's third marriage. As husband number three had a substantial stake in South Africa's steel industry, Karen had considered her daughter short-sighted.

'If you say so, Mum.' Alison had long ago ceased to argue with her mother about money. For all that she loved her mother, they had a completely different set of values. 'Things are still all right with Theo, aren't they?' She lived in dread of her mother's third marriage going sour.

Karen had sighed. 'I guess so. He's been very good to me. Just a teensy bit boring, that's all.' She'd looked around with an expression familiar to her daughter, one of longing filled with nostalgia. There was always something Karen wanted that she could not get her hands on. 'God, I love this flat. Your father would never have bought it if I hadn't persuaded him.'

That was true enough. Geoff had often acknow-ledged that his inclination was for a London base in a respectable suburb but his wife-to-be had a yen to live in a livelier part of town – and she'd got her way.

'I'd keep it on, Mum, if I thought it was going to be lived in. But I prefer Yorkshire and you're not likely to use it much, are you?'

Her mother had hugged her and said. 'It's a lovely thought, darling, but I'm not going to keep house when I come over. And Theo would hate it. He prefers the Connaught.'

Alison said nothing of this to Mariana. 'I've already got a house up north full of memories of Dad, I don't want this place too.'

'I understand. Too much baggage.'

Exactly. Mariana understood.

Alison stretched a leg in front of her – she was cramping up in this position.

'Are you OK? I could give you a massage.'

That was tempting. Mariana gave great massages – to humans and to horses. Alison didn't know if she was professionally trained but, whatever the cause, she had a magic touch.

'That would be nice. But later.'

'And coffee?'

'Of course.'

Mariana also made great coffee. After all, she was Brazilian.

Mariana ground beans and boiled the kettle. From the doorway of the kitchen she could see down the long stretch of carpeted hallway into the sunlit sitting room and the shape of Alison's curved back as she bent to her task. Mariana didn't think she was at any risk – Alison was a trusting sort – but for the next few

49

minutes she wanted to be sure her friend stayed just where she was.

She carried through a tray laden with a small cafetière and a plate of chocolate digestives.

'I mustn't,' said Alison as she saw the biscuits but she picked one up anyway, as Mariana guessed she would. All the woman she knew in England – the honest ones, that is – announced they shouldn't eat fatty foods and then did so. Then they looked at Mariana and said, 'I don't know how you keep your figure.' It was funny really.

As she left the room, adjusting the door so that Alison would have to get to her feet if she wanted to see what was going on down the hall, Mariana scolded herself for thinking mean thoughts. Alison had been a staunch ally in her conquest of Simon – and for the purest motives. She was a good woman and a firm friend who had been plunged into a nightmare. Mariana knew what it was like to lose a father she loved with all her heart. As far as she was concerned, Alison could eat as many biscuits as she liked. Not that it would make any difference to a slender woman like her anyway.

Mariana's ostensible task during the next few days was to help clear up the flat and put it in its most seductive state for prospective buyers. To that end, a couple of estate agents were due to assess its potential later that afternoon. Her unofficial role was to keep Alison company and provide a shoulder for her to cry on if it should be needed.

'I should come down with you,' Simon had said when they had discussed the trip to London. 'It's going to be horrible for her.'

But it was one of the busiest periods of the Flat racing calendar and Simon had his hands full at the yard. It was also true that he himself would find the job of clearing up his uncle's London home deeply distressing. Alison had assured him that she would manage very well with just Mariana for company.

Mariana was pleased about that. Though she missed Simon desperately, it gave her a better chance to do what she had to without being observed.

She walked back down the hall but, instead of returning to the kitchen, opened the door next to it at the end of the passage and slipped inside. The radio burbled faintly through the solid walls but there was no smell of freshly brewed coffee in here. And no sunlight; the curtains were drawn and the room was twilight dark, almost funereal – which was appropriate. This had been Geoff's bedroom and, so far, had remained undisturbed by the spring-cleaning activity that had been undertaken throughout the rest of the flat. Mariana knew Alison was leaving this room till last and, though nothing had been said, she realised the intimate task of tidying the place where the dead man slept should be left to his daughter.

All the same, she had no choice. She had to find the document, six sheets of A4 paper in a powder-blue folder, which Geoff had put into her hands back in June, a week before Royal Ascot.

'Read it,' he'd commanded as they stood in the office at Willowdale. It was mid-afternoon, a time when the yard was empty after a busy morning. Simon was racing at Redcar. Mariana had been working with Aquiline, giving him a body rub during a quiet period of the day, as she often did. Plainly

Geoff had been waiting for a moment to catch her on her own.

'It's a report from my solicitor,' he added as she stared at the folder in surprise. 'About you.'

She scanned the pages, rushing to the end to assess the extent of the damage. Half the content was printed off the escort agency website from two years ago. Even though her profile had long been removed she supposed there were still ways to access it. She'd called herself Fabiana and claimed to be Portuguese. Neither that nor the brunette wig were much of a disguise. There was no mistaking the wide-set nut-brown eyes and the smile of golden innocence. The effect was belied by a sidebar which priced her time from £200 for an hour to £1,500 for 'overnight'.

'Has Simon . . . ?' she began.

He shook his head. 'First I want to hear what you have to say.'

So it wasn't complete disaster – yet.

Geoff surveyed her with those cold stony eyes while she calculated – how should she defend herself?

'You have no right to pry into my private life. This is none of your business.'

'It's my business when you want to marry into my family.'

'But this is all in the past. I was desperate. I owed money and I had no choice.'

'There's always a choice.'

'You don't know what it's like to be poor in a foreign country.'

'That's true.' He stepped closer and she could see those grey eyes were not so cold after all. 'I'm going to give you a week then I'm going to talk to Simon. That gives you time to tell him yourself. If he's still happy to marry you then I shan't say a word to anyone.'

She supposed that was generous of him.

'You've got till we get back from Ascot.' He took the document from her grip. 'And if you don't tell him, I will.'

Standing there, watching through the window as Geoff walked away with the powder-blue folder in his hand, Mariana had had every intention of confessing to Simon. But when it came to it, she'd never quite managed to summon up the nerve for that make-or-break conversation with her fiancé. Then suddenly, in a twist of fate, she had been reprieved.

But she wasn't in the clear until she found that folder.

Alison was making slow progress. Whenever she determined to get this ordeal over with and began dumping things in boxes as quickly as she could, something would bring her up short. Right now she was contemplating a photograph of her adolescent self on horseback, grinning at the camera fit to bust, while her youthful cousin Simon stood by the horse's head, his face sombre. She remembered the day well, her first back in England after she'd returned to live with her dad following Mum's marriage to Theo, the boring Boer. She'd just been introduced to Skipjack, the horse she was to be allowed to ride out every day at Uncle Phil's yard, and reunited with Simon, her childhood companion from when she was little. It had been a triumphant day. She'd felt as if she'd redis-covered her past in returning to her real home, Yorkshire, where she was bound to be blissfully happy.

Of course, that was before she'd found out how ill Aunt Rose was. She'd already had her first stroke but Alison had been kept in ignorance about that. Looking at the picture now she could see the sadness in Simon's face. He wasn't trying to look moody and cool, as she'd thought then, he was bearing the weight of his mother's illness on his thin shoulders. She wanted to reach back in time and give him a hug.

The jingle of her mobile shook her out of her reverie.

'It's Claire Parker.' Detective Constable Parker of the Wandsworth police, a member of the specialist team investigating Geoff's murder. 'You rang earlier.'

Alison had called to speak to the senior investigating officer, Detective Chief Inspector Cliff Henderson. She'd met him on the night of the murder, after she'd driven from Yorkshire in a haze of disbelief, to be confronted by a man who seemed not much older than herself. He was short and handsome in a disconcerting way, with gelled black hair and a full girlish mouth. She'd felt as if she were in a movie and his appearance had only added to the unreality of her situation. He'd stared at her with blue-eyed intensity and announced, 'We're going to get these scum, Miss Hall, believe me.' And she had.

But as time went by and Henderson's investigation came up empty-handed, she had lost her faith. It would have helped if he hadn't made the pursuit of the killers seem like a personal crusade.

The inquiry had started well – if that was the appropriate word to describe the process of catching the men who had butchered your father. The attackers had been seen and remarked on by many people, on the train and at both stations. The returning race-goers had proved more than co-operative, all eager to provide statements, attend identity parades and, if required, to present their evidence in court. What's more, close examination of Simon's wounds had yielded good samples of DNA from the spiky-haired man who had inflicted the injury.

There were also clear CCTV pictures of the wanted men from the cameras on the platforms at Ascot and Clapham Junction, even of the attack itself, generated by the train's security system.

The murder had been national news for a couple of days and the story had played out for much longer in the London and racing press. It was later fuelled by captures from the CCTV film and by appeals from DCI Henderson, who made quite an impact on a TV screen, in Alison's opinion.

But . . . there had been no useful response to the publicity and there were no suspects in custody. All the CCTV and DNA in the world were redundant when there were no entries in the data base and no bodies in a cell. It was as if the men had vanished off the earth the moment they ran down the stairs from the platform at Clapham Junction.

'It's such a big station,' Claire had explained. 'The busiest in Britain, seventeen platforms, two thousand trains a day. And at the beginning of the rush hour on a weekday it's heaving with people. There's a pedestrian tunnel that runs north-south and links the platforms with an exit at either end. It's likely the two guys split up there, though one or both could have hopped on a train on another platform. But we've trawled through all the pictures and there's no sign they did that. Believe me, Clapham Junction has a state-of-the-art system – it can detect a graffiti artist within seconds of him defacing a train.'

They'd been sitting in this room in the Notting Hill flat for this conversation. Claire had produced these facts as if Alison should be impressed. She'd kept her thoughts to herself as the detective continued to explain why her father's killers remained at liberty.

'We think one of them exited the station on Grant Road and the other went out on to St John's Hill. It would have been humming at that time of day – shoppers, commuters, loads of traffic.'

'And more fancy cameras?'

'Yes, but we didn't spot them. We don't know how they did it – maybe they changed their appearance somehow or were just bloody lucky.'

'So you've got no more pictures?'

'Not useful ones, no.'

'And you don't know where they went?'

That had been a pointless question.

Since then Alison had called the investigating team regularly, all too aware that more cruel crimes were taking place in the capital every day and that her father's murder was no longer top of the list. Well, it was top of her list.

She always asked for Henderson but, as time went by, the DCI was increasingly difficult to pin down.

'He's a bit tied up at present,' Claire Parker explained unnecessarily. 'He asked me to send his apologies.'

Alison doubted if that was the way Henderson would have expressed it. But Claire was a decent woman and no doubt competent at what she did, even if she could bring no joy to Alison's heart. The fact was that, two months on from the murder, with other serious crimes clamouring for police time, the chances of catching her father's killers were receding fast. Alison feared that the hard-pressed police had now chalked the murder up as yet another knife crime statistic on the streets of the city.

She had called to give vent to her frustrations and to ask if there had been any further progress. Claire Parker could offer her nothing new. Though, to her credit, she heard Alison out and made sympathetic noises.

'Listen to me,' she said. 'I know it's terrible for you at the moment but you mustn't give up hope. We've got DNA, CCTV and solid witnesses. The moment one of these bastards slips up we'll have them. The clear-up rate for murder in this city is nearly ninety per cent.'

More statistics. It wasn't much comfort if your case was one of the unsolved ten per cent.

By the time Alison had finished the call, her coffee was cold. She drank it anyway.

Mariana's desire to assist Alison in her time of need stemmed from genuine sympathy. But there was no denying that being on hand to sort through Geoff Hall's belongings was convenient. Up in Yorkshire, she and Simon had moved in with Alison to provide what comfort they could. Now here she was in London by Alison's side once more. And in both instances being the handmaiden of grief had given Mariana a unique opportunity to save her own skin.

She'd not found that folder in Geoff's Yorkshire

home – and she'd hunted good and hard. So far, in the Notting Hill flat, she'd taken the opportunity while Alison was at a solicitor's meeting that morning to give the study a thorough going-over but she'd come up empty-handed. The bedroom was the last place left to look – it had to be here somewhere.

The most likely place seemed to be in the bedside cabinet but it yielded nothing of special interest – headache pills, an old camera, dusty tape cassettes, earplugs, tissues, batteries, blunt pencils and rubber bands, a travelling alarm clock stuck at ten past eight – the sort of half-forgotten stuff that collects in the back of drawers. In the bottom she found some letters, personal notes and thank-yous, a batch of them in a childish script with South African stamps on the envelopes: Alison's letters to her father after her mother had taken her away. Mariana did not open them, nor the more adult offerings with an earlier postmark in a flowing adult hand. From a woman, Mariana assumed. Probably that too-tanned ex-wife who had shown up for the funeral.

Was that all Geoff's love life had amounted to? This monkish little room with its single bed hardly spoke of licentious bachelor frolics. There weren't even any racy magazines tucked away at the back of drawer. His bedroom up in Yorkshire was larger and more comfortable but as bereft of a woman's touch as this one. For all his worldly success, Geoff Hall had gone alone to his bed at night, unlucky in love as he was to be in death. Mariana allowed herself a pang of sympathy. It was strange to find herself caring more for the man dead than she had when he was alive.

She quickly shut the bedside drawers and looked

around the room. The wardrobe contained only clothes and shoes; the chest of drawers, just underwear and sweaters. She felt into the corners and to the back of each shelf just to be sure.

There had been a difficult moment shortly after the funeral when Alison had asked Simon if he'd known how to open the safe in her father's office. A safe! Mariana had been terrified, convinced that was where Geoff would have put the detective's report. She had been on the point of confessing and throwing herself on Simon's mercy when Alison remembered where Geoff had kept a note of the combination. Since no repercussions had followed – Alison had continued to treat her as a trusted friend – she had assumed no file had been found.

But was there a safe in this room? There wasn't a sign of one on open view. She looked behind the desk and at the back of the wardrobe. She pulled up the rugs and examined the floorboards. Nothing.

She thought hard. If there was a safe it was unlikely she would be able to get into it. But it was better to know that it existed. Know your enemy. She'd tried so hard to find that incriminating file she couldn't just put it to the back of her mind. And if there was a safe tucked away somewhere she could be sure that was where her fate lay.

The room contained a small fireplace, long neglected as a source of heat but surrounded by late-Victorian tiles. Above the mantelpiece hung an oil painting of wheat fields at harvest time, a dusty old thing in Mariana's opinion and not to her taste. But, as she knew from many an old movie, it was big enough to hide the door to a safe.

She took the straight-backed chair from the writing table by the window and placed it in the hearth. Standing on it, she was able to lift the painting away from the wall and look behind. The Regency-striped wallpaper was a lighter shade behind the heavy frame, and dust flecks drifted down on to her face like flakes of snow. But the wall behind the picture was smooth and unmarked. There was no safe.

That was good news but it still didn't solve the mystery. Where was that incriminating folder? Unless she found it she would have to try to put it out of her mind and trust to fate. Trust that the time bomb of her past would not blow up before she'd made her future secure.

Then, still standing on the chair, looking to her right into the bookshelves that lined the alcove to the right of the fire place, she saw a glimpse of blue. Powder blue.

The folder sat on top of a row of books, invisible to the eye of a person standing by the bed but plain as day from her position.

She grabbed it.

Alison had not watched the CCTV of her father's murder. She had not asked to see it and the police had not suggested she should. Maybe they wouldn't have let her. The thought of it was terrifying – that it existed even, let alone the idea that it might be shown in a public court. But now the idea of any trial seemed hopelessly remote.

She should see those pictures, no matter how painful the experience. It was her duty as a daughter to share the last moments of her father's life.

Mariana, of course, had been there, had witnessed the slaughter first hand, had knelt in her father's life blood and screamed for his life. They'd not talked about it directly. She guessed her friend had held back out of respect for her feelings. She herself had distrusted her own reaction to what Mariana might say. Mariana was plainly the reason the men had picked on them. The ravishing girl in her summer finery had brought the beast out in them and Geoff had fallen protecting her.

She rejected this line of thought – it was dark and destructive and served no purpose. If she followed it, she'd turn away from a woman who'd been a rock in the biggest crisis of her life.

All Alison knew was that she wished she had been on the train. She could have taken time off work and gone down to Ascot with the others – it had been suggested. But the surgery had been short-staffed.

She knew there wasn't anything she could have done if she'd been sitting on that train. She couldn't have prevented her father from jumping into the fight and she couldn't have warded off the knife blow that had killed him. Just one thrust into his chest, piercing his heart – was it an unlucky strike or aimed with precision? She'd probably never know.

What she did know was that, by being a witness to the end of her father's life, Mariana had played the part that she should have played.

'I should have been there,' she murmured to herself.

Perhaps she'd ask to see that footage after all. In advance of any trial. The way things were going there might never be a trial at all.

She shook her head. She mustn't think like this,

allow herself to get bogged down in the despair of the situation. Yes, there would be a trial. They would catch those men and put them in court and make them own up to the pain and horror of what they had done. And if the police couldn't make that happen then she bloody well would. Somehow.

Whatever, it was time to shake the mud off her wheels. Stop grovelling on the floor and think positive. Get things done.

She got stiffly to her feet. Maybe she would accept Mariana's offer of a massage. It would make her feel better.

She picked up the coffee tray and headed for the kitchen, calling for her friend.

Mariana was still standing on the chair in Geoff's bedroom when she heard Alison from the hall. Oh no! To be discovered like this would be a disaster.

She shoved the folder behind her apron, down into the waistband of her jeans.

As she put the chair back in its place, she heard a clatter from next door. Could she slip out of this room without being seen?

'Mariana!'

No, better not risk it.

'I'm in here.' She yanked open the door.

Alison, in the kitchen doorway, stared at her in surprise. And suspicion maybe?

'Look, you've got to do something about this room,' she announced. Bold was always best.

'It's Dad's bedroom.'

'It *was* his bedroom. But you want to sell this place quickly, don't you? If you want to make the best impression, you've got to brighten it up. Draw the curtains, open the window, give it a good airing.'

'I suppose so.' Alison didn't look thrilled by the idea but at least she wasn't asking herself what Mariana had been doing in there.

'Look, leave it to me if it's too painful. I'll strip the bed and sort out your father's clothes – that's the worst bit, isn't it? But you should go through the bedside drawers, sort out any private stuff first.'

'You're right. I suppose I can't put it off any longer.'

'We'll do it together – if that's OK with you.'

Alison nodded. 'Thanks, Mariana. I'm so lucky to have you here to help out.'

Mariana squeezed her hand, then bent her head to kiss the other woman on the cheek. But she didn't get too close. No need to have Alison wondering what it was she had squirrelled away behind her apron.

Chapter Four

Fortunately for his peace of mind, Jeremy Masterton was not prone to guilty reflection. He'd often said, in jest, 'Thank the Lord I wasn't born a Catholic – confession's not my style.' He could have added that, had he been thus spiritually inclined, he would never have been short of material to offer up to his confessor.

Not that he was a bad man. He could say that with confidence. He'd done no evil in the purest sense – no lives had been ruined or lost due to his machinations. And if the occasional heart had taken a temporary battering and one or two balance sheets veered briefly from black to red thanks to the games he had played, well, that was life. Sometimes you win and sometimes you lose. And at the moment, he was delighted to admit to himself, he was on a winning streak.

The symbol of his current good fortune was close at hand in the stables of York racecourse, being prepared for another significant step in his racing career. Aquiline, winner of the Coventry Stakes at Royal Ascot, was about to fire his next shot at glory in the Gimcrack Stakes at the Ebor Festival.

Aquiline was by far the best horse Jeremy had ever owned. He'd had a share in one or two promising prospects in the past, but promise had invariably withered on the vine and, on the rare occasions when the animal had finished in the frame, he'd had to share the applause and what measly spoils there had been – never enough to cover the training fees, in his experience. As for the nags he had owned off his own bat, he was almost embarrassed to own up to them now.

Naturally, there was a good reason why this particular animal had come up trumps – he'd cost 50,000 guineas, five times what Jeremy had ever paid for a horse before. Not that he was mean with his money, he'd just never had enough for a decent investment. But even that outlay was a bit of a bargain price. Most of the Coventry field at Ascot would have sold for more and two of the runners left in Aquiline's wake that day Jeremy knew for a fact had changed hands at more than half a million pounds.

Given that, Jeremy thought himself entitled to a pat on the back. He'd always been a decent judge of horseflesh, a skill he'd picked up from trotting along to the races with Aunt Winnie and Uncle Clem when he was a nipper. They'd been horse mad and had been better parents than the bloodless old Widower, as he thought of his old man, left to bring up a vigorous boy child after his mum died. He'd known Aquiline had the makings of a decent racehorse the moment he'd clapped eyes on him. The colt had swaggered into the ring at Tattersalls as if he knew he was special. The bloodline had speed on the dam's side and he liked the way the horse carried himself – there was power even in the way he walked. Temperament was obviously an issue but Jeremy's trainer had a knack with difficult animals. And his judgement had been right, all the way down the line. Simon Waterford had handled the young horse sensitively and Aquiline had turned out to be a speeding bullet – which he had demonstrated at Royal Ascot.

Jeremy didn't like to think how much his investment was worth now, although he found himself dwelling on it a lot. If Aquiline never ran in another race he'd be worth a quarter of million easily at stud. And if he went on winning as a two-year-old and stepped up in distance at three, well, the sky was the limit. Rows of noughts in a bank balance filled Jeremy's mind.

Just as well he wasn't prone to guilty thoughts because, strictly speaking, those noughts did not belong to him.

The plan had always been – honestly – to pay the money back. It was sort of a short-term loan, diverted on its way from person A to person B with the aim of generating some extra bunce for J. Masterton en route. It was the way he'd always operated and hardly criminal. He'd run a book at boarding school, collecting the cash in the morning and cycling off to the bookies at lunch to get it on. Sometimes it wasn't always possible to cycle back before supper to pick up the winnings. And sometimes the picks were so daft that there wasn't any point in putting them on in the first place, not on that selection anyway. And nobody had ever taken him to task. Provided everyone thought they had their money down and they all got squared up in the end, then it was sunshine all round.

This thing with Aquiline was basically the same. Only, person A had been bumped off in a random assault on a train. And person B was not a person at all but a charity with a load of dosh sitting on deposit – they'd never miss Geoff Hall's money.

Just as well he wasn't the guilty sort really.

Planning her clothes for a trip to the races had been low on Alison's list of priorities after her return from London. She'd been tempted to duck the entire affair, except that her absence would be noted and people would put it down to her father's death. They would speculate on her mental state, say it was under-standable she wanted to avoid old friends and add that Geoff's murder had devastated her. All of which was, naturally, the truth. 'Poor Alison couldn't face it today – it's not surprising, is it?'

She was damned if she would allow herself to be an object of pity. Better to look people in the eye and say life was shit but she was dealing with it as best she could. That's what her father would have expected of her.

Geoff had loved York races, especially the big summer festival. He'd never had much luck with any of his own runners but he'd cheered home several famous winners saddled by Uncle Phil and he would never have missed the occasion. And, even as their family had become depleted – first Rose, then Phil – he'd made a point of showing the flag. Alison had no choice but to go.

All the same, she wished she had given more thought to her outfit – an aquamarine summer dress that left her shoulders bare. It was last year's number, substituted at the last minute because the weather had turned out to be foul. And though this year the rain had held off, there was still a cool enough breeze to raise goosebumps on her bare arms when she was out of the weak sunshine. She reminded herself how much her father had liked it – 'Just your colour, lass,' he'd said. He was right, the blue suited her rich auburn hair, her one feature that she admitted to be attractive.

'Miss Hall?'

She didn't recognise the man who'd appeared at her side out of the crush on the Champagne Terrace. He was huge, like a lumbering bear, uncomfortable in an ill-fitting suit.

'Have you got a moment?' He spoke broad Cockney. 'We've not met but you might know my name. Charlie Talbot.'

She shook her head. 'Sorry.'

'I knew your father,' the big man continued. 'I'm really sorry what happened to him. Bloody awful business.'

'Yes.' There was nothing else to say.

'Are you sure he never mentioned my name?'

'I'm sorry, I don't remember.' Geoff had had many friends and acquaintances, personal and professional.

'In that case, I apologise for intruding but, you see, we had some outstanding business, your dad and I. About a horse.'

'What sort of business?'

'Well . . . this is a bit embarrassing, Miss Hall, but your father owed me money.'

That took her by surprise. After her most recent

meeting with the solicitor, she thought she was up to speed with her father's affairs. It was quite possible, of course, that something had been overlooked.

'You'd better tell me about it then, Mr Talbot.'

'Charlie, please.' He looked sheepish, as if he was genuinely reluctant to raise the matter. 'A couple of years ago, your father and I bought a filly together, fifty fifty. She wasn't much cop, always injured. But this season she's been dynamite. You know who I mean? Jennifer Eccles.'

Alison knew very well. Jenny was now her horse and, according to Simon, the best of the half a dozen thoroughbreds that Geoff had owned. She had been due to run at Ascot before he had been murdered.

'My father left her to me in his will. I wasn't aware that anyone else was involved.'

'Well, I'm involved all right. Your father made me an offer for my share when she was on the sick list. But when she turned out to be a good'un after all, we came to an arrangement that he would pay me another instalment. I've got to admit he didn't want to at first.'

'Oh.'

'Believe me, Miss Hall, I am really sorry to spring it on you like this. But we came to an agreement at Ascot, the same afternoon he died. We shook on it before the Coventry and he promised he'd sort out the paperwork next day. Unfortunately he passed on before he could pay me.'

'How much?'

'A hundred and fifteen thousand pounds. I did say it was embarrassing but I'm sure you understand that's not the kind of money that can just be over-looked.'

Alison was stunned. 'No,' she said. 'No, indeed.'

'I did send your father an invoice in the first instance but I can send it to you again.'

She nodded. This was a complication she could have done without. She'd talk to Simon about it – he'd lived and breathed every moment of Jenny's existence since she'd come into his care. He'd know about this.

'You'd better send me the invoice, Mr Talbot. If my father owed you money, then I promise I shall honour his debt.'

As Mariana accompanied Aquiline and his groom out of the stables she was not surprised to discover Jeremy waiting by the gate. He was an owner who liked to be involved. He beamed at his horse as if he could hardly believe his luck. She could understand that. He was a fortunate man to own such a magnificent animal. She knew from talking to Meg that none of his other horses had ever amounted to much.

'Where's Meg?' she asked.

'She's not here. I'm fancy free.' He fell in by her side as they made their way out into the middle of the course. His pale blue eyes twinkled with mischief. 'Absolutely free,' he added, palming the cheek of her bottom through her jeans.

'Well, I'm not,' she spat and shoved him hard in the chest. 'You should be ashamed.'

'Really? It was a harmless gesture of admiration. I'm not ashamed of anything to do with our *friend-ship*.' He emphasised the last word and she wanted to hit him harder. Smack him in the mouth with all her strength. Men were such pigs. Some men anyway.

He smiled at her genially, amused by her obvious ill-temper. She'd risen too easily to his bait. It was stupid of her, she'd thought his little barbs were all in the past but clearly she was mistaken.

She took a deep breath, forced herself to unclench her fists and relax. She'd nearly threatened to tell Simon of his behaviour. But if she did that, well, Jeremy would have every excuse to give his side of the story.

The bottom line was that she had to keep in Jeremy's good books even if it meant putting up with some indignity when they were on their own.

She put a hand on his arm and smiled. 'I'm sorry, Jeremy. It's just that things are different now I'm with Simon. Your friendship does mean a lot to me.'

He nodded, considering the extent of her apology – was it enough?

'I guess I'm a bit wound up,' she added, 'about the race.'

'How is he?' he said, gazing at the horse in front of them.

'He'll be fine.' She said it with more confidence than she felt.

The stables at York are on the far side to the grandstand and the journey across involved traversing the undulating ground in the middle of the course. It was always a test of a horse's nerve to approach the packed grandstand and the noise from the Tannoy.

For a moment Aquiline began to fret but she laid a reassuring hand on his gleaming flank and began to sing him a song in Portuguese she'd learned from her mother. It soothed them both.

* * *

Simon was pretty good at keeping his nerves under control or, at least, keeping their existence from the knowledge of those around him. It was a handy trait, one he'd inherited from his father, for which he was grateful. In his opinion, keeping a cool head was an essential quality for getting the best out of humans and horses and, as events got underway at York, a Godsend in the present circumstances. He had runners in the first two races and an assortment of fires which needed fighting at the same time, but that was nothing new.

Holly, the groom who was leading up Closing Time for the first race, was in tears over something Beck, the travelling head lad, had said to her. Simon didn't want to know the details, though he suspected it was something to do with the horse, to which Holly was deeply attached. But he managed to dry tears and organise a truce while keeping an eye open for Closing Time's owner, Reg Hartley, who was accompanied by a man who fancied himself some kind of local historian. At any rate, as they stood in the parade ring, waiting for the horses to appear, the guest insisted on lecturing him about the Knavesmire, the ground on which York racecourse was built.

'Did you know they hanged Dick Turpin here?'

Everybody knew that. Simon had been coming to this course since he could toddle and it was one of the first things he'd been told – and sadly not the last.

Fortunately Reg's guest did not appear to require an answer, he was happy conversing with himself.

'In those days there was an assizes in York in August which all the mucky-mucks attended and naturally they wanted a bit of fun along with the hard work of sentencing the poor.'

Simon glanced at Reg, a local farmer who'd bred Closing Time himself and was in a permanent state of shock that he'd turned out to be a proper racehorse. Poor Reg looked in bits, fearful no doubt that the animal's lowly pedigree would be found out on this, the biggest occasion of his racing life.

'So, along with the gee-gees went other entertainments. Executing felons and cutpurses like Turpin. The legendary highwayman strung up for the edification of the masses.'

'He hasn't got a prayer in this company,' Reg blurted, plainly uninterested in executions. 'They're offering a hundred to one in the ring.'

Simon chuckled. 'I'd get some money on him quick then. That's a stupid price.'

'Do you think so?' The guest had given up on his lecture. 'I might go and put a few bob on.'

'Good idea,' said Simon, eager to get rid of him. 'Each way,' he called as he left.

Reg rolled his eyes. 'My brother-in-law. Goes on a bit, I'm afraid.'

Fortunately at that point Neil Fordham, the jockey, strode up with a big grin on his face. Though just a slip of a lad, Neil was never short of confidence. He thrust his hand towards Reg.

'Great to see you, Mr Hartley. I'm really looking forward to this. Lovely horse.'

This was standard Neil patter before a race but it always went down well and Simon was grateful. As Neil mollified Reg's nerves, Simon allowed his thoughts to drift to his runner in the next race. That owner wouldn't be nervous, he could guarantee, but the same could not be said with confidence of his horse. This was only Aquiline's third appearance on a racecourse and, despite his Ascot success, Simon feared the occasion might overwhelm him.

In an ideal world, he would have personally over-seen Aquiline's safe delivery from the stables on the other side of the course to the shade of the horse chestnut trees that overhung the pre-parade ring. But, with the first race off in five minute's time, he could hardly be in two places at once.

As he gave Neil a leg-up onto Closing Time's back and prepared to utter a few unnecessary words of advice for Reg's benefit, the phone in his pocket beeped. He glanced at the text on screen and the tension that had begun to build ebbed away. It was a message telling him all was well with Aquiline.

It had been silly of him to worry. He had asked Mariana to take care of the horse and he knew she would not let him down.

Jeremy took his place in the grandstand just in time for the Gimcrack Stakes, the only race on today's card that mattered, as far as he was concerned. Aquiline had not run since Ascot but the form of the con-tenders in the Coventry had worked out well and he was clear favourite for this race. Despite all the upheavals in Simon's life since the death of his uncle, the Willowdale yard had continued to run like clockwork.

'My trainer,' Jeremy frequently found himself saying, 'is top-notch. A chip off the old block – better if you ask me.' The claim was usually met with some scepticism, but even the senior followers of Yorkshire racing agreed that young Waterford had the touch when it came to horses.

One thing was sure, at present Willowdale runners were in good form. Closing Time had sneaked third place in the opener at a magnificent price which was a good omen. All Simon's staff were cock-a-hoop and Jeremy had promised a major celebration if Aquiline brought home the bacon. Whatever the outcome, he'd earmarked young Holly, Closing Time's lass, for some TLC at a later stage of proceedings. She'd been in floods of tears after the race – and before too, he'd been told – and he'd taken the opportunity to offer both handkerchief and shoulder. He reckoned there was further mileage to be run in that department.

After the little scene with Mariana he was a conscious of an itch that needed to be scratched, one that in this instance Meg could not take care of. That fleeting touch of Mariana's taut body had brought a lot of things flooding back. For all Meg's charm and skill, sometimes there was no substitute for a nubile woman in a man's arms. Meg was a valuable diversion but he fancied he could still afford to look for youth in a bed partner.

Simon knew his old mates – school friends and former co-workers – were fascinated by his relationship with Mariana. From the first, they had predicted it wouldn't last and they were still predicting, six months on. 'How on earth did he land a cracking lass like that?' was written in large letters on their faces whenever he took her down to the pub for an evening of booze and banter. There were plenty of Beauty and the Beast jokes doing the rounds, he was well aware. Aware, too, that they put it down to his relative wealth. After he'd inherited his father's yard, he'd become a fair catch. One or two local honeys had swapped snooty brush-offs for come-hither grins since he'd become master of Willowdale, so he knew the aphrodisiac power of money.

But Mariana wasn't like that. She insisted on paying her way and ran her own car, bought her own clothes and shared household expenses whenever he let her. The wage he paid her wasn't much so he was unsure how she managed. She'd told him she had savings but he couldn't believe they amounted to a great deal. He'd broached conversations about housekeeping allowances but she didn't appear interested. Once he'd slipped banknotes into her purse but she'd caught him and got angry. Puzzled, he'd never tried that trick again.

As for the disparity in their looks – something which appeared to obsess so many – he just shrugged it off. He knew he wasn't any kind of Adonis but he wasn't Quasimodo either, just an ordinary-looking skinny guy with a pale face and hair that wouldn't do what it was told. He didn't have much fashion sense or drive a snazzy car but he guessed that if Mariana had given any indication those things mattered to her, he could have invested some money in his image. But she hadn't and he knew he would have thought less of her if she had. And he didn't expect to think less of her, ever.

Mariana watched anxiously as Neil rode Aquiline out on to the course and away from the stands down to the six-furlong start. To the uninitiated the horse looked in fine shape, a smooth stride and a lordly bearing, head held high. But to Mariana, familiar with his every quirk, there were telltale signs that would signify that the tumult all around had got to him. She watched for an involuntary twitch of the ears or a flick of the tail that would signal alarm. But there was nothing.

The phone sounded in the pocket of her jeans – the arrival of a text message. She glanced at it and at once shut the implications from her mind. There was no time for that now. If she hurried she might just be able to watch the race by Simon's side.

Jeremy was counting all the reasons why it would not be a good idea for Aquiline to win the race. It was a habit he'd got into during his years as an owner and jolly useful it had proved too. He prided himself on being one of life's half-fullers and having a consolation or two at the ready was useful in moments of defeat. And it had worked to his advantage. He'd lost count of the number of times during his years as a horse owner that he'd been referred to as 'a good loser'. He'd had endless party and weekend invitations – and all the knock-on extras they entailed – out of coming over all Kipling at moments of equine disaster.

Naturally, he hadn't had so much practice at moments of sporting triumph – it was best not to anticipate them.

So, as he stood in the packed stand, hopping from one foot to another as if he were a small boy waiting for the toilet, he listed reasons why it would be better for Aquiline to fail.

His price would increase for his next race. For God's sake, if he won here he'd be impossible to back in the future.

That was one reason.

He was scratching around now but he had to come up with something more. Not that he was superstitious but it was bad luck not to list at least three things.

Well, obviously, it didn't matter if he won or lost because the horse wasn't really his. If he didn't win then it wouldn't be J. Masterton's loss but the JDC's, the Jockeys Disability Charity, for whom he was holding the animal in trust, sort of.

And a third?

The horses were loading now. Aquiline was already in the stalls (thank God) and there was only one other left to go. He had to be quick.

He had it – the owner of the winning Gimcrack entry had to make a speech at a grand dinner in York every November. If Aquiline won then it would be his job to entertain the racing aristocracy. God, he could do without that.

As the horses were finally loaded for the start of the race, Simon, unlike everyone else, relaxed. It was a gift, the ability to turn off when all around were strung out with nerves. The way he saw it, his job was over for the moment. The horse had been delivered to the start in the best condition that it was within his power to contrive. Whatever happened next was outside his control. The gates would open and thirteen runners would pelt as fast as they could down the centre of the course for six furlongs. It would be all over in around seventy seconds. It wasn't very long to have a breather. And after it was over, the whole damn thing would be back on his shoulders again. As he always did, he determined to make the most of it.

Mariana got to Simon's side just in time. She grabbed his hand and he wrapped a strong arm around her, hugging her to his side. That felt good.

The crowd was going crazy around them already and the horses were still only dots in the distance. She tried to make out the commentary above the hubbub but it was pointless. She craned her neck to get a glimpse of the screen.

'It's tight,' said Simon, bending to speak into her ear. 'There's at least six in a line.'

Then she could see for herself and she looked with hunger for Neil's red cap.

There. Slap in the centre of the jostling and pounding.

These were horses of quality, Group 2 two-year-old sprinters busting their lungs and guts to get to the line first in a naked, exuberant display of juvenile horse power.

They were all good but, by a fraction – the length of a horse's straining head – Aquiline was better.

'Oh Christ,' Jeremy heard himself saying to the backslapping crowd around him. 'Now I've got to give a sodding speech!'

He was secretly looking forward to it already.

After the presentation, the photographs and the first bottle of champagne – the first of many – Mariana slipped away to find a quiet corner. It was easier said than done. She stood under the trees during the next race and took out her phone.

Should she call back?

Did she dare not to? If she didn't respond there would be other calls and maybe not on her mobile but to Willowdale House – the number was widely available.

She didn't want Simon talking to this particular person. She got the message back up and tapped 'call'.

It was answered at once.

'*Chérie*, you rang me back – I knew you would.'

The voice was low and smoky. It sounded as seductive as its owner had once looked.

'Hello, Carla. How lovely to hear from you.'

Mariana struggled to inject enthusiasm into her voice.

Chapter Five

Alison was aware of a few sore heads at Willowdale as she arrived on the morning after the Gimcrack. Last night's party back at the yard – abundant refreshments supplied by Jeremy – had stretched on till the small hours, so Holly told her. Alison had cut the evening short. She wasn't much of a party girl these days, which was ironic. When she was nursing, she'd often stumbled into work at eight in the morning under the weight of a hangover. Nowadays, when she could afford to lounge around all day recovering, she only drank enough to be polite and ran for home early.

She promised herself she'd return to work soon. Her boss, Dave, would be happy to have her back at the surgery, or she'd find something else useful to do with her time. Return to work once they'd caught the men who'd killed her father. Maybe then she could have her life back.

'Is Simon around?' she asked.

Holly nodded in the general direction of the office. 'Just in from third lot,' she said thickly. The poor thing had plainly made the most of Jeremy's generosity. Alison patted her arm. She rather envied her.

Simon was in a rush as she knew he would be. He was due to return to York for the last day of the meeting, where he was saddling a runner in the big race of the afternoon, the Nunthorpe Stakes.

'I'm just going to collect Mariana, then we're off,' he said as he emerged from the office wearing his best suit, car keys in his hand. 'Are you coming too?'

'Does it look like it?' She was dressed in a check shirt and riding britches. Today was Ladies Day at the festival and half the county would be showing off their glad rags. It was typical of Simon not to be aware of that. Or, judging by the sly smile on his face, maybe he was.

'I just need a quick word.' She walked with him to his muddy Range Rover. 'Do you know a man called Charlie Talbot?'

He shot her a quick glance. 'Sure.'

'I ran into him yesterday afternoon on the Champagne Terrace. He said he was sorry about Dad.'

'So he should be.' Simon didn't look happy.

Alison was surprised. She'd rather expected Simon to find Charlie amusing. 'He looked a bit silly. He reminded me of a teddy bear in a dinner suit.'

'Only not as cuddly. What else did he say?'

'Just that Dad owed him money for Jennifer Eccles. Quite a lot actually.'

'A hundred and fifteen thousand pounds?'

'So you know about it?'

'I certainly do. Was he asking you for the money?'

'Yes.'

'And what did you say?'

Alison felt a flash of irritation. What had her father and Simon been up to? And how come she knew nothing about it? And why was Simon interrogating her all of a sudden?

'What do you think I said? If my father owed anyone money then it's my duty to clear the debt. It's not Charlie Talbot's fault Dad was murdered, is it?'

'I suppose not.' Simon was silent for a moment, clearly turning a thought over in his mind. 'Look, Alison, I haven't got time to talk about this now but, whatever you do, don't pay Talbot anything. Believe me, your father didn't owe him a penny.'

Alison watched him head off up the drive to the house, puzzled. It was good to hear that her father hadn't been in another man's debt but she didn't like to think of Charlie Talbot going round claiming the contrary. She wondered what she would have to do to shut him up.

Today Mariana was obliged to dress up. Simon had insisted she forget about her yard duties and enjoy the day out. But the high fashion event had eerie echoes in her mind of Ascot. She'd worn yellow that day and the image of the bright silk crimsoned with Geoff's blood as she knelt on the floor of the train was horribly fresh. Today she wore black, a plain summer dress with a matching straw sun hat, as simple as she could make it. All the same, she knew she looked good. The dress hugged her figure and her golden skin glowed.

Simon eyed her as she came out to meet him and

said, 'Bloody hell. If I'd known I'd have washed the car.'

She looked at him quizzically.

'That's Yorkshire for "Wow",' he added. 'You're looking good.'

She smiled. This was a big compliment coming from him. Then she had second thoughts. 'I don't look immodest, do I? I can cover up.'

'Don't you dare. Just make sure you come back with both your eyes.'

She stared at him, perplexed.

'Those other women,' he explained, 'the ones who've been shopping and planning their outfit and tarting themselves since daybreak – they're going to be jealous, see?'

She didn't really. Her English might be fluent but sometimes she didn't understand the expressions he used. On the other hand, she knew exactly what he meant. In the past she'd been showered with elaborate praise from men and she'd accepted it as her due. The flattery had been part of her payment.

She wanted to tell Simon that one word from him was worth all the compliments she'd received from other men, but that was dangerous territory. She'd talked little about her romantic past, beyond sharing the fact that she, like him, had suffered one major heartache. There was a symmetry to that. The men who'd paid for her company did not count. Simon was a better man in every way. He treated everyone in his yard equally, speaking to the stable lads as he did the owners. And he listened to what they had to say too. Not many men in his position did that.

She slipped her arms inside his jacket, circling his

waist, and kissed him. 'Thank you,' she said when it ended.

He held on to her. 'I wish we didn't have to go but we're late already.'

She nodded and got into the car.

She could never have imagined being with a man like Simon – uncool, unsophisticated, unaware of his public self. But honest, trusting and solid like a rock. Thank the Lord he didn't know how unworthy she was.

Now, she realised, would be a good moment to get a little awkwardness out of the way.

'I have a lunch appointment tomorrow – I hope you don't mind.'

'Of course not. You go ahead. Who with?'

'An old friend from London.' Better stick as close to the truth as possible. 'She's just up for a few days.'

'Great. Bring her back to the yard. I'd like to meet a friend of yours.'

The thought of that was appalling. 'I'll ask her,' she said, smiling brightly. She didn't like lying to Simon but sometimes it was a necessity.

She prepared herself for a barrage of queries. If she'd been in the car with a woman, Alison say, she'd never have got away with yielding up so little about her friend. But Simon didn't even ask her name. He was not the nosy sort and, right now, she could see he had something else on his mind.

She placed a companionable hand on his thigh as they drove to York in silence.

Simon should not have been surprised to see Charlie Talbot at York. He knew from Alison that he'd been present the day before and here he was again. All the same, the sight of Talbot's shaved head across the room distracted him from his conversation.

The big man turned in his direction.

'Simon!' Mariana pushed an elbow into his ribs. 'Mrs Conville just asked you why you didn't enter Aquiline for the Nunthorpe?'

There were good reasons – he grappled for them.

If he got the chance, he'd have a word with Talbot. Nip this business with Alison in the bud.

'Because I didn't think Aquiline could win a shorter race against more experienced opposition, Mrs Conville.'

But Ellen Conville, owner of Red River, Willowdale's one entry for the day, was not to be put off. 'Two-year-olds have won the Nunthorpe in the past,' she said. 'Quite recently, in fact.'

Talbot was coming towards them, carried their way by the crowd.

'You sound as if you'd like Aquiline to go up against your horse,' said Mariana.

The bugger was going to pass by, pretend he hadn't seen Simon.

Simon wasn't having any of that.

'Oh yes. I think it would be a marvellous contest. Perhaps we should arrange it. A race for a prize purse like in the old days. I'm sure that nice Mr Masterton would match my wager. What do you think, Simon?'

But Simon wasn't listening, wasn't even standing in the space he had occupied in their corner. As Charlie Talbot went by, he had seized his chance.

'Hey, Charlie, I want a word with you.'

Mrs Conville turned to Mariana and shrugged. 'I don't think he liked my idea very much.'

'What do you mean by hassling my cousin?'

The words came out more aggressively than he had intended but Simon didn't care about that. Neither was he intimidated by Charlie Talbot's bulk, at least he was able to look the big man directly in the eye.

'Keep your hair on, chum.' Charlie was grinning. 'This isn't the place to have a barney.'

'You started it. You approached her here yesterday.'

'We had a little talk, that's all. I told her about the Jennifer Eccles situation which I was a bit surprised to find she knew nothing about.'

They'd manoeuvred themselves out of the pedestrian traffic. A few yards away, Simon could see Mariana's back as she talked to Mrs Conville. The owner's bright eyes, alive with curiosity, flicked in his direction.

'There is no situation,' he said firmly, 'as you ruddy well know. You're just making mischief. Trying to take advantage of a poor woman who has lost her father in the most cruel way.'

'Bollocks,' said Charlie and took a swig from the champagne glass in his fist. It was dwarfed by his fat sausage fingers. 'You could say that it's you and her who's using poor old Geoff's death to avoid coughing up what he owed me.'

'He didn't owe you a thing. He bought you out fair and square when it didn't look as if the horse would ever race. In my opinion he was more than generous and look how you've repaid him.'

'Don't get superior with me, sonny. The pair of you bamboozled me and I aim to get what I'm due. And Miss Hall, I'm pleased to say, is more reasonable than you are. So I suggest you butt out of it and leave it to me and her.'

Simon took a deep breath. Talbot was right about one thing, here and now was no place to get into a slanging match. He had a job to do this afternoon.

'Let me make one thing plain, you'll get nothing out of her because Geoff owed you nothing. Have some decency and leave her alone.'

'Who's that gentleman Simon's having such an urgent conversation with, my dear?'

'I don't know,' Mariana lied. 'I've never seen him before.'

'He's awfully big. Rather uncouth, too. I'm not a fan of that shaven-headed look.'

Mariana had deliberately turned her back on the big man in the hope he wouldn't recognise her. But that had put him directly in Mrs Conville's sightline and she was clearly intrigued.

'I don't think I've ever seen Simon look angry. He's such an even-tempered young man as a rule.'

Mariana risked a look over her shoulder. Simon's pale cheeks flamed with a dot of pink, the way they did when he was annoyed. But she'd never seen him as upset as this. She could tell he was clearly holding his passion in.

Her eye found his. He would have read anxiety there – rather more than that, too, if he'd known the truth of the situation.

'Coming, Mariana,' he called and turned to hiss a

final comment in the face of his antagonist.

The big man shrugged and said something like, 'Please yourself.'

As Simon returned to join her, Charlie Talbot looked her full in the face.

Just as she feared, he had recognised her.

Mariana's afternoon was ruined. It had always been a possibility that she would run into a man she had met while working for Chrysalis Girls. She'd been uncomfortable at Royal Ascot for just that reason and had made sure she wasn't involved in the presentation for Aquiline's victory or the photographs that followed. But she'd assumed, stupidly, that she would be safer this far from London. There wasn't much logic to that – as she could see, the place was stuffed full of southerners. She hadn't realised what an event on the social calendar the Ebor Festival was.

It wasn't even being recognised that upset her. Most of the men she'd met through Chrysalis were civilised and well-bred. By definition they had money – her time was extravagantly expensive – and they usually had taste. She'd been squired to theatres, operas and art galleries, all kinds of cultural events she'd had no knowledge of, and she'd been forced to learn to hold her own in discussing them. It had been an education. Added to which, she had enjoyed the delights of fine restaurants and hotels and trips to villas in the sun. Certain kinds of men, moneyed, powerful men, loved to show off – to impressionable girls in particular. They even tried hard in bed – which was a mystery. Sometimes, she'd thought she was the one who should be paying.

To be recognised by a man like that would not have been a problem. In any case, most of her former clients would have been as keen to avoid her as she was them, seeing as they were nearly all married.

But not every man she'd come across in those days was civilised. Some were dangerous and she'd developed an instinct to detect them. And, of course, she'd been protected. Carla – whose own instinct was infallible – had seen to that.

She'd not thought Charlie Talbot one of the dangerous ones but he was crude. Mrs Conville had spotted it. He'd brand her a whore in a bar packed with race-goers, just for a laugh.

What was unjust was that she'd never slept with him. He'd never paid for a second of her time, yet he was just the kind of oaf who could make trouble.

She'd met him while spending the evening with a client called Derek, a property speculator who wanted an attractive dinner companion to impress a colleague in a new venture. 'He'll be so dazzled by you, he won't read as far as the bottom of the contract,' he'd said.

Charlie did indeed seem dazzled, notwithstanding the presence of his own female companion, a square-chinned blonde who looked almost as formidable as he did. 'The wife,' Mariana was told. In fact, Sharon was an unpretentious woman with a dry sense of humour who gossiped with Mariana in the Ladies so the men could talk business.

By the time they returned, there was a brandy bottle on the table and contract talk had been replaced by bawdy jokes. It was also clear to Mariana from the look in Charlie's suspicious little eyes that Derek had revealed the precise nature of their relationship.

The next hour had been long, with Charlie's remarks becoming broader and more personal as the brandy goblets were refilled. He asked how much Mariana would charge to pass him the bottle and, as his fingers deliberately brushed hers, suggested she put the gesture on Derek's tab. Finally, seemingly unconcerned that his wife was sitting next to him, he put his hand on Mariana's thigh under the table and thrust it up beneath her skirt. She kicked him on the ankle, jabbing the point of her shoe into the bone and was delighted to see the look of pained surprise on his fat face. He leapt to his feet, saying some folk had work to get to in the morning. Before he left he took a five-pound note from his pocket and pressed it into Mariana's hand. 'I think you're over-priced, darling,' he'd whispered in her ear.

The next morning Mariana instructed Carla never to book her with Derek again. Two days later, she was amazed to hear that a man called Charlie had been asking if she was available.

And here he was at York. Her one wish was to get away from the racecourse without clapping eyes on him again.

Standing in the parade ring before the Nunthorpe Stakes, Simon found it difficult to put the altercation with Charlie Talbot out of his mind. By his side Mrs Conville was taking a keen interest in proceedings and he forced himself to answer her questions properly. Though she only kept one horse at Willowdale, she was a valued owner and had known his father well. At the very least, he owed her his full attention.

'Be candid, Simon. Do you think there's a serious chance of Red River upsetting the odds?'

The bookmakers had the horse as an outside chance at 20–1.

'Candidly? No.'

'That's a relief. It's so much better when I don't have to get my hopes up.'

'I wouldn't write him off though. He's still a fine horse, Mrs Conville.'

'He's too old. I'm only keeping him going on sentiment.'

Simon thought that was a bit hard but it was true that at nine years of age the horse was the oldest in the field. He'd contested the Nunthorpe four times and once, in Phil's last year when he was in his prime, he'd come second. Simon would dearly love him to pull off a victory at his final attempt. An unexpected triumph was what he needed to wipe the image of Charlie Talbot's face from his mind.

Mrs Conville seemed to know what he was thinking.

'Cheer up. I'm just delighted he's still competing at this level. It's a tribute to your skill, young man.'

It was kind of her to say so but it didn't raise his spirits or stop the voice in his head that was cursing him for a bloody fool. He should not have spoken to Talbot, not on impulse like that, without considering what he might say. The other man had not yielded an inch. All he'd done was stir the hornets' nest and make things worse for Alison – which was the worst outcome of all.

Simon felt Geoff's absence keenly. There was a hole

in his life. He'd turned to his uncle more readily than he'd ever turned to his father and he'd never come away empty-handed. How much worse then was it for Alison? His cousin had been his best friend for fifteen years, ever since she'd come back from Africa to live with her father. She'd been the only person Simon had been able to talk to after his mother died, the only one on whom he'd felt able to dump his anguish and anger. He'd known he could say anything to her and she would understand because she loved him. Loved him better than a sister or a lover. He knew she was a true friend, one whose concern and advice would always be available to him as long as they both lived. Not that he'd ever dream of saying as much.

The way Alison's father had been stolen from her bled within Simon like a wound beneath the skin. He'd been right there on the train beside Geoff and he'd not been able to prevent the murder. Simon had apologised to Alison, over and over but she'd told him she did not hold him to blame. But, irrational though it was, Simon blamed himself. He'd do anything to ease Alison's pain. And what he'd done in this matter of Charlie Talbot and Jennifer Eccles was make matters worse. A fool indeed.

Red River, a gleaming black animal with a high step was making his final circuit of the parade ring.

'He looks magnificent,' said Mrs Conville. 'Maybe your lovely Brazilian friend will bring him luck.'

Simon fervently hoped she was right. 'So Mariana will take all the credit if he wins?'

'Why not?'

But Red River did not win – he came stone last.

In the circumstances, Simon was not surprised.

* * *

The moment Mariana had been dreading came right at the end of the afternoon. She'd been sticking to Simon's side, fearful of being accosted by the man called Charlie, though she'd wondered if that were the best course of action. If he came looking for Simon and insulted her in front of her fiancé, then what would happen? She was keenly aware of the events on the train, when she was the one who had attracted the attention of the men who had killed Geoff. Sometimes, it seemed her very presence was enough to spark trouble.

Simon hadn't mentioned the row and she didn't want to be the one who brought it up. She mustn't show any curiosity about this Charlie. She'd pretend that he didn't exist and maybe, after they left the course, she'd never see him again.

She'd thought she'd got her wish when, just before the last race, Simon said, 'Shall we go? Beat some of the traffic.'

She agreed eagerly.

They only split up for a couple of minutes but the big man with the shaved head was waiting for her as she came out of the Ladies toilet.

'Hello again,' he said. He was smirking, naturally. 'Fabiana, as I remember – or is it something different now?'

She gave him her haughtiest glare. 'You must be mistaken.'

She tried to push past. His bulk blocked her way.

'You're a bit out of your manor, aren't you? Or have you milked all the geezers dry down south?'

She didn't follow the words but the meaning was clear.

'Let me pass.'

'What are you doing with Simon Waterford? He's a wanky piece of Yorkshire piss.'

'Don't talk about him like that. Simon is worth two of you.'

'He's a crook. But the customer is always right, I suppose – especially in your line of work, eh?'

'He's not—' she cut the words off quickly. It was dangerous to say anything.

He gripped her arm in his great fist as she attempted to slip by. The corridor ahead was empty and she was aware of a roar from the crowd outside. The last race of the day was being run and they were momentarily alone.

'So he doesn't know about you? Don't tell me you've changed your career. Doesn't look like it in that dress.'

She could knee him in the testicles. She'd done it once before with a man who'd laid hold of her and wouldn't let go. It was a tactic that worked.

But there was a reason why she couldn't do that. She tried something else.

'How is Sharon? She's such a nice woman.'

'The silly slag booted me out of my own home, that's how nice she is. But let's leave her out of it. You're going to do me a favour.'

Mariana couldn't imagine anything she could do for this loathsome man. His grip on her arm was beginning to hurt.

'Me and your pal Simon have had a misunder-standing about a horse. Jennifer Eccles. Used to belong to Geoff Hall, now his daughter's. You with me?'

She nodded. Of course she knew Jennifer Eccles, the best filly at Willowdale.

'Geoff owed me money on that horse and your Simon is going to tell Alison Hall not to pay me. You'd better make him change his mind.'

'How can I do that?'

He laughed. 'You think I'm thick, don't you? Woman like you, with all your professional skills, you can twist a weak as water little twit like Simon round your – well, whatever you choose.'

'That's ridiculous.'

'Is it? It's all the same to me, love. You get me my money and I'll keep it zipped. Otherwise, I'll be delighted to tell him all about what you used to do for a living.'

It wasn't a surprise. She'd realised it was coming but it still made her sick. She played her last card.

'There's no point. He knows already.'

'Oh yeah? I don't believe you. And even if he does he won't have the whole story – not the one I'm going to tell him anyway. Your choice.'

And he released her arm.

Mariana found Simon waiting for her, impatient to get away. 'You took your time,' he said.

'Sorry. There was a queue.'

She could have told him she'd been waylaid by the man he'd been arguing with earlier. That he'd threatened to tell lies about her if she didn't persuade Simon to tell Alison to pay the money for Jennifer Eccles.

As they began the drive back to Willowdale, she turned it over in her mind. It wasn't too late. She could still try to get her side of the story in first.

But it was risky. She didn't know exactly what Charlie Talbot might say to blacken her name. He could, for example, get Derek to corroborate his story. They'd been in business together – they still might be. It was also possible Derek harboured a grudge against her. She'd refused to see him again after that night in the restaurant and she knew from Carla he'd regularly asked after her. He might be more than happy to confirm that he'd rented her body on several occasions a couple of years ago.

Besides, even if never proved, it was the kind of allegation that could permanently harm a woman in a man's eyes. Simon loved and trusted her, she was sure of it. She couldn't risk damaging that trust.

So, what was she going to do?

She had no idea.

They drove in silence. Simon was grateful that Mariana was not the kind of person to make conversation for the sake of it. She'd witnessed the row with Charlie earlier yet she'd not referred to it – he appreciated that, too. He supposed he ought to say something to her about it, at least give some explanation for his behaviour. Well, he would but not now. He didn't want to worry her. She'd been through one terrible experience since stepping into his life, he'd do all he could to protect her from another.

The reappearance of Charlie Talbot set off all sorts of reverberations. He vividly remembered the big man's visit to Willowdale when he claimed he'd been swindled. And his uncle's account of being watched on trips to London. The last time he'd seen the man had been at Ascot when he'd witnessed the effect

Talbot had had on Geoff. And then his uncle had been murdered.

Sometimes, when Simon was lying awake in the middle of the night and even the soothing presence of the sleeping Mariana by his side could not still the unhappy thoughts in his head, he'd considered the attack on the train. The police had said it was random, so did the press – and so did he himself in his rational daylight moments. The idea of two yobs assaulting race-goers dressed up in fancy suits fitted every profile of random violence going.

But suppose it wasn't random? Suppose their group – and Geoff in particular – had been targeted? Suppose those men had walked past every other extravagantly dressed passenger to pick them out *because they knew who they were*?

The police had assumed they must have been attracted by Mariana who, there was no denying, made an eye-catching sight. But there had been several other pretty women on the train, one or two, Simon had noticed as they'd waited on the Ascot platform, showing a lot more flesh than Mariana.

Then there was the man who had been knitting. A grown man knitting in public! Simon had never seen that before and it was surely worthy of note to youths out to make trouble. But they'd walked straight past him and made for where the three of them were sitting.

Simon knew very well that they'd done nothing to provoke the assault. The yobs had done that, just as the train was entering Clapham Junction. The timing was in their favour, giving them the opportunity to get off the train and vanish into the busy and complex station which, so it seemed, they knew well.

Maybe they had just been lucky. Or maybe it had all been planned.

The police had said they were confident of catching the killers. Sure, there were too many tragic knife assaults in the capital but they always – nearly always – caught the kids who perpetrated them. What with the excellent CCTV pictures and the unavoidable publicity, it would only be a matter of time before someone grassed them up or they fell into the police net. Young men like that would have records, would have left footprints somewhere on the system.

But they hadn't. No records, no footprints. No mendacious friend or guilty relative willing to turn them in. And time was passing. In the dead of night, Simon was not afraid to admit to himself that Uncle Geoff's killers would never be caught.

Then he'd go over the whole thing again in his head and try to come up with another line of thinking, one with a better chance of catching the men who had got away.

If the attack had been planned and his uncle was the target, then someone must have had a motive for the killing. Who would want to kill a fine and generous man like Geoff Hall?

Whenever Simon thought along these lines he could only ever come up with one name: Charlie Talbot. The business with the horse had obsessed the fellow. Witness the way he'd tried to bully everyone involved with the deal, from sending solicitor's letters to Dave the vet to putting watchers on Geoff's flat. Just talking to Charlie was an intimidating experience. The way he'd looked at Simon that afternoon, as if he'd love to pull his head off with those great bear's-paw fists.

But it wasn't just a gut antagonism. Geoff had told him before Ascot that Charlie's business was in trouble. That had not been much of a surprise, given the way the building trade had nosedived in the credit crunch. Maybe the pressures had got so bad, Charlie had come to see squeezing money out of Geoff as his only lifeline to some cash. And when Geoff had stonewalled him he'd snapped and arranged the incident on the train.

It wouldn't have been impossible. Charlie employed casual labour. He'd used his workers to keep watch on Geoff's flat. Maybe a couple of them were prepared to do more than that. And it didn't take a clairvoyant to have worked out that Geoff would be accompanying Simon to Ascot to watch Aquiline. Charlie himself could have kept an eye on when they left the course for the station.

If he spoke to the police, would they take him seriously? They could look at Charlie's phone records and interview his workers. Even if the men they sought had fled the country, they could maybe get a handle on who they were. And track them down – extradite them!

At that point in his midnight musing he would tell himself not to be stupid. If Charlie wanted to get money out of Uncle Geoff, what would be the point of killing him? And he'd conclude that he was getting carried away, turn over and finally get back to sleep.

But now, as he drove back to Willowdale, all those late-night suppositions came alive again.

The fact was that Geoff's death had not deprived Charlie Talbot of a shot at getting money out of Jennifer Eccles. Not if he pursued Alison for it.

It was imperative he spoke to Alison as soon as possible. He'd give her chapter and verse on Talbot's attempts to screw money out of her father. And he'd get her to promise not to pay the fellow a penny.

As for his suspicions about the murder, that was another matter. One that required a lot of consideration. You couldn't make casual accusations of that sort, even against a man as dislikeable as Charlie.

Then another thought surfaced. If his suspicions about the big man had any substance, and if Alison spurned his demands as her father had done, where would Charlie Talbot direct his murderous impulses next?

Back in London, fresh from his twin triumphs in York with Aquiline and that satisfyingly naive stable girl Holly, Jeremy made a beeline for his habitual watering hole, Hughie's wine bar in Hampstead. He had no trouble bagging his favourite seat in the window nook, which was par for the course this summer. He could remember past years when it had been standing room only of an evening, particularly on a night when musicians were booked to play in the basement room one flight down.

He put it bluntly to Hughie himself when the owner made an appearance.

'Hey, my friend from the north.' Hughie gripped Jeremy's hand and slumped into the seat opposite. He wore his jacket rolled to the elbows in his trademark style – one that was a good fifteen years out of date, in Jeremy's opinion. Not that he would ever voice it.

Jeremy caught the eye of the girl behind the bar and signalled for another glass.

'A bit thin on the ground tonight,' he observed.

'A bit thin every night. Except on the weekend when we've got a decent band.' The owner took a long pull on his drink. 'You need to drink this one quick, while it's still cold. The warmer it gets, the more it tastes like the horse piss it is.'

'Just as well you're here to help me then.' Jeremy topped up both glasses. The beauty of this place was that it was within staggering distance of his flat. And also that he and the owner went way back. There were some things he could talk about to old Hughie that were verboten in other company.

Hughie scratched his designer stubble reflectively. 'So, how's the harem these days?'

'Hardly a harem.'

'I don't know. More than one available woman counts as a harem in my book. And the way your horse performed yesterday you should be living it up like a sultan.'

As an ex-gambler, Hughie professed to have no interest in racing these days, but he was always well-informed.

Jeremy raised his glass – Hughie was right, the wine was thin – and said, 'To Aquiline. And the training genius who gets him on the track.'

Hughie's lip curled, as Jeremy knew it would. 'I'd rather drink to the birds you're shagging.'

Women were the abiding topic of their conversations. Hughie took a vicarious pleasure in hearing of Jeremy's exploits and Jeremy allowed himself to boast, just a little. He never would have got away with it with anyone else.

'How's that Meg? Still keeping her satisfied?'

'I like to think so. Though I'm going to have to tread carefully – I've just bagged a frisky new young friend in her neck of the woods. I can see that juggling the two of them might be . . .' he searched for the right word, there was no call to be uncouth, 'demanding.'

Hughie guffawed with pleasure and waved at the barista. 'Let's have something with a bit more body, shall we? And in the absence of your lady friends we'll have to make do with a Cabernet.'

The fresh bottle was brought and opened with suitable relish. Jeremy had never seen Hughie drunk though he was an assiduous sampler of the product he sold. He bought a few cases from Jeremy each year, which was another justification for his presence in this watering hole.

'And what about the Brazilian?' Hughie asked.

'Mariana? I hope you are not suggesting there's anything going on between me and her?'

'It's not beyond the bounds of possibility. Professional habits die hard and all that.'

'Mariana's in retirement. I squeezed her bum yesterday at the races and I thought she was going to put my eyes out.'

'So it's still full steam ahead with her and your genius trainer, is it?'

Jeremy confirmed that it was so. 'The wedding's definitely on.'

'And no one's told the groom he's marrying a tart?'

103

Jeremy shook his head emphatically. 'Who's going to tell him? Not me – why spoil a happy union?'

Hughie sipped his wine. 'You're a good man, Jeremy.'

Jeremy sighed. 'Sadly not. Just a broad-minded one – like you. I say, you're right, this is a much better drop than that last one.' He put his glass down and looked round with contentment, appreciatively eyed the girl who had served them – and her curvaceous colleague wrestling a cork from a bottle behind the bar. 'You know, Hughie, I'd burn out in six months if I worked here. Booze and beauty on tap. I'd be like a schoolboy in a sweet shop.'

Hughie turned a sardonic eye on him. 'And if you survived the six months you'd never put another sweetie in your mouth, I guarantee. They're all the same, these young girls, bundles of need and neurosis dressed up in a short skirt.'

'Oh dear, you sound a bit cynical.'

'Sorry, mate, sometimes the mask slips, especially when the lease is up and I've got the bank breathing down my neck. A moody little slut who gets in my bed looking for a pay rise wouldn't make life any easier.'

Jeremy topped up both glasses. Hughie might be off the girls but a drink was another matter.

'How about Carla?' he inquired, steering the conversation on to happier ground. 'Still seeing her?'

Hughie smiled. 'We continue to have a few mutual interests. Merchandisers of a good time, as you might say.'

Jeremy could see that. Carla might be a few years older than Hughie but, as in his relationship with Meg, there was a lot to be said for the mature liaison.

104

'It's like wine, isn't it?' he said. 'You can rely on a decent vintage.'

Hughie raised his glass. 'You certainly can, my friend.'

Chapter Six

Sitting at a table at the far end of the hotel garden, Carla could have been mistaken for a woman of Mariana's own age. The blond bell of her hair gleamed in the sunlight and her wrist arched elegantly as she raised her hand in salute. She stood up to welcome Mariana, showing off a chic navy two-piece suit nipped tightly round her tiny waist. Up close, make-up could not conceal the lines of years and hard experience. As Mariana bent her head to be kissed on both cheeks, a familiar perfume enveloped her; though liberally applied, it did little to mask the scent of cigarettes.

Carla surveyed Mariana's shirt and jeans with interest. 'The rustic look suits you.' The tobacco-rich voice brought a host of memories flooding back.

The table was laid for lunch and Carla poured wine from a half-empty bottle.

'It's not too bad,' she said as she raised her glass. '*Salut*. It's good to see you again, *chérie.*'

Carla's affectations were French but Mariana had heard several versions of her heritage. One thing was sure, it had its roots in poverty and desperation. Carla had scrambled her way up life's greasy pole and had no intention of sliding backwards.

A waiter appeared with menus.

'Order me something, will you?' Carla instructed. 'You know what I like.'

Mariana did as she was told. 'Crab salad for both of us.'

'Perfect.' Carla smiled and the waiter disappeared.

Mariana spurned the irrational jolt of pleasure that the word of praise had sparked inside her. The days when it mattered whether or not she pleased Carla were gone.

'I hope you've recovered from that terrible business on the train.' Carla took a cigarette from the packet by her elbow and lit it in one reflexive movement. 'It would have been too vulgar of me to bother you before but now, I hope, is not a bad time for us to enjoy a little reunion.'

Mariana could not quite bring herself to agree.

'What brings you up to Yorkshire?' she asked.

'Business.' Carla sucked in a lungful of smoke. 'You know.'

'The same business?'

'Why not? It's recession-proof.'

The waiter returned with their food and Mariana picked at it. She was uncomfortable. She wondered what the other woman wanted.

'I meant it when I said I was out of the game. Out of Chrysalis Girls, out of fashion, through with London. I've got a new life now. I'm getting married in November.'

'I know, darling. Congratulations. I shall expect an invitation.'

Oh no!

Carla laughed, a deep dirty familiar sound. 'Your face. I'm joking, don't worry.'

Mariana managed an awkward laugh of her own. Though, now she thought about it, maybe adding Carla to the guest list was not such a bad idea. At the moment her contribution was a little light.

'Felix has been asking after you,' Carla said as she forked her salad without much interest.

'Dear Uncle Felix.' Maybe he could come to the wedding too.

Felix Alves had been Mariana's employer before she'd left London for Yorkshire. Benefactor was a more appropriate term. He'd offered her a post in his fashion house when she'd turned her back on the escort world, and the job had been a lifeline. Mariana had known little about the marketing of beachwear but she'd been willing to learn and he'd paid her, she knew, far more than she'd been worth. She liked to think she'd done her best to earn it. Of course, she'd realised he'd had a crush on her but, by treating him as a respected elder, her relationship with 'Uncle' Felix had remained entirely proper. Not that she hadn't modelled the company's wares for him occasionally but she'd considered these private fashion shows part of her job.

Compared to some of the men she'd had dealings with, Felix had been a sweetheart and she'd felt a little guilty at vanishing abruptly from his business and his life.

'He's always talking about you,' Carla continued. 'Not that I see him all that often.'

Carla and Felix had roots in the past. Carla had

once revealed she'd worked in the rag trade as a girl and Mariana had no difficulty in imagining the youthful Carla modelling for Felix in a Soho basement a quarter of a century ago.

Mariana put nostalgic thoughts of Felix and guest lists to the back of her mind. Who was she kidding? At the moment the chances of the wedding going ahead were looking remote.

She emptied her glass. She'd not intended to drink but it helped. It was time to start putting a few cards on the table.

'Carla, can you please tell me what you want?'

Simon made the short trip to see Alison at lunchtime, after he'd dealt with the calls the yard secretary had left for him. The last on the list was Mrs Conville.

'I've decided to retire Red River,' she said. 'Yesterday was a race too many – I shouldn't have run him.'

'Don't blame yourself, Ellen, I was all for it. Anyway, he enjoyed himself.'

'I very much doubt it. He's never come last in his life before.'

Simon grinned to himself, even the most sensible people could be soft about their animals.

'Anyway,' she continued, 'I want you to know I'm on the lookout for a new horse and I shall have to find a good home for Red River. I shall be needing your advice.'

Simon reflected briefly on the conversation as he drove. Acquiring a new horse was always easier than resettling an old one but he'd do his best.

He turned into the drive and parked in front of his uncle's rambling old Victorian house. Of course, it belonged to Alison now but it was impossible not to think of it as 'Uncle Geoff's' - as it had been throughout his entire life.

As he waited on the doorstep he wondered, as he'd done frequently in the past two months, how Alison was managing on her own. The house was large, six bedrooms, two reception rooms, dining room, conservatory, study and countless other nooks and corners. It had provided a generous living space for father and daughter - they had both claimed that had its advantages - but now Alison must be finding its emptiness oppressive. Simon and Mariana had moved in for a couple of weeks after the murder but after they had returned to Willowdale, Simon frequently thought of his cousin in her loneliness. Yet, though she was selling her father's London home, she said she intended to remain here. If Simon could have had one wish in the world it would be for a good man to walk into Alison's heart and home and solve the problem. But he was keeping his mouth firmly shut on that score.

His reflections did not make him feel any easier about his regrettable behaviour of the day before.

She looked delighted to see him and dragged him into the kitchen. The table was covered in papers - bank statements and chequebooks, Simon noted - and the remains of an impromptu lunch.

'Help yourself,' she said, pointing to a loaf and packets of cheese and ham. 'There's beer in the fridge.'

Simon was tempted but first things first.

'I came over to say sorry about Charlie Talbot.'

'Oh, that's all right. I suppose you could have told

me about him but it was really up to Dad. He liked to protect me from unpleasant things, like I was still a little girl.'

'There's more to it than that. I ran into him yesterday at York.'

'He was there again?'

'Unfortunately. I'm afraid I rather lost my temper.'

She fixed him with a green-eyed stare. '*You* did? I wish I'd seen it.'

'It wasn't my finest hour. I told him to stop hassling you.'

'I can fight my own battles, Simon.'

'I'm sorry. But I know exactly what happened with Jennifer Eccles. Uncle Geoff bought Charlie out fair and square and now he's trying to con you. He's a bastard and you mustn't have anything to do with him. Leave him to your solicitor – Clive Silver can tell him where to get off.'

'I think,' she said, 'that you'd better tell me about the whole thing from the beginning – how Dad ended up owning a horse with him in the first place. I'd like to know exactly where I stand.'

Simon nodded and sat down heavily at the table. It was the reason he'd come over.

'Perhaps I will have that beer after all.'

Carla took her time, made a pantomime of lighting her next cigarette as if she hadn't heard Mariana's question. Finally she spoke.

'You don't think I am simply curious to see how my young protégée is faring?'

'You have many protégées.'

'And I like to keep an eye on them all. But, to be

111

candid, you matter more to me. You're not as tough as some of those other little gold-diggers.'

Mariana blinked with surprise. She wasn't sure whether to be offended or not. She said nothing.

'You see, we – Felix and I – don't think it is healthy for you to cut yourself off completely from your family.'

'I have no family.'

'You know that's not true, Mariana.'

So. Now she knew where this encounter was heading. 'No family I choose to acknowledge.'

'Paula is very sorry for the way she treated you. She would like the chance to mend things.'

Mariana poured the remains of the wine into her glass with an unsteady hand.

'No.'

'But she's your sister—'

'*Half*-sister.'

'The only sister you have – as you are to her. You need each other.'

'She ruined my life.'

Carla laughed. 'It doesn't look like it's ruined from what I can see.'

'I have another chance at being happy. I'm not going to let her screw it up for me again.'

Carla nodded, 'OK. I tried.'

'You've talked to Paula?'

'She asked me to make an approach to you – which I've done and you're not interested. So, let's have some more wine.' She raised a hand to the waiter.

Mariana felt the tension flood out of her. It made sense that Paula would try to reach her at some point, though she had not prepared herself for it. All her thoughts of danger had been focused in other directions. It was impossible, as a single person, to be on guard for threats from every quarter.

Suddenly it was a great relief to be sitting with a woman who knew the worst things about her. Carla had been her agent in the sale of her body. Had organised her dates, and made the phone calls to check she was safe, had advised her how to handle the difficult clients, had warned her off the dangerous ones and had ensured she always got paid. She'd watched Mariana's back with skill and cunning and never asked her to do anything she hadn't already done herself. With Carla, she didn't have to tell any lies because she already knew the worst about Mariana – and she still appeared to like her.

She allowed her glass to be filled. It was a long while since she'd let herself get tipsy. People said stupid things – unguarded things – when they were drunk.

Now, though, she had a unique opportunity to unburden herself. She could only talk to Carla about the matter that weighed so heavily on her today.

'Do you remember a man called Charlie Talbot?' she asked.

Carla drew on her cigarette. 'A gorilla,' she said. 'Not a premium client. Crude.'

'Yes, him.'

'He kept asking for dates with you and I had to say no. We had a row. Why are you asking about him?'

Mariana unbuttoned the cuff of her shirt and bared her forearm. The marks of the big man's grip made a bracelet above her wrist, puffy and crimson, with the red deepening at the edges with a hint of the blue to come.

113

'He did that to me yesterday.'

'My dear!' Carla looked horrified. 'Where was this?'

Mariana told her. It was good to get the story out, just to relieve the pressure that had been building up inside.

'He says he'll tell Simon about me working for Chrysalis Girls unless I find a way of getting him money from some horse sale. It's impossible.' She laughed. 'And here was I talking about a wedding. It's not going to happen, I know it.'

'What are you going to do?'

She shrugged. 'I don't know. I should tell Simon but I can't be certain he'll understand. It could ruin everything. But Charlie Talbot will ruin it for sure.'

Carla reached for her hand, squeezed with her thin bony fingers.

'If Simon loves you it will be OK. You will get through and it will make you stronger.'

'Maybe. But even if Simon stands by me, what if Charlie spreads it around? What will his friends say or the people who pay him to train their horses? What will Simon's cousin think? They are not so broad-minded here like people in London or Paris.'

They sat in silence for a moment. What could Carla say? There were no obvious solutions.

The older woman reached into her bag and pulled out an envelope. 'Considering what you said about Paula, I wasn't going to show you these. But, in the circumstances, you might as well see.'

She spread a handful of photographs across the table top. They showed a young woman, dark and pretty, in a prim skirt and high-buttoned blouse standing in front of a two-storey building with a crest over the arched wooden door. In a couple of shots she was sitting at a table by a computer. In another, looking up from an exercise book covered in close-written script. In these she wore spectacles.

'Paula has gone to college,' Carla explained. 'She says she knows she's left it too late to be a doctor but she's training to be a teacher.'

'Oh.' The images were far removed from the ones Mariana carried in her head. In those, young Paula was visible in smoky interiors behind beer bottles and between amorous boys. She wore no spectacles and no high necks in those.

'She's still very young,' Carla said. 'Just twenty. And when she let you down she was off the rails. I think she's back on track.'

Mariana found herself smiling. 'You never give up, do you?'

'I just think – especially after what you've just told me – you can't allow yourself to get isolated in life. You may not be proud of your roots but they can still give you strength. You're going to need that, from the sound of it.'

'Yes.' She sighed heavily. 'You think my best bet is to confess to Simon?'

Carla shook her head. 'Not yet. Charlie won't tell him, surely, until he's certain he won't be paid.'

'But he won't be. I overheard Simon telling him he'd get nothing.'

'Still, I would keep very calm. Decide in your mind what you will say to Simon if you have to throw yourself on his mercy. If you think it will help, I can talk to him.'

'But what would you say?'

'Men don't always see things from a woman's point of view. There were reasons why you did what you did.'

Mariana appreciated the offer. All the same, it wasn't reassuring.

'There is one other thing you should do.'

'Yes?'

'Pray.'

Mariana would have laughed but she saw the older woman was serious.

Alison listened carefully. She wasn't surprised to hear that her father's conduct in the acquisition of Jennifer Eccles had been blameless. The way Simon told it, Geoff had started off trying to do Charlie a good turn by sharing the cost of a promising horse. Then, when it looked as if the animal didn't have a racing future, he'd made it easy for the builder to walk away with no financial loss.

When she'd begun the loathsome task of sorting through Geoff's belongings, Alison's fear was that she would discover things that would belittle her father in her eyes. She was aware she held him in an almost unhealthy regard. Friends she had spoken to about their parents had always found aspects of their life and character to criticise – God knows, she was critical enough of her mother. Nobody could be without flaws and it was as important to love someone's minuses as their pluses, otherwise how could you claim to really know the sum of a person?

She'd gone through a phase in her mid-teens when she'd tried hard to hate her father. Aunt Rose had died the year before and she'd seen the hole it had left in her family's life. Suppose she should lose Dad in the same way? He and Rose were brother and sister – maybe the stroke that killed her was genetic? She didn't want to go through the trauma that had steamrollered Simon.

So she had tried hard to diminish her father in her eyes, to make his loss less painful when it came. But hating him was difficult. They had plenty of shouting matches – he was a good shouter – but somehow they always finished with his arms around her, telling her how much he loved her.

The hating-dad phase hadn't lasted long and she'd come to accept that she had more regard for her father than others had for theirs. So losing him was a horror – as she'd always known it would be. And part of it was being faced with the remains of his life. Would his goodness stand up to scrutiny? What evidence would there be of private vice that would undermine his memory?

So far there had been nothing – unless you counted a secret addiction to Werther's Originals; no packets of porn or incriminating letters from mistresses or rent boys. She'd laughed about that possibility with Mariana as they had travelled back from London.

Mariana had been scandalised that Geoff had had no serious romantic relationships since he'd broken with Karen. 'Just think of it – twenty years without sex.' She'd said it as if it were the most unnatural thing in the world and Alison had not contradicted her. But she respected her father's self-restraint – he had never met another woman he cared for sufficiently to turn his life upside down. A sexual relationship for him was a serious undertaking and that was how she felt herself. Which explained why she, too, had slept alone for the past three years. But she'd not gone into that with Mariana who – you could tell just from looking at her – probably thought a day without a hot embrace as unsupportable as a day without water or wine.

But people's secrets did not just involve sex. And when Charlie Talbot had come blundering out of the crowd at York races with his story about Geoff owing him money on a horse, it had struck a chord in Alison. Was this the blow to her father's reputation that she'd been preparing herself for? Of course she didn't want it to be that way, but she was prepared.

So, despite Simon's assurances yesterday morning, she had steeled herself against the possibility that Talbot had been telling the truth. And then she had gone to look for evidence to refute it.

'I've been going through Dad's records,' she said, pointing to the mess of papers on the table. 'He kept his business and personal stuff separate. All his outgoings to do with horses were drawn on his personal account.'

Simon looked surprised. 'What are you looking for?'

'I started off thinking there might have been a mix-up and Dad had already paid Charlie Talbot.'

'I told you he paid him fifteen thousand pounds.'

'Yes, I found a record in an old chequebook. It's here.'

She showed him the stub. On it was scrawled the sum, with 'Talbot' on the payee box.

'As I said.'

'And there's also a cheque in this book for a hundred

thousand. Made out to JDC. Do you think that's got anything to do with Charlie?'

She showed it to Simon, who studied it and then began to smile.

'JDC stands for Jockeys Disability Charity. Your dad was making a donation.'

She felt foolish, not so much for failing to recognise the initials – Geoff had left the charity more money in his will – but for looking for a misdemeanour on her father's part. All she had unearthed was an act of generosity that, had he lived, would never have come to her notice. How typical.

'I just thought I might turn something up,' she said. 'The invoice Charlie told me about or maybe a note in Dad's desk diary. But this was all I could find. I suppose there wouldn't have been anything in writing because Charlie said they'd only come to an agreement at Ascot, just before Dad was killed.'

'Jesus.' Simon's face flushed pink. 'Is that what he told you?'

'He said they shook on a deal just before the Coventry Stakes.'

'That's an absolute lie. I was with your dad all the time and he did no such thing. Talbot was there all right but they didn't speak. Your dad deliberately avoided him.'

'Oh.' The notion of this man telling lies about her father was as upsetting as him making unfounded demands for money. Whether he was just mischievous or deluded, she had the feeling it wouldn't be easy to shut him up. He looked the kind of person who'd keep coming after her and Simon, making scenes, pressing his imaginary case. And, if she paid him something to get him to go away, it would look like an admission from her side that her father really had owed him money.

She didn't say any of this because there was a bubble of panic in her throat, blocking the words.

Simon read her distress in her face and reached across the table to cover her hand in his.

'Maybe it's a good thing this has happened,' he said.

'What do you mean?'

'I've been puzzling over things. About your dad and Charlie Talbot. I think it's time we talked to the police.'

Alison stared at him. What did this have to do with the police?

Then he told her.

It was early evening by the time Simon arrived home. He'd spent the afternoon with Alison, setting out his theory that Geoff's murder might not have been a random act, that it could have been carefully planned. By Charlie Talbot.

He had rather expected that unveiling his midnight fears in daylight would show them to be weak and silly, as insubstantial as dreams. But, as he ran through his argument for Alison, he found the opposite to be true. By the time he had finished, he had convinced himself.

'What do you think?' he'd said. 'Am I being stupid?'

She shook her head. 'I suppose we'll have to see Henderson.'

It was agreed Alison would get on to the Metropolitan Police in the morning and he'd drive down with her as soon as a meeting could be arranged. Ken and the others could mind the fort at Willowdale.

He'd dropped into the yard on the way back, expecting to find Mariana but there had been no sign of her. Now, as he drove up to the house, he could see her car was missing from its usual spot. Lunch had obviously turned into something of a marathon.

Just who was this old friend she'd met? he wondered. Mariana had only told him it was a woman she'd worked with in her rag trade days. It was the first time she'd been in touch with anyone from her previous life and he counted that as a good sign.

It had always been clear to him that she'd been running away from her past but he'd been too happy that she'd chosen Willowdale as sanctuary to ask why. And as their romance had progressed he had put off any earnest inquiries. There would plenty of time for all that – she would tell him when she was ready. He realised he was unique in holding this point of view. Geoff had begun a serious campaign of questioning her suitability as a wife shortly before his death. Simon had assured him he had absolute faith Mariana would reveal her secrets in time. And he'd been on the point of asking a few pointed questions himself when Geoff had died. Had been slaughtered in front of them, to be accurate, binding them with bonds of fear that made whatever might lie in her past irrelevant. He wasn't the only one, he was aware, who frequently lay awake through the small hours, reliving the horror of his uncle's murder.

He found Mariana upstairs, lying half dressed across the bed, her jeans in a crumpled pile on the floor. Her burnt-blond ringlets lay in a cloud across the pillow and her long olive-brown legs stretched almost to the foot of the bed. The sight of her like this was still a shock. He wondered if he would ever get over her exotic beauty.

He kicked off his shoes and lay down carefully beside her on the bed, so as not to wake her. He put his face to hers to drink in her sleepy perfume and detected wine and tobacco. This was a first. He didn't care – she was still irresistible.

Her eyelids flickered and she woke. Her limbs stiffened and, as a reflex it seemed, she thrust him away from her hard. For a split second there was no recognition in her eyes.

'Jesus, Mariana!' He clutched at the bedpost, so surprised he almost ended up on the floor. 'It's only me.'

As suddenly as she had lashed at him she lassoed him in a long-limbed hug. 'I'm sorry, I'm sorry,' she moaned. 'I was so asleep. I thought – I don't know. Forgive me.'

She kissed him fiercely and he held her tight, excited by the passion in her. She was as unpredictable as any of the skittish animals in his yard, quite unlike the other girls he'd known. Was it any wonder he was so hopelessly in love?

They lay skin close, the full weight of her on him. It was perfect.

'I stink,' she said.

'Have you been smoking?'

'It was Carla. And she got me drunk. I had to call a taxi to get back.'

So that's why there was no car outside.

'Tell me about Carla.'

Would she fob him off? But it was a reasonable question.

'She knows Uncle Felix who owns the company I used to work for. He's not my uncle but that's what I used to call him. He's a lovely man. A bit tubby with no hair – he must be seventy.'

Simon smiled inwardly. This was a lot of information, almost unprompted. 'How old is Carla?'

'Fifty or so, I suppose.'

'If he's your uncle is she your aunt?'

She laughed. 'I'd never dare call her that. More my big sister. I thought,' her voice became hesitant, 'I might ask them to the wedding.'

'Great,' he said. And it was. The idea of her being completely outnumbered had been preying on his mind. 'You know what, I can't wait till we get married. What about you?'

'I suppose so.'

'Bloody hell, Mariana. You're meant to sound more enthusiastic than that.'

There was a pause.

'Listen, Simon, I've got a confession.'

A confession?

'There's something you should know,' she continued. 'Something I should have told you a long time ago.'

He looked at her in confusion.

She seemed to hesitate, then suddenly reached across him and picked an envelope off the bedside table.

'Look.' She took out some photographs and spread them across the bedsheet. 'I have a sister. A half-sister anyway. I should have told you. I'm sorry.'

The pictures showed a pleasant-looking girl, neatly dressed, a hard-working student from the look of her. He peered closely, seeking a resemblance with the woman in his arms. Yes, could be.

'Fantastic,' he said. 'What's her name?'

'Paula.'

'Well, Paula is coming to the wedding too. I can't wait to meet her.'

The summer sky outside was still light but the half darkness of evening thickened the bedroom. By her side, Simon dozed, his arms still round her. Mariana lay wide awake, her insides in knots.

She'd almost told him. Had got as far as saying she had something to confess. Then caution had got the better of her and she'd played another trick. Paula had saved her. It was the least that scheming little devil owed her.

No, she mustn't be unfair. Maybe the kid was serious about studying and being a teacher. If only she could believe it.

But Paula was an irrelevance in this situation, particularly after what Simon had gone on to say about his afternoon with Alison. The two of them were going to London to tell the police about Charlie Talbot. It sounded ridiculous to her. She had no doubt Charlie could kill someone – it was plain from his mean piggy eyes and the way his great ham hands had casually crushed her flesh. But when Charlie killed, it would be in anger, in the heat of a passion he couldn't control. Not a cold-blooded, carefully planned assassination.

No, those two men on the train had used her as a

focus for their evil natures – that's what some men did.

Thank God for good men like Simon. She'd give anything to be his legitimately. To be his wife and live by his side, working to be the best person she could possibly be.

She did love him, she was sure of it. Loved him in the way he deserved, as he loved her. That was ironic, because she didn't see how they could possibly be together once the truth came out.

And it was bound to come out now. Simon accusing Charlie would only hasten the end. Once the police talked to Charlie, he would have no reason not to tell everything he knew about her – and whatever else he could make up. He'd blame her and pile the poison on. It was going to be terrible.

She closed her eyes and followed Carla's advice. For the first time since she was a little girl she began to pray.

Chapter Seven

Charlie Talbot stumbled out of bed and grazed his shoulder against the door of the en suite. He sat on the toilet to relieve himself, taking care not to bang his chin on the washbasin. He'd intended to have a shower but when he contemplated squeezing himself into the standing area in the bath and cricking his neck to get under the water jet he thought better of it. The fact was this place – this uniquely affordable property offering a high-end experience of contemporary city dwelling – was too effing small for a man of his build. Too small for all but midgets and shrunken pensioners, to tell the truth. And neither of those sections of the population featured high in the property-buying demographic. Especially in a housing depression.

But at least the show flat in this development of one- and two-bedroom apartments had been available when Sharon kicked him out, on account of it was his development. So he hadn't, thank Christ, had to go and rent some sad-sack bedsit or, worse, end up back in his sister's spare room while her bloody barrister live-in looked down his long nose at him. It was bad enough everybody knowing he was losing Sharon and the kids without letting them see up close just how badly things had fallen apart.

He'd loved this project. Sure, the flats were titchy but they were aimed at young thrusters getting their feet on the property ladder. Kids in shiny suits who'd spend all day in their City offices – less than half an hour by tube from vibrant Gant's Hill – and all night lashing it up in bars and clubs. They'd only be here to sleep off their hangovers. He'd called the development Quiesco, which was one of those bloody silly style names which had been all the rage last year when he'd dreamed this caper up. It meant 'rest' or 'calm' in Latin, or so he'd been told by one of the plumbers whose dad had wasted money buying him a fancy education. Young Col had been able to make a damn sight more money fitting U-bends than teaching snotty brats dead languages.

Charlie pulled on some manky old tracksuit bottoms and shambled into the kitchen to knock up a Nescaff and Weetabix, taking care to keep spillage on the plastic sheet that covered the chic birchwood-style finish of the pull-out breakfast nook table. Sharon would have been amazed to see that the sink was empty of used tea bags and fag ends and no greased-up piles of food plates had collected on the surfaces. Singledom had turned him into a house-proud homebody. Of course, he still had hopes, faint though they may be, of selling the place.

Maybe tomorrow some genius in government would wave a magic wand and he'd be waltzing happy house-buyers round this gleaming little show dwelling, talking of waiting lists and quick offers and deposits. And Quiesco, his dream development, would save his bacon. Who was he effing kidding.

He moved, in a couple of strides, into the living area, carefully placed his coffee mug on an old *Racing Beacon* on the table nest, and switched the TV on to the racing channel. That was one good thing about this place – he'd had it cabled and wireless-connected to the max to attract the twenty-first-century techno generation. At least now he had home entertainment on tap to keep him from going completely crazy.

He knew he was losing it a bit, sitting here in front of the telly looking like some old dosser and the clock past noon. In the old days he'd have been kicking arse since daybreak, juggling clients, bullying money out of slow payers and fielding calls all day, shouting, cursing and having a few laughs. Now, his work team had broken up, he had no clients left and he kept his phone turned off to avoid people calling *him* for money. And, of course, he had no loving wife and jolly nippers to return home to any more. Not that it had been all that loving or jolly of late.

Trying to go big time had obviously been a bit of a mistake. He'd chanced his arm on this place and caught a cold. He'd have been better sticking to the bread and butter. Some guys were probably still rubbing along on loft conversions and conservatories. Buying and selling might be a disaster right now but people still moved in with each other, had babies, found they had to put up their ageing mums. If they couldn't move somewhere bigger then they looked for ways of making the most of the space they were in. If he were running modest jobs maybe he'd still have his head above water. He certainly wouldn't have a dozen half-built, unsellable studio apartments on his hands and eye-watering monthly outgoings to the bank.

His losing streak on the horses didn't help. He'd never chased his losses before – number one rule in his book – but he'd had no bloody option seeing as how he couldn't afford to lose. And so he'd lost more.

All the same, that was no excuse for hitting Sharon. There were lots of people he'd like to hit and many, in fact, he'd enjoyed thumping. But not women. And particularly not one he happened to be married to.

He took a deep breath and tried to change the direction of his thoughts. He'd gone to York to shake himself out of this rut of self-pity. He'd dug out his best racing togs and put on a show like it was the old days. And, apart from the horses, you might say it had paid off.

When he'd first demanded money from that sanctimonious prick Geoff Hall, it had just been payback for the way he'd been treated. Him and his nephew the trainer. A pair of conniving, chiselling Yorkie bastards – they'd seen him coming all right.

But he'd never actually expected to get any money out of Hall, unless he could make himself enough of a nuisance to persuade the old sod to pay him to go away. But Hall was no pushover and Charlie had come to the conclusion that pursuing the matter was more trouble than it was worth. Then Geoff Hall had up and got himself killed. A shocking event, of course, but he'd be happy to buy the guy who'd done it a beer. He'd had a good laugh the night he'd heard, until he'd realised that there had gone any remaining chance of getting paid out.

But running into the red-headed daughter at York

had revived certain ideas. She was no hard nut like her father. Getting money out of her was a different proposition and, by God, how he could do with it right now. A hundred and fifteen thousand smackers would be a lifeline back to some kind of self-respect.

The run-in with Simon the trainer had looked like scuppering things until he'd spotted the bird. Funny how things worked out sometimes. Back in June, when he'd been following the story of the Ascot murder, he'd not paid much attention to the girl in the pictures, beyond noting she was a smart bit of upmarket totty. But seeing her up close at York in that skimpy black dress he'd clocked her for who she really was – that fancy tart old Derek had been knocking off. 'A high-class hooker' Derek had called her that night in the restaurant. High-class simply meant overpriced in Charlie's book but he'd been prepared to dig into the Talbot piggy bank to see if she lived up to her billing. And the bitch had turned him down.

So it would give him a deal of pleasure to shop her to Simon Waterford. A pleasure he would be prepared to forgo only on receipt of a cheque for Jennifer Eccles. For the first time he had realistic hopes of getting one. A woman like that, samba sex on knockout legs, could surely get Waterford to dance to any tune she chose. Bottom line was, it wouldn't be Waterford's money, it would come out of Geoff Hall's estate. The daughter would never miss it – it might help to bring down the death duty bill – so, everyone would be a winner.

Charlie sipped his coffee. Get a grip, no need to get carried away. Think it through. Suppose they didn't pay and he spilled the beans about the Brazilian.

She'd get her pretty arse kicked out of Yorkshire – serve her right – but where was the lasting satisfaction in that? Revenge might be sweet but it would be sweeter if it paid a few bills.

It didn't take all that long to come up with something. It would entail a bit more legwork on his part but what else did he have to do with his time?

Alison could tell right from the start that the meeting wasn't going as they had hoped. They were in an unfamiliar interview room in a police station on the south bank of the river. It had been a struggle to get a piece of DCI Henderson's time and it was plain he would rather have delegated the chore to DC Parker. All the same, he had put a decent face on it, shaking hands warmly and opening with bold sentiments about steady progress and keeping the faith and the continuing commitment to justice. It was plain he was expecting a whinge from Alison and Simon about the failure to find the suspects in her father's murder and he intended to get his defence in first.

But, for all their frustrations, that had not been their purpose. The idea was to ask the police to consider the possibility that Geoff had been deliberately targeted by killers working for Charlie Talbot. And it had been agreed between them that Simon would make the case.

She couldn't criticise the way he went about it but she could see that Henderson wasn't buying. For a poker-faced detective, his thoughts weren't hard to read. As Simon explained in some detail the sequence of Jennifer Eccles' injuries and the financial arrangements between the owners of the horse, the policeman's bright gaze dulled and he began to chew on his lip. He must have already concluded that their theory wouldn't float. It didn't help that he was being regularly nagged by calls on his phone which, to his credit, he did not take.

'So you're alleging that Mr Hall owed money to Mr Talbot for a horse,' he said, cutting into Simon's monologue, 'and as a consequence Talbot hired two men to stab Mr Hall on the train.' He made it sound far-fetched.

'Actually,' said Simon, 'Geoff didn't owe Talbot any money at all – Charlie was just trying it on. But, yes, I think it's possible he paid the men to kill him.'

Henderson folded his arms and leaned back in his chair. 'If I was thinking of arranging a murder I'm not sure I'd ask for it to be done in a carriage full of passengers on a railway equipped with some of the best security cameras money can buy.'

'But they got away with it, didn't they?' Alison couldn't help herself. 'All the photos in the world don't help unless you've got a suspect.'

'They were just lucky, Miss Hall.' There was sympathy in his pale blue eyes – maybe he thought grief had driven her to this desperate clutching of straws. 'You'd never plan it like that. Anything could have gone wrong.'

'But it didn't.' She heard the pain in her voice. She was going to make a fool of herself in a moment.

The silence was short but it seemed to stretch on.

Claire Parker broke it. 'Can we just recap on Mr Talbot's possible reason for arranging the attack? If he believed he was owed money, there wouldn't be much point in commissioning Mr Hall's murder, not if he wanted to get paid.'

'But he's still asking for money. He accosted Alison at York races.'

Alison nodded. 'Clive – my solicitor, Clive Silver – got a new invoice from him just this morning.'

'So you see,' Simon added, 'he revenged himself on Geoff and now he's continuing with his bogus claim.'

This time the silence was lengthy, broken eventually by the signal of Henderson's phone.

'Sorry,' he said, glancing at the screen, 'I really must take this,' and he left the room at speed. They all knew he would not be coming back.

'He thinks we're kidding ourselves, doesn't he?' Alison said.

Claire offered a smile. 'I'm sure he doesn't. He's frustrated that we haven't made the kind of progress in this investigation that we would like. Sometimes these things take time.'

'But,' Alison cut in quickly to prevent a trip down a conversational alley that was all too familiar, 'we're asking you to come at this from a different angle. Charlie Talbot had a grievance against my father. At least consider that he might have acted on it.'

'You could go and talk to him, couldn't you?' Simon asked.

Claire didn't commit herself. 'Can you leave it with me for now? I promise I won't forget. It's important that you come to us with anything you think relevant.' She got to her feet. The interview was plainly over.

They shook hands at the door and Alison managed

to offer a thank you to the officer for sparing the time.

Claire looked faintly embarrassed and said, 'This investigation isn't dead, I promise you.'

How Alison wished she could believe her.

'Derek, how goes, me old mate?' Charlie put maximum cheer into his voice down the phone.

'Good Lord.' Derek was suitably surprised. 'How the devil are you, Charlie? I thought you'd skipped the country – or died.'

Charlie gave it the hearty laugh. 'I'd have let you know if I'd kicked the bucket.'

They both laughed this time. Good old Derek sounded pleased to hear from him. But then, he didn't owe Derek money.

'So how are you, Charlie?'

'I've been better. Me and Sharon split.'

'I heard. Any chance of—'

'No.' He shot that down quick. He'd had the divorce papers from the court.

'I'm sorry, Charlie.' Derek sounded sincere. 'And your development in Gant's Hill? Placebo or whatever you called it.'

'Quiesco. Actually it's too bloody quiesco – nothing doing at all. The world's gone skint. But,' he added quickly, mustn't start bleeding down the phone or he'd get nowhere, 'that's not why I rang. Do you remember a few months back when you wanted to put that feller on to me? The one who was asking you about the birds from Chrysalis?'

'Can you hang on a moment?' There was a thump and the muffled sound of voices. Charlie guessed he'd caught Derek at his office and he was clearing the room. Derek confirmed as much when they resumed. 'Yes, I remember.'

'Have you got his number?'

'What for?'

'I'd rather not say at the moment, mate – all will be revealed in the fullness. He was researching escort girls, wasn't he?'

'He was looking for the lovely Fabiana, that Brazilian girl you spooked. He said he was working for a solicitor and she might have money coming to her from some bloke's will.'

'That's right. Sounded fishy.'

'Quite. I'll give you the number but are you sure you want to get involved? I mean, suppose Sharon finds out about you and Chrysalis Girls.'

'It won't make a blind bit of difference. She's going to crucify me anyway.'

Derek gave him the number and made his excuses before Charlie could elaborate. He couldn't blame him.

Claire Parker looked up as Henderson leaned over her desk. 'Sorry to abandon you in there,' he said.

'It's OK. You'd heard it all anyway.'

'Bloody people. They've been watching too many movies.'

'I feel sorry for them. They're desperate.'

'Maybe.' He squatted on the side of her desk, an irritating habit of his. 'And maybe there's more to it. Have you considered that they might be trying to get out of paying this bloke Talbot the money for the horse? Sounds like his word against theirs. They might think that if they sick us on Talbot it will scare him off.'

That hadn't occurred to her. 'I can't believe Alison would do that.'

'If she wouldn't, her cousin Waterford might. He's a Yorkshire horse trainer – a canny bugger like that won't miss many angles. I bet it was his idea to bring Talbot to us – he did most of the talking, didn't he?'

Claire agreed that he had. Maybe Henderson had a point.

'Are you just going to ignore it, then?' she said.

'I didn't say that. You check Talbot out. Just bear in mind that there might be a whole agenda here that has nothing to do with the murder. Have a gentle word and see if any of what Simon Waterford told us stacks up.'

'Yes, sir.'

'And try not to get bogged down in the horsey details. When it got a sore knee and where it was placed in the Two Thousand Guineas.'

She concealed a smirk, obviously not very well.

'What's funny?'

'The Two Thousand Guineas is for colts and Jennifer Eccles is a filly. You mean the One Thousand Guineas.'

'Well, excuse me. You know all this horse crap?'

'Yes, sir.'

'In that case, Claire, I'm expecting you to solve the whole bloody case.'

Loughton, to the east of London – the address she had been given for Charlie Talbot – was not exactly on Claire Parker's regular beat. She was a south-of-the-river girl by breeding and experience. Ask her to navigate the remotest corners of Kent and Sussex and she was in her element. Essex, on the other hand, was alien territory.

She located Talbot's house in a road of Victorian semis – it was the one with a half-demolished perimeter wall and dusty bags of sand and cement that looked like they had taken root in the bare front garden. She could imagine that the neighbours – when out watering their hanging baskets and climbing roses – weren't overjoyed by the sight.

A belligerent bottle blonde eventually answered the door. From down the hallway behind her echoed the sound of squabbling children.

'Mrs Talbot?'

'Who wants her?'

There was no point in asking if this was a convenient time to call – it looked as if no time would qualify.

Claire showed her warrant card and introduced herself.

'It's about Charlie, isn't it?'

'Yes, I wonder if—'

'What's he done? He's all right, isn't he?'

'As far as I'm aware, Mrs Talbot. I was hoping to catch him at home.'

'This isn't his home any more.'

The child decibels increased behind the woman, followed by thumping footsteps down the hall. Two small red-faced boys appeared by their mother's side.

'What you after?' the bigger of the two piped up.

'Don't be rude, Jack. This lady is looking for your father.'

'Daddy!' shrilled the other lad. 'Daddy, Daddy, Daddy!'

Claire smiled weakly at the kids. 'I apologise, Mrs Talbot. I can see this is a bad time. If you could just tell me where to contact Mr Talbot, I'll leave you in peace.'

The woman rattled off an address which Claire had to ask her to repeat. As she scribbled it down, the two boys stared at her with frank interest.

'Is she Daddy's new bit of stuff?' the elder one asked.

The mother prodded him with a finger. 'Shut it, you,' she commanded.

Claire retreated with the sinking feeling that she was intruding on someone else's horrible domestic mess. It was something she was used to in her job.

To cap it off she could raise no response from the address the woman had given her, a new development near Gant's Hill with a distinctly unfinished air. Only one dwelling had curtains and showed signs of being inhabited. But Charlie Talbot was not at home. Probably round at his new woman's place, she thought cynically.

As she drove back into town she promised herself never to get married.

Mariana had spent the day in turmoil. She tried not to let it show as she massaged horses and busied herself around the yard. But the horses did not respond as they usually did – they could tell she was unhappy. And when Holly asked her if she was feeling all right and insisted on bring her cups of sugary tea, she realised she wasn't fooling the humans either.

Simon was in London with Alison, urging the

police to interview Charlie Talbot – a pointless activity, in her view, guaranteed to make the rift with the big man absolute. And when that happened he would pull the rug from beneath her out of simple spite. If only she'd been nicer to him that evening with Derek. But being nicer would have meant putting herself at the mercy of his fat-pig body. It was ironic. She was about to be exposed for being a prostitute but if she'd been a true whore she would have taken his money and let him use her as he liked. That would have been the professional course of conduct. And if she'd done that she would not be branded as his enemy.

But he was a coarse and horrible man, it probably wouldn't have made any difference. She was glad she'd never sold herself to him.

Charlie Talbot was not the only demon haunting her. The memory of yesterday's meeting with Carla had dogged her all day. When she got home she made straight for the drawer in the bedroom where she had put the envelope with the photographs of Paula.

She spread them out on the desk top in the study and peered hard at her sister's face. What was it she could read in that expression? Pride? Happiness? Resolve?

Or deceit?

Paula had been the lucky one when their father had died – that's what she had been told. There was family on Paula's side, an aunt and uncle who would take the girl in and pay for her to attend a decent school in Rio. Mariana, on the other hand, had to make her own way in another country. So they'd parted and it had been hard. Mariana had sent money home – the thought of her little sister in another land had been one more reason to take on the best-paying work that she could. She had thought her sister might be grateful and committed enough to the days of their childhood not to betray her. But she'd been wrong.

And now time had gone by and here were these photographs to bring back memories and to revive hopes. Among the prints, she also discovered an address.

She took notepaper from the drawer and considered what she should write.

She had sworn never to have anything to do with Paula again. But that had been two years ago when her heart had been broken and the wound had been fresh. Maybe, on reflection, Paula's behaviour had not been so bad to warrant complete severance. Was her life so rich – with disaster waiting around the corner – that she could afford to ignore the one member of her family who was still alive?

Besides, she was the elder sister. It was up to her to be the bigger person. To understand past mistakes and hold out her arms in forgiveness.

Not that she would put it like that in her letter.

Writing it proved difficult, like squeezing water from a stone. What could she say that didn't sound like a reproach or opened old wounds or was simply inappropriate? 'I'm glad to see you have given up nightclubs and gone back to college' – well, who was she to talk? She couldn't pretend to Paula that she herself had always been a responsible citizen when the girl knew the truth – and had thrown it in her face when they'd last spoken. Of course, what she really wanted to say was, 'Are you sorry for the way you betrayed me?' but that wasn't the way to rebuild a bridge that had been burnt.

In the end she kept it simple. She explained that she was living a completely different life to the one she had lived before. She had met a new man, Simon, who trained horses for races at all those English courses Daddy used to talk about so fondly. They lived in the country in the north of England and she worked every day at the stables. She was pleased Paula had gone back to school – Carla had given her some photos. 'Please write and tell me how you are getting on with your studies and any other news.'

And while you're writing, you could sincerely ask for my forgiveness. But she didn't say that.

Mariana folded the single sheet of paper and placed it, with a photograph of her and Simon that she had selected, into an envelope. Then she carefully copied Paula's address on the front from the slip of paper Carla had enclosed with the shots of her half-sister.

When she heard Simon's car purring in the drive she put the envelope on the hall table as she rushed to meet him at the door. His pale face was weary and drawn but it broke into a smile as he wrapped his arms around her. He was still hers for now, it seemed.

'How did it go?' she asked, trying to make it sound casual.

He bowed his head and kissed her.

'Well?'

'They didn't believe us,' he said. 'A complete waste of a day – we flogged all the way there and back for nothing.'

She made sympathetic noises but, inside, for the moment, all she could feel was relief.

* * *

Gabriel Silver leaned back in the leather seat of the hotel bar and admired the display of roses – a confection of pink and scarlet buds erupting from the mouth of a vast crystal goblet – displayed on the marble slab of the drinks counter. He'd rarely been in such an extravagant setting and the price of the Coca-Cola fizzing in front of him was eye-watering. He hoped, however, that his new client, Mr Charles Talbot, would be picking up the tab. After all, this ritzy West End venue had been his suggestion.

Gabriel was enjoying the décor and the scenery. Yesterday had been spent in two greasy spoons and a dingy pub in Acton waiting for the right moment to serve court papers on a car dealer more slippery than Arthur Daley. At least you could say this line of work was varied.

He didn't think of himself as a private investigator. He'd only started doing odd jobs for his uncle after he'd packed in his accountancy exams and began casting around for a more congenial way to spend his working day. There was no doubt in his mind that hanging around in places like this qualified as congenial. And as the exception to the rule.

At the next table a fair-haired woman in a dark suit picked hastily at a plate of smoked salmon while quizzing her nanny on the mobile. Opposite, two overweight men made notes on sheaves of paper while another consulted a laptop. The stressed-out business community on their lunch break – none of them appeared to have noticed the flowers.

Mr Talbot was late but Gabriel wasn't bothered. One thing this work had revealed to him was that, when required, he had an infinite amount of patience. He was also observant. The harried blonde lady had disturbingly good legs.

He knew the big man was his client the moment he barrelled through the door, tucking a phone into his jacket pocket, gazing around with a welcoming grin. Up close, as Gabriel stood to grip flesh, there was anxiety behind the grin. That was no surprise – he was unlikely to have arranged this meeting otherwise.

The call had come out of the blue the day before. Had Mr Silver not been involved in an inquiry that touched on the affairs of the Chrysalis Girls escort agency? Would he mind meeting to discuss a related matter?

Gabriel had been happy to oblige once it was established that a fee would be involved, though maybe only a minimal one as this wasn't a complex proposition. All of which was fine by Gabriel. The Brazilian Tart Affair, as he liked to think of it, had been far and away the most interesting project he'd undertaken for his Uncle Clive. His only regret was that he'd never met the girl in the flesh. From the photographic evidence he'd researched, this was one surveillance suspect who would be worth watching.

'Look, I'll get right to it, Gabe.' Mr Talbot – Charlie – was a congenial sort, though there was a niff of the unwashed about him and a clamminess in his handshake that was off-putting. 'I understand you were looking into the activities of one of the Chrysalis escort girls. She called herself Fabiana.'

Gabriel confirmed that this was so and, in response to further questions, he revealed that he had completed his investigation for his client.

'I dunno who you were working for before – that's not my business,' said Charlie. 'But I'm also interested in this woman. I presume you wrote up some kind of dossier on her.'

Gabriel agreed that he had submitted a report.

Charlie's face lit up. 'Exactly. And that's what I'm after. Let me have a butcher's at it and then I can decide whether I want you to dig up any other dirt.'

'I'd have to give that some thought.'

'Why? You're in business to make money, aren't you? You've already done the legwork – this is money for old rope.'

'I'm not sure about the ethics of selling you a report I've compiled exclusively for another client.'

Charlie rolled his eyes to the heavens. 'Bloody hell. You're a private bleeding detective. You spend your time peering through keyholes and sniffing dirty knickers, don't you? All I'm asking is to read a copy of a file you can probably print off in two minutes.'

Gabriel didn't bother to put him right about the keyholes and knickers – thank goodness his uncle did not handle divorce work.

'I'm not saying no, Charlie. I just want to consult someone else to make sure I'm not infringing any third-party rights.' That sounded good though Gabriel doubted if it held any water. He just needed time to think it over, maybe he'd refer it to Clive. Although the party who had commissioned the original report was dead, maybe his estate still had exclusive use of the material.

'Huh.' Charlie leaned back in his seat, setting the leather creaking. He looked at his watch. 'Look, I gotta go to a meeting. Just don't take too long in this consulting. There's a monkey in it for you but that's top whack, OK?'

Gabriel watched the big man barge his way out of the door before draining the most expensive Coke he'd ever tasted. Which, he realised with wry reflection, he would have to pay for himself.

Charlie fumed as he sweated in the summer swelter of the Central Line back to Gant's Hill. He'd wasted his time on that Silver kid. At his age he'd have jumped at the chance of making money easily. Sell a job twice over? If only he worked in a business where that was possible.

Maybe, after Silver had asked permission from whoever pulled his strings, he'd let him see what he had on Miss Copacabana. He wished he hadn't offered that much money – he couldn't afford it though he reckoned he could get it back. If that report held the right kind of sleaze, surely it would be worth a few bob to a paper. Even if he couldn't get a national interested, the Yorkshire rags and the racing papers would go mad for a scandal on the top trainer in the county. And going public would be an even more satisfactory method of scuppering the little bitch than simply telling Simon Waterford – though that was still an option.

When it came down to it, he still had enough to sink her off his own bat.

He reminded himself that sinking Mariana wasn't the point. But if he couldn't get money out of Alison Hall, it would give him a lot of satisfaction. And maybe, once the cheque had cleared, he'd do it anyway.

Back at the flat, he set about tidying up. He'd not been lying when he'd said he had a meeting. Some guy was coming round to look at the flat – he'd put a note through the door requesting a viewing at four. Charlie didn't have much time but, thanks to keeping the place neat, he didn't need much.

If he could sell just one of these flats it would be a start he could build on. A removal van outside, visitors coming and going, signs of habitation like vases on window sills – window boxes! The little things counted, would show Quiesco was alive and not some dead-end symbol of financial ruin. And buyers had friends, didn't they? Maybe friends who were also thinking of moving house. This could be a turning point in his fortunes.

Once he had straightened out his finances, he'd get his team back together for more modest jobs – loft conversions and new kitchens, like he'd been thinking. He'd have to pay the boys what he owed them, of course, and maybe a bit more, sort of a loyalty bonus for sticking by him in times of trouble. Not that they had, exactly. He still had ringing in one ear from when Roy had gone for him outside the pub last week. But it wasn't serious, more like a family squabble.

And maybe, if he could pull it all together, his other family might not be out of reach. Sharon's bark was worse than her bite. If he could sort himself out she'd see the sense in tearing up that divorce petition and letting him come back. Surely a man – a hard-working, honest man – belonged at home with his wife and kids.

He'd stowed all his toilet stuff under the sink in the

bathroom, bundled the bedding on top of the wardrobe and cleared the plastic sheeting off the kitchen surfaces. He left some of the newspapers on the coffee table in the living area to make the place look more homely and arranged the yellow carnations he'd bought outside the tube.

There – the place didn't look too bad. He'd *make* this bastard buy. Well, he'd offer a bloody good deal at any rate. It would be worth it.

The doorbell rang, spot on four. That was a good sign – this character must be keen.

He flung open the door. There were two of them on the doorstep. Blokes in their twenties, he guessed, one was tall and thin with dark messy hair; the other short with well-muscled forearms beneath his short-sleeved shirt. Yuppies on their day off, no doubt.

For once these days the good humour he exuded was entirely genuine.

'Come in, gentleman,' he boomed. 'Welcome to Quiesco!'

Claire found the journey back to Gant's Hill as tedious as the day before, even though the afternoon traffic in town was summer light. She hoped this wouldn't be another wasted journey. She could have rung this Talbot to fix a meeting – his wife had given her a mobile number – but it was always best to take people by surprise, before they'd had a chance to prepare what they might say. Not that in this case she expected him to say anything incriminating. The more she considered Simon Waterford's allegations, the more she agreed with the DCI – there were easier ways of setting up a murder than on a train.

The first thing she noticed as she walked up the short path to the door was a glint of yellow in the window. The flowers had not been there yesterday.

But Talbot still wasn't in – or at least it was taking him forever to answer her repeated ringing. She stepped off the path and walked along the parched grass verge to peer through the window.

A big man in a suit lay flat on his back on the carpet between the sofa and the television stand, staring at the ceiling. His jacket had flapped open and his white shirt was a blood-red rag. Beneath the bulk of his body, the beige carpet was soaked dark crimson.

Talbot was not absent, as she had feared – though it would have been preferable if he had been.

Even as she called the emergency services, Claire doubted that a life remained to be saved. She had attended a few murder scenes, had observed the body in situ in the company of other officers. But she'd never before discovered a corpse herself.

This was a first.

Chapter Eight

Simon was a good furlong off from the string of horses who were working on the gallops above Willowdale. All the same, like a sixth sense, he knew immediately when something was wrong. His father had possessed the same awareness. Or maybe they both lived in fear of the thousand and one niggles that could afflict a thoroughbred racehorse, expecting disaster to arrive out of the blue at any moment. As it did now to the small horse at the back, the chestnut with the powerful action.

Jennifer Eccles' problem was confirmed a moment later when the jockey pulled the horse up and dismounted. Simon raced back to the old Land Rover and drove across the gallop towards them. This was a blow. The filly's next race was only a couple of weeks off.

Neil, the jockey, was walking beside her, following the rest of the string home.

'What's she done?'

'I'm not sure. She was working fine then suddenly lost her action just as we were about to pull up.'

Simon watched the filly carefully as she walked.

149

She seemed sound now but horses were no different to humans when it came to injuries. What hurt when you ran didn't always hurt when you walked. He'd be disappointed if she couldn't run at Haydock; so would all at Willowdale. And the owner. Maybe he could put off calling Alison until the vet had had a chance to look the horse over. The thought of telling his cousin was not the least of his concerns. She could do without further disappointments.

But when he got back to the yard he found that Alison was already there. Maybe she had that sixth sense too. She made a beeline for the Land Rover.

Before he could break the news about the horse, she gripped his arm, her face tense. 'Have you heard about Charlie Talbot?'

He froze, his concerns for Jennifer Eccles instantly pushed to the back of his mind.

'What's he done now?' The man was a menace. It was a mystery how his uncle had ever thought him worth befriending.

'He hasn't done anything. He's been murdered.'

Mariana moved slowly in the half light of the horse's stall as she prepared to begin her massage. It was important to get in the correct rhythm and not disturb her patient more than necessary. She prided herself on being able to attune to a body's needs, in spirit as well as with her hands, and to leave a patient, horse or human, feeling better with the world once she had completed her ministrations. She'd massaged Simon last night after a day at the races that had been highly stressed. When she'd finished he'd wrapped her in his strong arms and held her in a protective embrace that had, for just a few minutes, stilled her fears that any day now she was about to lose him and this wonderful new life.

Of course, there was no way of being sure that her horse patients were relieved of their worries and tensions but she just knew they liked what she did to them. Anyway, I've never had any complaints, she said to herself.

This particular horse, Red River, who was due to leave the yard soon once a new home was found for him, butted her shoulder gently with his great black head as she laid her hands upon his neck. This was what she enjoyed – the close companionable contact with these big creatures. If she got it right, settled on to their wavelength and eased their pains, it soothed her demons too.

Those demons were hard at work today, torturing her with the thought that maybe it would be her last at Willowdale basking in the protective circle of Simon's love. Charlie Talbot could expose her at any time.

She'd been racking her brains, trying to make plans for her inevitable expulsion. Where was she going to go?

She could return to Brazil. After all, in writing to Paula she had taken the first step in mending the breach with her sister. But she couldn't just flee from Yorkshire and go straight to Brazil. Maybe that would be a long-term plan but what would she do if she was thrown out tonight?

She'd go back to London – that was the obvious place to go. At least she still had some of the money she'd saved from her Chrysalis Girls days. It wasn't a lot but would be enough to sustain her until she found work. The thought made her heart sink. She'd found the work she wanted to do and it was here, with horses. But would the horseracing world be closed to her once her past became known? She didn't doubt that Charlie would ruin her reputation as widely as he could – he'd make a point of it.

Maybe – and she'd been trying hard to ignore this pernicious little thought – she should try to persuade Simon to change his mind about Jennifer Eccles. She could even try talking to Alison, who was the one who would be paying the money.

She rejected the idea. Even if she was successful, Charlie would still know. The blackmailer would never go away.

She'd rung Felix. He was her trump card. Her former employer who had been more than generous to her in the past. She'd not been much good at the office grind of marketing his goods but he'd always been kind and encouraging. As if providing for her needs had been more important than using her in his business. And she'd walked out of his world with the barest of notice and scarcely given him a thought.

She began with effusive apologies for not staying in touch.

'My darling, it's OK,' he said in his soft, whispering tones. 'You are young and have a new life to live. Carla has told me all about it. Many congratulations.'

She'd burst into tears at that and confessed that her new life was about to blow up in her face. But he'd talked to Carla – he knew that too.

It was a comfort to speak to him and she said much more than she had intended.

At the end he said, 'You know that you are welcome back here. The flat is empty and I can always find work for you in the office.'

So, her old life was still there waiting for her. A bolthole.

'But Mariana,' he continued, 'you should not upset yourself so much. Maybe all this will work out just fine.'

She didn't see how.

Simon sipped coffee in the tack room with Alison as they discussed the extraordinary news. Charlie Talbot murdered. It was about the last thing he had expected to hear from her as she'd rushed to meet him.

He'd fetched the radio from the office and they'd listened to the news on the hour. The murder got a brief mention, the fourth item down, in the shock-horror context of London's burgeoning knife crime.

'Is this how you heard about it?' Simon asked.

'No. Henderson rang me. He asked where I was yesterday afternoon. You too.'

It took a moment for Simon to work out the implications.

'Seriously?'

'I suppose so. He didn't tell me about Charlie's death till I'd told him we were both at Chester yesterday.'

'He couldn't possibly think we had anything to do with it.'

'Why not? After all, we do have a motive.'

He laughed. The idea that he or Alison could kill

anybody was preposterous. And yet they had sat in a police interview room just two days ago suggesting that Charlie could have arranged a man's death. On reflection, with the poor fellow dead, that now seemed a pretty stupid idea.

Her face was pale and unhappy as she turned to him. 'It just gives me the creeps. I'm beginning to think Jennifer Eccles is jinxed.'

He looked at her with concern. She was a bright, rational woman, he'd never heard her give an inch to superstition before.

'Don't be daft, Alison.'

'Dad and Charlie owned her and now they're both dead.'

'That's just a weird coincidence,' he said.

'I suppose.'

Across the yard, he saw Jennifer Eccles being led to her stall. Then he remembered that he'd not yet broken the news of Jenny's latest mishap.

Alison simply nodded when he told her. 'See what I mean?' she said. 'Jinxed.'

He didn't argue with her this time.

Gabriel was nursing half a bitter at the back of a pub in the Elephant, not his normal hangout at eleven thirty of a weekday morning but better than many he could think of. He was pretending to read a copy of *Metro* which had been lying on the table, a handy discovery since it provided some cover while he kept an eye on a portly gentleman playing darts on the other side of the taproom.

He'd read more newspapers in his fledgling career as a snoop than ever before. They not only passed the time but were some protection against casual acquaintance. He didn't know what it was about him, maybe his youthful looks, but he seemed to invite conversation from strangers. Though he was well over six foot, he possessed abundant curly hair and smooth boyish cheeks and was invariably asked for ID before he bought a drink. His appearance had its advantages, however, for no one ever perceived him as a threat. The downside was that his natural inclination was to respond to social overtures. Only the week before he'd been so busy trading cocktails with the off-duty girls from a car-hire firm that he'd completely lost the guy he was meant to be observing.

Today, though, he was determined not to be sidetracked and, from behind his paper, he kept an eye on his subject's prowess on the oche. Seeing as Gabriel was being employed by a motor insurer to assess the fellow's claim for impaired vision following a shunt on the A41, the activity was fortuitous. Gabriel marvelled at the facility with which his target could hit double top in his handicapped state. The chap must have been some kind of champion before the accident.

He looked down at the paper to hide the smile that had crept on to his face and, for the first time, took in the words on the page spread before him. 'I don't believe it,' he muttered to himself as he read it through again, with rapt attention this time.

It was an account of murder in Gant's Hill and it wiped the darts game from his mind. Property developer Charles Talbot – described as a 'larger than life character' and 'a devoted family man' – had been knifed to death in the show flat on the ground floor of his new building. A police statement revealed that the body had been discovered at approximately four thirty the previous afternoon and that there were some indications of a struggle.

Two photographs accompanied the report, one of a nondescript suburban building with a For Sale banner on its frontage; the other of the man Gabriel had met yesterday, rigged up in top hat and tails with a pair of binoculars around his neck. The caption stated that Talbot – 'Champagne Charlie' to his friends – was a familiar face on the horseracing circuit.

Gabriel digested this information in a state of shock. Charlie had left him at about two thirty and just over a couple of hours later he was dead. On the assumption he'd gone straight to Gant's Hill, the journey would have taken about an hour. What had the big man said before he left? That he had to go to a meeting. With his killer maybe? That was one meeting he'd have done better to avoid.

Whatever had happened, Gabriel must have been among the last people to have talked to Charlie. Which meant that the police would soon be wanting to talk to him. He wondered how long it would take for them to track him down. Just as long as it took them to consult Charlie's mobile phone, he assumed.

He folded the paper and got to his feet, abandoning his drink. Across the bar, the podgy dart-player checked out with another tricky double but Gabriel was no longer interested – he had enough on him anyhow.

As he hoofed it up the road to the tube, he reflected that this summer stop-gap job certainly had its moments. He'd come face to face with a man who'd been knifed to death and, as a consequence, would soon be making a statement in a murder inquiry. His parents would be appalled – they thought Uncle Clive had found him a nice little office job. Gabriel couldn't deny he was apprehensive but it also gave him an undeniable buzz.

Maybe he'd stick at it a little longer.

'Ah, there you are.' Simon's voice cut into Mariana's thoughts as she manipulated an appreciative Red River. 'I wondered where you've been hiding.'

Was there reproach in that voice? He looked serious and stern.

'Simon,' she said, 'is everything OK?'

From across the yard came the sound of a car and the rattle of a handbrake.

'There's the vet,' he said, already moving away from the stable door. 'See you in a moment.'

He hadn't answered her – maybe he knew.

But if Charlie had told him about Chrysalis, surely Simon wouldn't be so unemotional. Any man who discovered his wife-to-be had recently been working as a prostitute would surely shout or weep – show some kind of emotion, at least? Or maybe this was the way of these Yorkshire English. She hadn't thought of her Simon as cold and cruel but who knew how he might react to a woman who had just broken his heart?

From the way Henderson was grinning as he approached her desk, Claire knew some sarcastic remark was coming. He didn't disappoint her.

'Jesus, Parker, I told you to check Talbot out, not finish him off.'

She raised a weak smile in response. She felt like shit and probably looked it too. It had been way into the evening before she'd extricated herself from the clutches of the Ilford police and the long drive back to her home in Streatham had been no fun. She'd hardly slept. She'd thought she was hardened to police work but finding a man with his torso reduced to mincemeat had had its effect.

What had really knocked her for six was the thought that, as she had stood on Charlie Talbot's doorstep, the door might have opened on the butcher who had carved him up. What would she have done then? More to the point, what would he?

This realisation had surfaced during the course of a conversation with one of the detective team who had arrived to investigate, DS Steve Gill. He'd been attentive, plying her with coffee and biscuits, offering to summon up a medic.

'What for?' She'd sounded more indignant than she felt.

'Shock. Just because you're on the job doesn't mean you're immune.'

She'd brushed off the suggestion but, on reflection, he'd been right. She'd been in shock last night and she didn't feel a hundred per cent right now. And she could do without Henderson's leaden wit.

The DCI plonked himself on the desk. 'So what did you tell them?'

'Just the basics. How I looked through the window when no one answered and saw the body on the floor.'

'You didn't say why you were there?'

'Just that Talbot's name had come up in another inquiry. They were more concerned to find out if I'd seen anyone near the flats as I arrived. They didn't have a time of death, of course, but it might not have been that long before I turned up.'

'Nasty.' He pulled a face.

'I promised I'd talk to them today though.'

Steve Gill had sent her home last night after she'd insisted she was fit to drive. Though she'd bristled at his attentions, in the cold light of day she appreciated it. He was a more sensitive man than the one now sprawling on her desk.

'Just make sure,' he said, 'that they repay the favour.'

'Why? You don't think there's any connection between the Hall murder and this, do you?'

'I don't think anything at the moment. Beyond the fact that our Yorkshire visitors fingered the guy one day and he turns up dead the next. It's quite a coincidence.'

'You're not suggesting—'

'No, I'm not. In any case, Miss Hall and Mr Waterford were both at Chester races yesterday afternoon – we've checked. It's just that now, with Charlie gone, they don't have to worry about coughing up a hundred grand. That's the kind of thing that makes me curious.'

It made her curious too.

'I'll call Ilford,' she said, 'and let you know how I get on.'

Apparently satisfied for the moment, he got off her desk and sauntered away.

When Mariana had finished with Red River, she

found Simon with Alison and Dave, the vet. The three of them were grouped around a familiar chestnut horse with a white blaze down her nose – Jennifer Eccles.

'Ah,' said Dave as she joined them, 'the answer to our prayers.'

Simon shot her a look that, no matter how she tried to interpret it to her disadvantage, was fond. More than fond, it was full of love and pride.

So she hadn't been found out yet.

'Jenny pulled up on the gallops,' Simon explained. 'Dave thinks it's a pulled muscle in her shoulder. She's due to run at Haydock in a fortnight.'

'I can give her a painkiller,' the vet said. 'But it would be better not to mask the pain – we wouldn't want to damage her long term. Massage might be a better way of dealing with it.'

Mariana put her hand to the little horse's face. 'I'll look after her. I would love to.'

'Just do what you can,' said Alison. 'I'm not going to run her if there's any risk.'

'Of course not,' said Simon.

Dave indicated to Mariana exactly where he thought the problem was.

'I can't work miracles,' she said.

'Don't sell yourself short, love,' said Simon. He was grinning.

'I'll come back at the weekend and see if there's any improvement.' Dave turned towards his car.

'Hey, Dave,' Simon called to him. 'Do you remember the guy who used to own Jenny with my uncle? Charlie Talbot.'

'The property dealer? Sure. A most unpleasant fellow.'

'You're not the only one to think so – he was found dead yesterday. Murdered.'

'Good Lord.' Dave looked genuinely surprised.

'Looks like he was attacked showing people round a flat he was selling. The police rang Alison this morning.'

Dave asked for more details but Mariana took no further notice of the conversation. She pretended to be immersed in stroking the horse – after all, she wasn't supposed to have any personal acquaintance with the dead man. But it was all she could do to remain upright, her body was shaking so much.

Her prayers had been answered. She should be jumping for joy not quivering with fear.

She'd been saved again.

As a rule, Gabriel avoided too many trips to his uncle's office in Holborn. The atmosphere of worthy concentration reminded him too much of the accountant's office where he'd been a trainee. In any case, Clive didn't want him hanging around the place when he could be out on the street, doing something useful.

He kicked his heels in the outer office while some dull meeting ground on. Finally, after about three-quarters of an hour, the visitors left and he was able to take a seat across the desk from his uncle.

He placed the newspaper on the desktop. 'Take a look at that.'

Clive, a heavy man with paunchy features, gave the page a quick glance. 'I'm not surprised,' he said. 'Mr Talbot had a talent for pissing people off.'

'You knew him?'

'Only by letter and phone. He was trying to extort money from Alison Hall, Geoff's daughter.'

It had not occurred to Gabriel that his uncle would be aware of Charlie Talbot, though maybe it should have done. There weren't many things or people Clive did not appear to know. But, on this occasion, Gabriel had one up on him, considering that he had met Charlie face to face.

He relayed the facts of yesterday's encounter in the hotel bar and was gratified to see that he had all of Clive's attention.

'The police will need a word with you,' the solicitor said.

'I know but there's not much I can say that's going to help their inquiry. Just that Charlie said he had to go because he had a meeting.'

Clive thought that over. 'That might be very useful knowledge. If the person he had arranged to meet then killed him, it mitigates against a chance assault. By a burglar, for example.'

Gabriel had worked that out for himself and it wasn't the reason he hadn't yet picked up the phone to the Ilford police.

'Do I have to tell them why Talbot wanted to see me?'

'Why did he?'

Gabriel recounted their conversation.

'What did you say to his offer?' Clive asked.

'I said I'd have to think about it. I wasn't sure whether we had the right to flog the report to a third party, even if the guy we wrote it for was dead. I didn't say that, of course.'

'And you weren't tempted just to go ahead and pass him a copy for the money he offered you?'

'No.' It was the truth but he wondered if, in his position, Clive would have felt the same. 'I was going to run it by you, actually.'

'Very wise.' Clive fingered his jowls. 'Let's think it through then. A few months ago my longstanding client Geoff Hall asked if I could recommend a discreet private investigator to run the rule over the girl his nephew wished to marry. That investigator was you and your findings, as I recall, were damaging to the lady's reputation. I passed on the information in the expectation that the engagement would soon come to an end. However, it didn't and as far as I'm aware the marital arrangement remains in place. I can only assume Geoff had second thoughts about showing your report to his nephew. Or maybe he was still considering what to do with it before his unfortunate death. Of course, it is possible that Simon Waterford was unmoved by these revelations – she might have already informed him of her shady past. Though, personally, I doubt it.'

'Why?'

'Because I've met Mr Waterford. An upstanding and impressive young fellow, only a few years older than you. But he doesn't strike me as a sophisticated man with the ladies. I also think that should Miss Hamilton's unconventional history come to light it might be damaging to his business. Lots of snobby society people own horses.'

Gabriel nodded. He'd wondered what had become of the information he'd dug up on the Brazilian girl. Not much, it seemed. Not yet anyway;

it might still be something of an unexploded bomb.

'In the meantime,' Clive continued, 'Mr Talbot was pursuing a fictitious claim for compensation over a horse he once owned jointly with Geoff. Geoff bought him out when the animal was sick but when it got better and started winning, Talbot came back for more. He submitted an invoice for over a hundred thousand pounds and Geoff passed it on to me, asked me what to do to get this nuisance off his back.'

This was all news to Gabriel. 'Charlie never mentioned horses to me.'

'He had no need to but I'm sure his desire to see the information you unearthed was connected to this demand. In the past week he has renewed his claims to be paid and confronted Geoff's daughter Alison and his nephew, Simon Waterford.'

'The trainer?'

'Who is engaged to Mariana, a half-Brazilian young lady known in some quarters as Fabiana. As you know.'

Gabriel shouldn't have been surprised. It was plain Charlie would not have had a benign purpose in seeking to acquire the report.

'How do you think he was going to use the information?'

Clive shrugged. 'It's possible Simon knows about Mariana's past and accepts it. But he might not be so happy for others to know about it. You can imagine the stir it would cause in the world of racing. I doubt if his owners would be impressed.'

'Blackmail then?'

'Indeed. Or revenge. I gather he made threats. Maybe he just wanted to get his own back.'

Gabriel considered the point. Would he say, on his short acquaintance, that Charlie was a vindictive character? Definitely.

Clive shot him a quick, penetrating glance. 'What are you intending to tell the police?'

'Beyond the basic facts, you mean? I won't mention the report – unless you think I should.'

Clive shook his head. 'Given its sensitivity, I'd rather it didn't leak into the public domain. Do you think you're capable of keeping quiet about it?'

'I don't see why not. I'm just volunteering what I know, aren't I? They won't be talking to me under caution.'

'So why did you meet? What will you say?'

Gabriel grinned. 'That Charlie wanted to hire a private investigator but didn't say what for. And he didn't seem impressed with me. Don't worry, Clive, I've failed a few job interviews – I'll make out that this was just another.'

His uncle nodded. 'Better call them quick before they call you.'

Claire met DS Gill in a fancy Italian café near Smithfield Market – his choice of venue. 'Neutral ground,' he'd said as he'd issued directions. 'Not my patch or yours and they do a good coffee.'

They did more than that but Claire contented herself with just a mouthful of Steve's lemon cake. He was easy to talk to and there was a hint of more than professional interest in his eye as they discussed Talbot's murder.

She repeated her account of discovering the body, preceding it by a swift description of her trip to

Talbot's former home and her encounter with Mrs Talbot and her children.

Steve pulled a face. 'The Family Liaison bods are babysitting her at the moment. I don't think the kids know yet. I wouldn't have their job for all the tea in China.'

He looked like a family man – capable, comfortable in himself, attractive in a laidback way. And with a quaintly old-fashioned way of expressing himself. Tea in China?

'Do you have children?' she asked.

'No fear. Not yet anyway. Got to find the right woman first.'

'Well, it won't be me. After I came away from meeting Mrs Talbot I swore I'd never get married.' She didn't know why she'd said it. Best to get your cards on the table though.

'That so?' He was grinning

'Those boys. Right little bruisers but you could tell they loved their dad. They just wanted him home.'

He didn't say anything, which was as well because it was the one thing about the Talbot affair that made her a bit misty-eyed and that was distinctly unprofessional. She'd never live it down if news of her tearing-up got back to Henderson.

Steve drained his coffee. 'Suppose I bring you up to speed with what we're thinking and then maybe you can fill in some gaps?'

'OK.'

'It all happened in that titchy front room. The TV's been knocked off its stand and a little table's been kicked over and, of course, it's where the body was lying. As you saw, there's plenty of blood. Everywhere else is spick and span except the bathroom where there's a bloody towel in the sink. It looks like he was attacked and killed in the living room. The killer then washed himself off in the bathroom – hence the towel. Naturally, forensics are all over it but we don't have any results yet. There's no sightings of anyone coming or going, unfortunately.'

'Cameras?'

'The security system in the block is not onstream yet. The other flats in the building are empty – never been lived in. So there's no neighbours and no witnesses. According to his wife, Charlie had been living in the show flat since he'd left home two weeks ago and we found bedding and toiletries stowed away out of sight. We're working on the theory that he was expecting a prospective buyer yesterday afternoon and that person killed him.'

'You think the killer made an appointment?'

'As I say, the place had been spruced up. There was even a vase of flowers.'

'Yellow carnations. I saw.'

He nodded approvingly. 'He bought them as he left the tube station at about a quarter past three. The flower-seller remembered him. We also know where he was earlier in the afternoon – meeting a guy in the bar of the Rainsborough Hotel up west.'

'How did you find out?'

'The guy's called Gabriel Silver. He read about the murder in the paper and rang us up. He's tied in to a solicitor called Clive Silver who uses him to serve court papers and check up on witnesses in insurance cases.'

'An inquiry agent?'

'Right. He says Talbot had arranged to see him at two but he turned up ten minutes late. Then he left at around half past saying he had to go to a meeting. The timing checks out. It's a five-minute walk to Oxford Circus station from the Rainsborough and half an hour or so on the train puts him buying flowers at Gant's Hill at a quarter past three.'

'What's the connection between Silver and Charlie?'

'According to Silver, Talbot rang him out of the blue and fixed the meeting at the hotel. He said it was like a job interview with Talbot sounding him out but he never discovered what sort of job because Talbot cut it short. He assumed Talbot wasn't that impressed. When he read about the murder he realised he'd been among the last people to see him and called in.'

'Silver, you say?' That rang a bell.

'Gabriel Silver.'

That didn't.

'Your turn.' Steve was looking at her with sympathetic brown eyes, inviting her confidence. She'd bet he was damn good at dealing with female witnesses. 'Why were you interested in Charlie Talbot?'

Despite Henderson's caution, she didn't see that there was anything to hide. When she began to talk to Steve about Geoff Hall, she saw those eyes fill with interest. Everyone was intrigued by what the papers called the Ascot Murder.

'We're sure it's got nothing to do with the usual gang stuff, however it may look. We've been banging heads and leaning on street kids for months and nothing has come out of the woodwork at all. To be honest, they're as puzzled as we are. We've got great CCTV and DNA but no bodies and no leads. As a result we're frustrated and so are the relatives. The murdered man's daughter and nephew came to see us a couple of days ago with a theory that the murder was revenge for a horse deal that had turned sour. They mentioned Charlie Talbot. Apparently he once owned a horse with Geoff Hall and claimed he was owed money as a result. My boss thought the idea was pretty outlandish but I was detailed to have a chat with Talbot and get his side of the story. I found he'd left the family home but Mrs Talbot gave me the Gant's Hill address. I went there the day before yesterday and he was out, so I returned yesterday afternoon – as you know. I doubt if that helps you much – or me for that matter.'

'I'm not sure.' Steve said. 'So the relatives were suggesting that Charlie had killed your victim?'

'Not him personally but that he could have paid for the murder.'

'If he did then you just lost your only suspect.'

That was true though she hadn't thought of it like that.

'On the other hand,' Steve looked at her steadily, 'how many people attacked your victim?'

'There were two. One of them had a knife and he killed Geoff Hall.'

'Well, like I said, we don't have all the forensics yet but we've got a preliminary report from the pathologist. Talbot put up a fight and there were at least a dozen stab wounds. From two different knives.'

Claire digested the information. 'Two killers then –
unless the guy had a knife in each hand.'

Steve shook his head. 'We've ruled that out. The
blows came from different heights and different
angles. Two killers for sure, like your case.'

'It doesn't prove anything. What connection could
there possibly be?'

'That's for us to find out, I guess. More coffee?'

She knew she ought to get back. But sod that.

Gabriel had a desk in the offices of Silver & Co. but on
the days he showed up to see Clive, he often found it
occupied by a temp secretary or covered in files in
transit to somewhere else. On one occasion it
appeared to have vanished completely until he
realised it was walled in behind a delivery of loo rolls
and towels for the toilets.

He liked having his own desk, however. It contained
a drawer which doubled as a filing cabinet. When he'd
first started his work for Clive he had been assiduous
in keeping that cabinet fed, thinking that maybe
Clive would need to inspect his records. He'd soon
realised, however, that Clive had little interest in
office bureaucracy and, in recent months, he'd kept
his notes at home

Now he pulled out the file he'd originally created
for Geoff Hall's inquiry. There was precious little in it
beyond some pages he'd printed off the internet and
some scribbles torn from a notebook.

He'd not looked in here since he'd presented his
dossier to Clive for onward transmission to the client.
He'd been working to a deadline and so not every lead
had been followed up. The scribbles were lines of

investigation that could be expanded should further information be required. But Geoff Hall, poor fellow, had not asked for more work to be done and Gabriel had forgotten all about his promising future leads.

Until now.

Chapter Nine

Clive Silver reflected, as he frequently did, that there are some professions in which the death of a client does not necessarily mean the end of a working relationship. A solicitor's job was one of them. Geoff Hall may have passed on but the responsibility for administering his estate remained with Clive – and other commitments too. For more years than he cared to count – more than a quarter of a century, that was certain – Clive had shared the ups and downs of Geoff's existence. The ups had encompassed his business ventures where every project he had embarked on had turned out well. Geoff had not been a get-rich-quick merchant. He had planned his moves with care and foresight, kept his pledges and built relationships to last. As a result he'd made a lot of money.

But, in applying the same diligence to his personal relationships, somehow Geoff had been left empty-handed. Here were his downs and most of them could be laid at the door of bad luck – the deaths from accident and illness, his own random murder, were not Geoff's fault. Only his choice of a wife, in Clive's opinion, had been a poor decision. Though that, to be fair, had resulted in the most satisfying and successful relationship of Geoff's life, with his daughter, Alison, a girl whom Clive had admired ever since her father had brought her to visit as a toddler, her red curls and joyful giggles brightening the dry atmosphere of his office.

Alison still had the same curls, though these days her visits did not contain much merriment. Despite the size of her inheritance, here was one surviving relative who genuinely could not care less about the hefty bank balance that now took the place of her father.

Clive's concern for Geoff, personal and professional, transferred seamlessly to Alison. As committed as he had been to the father, so Clive was to the daughter and her affairs. He considered it a duty born of long association.

In this connection he now pondered the investigation Geoff had instigated into his nephew Simon's intended wife. Geoff had come to him with his concerns about Mariana and Clive had suggested the option of employing his own nephew, a young man who'd proved resourceful in a variety of clandestine tasks, and Geoff had taken his advice. Clive had scarcely given the matter any thought since he had handed Gabriel's dossier of findings to Geoff. The murder and its ramifications had driven all thought of Mariana's secret past from his mind. In any case, it was hardly his business.

He thought now he had cause to revise that opinion. Mariana was still involved with Geoff's family and likely to become securely embedded, to the point where her removal would be costly and painful, unless steps were taken. Geoff had begun the process of dislodging the former prostitute but fate had intervened to prevent him following through. In the circumstances, as a trusted family adviser, it was surely part of Clive's job to continue the process. And that was the reason he had instructed Gabriel to continue his research.

It could be argued, Clive mused, that he should first talk to Alison. But she, as far as he could tell, was in ignorance of the matter and to speak to her was to let the cat out of the bag. It made more sense to review the investigation and see what else Gabriel could discover. Maybe then a word with his client, just to sound her out on the subject, would be in order.

Clive was well aware that Alison was close to her cousin and, from remarks she had let slip, that she approved of the girl he proposed to marry. She plainly liked Mariana and had only spoken of her in positive terms. Maybe she knew of her colourful past and didn't see anything wrong with it. Maybe Simon knew too and didn't count it of significance.

If that was the case then it was all the more reason for Clive to play his cards cautiously. It wasn't his place, however he might feel personally, to pass judgements on the private lives of others. However, it was his function – and his longstanding duty to his old friend Geoff – to ensure that the next generation had all the facts at their disposal to make the most of their lives. And somehow he didn't think welcoming a former escort girl into the family would be accomplishing that. He could only imagine how his sister and brother-in-law would react if Gabriel were to fall for a girl with Mariana's history. It didn't bear thinking about.

Gabriel had been surprised to get a positive response from the number at the bottom of the list in the file. He'd been given it months back by a Chrysalis punter desperate to cooperate lest his wife discover the true nature of the sport he pursued on his golfing weekends. Most of the contacts the fellow had supplied had turned out to be duff but this call had been answered by a woman with a soft Irish accent who appeared to swallow his story about researching a television play. In response to his request for a meeting, she'd replied with a cheery, 'Why the heck not?'

He'd agreed to Nadine's rendezvous – a first-floor coffee bar in an Oxford Street bookshop – and, arriving early, took a seat where he could keep an eye on the customers stepping off the escalator. After half an hour he'd begun to conclude that she had thought better of her hasty agreement. That would be a pity, he was looking forward to meeting the owner of that seductive voice.

He discounted the heavily pregnant redhead even as she made directly for where he sat by the window. He was the only lone male in the place.

'I know, I'm late – I'm sorry. It takes me bloody ages to get anywhere like this.'

'Nadine?'

'Don't look so damned shocked.' She eased herself on to the chair opposite him. 'Even ex-hookers get knocked up, you know. Get us one of those strawberry frappucino things, would you? I'm boiling over.'

175

He did as he was told and admired the way she dispensed with the straw and gulped half of it down in one draught, decorating her full red mouth with a moustache of pink froth. Her sea-green eyes danced with good humour as she watched his reaction. Her sweating, fecund presence was not what he had been expecting.

His previous attempts to talk to escorts who knew Mariana had met with little success. They'd closed ranks and brushed him off. Even when Geoff Hall, through Clive, had authorised the purchase of an hour of a girl's time, she had been happy enough to yatter on in general terms but scarcely told him more than he had discovered already. Nadine, he hoped, would be much more forthcoming and all for the price of a milky drink.

She had married a client, she told him, a German artist who Gabriel had never heard of. He specialised in architectural sculptures and large public installations, playing the corporate bohemian to his advantage. He didn't give a hoot for his wife's past profession and, according to her, enjoyed scandalising some of his more strait-laced business clients with tales of her adventures.

Gabriel's call had come at a good moment for Klaus was working and Nadine was bored. She'd been instructed to 'rest' until the baby came and her due date was three weeks off.

'I expect I'll be late,' she announced. 'I've been late for just about everything else in my life so why not?' She raised her glass and sucked at the remaining chips of ice. 'So, you're a writer?'

Gabriel made a quick decision to change his story –

sticking, as close as possible to the truth was always a good idea. He produced his business card.

'Only an amateur one. I work for a solicitor.' He pushed his card across the table. It revealed little but implied he was rather more important than was the case.

She pinned it to the tabletop with a long, exquisitely painted fingernail and read, 'Gabriel Silver, Silver & Co., Solicitors'. The ever-present smile was present no longer as the green eyes assessed him anew.

'I *am* researching the escort business, however,' he said hastily. 'We're handling a legacy and I'm trying to trace someone who I believe you used to know.'

She nodded but there was apprehension in her face now. 'Oh yes?'

'Mariana Hamilton.'

Nadine shook her head. 'I don't remember.'

'She used the name Fabiana when she worked for Chrysalis.'

'I don't think I can help. Sorry.' She put her empty glass down on the table. 'Do you mind if I go to the loo?'

How could he? She was already halfway to her feet.

'Would you like another drink?' he said, suddenly anxious that she might be heading straight for the exit. He'd obviously spooked her.

'Sure,' she said and made for the door to the left of the counter with surprising urgency.

He bought another frappucino and a coffee for himself which he finished as he waited for her return. The minutes stretched on and his worries began to crystallise. How stupid of him to have switched identities. A solicitor was much more threatening than a fluffy TV writer. And then to have plunged straight into asking after Mariana – he should have got to her in a more roundabout fashion. He must have scared Nadine off.

But he'd liked her and wanted to lie to her as little as possible. And he'd felt instinctively that she'd prefer a no-bullshit approach. Plainly he'd been wrong.

Twenty minutes had gone by. He approached the girl on the till.

'Is there a way out through there?' he asked, pointing at the door through which Nadine had disappeared.

She shook her head. 'No, it's just the toilets.'

Gabriel was relieved. So she hadn't walked out on him. On the other hand, what was she doing?

The girl was considering him. 'Your wife's pretty far gone, isn't she? Would you like me to see if she's all right?'

Gabriel considered correcting her but simply said, 'Yes, please.'

In two minutes she was back, an arm hooked through Nadine's. The Irish girl was pasty white and the smiling mouth was set in a letterbox of pain. She reached for Gabriel and hissed, 'Get me to Saint Catherine's quick.'

'Right you are.' He supported her weight and led her away with a smile of thanks for the girl who had come to the rescue. 'Saint Catherine's church? Where's that?'

'The hospital, you eejit. In Paddington. I'm having the sodding baby.'

Many things went tumbling around Gabriel's head as he manhandled Nadine through the Oxford

Street crush and flagged down a taxi. First was the relief that she hadn't been trying to get away from him at all and second that she'd been wrong when she'd stated with such confidence that she was always late. But the overwhelming feeling, as she dug her pink-lacquered fingernails into his hand on the back seat of the speeding black cab, was that his chance of learning anything useful from her had just vanished.

Between contractions, as they neared the hospital, Nadine made frantic phone calls – none of them successful. Her downstairs neighbour was out and her husband had his phone turned off.

'He's in a meeting,' she blurted. 'With a really important client.'

Gabriel calculated that, once he had safely delivered Nadine to the hospital, he'd have to curb his impatience for a couple of days. He could phone after the happy event and resume his inquiries. The Mariana investigation had been on hold for three months so a further delay would hardly matter.

'When does his meeting finish?' he asked.

'I don't know exactly. There's a six-hour time difference between here and Bangladesh.'

Jesus. Gabriel made a note for future reference never to turn off his phone with a partner eight months pregnant. It didn't help, of course, that the fellow was halfway round the world.

Nadine had more luck with her mother, though it turned out that she was in Kilkenny and it would be well into the evening before she could possibly make it to London.

'Haven't you got some friends here in London you could call?' he asked.

But they were drawing up outside St Catherine's and Nadine was whimpering with pain. He jumped out of the cab and fumbled for the fare.

He helped her out and hauled her into the reception area.

'Thank you,' she mumbled. 'I'll be all right now. You can leave me here.'

'Oh sure,' he said, spotting a freshly abandoned wheelchair by the door. He grabbed it and plonked Nadine on the seat. 'Now, which way's maternity?'

Mariana sang one of her Brazilian songs as she rubbed down Jennifer Eccles, a happy song that had just arrived in her head out of nowhere. She'd not sung it for years.

'You sound cheerful.' Alison stepped into the box.

'Sorry.' Mariana didn't know why she said it, except that she was conscious that Alison was still grieving for her father – a man who, to her shame, Mariana had wished dead in the moments just before he had been killed. That, in itself, was another reason to say sorry.

'Don't apologise, it's a lovely sound. Jenny likes it too.'

Who could say what the animal really thought but she did appear contented as Mariana smoothed her coat.

'Maybe she'll be OK for the race,' Mariana said. 'She's not in pain.'

Alison shrugged. 'I don't mind if she doesn't run. I'm thinking of selling her.'

'Oh no. Why?'

'Because, considering what a sweet horse she is, she causes trouble. My father and Charlie Talbot fell out over her and now they're both dead. I have the feeling she's bad luck. You probably think I'm silly.'

'No.' Mariana was surprised to hear Alison talk this way but she didn't think her friend was silly. Far from it. Alison's admission gave her sudden confidence. 'It's strange that man Charlie is dead. I know it's wrong but I'm glad.'

Alison looked at her closely. 'I didn't think you knew about him.'

The urge to talk about it was strong. 'I met him at the races and he was horrible to me.'

'You met him?'

'He saw me with Simon and he got me on my own. Look.'

The bruise on her wrist had turned a malevolent purple and was plainly visible in the dim light of the stable.

Alison sucked in her breath. 'He did that? Why?'

'Because he wanted me to change Simon's mind about Jennifer Eccles. Get Simon to persuade you to pay up.'

'What, by twisting your arm? I hope you reported it. You could have had him arrested.'

'Oh no. The bruise has only just come out actually. It looks much worse than it is.'

'What did Simon say?'

'He doesn't know that's how I did it. I didn't tell him.'

'Why ever not?' Alison said.

'Because he'd probably have got into a fight with

Charlie and I didn't want that. And it doesn't matter now anyway, does it?'

'I suppose not, not the way it's turned out.' All the same Alison looked a little oddly at Mariana who was regretting the impulse to talk about Charlie. There was a lesson in this, she realised. Even now, on a day when it seemed all her troubles had been magically blown away, she had to watch her every step.

Calm – on the surface at least – prevailed in the maternity unit. The moment Gabriel and Nadine barrelled through the double doors, hospital staff intercepted them and assessed the situation at a glance. Within seconds Nadine was detached from the wheelchair and led away for assessment. Gabriel was instructed to wait.

This was his chance to leave and Nadine could hardly hold it against him if he did. He'd delivered her into the hands of the professionals and from here on she could safely be left on her own.

He didn't like the sound of that, for all sorts of reasons. He imagined his sister Becky, married to Lawrence and expecting her second this Christmas, in a situation like this. It could happen, with Lawrence on one of his conferences and their parents off on some jaunt. Becky wouldn't want to be on her own. A strange face, if friendly, was better than no face at all. He'd hang on for a few moments and see if he could be of use to Nadine. He could at least call someone else for her.

A nurse appeared by his side. 'Would you like to come through, Mr Adler? We've made your wife comfortable.'

'Actually, she's not my wife.'

But the nurse was in a rush, she trotted on ahead at speed and Gabriel followed.

Nadine was in a bed in an alcove screened off from the rest of the small ward. Her face was flushed and her fringe hung in damp auburn strips across her forehead. She managed a thin smile and grabbed his hand as he sat beside her.

'How are you doing?'

'It hurts,' she said. 'And I hate this horrible hospital gown.'

Gabriel thought that was the least of her problems.

She reached into her handbag on the bed table and pulled out a keyring. 'Would you do me a favour? Fetch my hospital bag. It's got all the stuff I need, shampoo and socks and things. I packed it ages ago. It's blue with a black stripe, just under the hall table.'

She put the keys into his hand. 'Hurry, please – I don't think it's going to be long.'

The nurse was back, taking her pulse, and another was fussing around.

'I'll be as quick as I can.' He bent his head to Nadine's anxious pink face. 'Where do you live?'

Fortunately Nadine's apartment wasn't far, a ten-minute taxi ride to a large service block overlooking Hyde Park. The Adlers lived on the top floor. Thinking of all the kiddy kit his sister carted around, Gabriel hoped for Nadine's sake that the lifts never broke down. It would be no fun lugging a baby buggy up twelve flights of stairs.

The bag was in the hall, exactly where Nadine had said it would be. Once he had located it, there was no legitimate reason for Gabriel to remain. But he was curious and, besides, he was being paid to snoop around. A couple of minutes' delay wouldn't harm.

The top-floor flat was spacious and filled with light from high front windows and French doors at the rear which opened off a messy studio on to a nifty roof terrace. Gabriel could see the appeal for Klaus Adler the artist, though the heavy heat would not be pleasant for his pregnant wife. He noted the fan angled towards the white leather sofa in front of a vast plasma television screen in the front room. And the jumble of DVDs on the floors. Was this what Nadine got up to as she sweltered her way to full term – sprawl on the sofa through endless series of *Sex in the City*?

The studio wasn't Gabriel's idea of an artist's lair. There was no mess, no smell of paint and not a canvas in sight. The room was filled by desks, a designer's table raised at an angle and a bank of computer screens. The place seemed neat and ordered with shelves of books and files stowed in order. He moved on, there was nothing of Nadine here.

Surprisingly, there didn't seem much of her in the bedroom either, beyond the obvious – make-up on the dressing table and toiletries in the adjacent bathroom. Doubtless the fitted wardrobes contained a cascade of female finery but clothes weren't his interest. He pulled open a few drawers, feeling shitty about it. But if he saw a diary or an address book he knew he'd thumb through it.

He found the thing he'd been subconsciously looking for in the kitchen. He was acutely aware now of Nadine back at the hospital, giving birth in pain on her own. As her apparent stand-in for friends and family he should hurry up and return.

But first he took a moment to inspect the notice-board on the wall by the kitchen table, thumbtacked with phone numbers, a calendar, old concert tickets, a list of recommended foods and photographs – lots of them.

Nadine sure was a great-looking woman, Gabriel reflected. Even her puffy-faced, over-heated, pregnant state couldn't disguise her loveliness and the old holiday photos on display revealed her in all her former glory. Klaus Adler was a good ten years older – at least, Gabriel assumed the professorial type with grey hair and steel-rimmed glasses with his arm round Nadine's waist was her husband. He was the only man in the pictures. But there were several other women, none of them as attractive as Nadine unless you counted the tall bikini-clad beauty with honey-blond ringlets standing next to her in a beach shot. They were laughing, having a pretty good time from the look of it.

Pregnancy must do funny things to your mind, Gabriel reflected, if it wiped friends from your memory.

Claire caught the finger-across-the throat gesture from Henderson and wound up her conversation with Steve Gill. It was true she had been on the phone for some while but she managed to look indignant as the DCI snarled, 'Romance the boyfriend on your own time, darling.'

'He was only giving me an update on Talbot.'

'Yeah, sure. Just tell me the expurgated version – the one without the lovey-dovey crap.'

Tempted though she was to take the bait and make a smart-ass comeback she knew better than to mix it with her boss. He had a mean streak.

'They've got nothing on who may or may not have made an appointment with Talbot to see round the flat. They still think it's likely he had an arrangement to meet a possible buyer, or someone who was posing as a buyer, if only on the basis that the place was spruced up. His wife says he was desperate to sell. He was up to his neck in money troubles. But there are no likely contacts on his phone. They've traced all his recent callers and they're all listed in his address book apart from Gabriel Silver, the man who met him for lunch on the day he was killed.'

'He's the character who called in, right? The solicitor's snoop.'

'Yes. But they're not looking at him as a suspect. For one thing, it appears there were two killers. They're thinking it might be down to some of the lads who used to work for Charlie. He owed them all money and there was a fight in a pub the other night about it. Maybe a couple of them set Charlie up and killed him because he wouldn't pay them what he owed. That's what Ilford are thinking anyway.'

Henderson said nothing for a moment, just scrutinised Claire. 'So what do you think?' he said eventually.

'I think they're barking up the wrong tree. I can understand Charlie's workers being upset if they're owed and they might do him over in a spur-of-the-moment fight. But they're unlikely to set him up like this. It's too cold-blooded – and pointless if you want him to pay what he owes. Anyway, the forensics will sort it out. We've got DNA on Hall and they've got some on Talbot. When the results are in I reckon we'll have a match.'

'Same killers?'

'Yes, guv. The knife wounds might match too but the DNA should prove it.'

He nodded. 'I reckon you're right. Got any idea why?'

'Why they might be connected? Not the foggiest actually.'

Foggiest? Why had she said that? It was the kind of thing Steve would come out with.

'The DNA results shouldn't be long apparently,' she added.

'How nice for you.' Henderson was giving her his sarcastic grin.

She had no option but to respond as expected. 'Sir?'

'You've got a good excuse to keep ringing your boyfriend in Ilford, haven't you?'

Gabriel had barely been gone an hour, he calculated, by the time he returned to the hospital. Would that be time enough for the birth to have taken place? The way things had been going it wouldn't have surprised him. His only first-hand experience (sort of) had been with Becky when he'd been alerted by a phone call from his breathless brother-in-law. But seventy-two hours later little Tina had still not made an appearance and the baby had had to be induced. Who knew what would happen to Nadine?

She had been moved out of the ward into a poky single room. The contractions were coming at ten-minute intervals and she was clutching a face mask to gulp in gas and air and take the edge off the pain. When she saw him in the doorway she squealed in delight and he felt irrationally pleased.

'Thank God you've come,' she said. 'I've been on my own for the past half hour.'

It turned out there was an emergency down the hall and the midwife was an old boot who only stuck her head through the door to tell Nadine to push harder.

The enclosed space was as stuffy as a boiler room and the feeble old fan on the bedside table simply circulated the hot air.

He set about trying to make her more comfortable, running a flannel under the tepid water of the cold tap and bathing her forehead.

'God, thanks,' she murmured and jammed the mask over her face as the next contraction gripped her.

The door opened and a lean, square-jawed woman took in his presence. 'About time you turned up,' she observed. 'Your wife needs all the support she can get.'

'We're not married, actually.'

The midwife gave him a steely glare. 'Well, it's none of my business, I'm sure,' she said and marched briskly away.

'Do you think we ought to put them straight?' he said.

'Uh?' Nadine looked at him with glassy eyes.

'It doesn't matter to me if they think we're married but what's your husband going to say when he turns up?'

She shook her head, as if the issue wasn't any kind of priority, which in her condition it probably wasn't. 'We'll sort it out later. Stay with me, please.'

'Of course. I'll stay as long as you want. Until your mother gets here anyway. Is that OK?'

But she wasn't listening.

Mariana called Carla. There was no one else she could talk to honestly about what had happened.

'I took your advice about Charlie,' she said, 'and it worked.'

'What was it? I can't remember.'

'I prayed, like you told me to, and now Charlie's dead.'

There was a sharp intake of breath on the other end of the line. Obviously Carla had not heard about the murder and Mariana had to explain.

'So now you feel guilty?' Carla said.

'In a way. I feel bad that I'm happy a man is dead.'

'But it's not your fault – how could it be?'

'I know. It's just that I prayed to be saved and this happened.'

Carla chuckled. 'Don't be silly, *chérie*. You have been saved by fate and you deserve it. Don't think about Charlie, think about the nice man you are going to marry and be happy.'

Mariana was pleased she had spoken to her old friend. She put the phone down with a glow of well-being, determined to take her advice. She should be grateful that, for once, a good angel was watching her path, removing obstacles like Charlie Talbot.

And Geoff Hall. She had not told Carla that Geoff had been threatening to expose her too. But that was fate too – it had to be.

She went downstairs to find Simon and make the most of her newly charmed life.

* * *

It was no cooler in the room where Nadine was struggling to give birth but the atmosphere, by some magic, was less tense. The expectant mother was in a trance, somehow coping with the rhythm of her contractions. Gabriel was in awe of her capacity to take the pain and he murmured basic words of encouragement to her over and over as he sponged the sweat from her face.

Earlier – he didn't know when, time had become irrelevant – there had been discussions about pain relief. But Nadine had clung to her gas and air mask and said no to everything else. She'd dismissed the offer of an epidural with a strained smile. 'I've often wanted to be dead from the waist down,' she'd hissed to Gabriel, 'but I'm going to bloody well manage this.'

That was the last coherent thing she'd said to him and he'd made no attempt to make conversation. At first he'd considered trying to pump her for information about Mariana – 'Come off it, you do know her, you've got a photo of her in your kitchen!' – but on only a brief consideration the notion was ridiculous. He remembered what Becky had told him after the birth of his niece, that Lawrence had kept trying to get her to talk. 'He thought he'd take my mind off it hurting. As if there was anything else I could think about, the flaming idiot.'

So he asked no questions of Nadine, just swabbed and soothed and murmured that she was fantastic and listened to her moans of pain.

When the moment came, everything happened fast. Suddenly the room seemed full of people and he was happily irrelevant, declining the invitation to 'have a look at the business end', as the midwife put it. He didn't think his short acquaintance with Nadine entitled him to such intimacy. He wasn't exactly unhappy about it.

The baby was male, pink and noisy, to everyone's satisfaction, and Gabriel watched the professionals go about their business with relief. He felt knackered but happy, as if he really had had a hand in the birth of his own son.

'Congratulations, dad,' said the paediatrician who checked the baby over.

'Thanks, but—'

'I thought you were going to be trouble,' the midwife interrupted, 'but you did all right in the end.'

Suddenly the room cleared and there were just the three of them, the baby lying on Nadine's breast, seemingly content with his new situation. It hardly seemed the moment for Gabriel to ask the new mother about her previous life as an escort girl. Instead he fished a camera out of her bag and took several photos of the pair of them.

'You take him,' she said, offering up her bundle. 'I want one of you together.'

He hesitated. 'Is that a good idea? I mean, what's your husband going to say?'

'He's going to bloody well say thank you. If you hadn't been with me I'd have gone bananas. Take him.'

So he did. Fortunately he knew about holding newborns from his experience with Tina.

She took two shots of him grinning and the baby snuffling happily.

'I've got a confession,' she said as she put the camera down and reclaimed the baby. 'I thought you were just some nosy parker before. I didn't trust you.'

I am a nosy parker, he thought, but kept his mouth shut.

'I lied to you,' she said. 'I do know Mariana – at least I did. She used to be my best friend.'

'Used to be?'

She would have answered, he was sure of it, but at that moment the door was flung open and a large, square woman with wild brassy hair burst into the room.

'Oh Mam!' squealed Nadine and Gabriel's chance had gone.

Chapter Ten

After Simon had concluded the phone call he left the office and returned to the house. He made himself a mug of tea and walked out of the kitchen. He needed to think undisturbed.

The garden had been his mother's preserve and her chief interest in life beyond her family. As a boy, Simon and his friends had been banned from playing ball games at the back of the house and banished to the meadow on the other side of the bridle path where his dad had made a bit of a playground with goalposts and swings. He'd been such a lucky little bastard.

All the same, it hadn't stopped him and his pals from wreaking occasional havoc among his mum's delphiniums. And nicking fruit had been a summer sport. 'Who's had all my raspberries?' was his mother's annual complaint. In time, Simon had come to appreciate what his mother was doing. She had green fingers, a genuine talent for growing and nurturing plants, and had been delighted to discover a willing apprentice in her son. The afternoons Simon had spent with her in the greenhouse and kneeling by the flower beds had earned him many maternal Brownie points.

Now he took his tea down to a bench by the old garden wall and sat by the fig tree whose glossy olive-green leaves gleamed in the morning sunlight. He could see a mass of fruits ripening – 'Looks like a good year, Mum,' he said to himself – and thought briefly of long-off hot summers when they'd filled baskets with ripe figs from just this one tree. Maybe such bounty would return this year. That would be something.

The substance of the phone call weighed on his mind – as it should. It was not every day that someone offered to buy one of the horses in his yard for almost a million pounds.

He knew many trainers whose first impulse would be to put the champagne on ice and call the owner. Indeed, he would shortly ring Jeremy Masterton but the champagne could wait. He wanted to think the matter over.

Aquiline was undoubtedly a star two-year-old with a brace of fine victories to his credit in the Coventry Stakes at Ascot and the Gimcrack at York. But there was no guarantee he would continue to improve and win any of the Classic races for three-year-olds, which was where the real glory – and riches – lay. For one thing, he was temperamental and contrary, it took enormous effort to get him to the course in a state to race. Simon was well aware that the colt had only just squeaked home ahead of his rivals at York. Maybe that success was destined to be the pinnacle of his career.

So far Aquiline's victories had been in six-furlong sprints and, though next year he would be bigger and stronger, there was no guarantee he would make the step up to a mile to land a classic. Simon knew plenty of horses who had performed like world-beaters at two and also-rans the following season.

Then, of course, there was the possibility of injury. Horses were masters of their own destruction, constantly finding ways of hurting themselves no matter how closely you watched over them. Two weeks before the Gimcrack, Aquiline had got loose at exercise and galloped home flat out – he could easily have hurt himself. The bottom line was that anything could go wrong with a horse and only fools and optimists would risk serious money on their future prospects. And a million pounds counted as serious. Would Jeremy be tempted?

Simon didn't spend much time pondering the question. Jeremy didn't strike him as a fellow in need of cash but, these days in particular, who knew? However, it was his own feelings he was exploring at the moment. His ten per cent of the sale price was not to be dismissed lightly, yet it might look insignificant should Aquiline train on. In that event, the horse's stud value would go through the roof.

As far as Simon was concerned, the money wasn't the real issue. There was a bigger picture – the future of the yard he had inherited from his father. It was important to have horses like Aquiline at Willowdale. Victories in the top races advertised his training skills in the best possible way, attracting other classy horses for the future and perpetuating the chain of success. To lose Aquiline from his stable for next season would be a blow, not just for him but for the Willowdale team. Star horses and big wins lifted the morale of the entire yard. Mariana in particular would be upset if he were to go.

So, when it came down to it, he numbered himself among the optimistic fools.

He put down his mug and fished out his phone. Time to make the call now he knew where he stood. If necessary, he'd argue against the sale – Mariana would be disappointed if he didn't and he had no intention of letting her down.

Claire was irritated with Henderson, which was nothing new. His hobnail-boots approach to personal relationships had been a source of annoyance ever since she'd started working for him. He'd made an oafish pass at her within the first week of their acquaintance – 'You look like you work out – how about working out with me sometime?' – and had taken her refusal in similarly boorish vein: 'I'm just testing, sweetheart, don't flatter yourself.'

That had been almost a year ago and, to his credit, he'd got over the fact that she plainly didn't find him as attractive as he found himself. But she'd been using her work as therapy to get over the last hideous cock-up of her so-called romantic life. Finding her then-fiancé in bed with her sister had been reason enough to bin most kinds of emotional attachment and focus on her career, if that's what working under Henderson's cosh could be called.

At any rate, they'd arrived at a reasonable working relationship and she felt she could get away with more than anyone else on his team. The main reason was that she had effectively de-sexed herself in his eyes. She didn't go on dates, she didn't have boyfriends

– or girlfriends, for that matter – and she took on every graveyard-shift task with masochistic zeal. It had got to the point where, for the most part, he left her alone, trusting her to do the right thing without his beady eyes on her 24/7.

But that had just changed and she knew why. Henderson was a domineering leader of the pack with all the subtlety of a bullet-proof vest, but he had well-attuned instincts, especially where the female members of his team were concerned. Claire's romantic impulse might have been dormant throughout their entire relationship but the moment it showed signs of waking, Henderson was on to it almost quicker than she was. Suddenly her boss seemed to be clocking her every move. She could feel his eyes on her now through the glass of his office partition while she took the phone call from Ilford police.

She couldn't explain why Steve Gill, a dependable by-the-book copper ten years her senior, had aroused her interest. Close-cropped receding hair had never appealed to her. He probably preferred cycling in Cumbria to a carnival weekend in Rio and she'd bet his iPod was filled with instantly recognisable stuff her parents used to play. She knew she wasn't the most stylish 25-year-old in London but she had some taste, she told herself.

Yes, but it's bad taste, she'd respond in the internal debate that was playing on a loop inside her head. The kind of taste that had led her into the arms of a cutting-edge dude who had no qualms about looking down her sister's party dress. And then taking it off.

She didn't think Steve would do a thing like that. That surely was the only reason she felt drawn to him.

It wasn't a good enough reason to drop her guard – or to stir up Henderson's interest.

'Yes,' she barked into the receiver. She could do without the hassle.

'Hi, Parker. Just reporting in on Charlie Talbot, as requested.' Steve's voice was warm and friendly. 'I think you're going to like this.'

'Spit it out then.'

'We've got the DNA results back and there's a match.'

'On the data base?'

'No. With your sample. One of the guys who killed your man left DNA on Talbot.'

Wow. All the theorising in the world didn't change a thing. But this, a concrete result, turned the Geoff Hall case on its head. The thug with spiky hair who had assaulted Simon Waterford had also been party to the murder of Charlie Talbot. It raised more questions than it answered but they were new, fascinating questions. There was movement in the investigation at last.

Claire turned to look at Henderson across the office. He was staring at her, just as she knew he would be.

'We need a proper pow-wow,' Steve was saying. 'Now it looks like we're looking for the same perpetrators. Your governor's got to talk to mine.'

'Leave it to me, Steve,' she said, already out of her seat. She was halfway towards Henderson's door when she realised she hadn't even thanked him.

Mariana clicked open the email in a state of disbelief. *Paula1988@hotmail.com* couldn't be what she suspected, could it?

It could. She'd added all her contact details in the letter to her sister and, plainly, it had paid off.

Cara Mariana –

I am so happy to get your letter this morning that I have to mail you at once.

First I have to say that I am so, so sorry for the way that we fell out and that I accept the blame entirely for what I did. But – I am not trying to excuse myself – I was different then. I like to think I am wiser now and less selfish. I haven't done drugs for a long time and I don't go to clubs and bars and run up debts anymore. I don't want to come over like a suck-up goody-goody but I think I've learned that money is not everything in life. So I say again, I am sorry for what I did and I hope that you can forgive me because there is a great hole in my life without my big sister to look up to.

I am writing this on my computer – the one you saw in the photos. Even though it is vacation time I get to my desk by nine o'clock nearly every morning because I have a lot of studying to make up. Can you imagine that it is your naughty little sister saying this? The girl who thought every teacher was a boring fart-faced person and that books were only good for lighting bonfires – yes, I can remember saying some pretty stupid things – they make me blush with shame now. You are the only person I can confess these things to because you know me so well and I cannot hide the truth from you.

So you must know that I am serious about

becoming a teacher myself. It is hard for me because I neglected my studies for so long but now I see a real purpose in learning for its own sake and passing on that knowledge to others – so they will not make the mistakes that I made.

I'm going to stop now before I say anything too embarrassing – and before I think better of pouring my heart out to you in this way. But you are my only sister and if you do not understand me then who can?

With big hugs and kisses from your sister
Paula

P.S. Your Simon sounds marvellous – I am so happy to hear you have found a good man. It would be so wonderful to see you again and to meet him. It may happen sooner than you think!

Mariana read the mail through twice more, savouring the message and all it implied. It was all she could have hoped for.

'You're looking particularly smug today, Jeremy.' Meg sprinkled lemon juice on her asparagus and reached for the pepper. 'Would you like to let me in on the secret?'

Jeremy was not offended by her words. It was part of their regular repartee. 'You like me smug,' he'd say in response. 'It's only another way of saying self-confident. Admit it, Meg, you like a man who knows what he's doing.'

As a rule these discussions were carried out in bed, where Jeremy undoubtedly knew what he was doing and his post-coital smugness was well-merited.

On this occasion, however, they were dining at the Perfumed Olive, the newly refurbished Michelin-starred restaurant in the grand old Belville Castle Hotel on the outskirts of Leeds. This calibre of eaterie was usually beyond the reach of Jeremy's pocket and only to be patronised when Meg deemed that he had earned the privilege. But today Jeremy intended to pick up the bill.

The invitation to Meg had been issued in advance of the news he had just received from Simon and had been prompted by guilt. He had been deficient in his attentions recently and this was his way of making it up to her. The fact that she would have probably preferred a picnic in her bedroom was beside the point. He needed a sustaining lunch after last night's exertions with young Holly. A fellow had only so much smugness to go around.

He smeared his asparagus with a creamy wodge of hollandaise and almost squealed with delight as the classic combination seduced his taste buds. Positively ravishing. The simple things done to perfection, that was all he asked of life. Simple like the yellow and green combination on his plate, like the buttery smoothness of the skin of Holly's thigh, like the row of noughts on a banker's draft made out in his name. Simply exquisite.

'Well?' said Meg briskly, putting down her fork. 'What's going on? You haven't dragged me all the way over here just to watch you fill your belly, have you?'

Though this was indeed close to the mark, Jeremy rolled his eyes and snagged another asparagus spear. Then he told her about the offer for Aquiline.

'Clever,' she said. 'Pitched at the right level to tempt the novice.'

It wasn't the reaction he'd been expecting.

'That's a bit harsh, Meg. I'm hardly a novice. I've owned horses for years.'

She wrinkled her nose. 'And all of them rubbish except this one. I suppose you want to take the money.'

Of course he wanted to take the money. A million quid – well, almost. Less Simon's share and the amount he was holding in trust, as it were, for the JDC. What's more, he could afford to pay the charity a handsome dividend for the loan. He could double their stake, pay Simon and still put some hefty change in the bank. It was a no-brainer.

But he said, 'I promised Simon I'd think about it. You know, consider the offer from all angles.'

That was partly true. Simon had insisted he didn't just leap in and grab the dosh, said it was bad tactics to agree immediately. Jeremy had seen the sense in that, sort of, and promised to sleep on his decision. But frankly it was yes all the way down the line.

She regarded him shrewdly. 'I don't suppose Simon was all that keen.'

Well, no, he hadn't been. He'd gone out of his way to say what a smashing horse Aquiline was and, provided all went to plan, how he might land a Classic next season and put his price up. But, when pushed, Simon couldn't name that price and the phrase 'provided all goes to plan' had stuck in Jeremy's mind. It had a decidedly iffy ring to it.

'Simon said it was a good offer.'

'But I bet he wasn't begging you to accept.'

'Simon's got his own agenda. He'll lose a top horse from his yard, which is a bit of a blow.'

Her eyes lit up as he conceded that she'd been right in her assessment of the trainer's attitude.

'I take it then,' she said, 'there's no chance the new owner will keep him in training at Willowdale.'

'No.' That had been made abundantly clear, apparently. 'It's one of the Arab outfits and they've got their own set-up.'

Meg sipped her wine – he'd offered her a top-notch champagne but she'd insisted on a premier cru Chablis. She had taste, Jeremy conceded. She knew a bloody sight more about trading in top-flight horses than he did, that couldn't be denied.

'I'd be surprised if anyone else but Simon could get the best out of Aquiline. He won't do much if he leaves Willowdale.'

Jeremy chuckled, he couldn't help it. 'That won't be my problem, darling.'

Meg's face registered disapproval. 'What about Aquiline? Sometimes I think you have no interest in the animals themselves. One horse is the same as the next as far as you are concerned.'

Give or take small matters of who owned what and how much he was in for, that just about summed up Jeremy's attitude. But it was important not to let Meg, and the many who listened to her trenchant opinions, think so.

'Good Lord, no. Horses are in my blood,' he stated vehemently. It was true enough. The Widower had secretly confided to Jeremy that he'd put him through boarding school courtesy of William Hill and Jeremy had no reason to doubt it. Dry as he was, the old man could pick a horse, all right. And it seemed as if, in Aquiline, Jeremy had triumphantly emulated his old man's talent.

'Every few seasons,' Meg continued, 'a two-year-old catches my eye who I just know is going to be a world-beater. I've not been wrong yet. If he stays injury-free, Aquiline could clean up at three. He's big and strong, got the build of a Derby winner, maybe an Arc. If I had the money I'd buy him from you like a shot. If I'd realised you were thinking of selling I'd have made you an offer before the Gimcrack. I've always wanted a runner in the Breeder's Cup.'

Breeder's Cup! If Aquiline won a race in the States that would lift his stud price into the stratosphere.

'Er, Meg, what do you think he'd be worth if he does all that? The Derby and the Breeder's Cup?'

She mulled it over. 'If he were better bred, the sky's the limit. But probably ten times what they're offering now.'

'Ten million!'

'Absolutely. I suppose Simon was reluctant to spell it out to you so you wouldn't reproach him if it didn't come off. But I don't see why not. Aren't you going to finish your asparagus, Jeremy? It's not like you.'

But Jeremy wasn't hungry at all. Suddenly a million pounds didn't seem such an impressive figure.

Claire was tired, but elated too. She'd been hard at it all day since the news of the DNA match-up, reviewing the Geoff Hall murder case from scratch. At last there had been a significant development. If the men who had killed Hall had also killed Talbot, that turned an act of spontaneous violence into – into what? That was the question.

Talbot's murder looked like a set-up, a premeditated and planned assassination. Was the same true of Geoff Hall's?

And was there a link between the two deaths beyond the identity of the murderers?

After she'd given Henderson the good news from Ilford he'd jumped right on it, calling Steve's boss, an Inspector Thomson, to set up a meeting. On Thomson's invitation he'd headed straight over to Gant's Hill to inspect the Talbot crime scene, taking with him DS Shepherd in preference to Claire. 'Sorry you won't get to see lover boy,' he muttered to her as he left, 'but you're already familiar with our friends from out east.' He'd lingered over the word 'familiar'. He thought he was so funny.

Claire had carried on working into the evening when she got home, resisting her father's invitation to watch a movie with him that he'd rented. Since she'd moved back she'd got into the habit of curling up on the sofa downstairs with, as she said to her Friday-night drinking mates, 'the two most dependable men in my life' – her dad and his cat. Except that she didn't make that joke any more. After a year of sleeping on her own, it no longer seemed funny.

She poured herself a glass of wine and took it into her bedroom. It was the one she'd occupied in her teens and still carried the scars of her schoolgirl presence – a row of biro hearts on the wall above the desk, shelves of books she'd never open again and a pile of CDs she no longer played. She'd not bothered to update the décor, reasoning that her stay was only temporary. She'd once read an article about people in her situation, young adults who ended up living back in the parental home – boomerang kids. So that's what she was. It seemed like the ultimate insult.

She propped herself up on the bed and thumbed through the address book on her phone. She'd never called Steve out of office hours before, even though they'd exchanged mobile numbers at their café meeting. She'd thought about it but she'd never had a reason that hadn't seemed transparent, but now she did.

She wasn't calling for personal reasons. This was work but, given Henderson's irritating scrutiny in the office, best conducted on her own time.

It rang for long enough for her to fear that Steve was not available. Then the warmth of his voice came down the line.

'Hi there, Parker,' he said. 'Where are you?'

'I'm not in the office with Henderson breathing down my neck, if that's what you mean.'

He chuckled. 'He turned up at our place this afternoon. He seems to think you and I have got a thing going.'

'He gets the wrong end of every stick.'

'Bang goes our double murder investigation then. My boss is letting him take the lead.'

'Oh, I just meant . . .' she wasn't really sure what she meant, except that she was fed up with Henderson's insinuations. She was beginning to get fed up with Steve too. If he was interested in her, why didn't he ask her out? She put the thought from her mind.

'If it's a joint investigation,' she continued, 'then we're both scratching our heads to find a link between Geoff Hall and Charlie Talbot.'

'Come up with anything?'

She wished she had. 'The only connection seems to be this horse they had a row about. But I don't see why that would lead to a third party wanting them both dead.'

'How about Hall's daughter?'

'Alison?' Claire was shocked at the thought. 'That's ridiculous.'

'Are you sure?'

'Absolutely positive. She was completely knocked for six by her father's death.'

'You mean she's very convincing in her grief.'

Claire was outraged. 'Are you saying you don't believe me?'

'No. I'm saying I'm always amazed how convincing guilty parties can be, especially relatives. Just step back a bit and consider how much she has gained. She's copped all of her dad's money and now Charlie, who was turning out to be a bit of a nuisance, is out of the way too.'

She forced herself to consider the idea of Alison as murderer – and rejected it.

'Impossible. I was with her right from the start. I held her in my arms while she cried her heart out. She was devastated.'

'Killers cry too. She could still have fixed it.'

'How?'

He thought for a moment. 'She's mixed up in racing, isn't she? Lots of dodgy characters in that world. Maybe she hired a couple.'

'I don't buy it.' But his remarks were already forcing her to reassess Alison Hall. However, just supposing Alison was responsible for the killings, why would she have pointed the police in the direction of Charlie Talbot just before sending round men to murder him? Unless maybe Simon Waterford was so fired up about Talbot that Alison had had no option but to go along with his accusations.

But, to be honest, it didn't stand up. She was going to take a heck of a lot of convincing that Alison was anything other than a victim.

She didn't pursue this further with Steve. She had the feeling he was just playing devil's advocate for the fun of it. She suspected it was his style to be provocative. In which case, if he asked her out she'd tell him to stuff it.

'Henderson said you were reviewing the files,' Steve said. 'Have you found anything new?'

'There's a witness I'd like to talk to. A guy who was in the carriage when Geoff was killed. His statement's on record but I have a feeling he might have more to tell us.'

'Why do you think that?'

She considered her words. She'd not interviewed the witness personally, he'd given his statement to Shepherd. Henderson had also spoken to him and had later dismissed him as 'a fruitcake'.

'He wasn't a race-goer like most of the other passengers. He was travelling to London for a business meeting. And he was knitting.'

'You mean knit one, purl one type knitting?'

'Indeed. An olive-green sweater with a circular needle.'

Steve laughed. 'And you want to talk to him to get the pattern.'

'I want to talk to him because he gave us the best

description of what went on. We've got a dozen statements from people in that carriage, some of them inches from the assault, and if you compared what they said you'd be hard pushed to come up with a coherent picture of events. One person swore blind the tall guy with spiky hair had a beard, another said the short guy wore a blue denim jacket, someone even said there was a third guy with a machete. Thank God for the onboard CCTV.'

'But your knitter got the details right?'

'More than that. He said it was likely the tall man played the guitar because the fingernails on his right hand were significantly longer than on his left. I've gone back to the pictures and they are.'

'That's right.' Steve sounded impressed. 'Some acoustic guitarists do grow the nails on their picking hand. Is this knitting fellow called Sherlock by any chance?'

'No. Darren Butterworth. He's some kind of journalist. Henderson thought he was an oddball and said that knowing the guy played the guitar was about as useful as an ashtray on a motorbike. But I'm thinking another visit might help us.'

'Sounds like a good idea. How about I come too?'

'If you like,' she said, trying to sound as if she didn't care one way or the other. Not that she did, of course.

Claire had made an appointment to meet Darren Butterworth at his place of work, which was down a cobbled mews street in Mayfair. The sign on the door read 'Artefact – the magazine for the Fine Art connoisseur'.

A stick-thin girl heavy on the eye make-up ushered

them into an upstairs room at the back with some chairs and a stained but comfy sofa, boxes full of magazines and a water cooler. She announced that Darren would be with them shortly.

Steve took a copy of *Artefact* from the box and thumbed through it quickly.

'What does this bloke do?' he asked.

'I think he's the art director.'

Steve studied a photo that looked to Claire like a Fabergé egg. He tested the thick glossy paper between finger and thumb. 'Nice. I wonder if it makes any money.'

'No,' said a small dapper man in a candy-striped shirt and linen trousers as he stepped into the room. 'It's owned by an American billionaire who's a casualty of the credit crunch. He's looking for a buyer now he's down to just three houses and a villa in Palm Beach.'

Claire recognised the pale oval face from the CCTV as their witness. She was disappointed not to see him wearing a hand-knitted sweater but, given the muggy late-summer day, it would hardly have been appropriate. She introduced herself and Steve. Butterworth took time to scrutinise their warrant cards.

'I gave a full statement back in June,' he said irritably.

Claire smiled pleasantly. 'I'm sorry to trouble you again but sometimes a follow-up interview can be useful.'

'Really?' He didn't look convinced. 'But I related everything in detail to Deputy Chief Inspector Henderson and Detective Sergeant Shepherd. I'm not sure that there's anything I can add.'

Steve spoke up. 'What my colleague means is that sometimes a person's memory is refreshed after he's had time to recover from the trauma of the event itself. You know, odd things come floating into the brain that you didn't mention the first time around.'

'Not my brain, officer.' Darren Butterworth appeared to be a fellow who admitted little room for doubt – at least where his own opinion was concerned. It was no wonder, Claire reflected, that his pedantic manner had rubbed Henderson up the wrong way. That and the knitting, of course.

'All the same,' she said briskly – there was no point in trying to soft-soap him – 'it would be useful for us to hear your version of events again. Especially since your statement was by far the most reliable of those we obtained.'

'Is that so?' The irritation had vanished from his tone.

'Absolutely,' she said with enthusiasm, delighted she had found a button to press. Flattery often worked wonders. 'We were very impressed by the clarity of your observations.'

'The fingernails were brilliant,' Steve chipped in. 'You should be doing our job.'

'I used to play the guitar myself. It's quite common to grow the nails of one hand for a certain style of playing. I trust you have found it useful when interviewing suspects.'

'Oh yes,' said Claire. She'd always been able to lie with conviction. The fact was, Henderson had been so dismissive of Butterworth that no notice had been taken of his statement at all. In any case, as Steve had remarked on the way over, what were they meant to do, hang around folk clubs on the lookout for blokes with long nails?

At least this interchange broke the ice with their witness who relaxed enough to perch on the edge of a chair and answer the questions Claire put to him. She began by asking him the purpose of his journey – he'd been working from home in Reading but had been summoned to the magazine office for an emergency meeting with the American owner – before getting him to relate his recollection of the murder itself.

Butterworth stuck to his previous version almost word for word, leaving nothing out but adding little that was new. He ran through a description of the two attackers, their clothes, their build, their manner – the fingernails – as if he were ticking off items on a list. It was a long list.

'Have you got one of those what-do-you-call it memories?' asked Steve.

'An eidetic or photographic memory. It's quite possible. I've never had it diagnosed, however.'

His self-satisfaction was unnerving.

'But you've forgotten something, Mr Butterworth.' She enjoyed putting a spoke in his wheel.

He blinked at her. 'What would that be?'

'You've not mentioned the bracelet. The shorter man, the one in the white vest, had a silver bracelet on his left wrist.'

A witness had mentioned it and Claire had verified the bracelet on the CCTV film.

For a moment Butterworth seemed at a loss. His face twisted in puzzlement. 'Did I not mention it?'

'Not in your statement or now. It's the only significant detail you've left out.'

'I'm awfully sorry. I suppose I have just been going through in my mind what I recall telling you in the first place.' Suddenly he looked at them with wide-eyed panic. 'I really don't want to have to visualise it all over again. It creeps up on me sometimes. Like when I'm falling asleep. I'm trying to train myself not to think about it.'

Claire's antagonism vanished. There were many casualties in the brutal slaughter of a man, not just the victim himself. A witness who could not get the horror out of his head would suffer in his own way, particularly one as sensitive as the slender little man in front of them.

'I'm sorry, Mr Butterworth,' she said. 'It must have been a terrible experience.'

He nodded. 'I wish I could have done something. I keep thinking that I could have attacked them with my knitting needle.'

By her side Claire heard Steve's intake of breath – it was the first time this strange witness had mentioned his incongruous activity.

'It's a very good thing you didn't,' she said hastily. 'You could have got yourself killed.'

'That's true. I've never been the macho type. Not very brave, I'm afraid.'

'I don't know about that,' said Steve. 'If you could bring yourself to go over what happened, maybe tonight, just to see if that photographic memory of yours can recall anything you've not mentioned, that would be brave enough. You don't have to go thumping villains to bring them down.'

'OK.' He looked suddenly more cheerful. 'I'll do that. I promise.'

They stood to go and shook hands.

Before they left, Claire said – she couldn't resist, 'I don't think I've ever come across a gentleman who knits before.'

'I always knit on trains,' he replied. 'I've got three hobbies. Knitting. Bird-watching. You can't do much bird-watching on a train.'

There was something odd about that statement.

'What's your third hobby?' she asked.

'Actually, I'm a naturist.'

Which you couldn't do on a train either. Claire didn't dare catch Steve's eye as they descended the stairs. It would be rude to laugh.

Chapter Eleven

Gabriel had felt curiously deflated for the past forty-eight hours, since he'd left St Catherine's Hospital. He longed to know how Nadine and her baby were doing. It was as if he were the father and had been suddenly banished from the presence of his wife and son. Which was daft.

He'd rung up his old girlfriend Chloe, who'd listened to his recitation of the birthing drama and pronounced the whole thing ghastly. 'You sound broody,' she'd said, then announced she was off on a hot date and suggested he get one too. 'Chance would be a fine thing,' he'd muttered and got drunk with a football mate instead.

Hungover the next morning, he'd called the hospital and learned that mother and baby had been discharged.

The question was, how soon could he go round to the flat overlooking Hyde Park? Apart from his desire to see how Nadine was getting on, he needed to speak to her about Mariana. She'd been about to spill the beans when her mother crashed in; he had to recapture that moment when he'd had her confidence.

He was reluctant to pitch up out of the blue. Who knew what delicate eating/sleeping regime had been put in place around the baby? Turning up unexpectedly could backfire. Likewise an ill-timed phone call – the new mother might be asleep or involved in some delicate bonding thing. He remembered his sister in the days after she had given birth. Neurotic didn't cover her behaviour, though it had come second place to his antsy brother-in-law.

He sent her a text. 'How U doing? Wd love to visit – say when. Gabriel.' He'd wondered whether to add his surname. She'd remember him surely.

He needn't have worried. The reply came instantly. 'Come now. Nxxxxx.'

He turned up at the flat an hour later clutching flowers, chocolates and a small plastic pig with a goofy face similar to one he'd given his baby niece. The door was flung open by Elaine, Nadine's mother, who looked considerably less flustered than the last time Gabriel had seen her. He started to introduce himself but she shut him up by hooting, 'I know who you are – the angel Gabriel!' And she clasped him in a hug that threatened to destroy both flowers and chocolates. From down the hall came a more familiar cry, Nadine yelling for him to show his face. Evidently there was no neurosis here about keeping the noise down for the baby's sake.

Nadine was reclining on the sofa, the baby in a Moses basket by her side, fast alseep, his pink face puffy and peaceful.

'Sure, *he's* no trouble,' said Elaine darkly as she set up a side table for tea.

'She means that I'm difficult,' Nadine explained.

216

'And that husband of yours,' Elaine added. 'Why isn't he here?'

'Klaus is out wetting the baby's head,' Nadine explained.

'He's hardly been here since he got back from wherever he was,' Elaine added as she produced a tray with cups and saucers and returned to the kitchen for more.

Gabriel offered to give her a hand.

'Leave her be,' said Nadine. 'She's waited the best part of thirty years for this so let her enjoy it.'

Finally Elaine left them in peace. Gabriel sipped tea and nibbled cake. The baby made a snuffling sound but didn't wake. He surveyed Nadine.

'I know, I look bloody awful.'

That was far from the truth and he said so.

'Well, not the glamour girl you were expecting a few days ago anyway.'

That was true but thank the Lord for that, he thought. Was now the moment he could ask his questions?

She beat him to it. 'You want to know about Mariana, don't you? When I was working for Chrysalis, sometimes clients would hold parties and hire a few of us at a time. They were mostly in West End hotels, lots of booze and dope. And we weren't paid simply to look good.'

'Sounds very *News of the World*.'

'Oh, it was. Anyhow, that's how I got to know Mariana, though I didn't know that was her name at the time. We went to a couple of these things and on more exotic trips too – yachts and villas in the sun. And we'd look out for each other. You know how it is with some people, we just clicked. I didn't even care that standing next to her made me look ordinary.'

Gabriel protested and she waved his words away, unconcerned.

Elaine poked her head round the door to see if more cake was needed and Nadine told her to leave them in peace.

'Mam doesn't know. She thinks Chrysalis Girls was for office temps. They sent me some fantastic flowers and Mam was all for ringing them up.' She pointed at an elaborate display of blooms in a basket on the other side of the room. They rather put his own offering in the shade.

'So you're still in touch with them?'

'Occasionally.' She shot Gabriel a defensive look. 'Don't go reading anything into it. I was so excited about the baby I've been ringing everyone I know. I couldn't leave Carla out – she's the woman who runs the agency.'

Gabriel was aware of that. 'Are you still in touch with Mariana then?'

Nadine shook her head. 'Klaus forbade me to see her. There was trouble to do with a friend of his and, out of loyalty to him, I'm not to have anything to do with her.'

'But you've got a picture of her on your fridge.'

Her face registered confusion, then suspicion.

'Sorry,' he said hastily. 'But I couldn't resist a quick look round when I picked up your bag.'

She nodded. 'I see. Well, I'm allowed the photo because Emile never comes here. He lives in Majorca.'

'So Mariana and this Emile fell out?'

'You could say that. They were going to get married

and then everything blew up. She was living with him in Majorca but then his father found out about the kind of work she'd been doing and paid her off. It turned out quite ugly in the end apparently. I can tell you how to contact Emile, if that's any good to you.'

Gabriel thought it might be.

On receiving the text from Steve, Claire called him back on her phone from the hall, away from Henderson's baleful glare.

'Darren's been on the phone,' he said at once. 'He's been delving back into his fancy memory to see if he can help us.'

Claire was a bit miffed. 'Why didn't he call me? You were only along for the ride.'

'I think he warmed to my particular insights. The way I deduced he had a photographic memory and all that.'

'Crap.'

'And the fact that you work directly for Henderson. He seems to have sussed that out.'

That made more sense. Claire felt mollified. 'So has he come up with anything new?'

'Not much. Only about the bracelet.'

'So, he remembers it now, does he?'

'Better than that. He can visualise it. It's the way the eidetic memory works, you see.'

'Get to the point, Steve.' She wasn't in the mood for time-wasting bullshit, especially from him. For all the jokes and eye contact and playful innuendo, he still hadn't asked her out.

'He says he's remembered something else too but he was a bit coy about telling me over the phone. I think he wants someone to pat him on the back in person. Said he was making a drawing which should be ready any time now. He's at his office.'

'Great. I suppose I'd better go and pick it up.' And she ended the call before he could muscle in on this interview too.

Alison and Meg stopped by the gate of the paddock behind Alison's house and regarded its occupant, Red River.

'He's certainly got enough space,' Meg said. 'Though I'd have thought he might get a bit lonely.'

'He's not going to be the only one. Ellen Colville has an old hunter she's planning to retire. The two of them can keep each other company.'

'Ellen's happy with this set-up then?'

'Yes. She says it's a relief to know they have a good home. I think she's had a problem rehousing her old horses in the past.'

Meg looked sceptical. 'Remind me again who's going to look after them?'

'Me. I'm sure I can rope in some help but I'll be the principal carer. I've got endless amounts of time.'

They resumed their walk along the path by the field, heading for the river which marked the boundary of Geoff's – now Alison's – land. Alison's remark hung in the air.

'So you're not going back to work?' Meg said.

'Dave's got a replacement nurse at the surgery. He said he couldn't afford to wait while I made my mind up about going back.'

'And you couldn't go back because . . .?'

Alison looked her square in the eye. 'Because of

Dad. I worked there when Dad was alive. I don't know that I could go back to that routine and come home to an empty house.'

'You could always get another job.'

'Yes, but I don't know how hard I could commit myself. Not while Dad's killers are still out there. I feel I need them to be caught and found guilty before I can get on with the rest of my life. Do you understand?'

Meg patted Alison's arm. 'Of course. But you could be waiting a very long time, could you not?'

'For ever.' She sounded bitter but it was her worst fear, that those men who'd brazenly murdered her father in full view of a carriage full of people would never be caught. They were out there somewhere. Unpunished. Free to ruin more lives.

'You can't just stagnate, my dear. You're young, lovely-looking and, dare I say it, not short of a bob or two. You've got to make plans and do something with yourself. You'll be letting your father down if you don't.'

The little lecture irritated Alison and not simply because she knew Meg was right.

'That's why I'm looking after Ellen Colville's horses. I might take on more. Use this land as a home for retired horses.'

Meg didn't look impressed. She pursed her lips but managed to keep her thoughts to herself. Alison knew she was liable to get the benefit of them before long.

They'd reached the river and were following the footpath beside its bubbling length. It took them round in a loop behind a small copse to an empty and battered-looking cottage.

'Is that yours too?' asked Meg.

Alison nodded. 'It's the old mill cottage. Dad was going to do it up at one point and let it out to holiday-makers. But he never got round to it. He used to rent it to workers on the farm up the road but there was a burst pipe last winter and the kitchen ceiling came down. It's been empty ever since.'

'Can I have a look inside?'

Alison was surprised by Meg's interest but happily led her round to the back door.

'I imagine it's locked up,' she said.

But the wood around the old Yale lock was splintered and the door creaked open at her touch. In the front room to the left of the door there was the remains of a fire in the hearth and a row of empty Guinness bottles on the hearth. The room still contained some furniture – a ragged, lumpy sofa and a dark wood table and chairs. A threadbare rug covered the floor.

Alison touched the faded chintz curtains still hanging in the window; they were stiff with age and dirt.

'Simon and I used to hang out here sometimes when we were kids. He once caught a trout in the stream and I tried to cook it on the fire. It was a bit of a disaster.'

The place had hardly changed since then, just got dirtier and more neglected. A hole gaped in the kitchen ceiling and tendrils of bindweed poked through a broken window. From the dusty bedrooms above could be heard cooing and fluttering. Nature was taking over.

'Well,' said Meg in her brisk manner, 'here's something useful you could do for a start. The walls seem sound but you could rip out the rest and start again.'

Alison groaned within. Making the place over from scratch was a daunting thought. And what would she do with it then?

'I don't much fancy running a holiday let,' she said.

'You don't have to,' said Meg. 'I've got something much more useful in mind.'

'You want to go where?'

Gabriel knew his uncle had heard him perfectly well the first time but he'd been prepared for some resistance to his proposal.

'Majorca,' he repeated. 'That's where this Emile bloke lives.'

Clive regarded him grumpily. 'That doesn't mean you have to go there. Talk to him on the phone, for God's sake.'

'I've tried that.'

Nadine had given him an address and a number. 'He's got this place up in the hills on the north coast of the island,' she'd said. 'It's absolutely gorgeous, only twenty minutes from the marina where he keeps his yacht.'

'What does this fellow do?' Gabriel had asked.

'Not much. Not if you mean, how does he make a living. He was one of Kurt's students at an art college in Paris – that's how they met. Emile paints but I don't think he sells much.' She'd pulled a face. 'I mean, his paintings are a pile of old pig's poo if you ask me.'

'But he lives in a villa on Majorca and has a yacht?'

'He only lives there in the summer. He spends the

winter in LA, or New York because it's artier. But cold, of course.'

He'd looked at her with some incomprehension and she'd burst out laughing. 'You don't understand, do you? A guy like Emile has money. At least, his father does. He's a big-deal industrialist.'

Gabriel had called the number that Nadine had given him. The first few times he'd called, there'd only been an answer service and he'd rung off. He didn't want to leave a message that could easily be ignored. On the third try, he'd got a pleasant-sounding Frenchman on the line.

'Monsieur Emile Lambert?' Gabriel had put on his best accent.

'Ah, *oui.*'

'Er . . .' His confidence had collapsed at that point and he'd reverted to English. Nadine had told him Emile spoke it 'better than I do' so there didn't seem much point in persevering with his dodgy GCSE French. 'I'm calling from London. Gabriel Silver from Silver and Co., solicitors.'

'How can I help you, Mr Silver?'

He'd been charming and his English effortlessly fluent. It seemed Gabriel had caught him in a good humour because he'd immediately made a joke at the expense of London weather. Gabriel had mentioned Nadine's name and conveyed news of the baby and so the conversation had proceeded on a happy footing until Gabriel had got to the point of his call.

'I'd appreciate it if you would help me in some inquiries I'm making into a young lady I believe you know.'

'I know lots of young ladies.'

Gabriel had no doubt about that. 'This one is called Mariana Hamilton though I believe you may know her as Fabiana.'

'I know exactly who you mean, Mr Silver. Goodbye.' And he'd put the phone down.

Gabriel had sat in shock, debating what to do. There was one thing to be said about Mariana aka Fabiana, former escort girl, she had an effect on people.

Before he'd formulated any plan of how to revitalise a line of investigation that had just died in his hands, the phone rang. It was a woman with a French accent.

'I believe you were talking just now to Monsieur Lambert. He has asked me to call you back and apologise for his rudeness in terminating your call.'

'Oh. That's all right. Who am I speaking to?' Whoever she was, this woman sounded very efficient.

'I am Sylvie, Monsieur Lambert's personal assist-ant.' She sounded middle-aged and frosty. 'I understand you wish to ask some questions regarding Mariana.'

'That's correct.'

'And you are a London solicitor?'

'Yes.' Sort of.

'Are you representing Mariana in a court case?'

'Not exactly. I'm making inquiries on behalf of another client who has had dealings with her. It's a matter of legitimate family business.'

'And this family are in dispute with Mariana?'

'Not at present.' It was reasonable to assume that the Frenchman would be more likely to help him if he thought Gabriel was acting against Mariana. Which he was. 'My client's family is well-established and very respectable. They have a lot to lose if they make the wrong kind of liaison. That's why I am curious about Ms Hamilton's past.'

'Wait. I will call you back.'

And Gabriel found himself cut off again, this time in a happier frame of mind. At least this Sylvie had heard him out. And, for all that he had seemed like a nice guy, the way Emile had hung up on him suggested that he was steamed up about Mariana. In which case, why wouldn't he want to get it off his chest?

The woman had rung back five minutes later. Gabriel felt as if he had passed some kind of test – which he obviously had. 'Mrs Adler speaks well of you. She says you assisted at the birth of her baby.'

'Er . . .' Something must have got lost in translation – holding a screaming woman's hand and averting his eyes hardly counted as assistance. But Gabriel wasn't going to argue if it got him what he wanted.

'Emile cannot discuss a matter as sensitive as this over the telephone.'

'It won't take long, just a few minutes of his time.'

'That is not the point. It is delicate. But if you are agreeable, I will make arrangements for you to visit us here. OK?'

Gabriel supposed it was. It was no skin off his nose anyway, provided he could swing it with Clive.

The conversation with Emile and Sylvie had taken place in the morning and it had taken until mid-afternoon for Gabriel to get in to see Clive between his appointments. His uncle was already clock-watching, irritated that his time was being wasted on a daft request.

'Sorry, Gabriel, I can't justify sending you off on some Mediterranean jaunt. We shouldn't really be doing this without Alison's say-so anyway. I can't ask her to pay for it and I'm not going to.'

'But neither of you have to. Emile's paying. He's flying me out and putting me up at his villa in the hills, fantastic sea vista apparently.'

Clive's face was a picture. 'You jammy little bugger. How on earth did you swing that?'

Gabriel grinned. It was a satisfying moment.

Alison allowed herself to be quizzed by Meg as they tramped back to the house.

'Your father did pretty well for himself, didn't he?'

He had done. Better than Alison had expected and she said so.

'Well, good for him. And it's all coming to you, isn't it?'

Alison agreed that, excepting charitable donations and sentimental bequests to his ex-wife, that was the case.

'I'm not yet sure how to handle it,' she added. 'I'd give some of it to my mother if I thought she needed it. But her current husband has pots of money and there's only so many outfits you can wear and cruises you can go on.'

'Huh.' Meg didn't sound impressed. 'I think if you're lucky enough to be well off you've got a responsibility to put your wealth to use.'

Alison smiled. This was evidently her cue to agree. 'What do you think I should be doing with Dad's money then?'

'You've heard of the Jockeys Disability Charity?'

'Of course. Dad left them money in his will.'

'Did he? Excellent.' Meg seemed bucked by the information. 'I imagine all the charities have been feeling the pinch in the credit crunch. They'll need all the donations they can get.'

They picked their way across Red River's field to say hello.

'Oh dear. So you think I should be giving to them?'

'In a way. But money's only part of it. They provide housing for disabled jockeys. Accommodation specially fitted out for use by people who are wheelchair-bound or worse. Preferably in a horsey environment that's familiar and where injured racing people can be of use.'

Alison was aware of this though she still didn't see the connection. They stopped by Red River's side and he allowed himself to be petted, watching her hand in case it should produce a carrot or an apple.

'You're out of luck today,' she told him.

'What I was going to suggest,' continued Meg, 'was that you considered refurbishing and equipping your cottage for the JDC. It's better than giving money because it's right here, on your land. You could oversee the project and involve yourself with whoever went to live there.'

'Oh,' she said. It was an interesting idea.

Alison enjoyed the feel of the horse's silky coat beneath her fingers as she stroked his side. A rest home for retired racehorses *and* accommodation for injured jockeys, side by side. It was more than interesting.

'Of course, you'll have to talk to an architect. Do some costings, sound out the charity and so on.' Meg stopped abruptly. 'Sorry, my dear, I'm getting carried away. It's your business, not mine.'

'Yes,' Alison said. 'It does sound like my business.'

It felt right the moment she said it.

Claire had expected Darren Butterworth to be rather full of himself, given Steve's remarks on the phone, but on her return to his office he struck her as simply neurotic.

'I forced myself to go over that afternoon, as your friend DS Gill suggested.'

'Thank you, Mr Butterworth. It is appreciated.'

'I can't tell you how horrible it was and I've hardly slept a wink for the past two nights. I'm going to have to try very hard to forget it all again.'

'And did anything new occur to you?'

'It didn't *occur*, officer, it was there in front of my eyes in technicolour detail. I told you I have vivid recall.'

She wasn't sure whether she was meant to be sympathetic or simply grateful. But she was becoming impatient.

'What exactly did you remember, Mr Butterworth?'

'This.' He produced a piece of paper with a flourish. The drawing was of a capital B in which the upright of the letter had been drawn in the shape of a gun.

'It's an old-fashioned tommy gun,' Darren explained eagerly. 'Like in George Raft movies.'

Claire had never seen a George Raft movie but she knew what he meant. She still didn't understand what he was getting at.

'It's a tattoo,' he explained. 'The man in the T-shirt had this symbol tattooed across his bicep.'

She looked at him sceptically. She'd studied the pictures and not seen anything like this.

He read the look on her face. 'High up on his right arm, just visible beneath the short sleeve. Go back to your photographs.'

His *right* arm? Well, it was possible; the CCTV couldn't capture everything.

Or maybe Butterworth was a bit of a fruitcake after all, as Henderson had said.

Gabriel was booked on a budget airlines flight out of Gatwick. It was still holiday time and the airport was heaving with families and tipsy youth. Although their departure time was delayed, Gabriel didn't care, he was too excited by this sudden change in his fortunes. He'd not had a holiday in over a year and this was probably as close as he was going to get this summer.

Not having a girlfriend didn't help. There was a football trip in Holland planned for the autumn and a stag weekend in Dublin pencilled in for next January but they hardly counted. Back in the days when he was going out with Chloe they'd had a fantastic ten days in Crete – that was his idea of a holiday.

The funny thing was that he could have brought a girl with him on this trip if he'd had one to bring. When Sylvie had rung to discuss travel arrangements she had surprised him by asking if he was travelling alone. 'You are not bringing your assistant with you?' she'd asked and he'd assured her that no, on this occasion, he would be unaccompanied.

The thought had entertained him throughout the long evening hanging around the departure lounge and during the flight. If he'd still been with Chloe he could have called her up – 'Fancy a freebie in Majorca? Just pretend to be my secretary.' In fact, he'd been tempted to ask her anyway until he'd come to his senses. What a mistake that would have been. As he wearily shouldered his bag through Palma airport at one in the morning, he was glad not to have a moody ex trailing along by his side.

He mooched around in the arrivals hall while the other passengers disappeared. He was expecting to be met but maybe the flight delay had disrupted arrangements. He scrabbled in his pocket for Emile's address. It would have to be a taxi.

'Excuse me, but are you Mr Silver?'

The tall woman had materialised out of nowhere. She was well-groomed: tight black skirt, dazzling white blouse, neat throat scarf and shoulder-length blond hair which appeared creatively tousled. She looked as if she had stepped straight out of some makeover salon for glamorous business execs. In comparison, Gabriel felt grubby and travel-stained. He registered her look of surprise when he conceded that he was indeed Mr Silver.

'Really?' She offered a warm dry hand. 'I'm Sylvie. We spoke on the phone. I was expecting an older gentleman in a pinstripe suit with a briefcase – like a proper London solicitor, you know?'

Gabriel was tempted to say that was because he wasn't a proper London solicitor. And to add that she didn't chime with his expectations either. However, he was simply happy to fall in step with her energetic stride out into the car park where she ushered him into the passenger seat of an open-topped sports car.

'It's a few miles,' she said as she started the engine.

'But it won't take too long at this time of night. You don't mind if I go a little quick?'

It wasn't really a question so it was just as well he didn't. But she drove smoothly as well as fast and didn't talk, for which Gabriel was grateful, especially when they left the main roads behind and began to ascend into the hills on a narrow and winding track. The air was balmy and fragrant and Sylvie's no-longer-groomed blond tresses streamed behind her in the wind. He felt a million miles from London. As if he were in a movie.

Sylvie glanced his way. 'Don't worry. We'll be there soon.'

Gabriel muttered something sleepy and meaning-less. He didn't care if this journey never ended at all.

Whatever her previous misgivings about Darren Butterworth and his freakish sense of recall, Claire arrived home feeling only gratitude towards him. It was late and she was happy-tipsy and the guy who was dropping her off had been an ideal companion for the rousing evening she'd just spent – and she had Darren to thank for it.

Armed with his drawing of the tattoo, she'd gone back to the CCTV footage. As she had suspected, the camera angle was such that the short killer's right arm was obscured for most of the time. But she'd slowed the footage down and found just one sequence which showed the man's right side as he turned to get away. And there, just below the sleeve of his T-shirt, across the bicep as Darren had claimed, she could see the marks of a tattoo. She'd blown up the image. The result revealed only the bottom portion of the mark on the skin but it bore a striking resemblance to the drawing Darren had given her.

Henderson had not been impressed – surprise – though he had grudgingly admitted that it looked as if the suspect did indeed have a tattoo on his upper right arm. She knew that the Butterworth connection had put him off. Perhaps she shouldn't have mentioned George Raft.

Steve, on the other hand, had been excited. So excited he'd picked her up from her flat at eight that evening and taken her to a Brazilian club in the West End.

'I've done some research,' he'd announced as he drove up west. 'I've been on the internet checking out that image and, guess what, it's the logo of a group called Bandeira. It's the name of a mountain in Brazil.'

She'd only been half listening at the time, being a bit miffed that he hadn't properly appreciated the efforts she had made to transform her everyday appearance – new spray-on tight jeans, slinky top with flirty neckline and her special-effort eye make-up. 'Nice outfit, Parker,' he'd said casually as she'd walked to the car. 'You'll blend right in.'

He'd gone on to explain that the Bandeira group played the kind of music they'd be hearing at this club and it might give them an insight into the mind of the killer – which, Claire thought, was bollocks. On the other hand, if that was the excuse Steve needed to show her a good time then she was all for it.

And a good time had indeed been shown. Since she'd considered herself distinctly off duty she'd not stinted on some Brazilian cocktail containing a lot of lime juice and booze. Steve, being the driver and a sensible fellow, had not touched a drop of course. As a result the music had passed her by in a sultry rhythmic blur but that had been fine because Steve, it turned out, was a pretty smooth mover on the dance floor. 'You're not bad for a flatfoot,' she'd told him, which was dangerously close to a compliment.

So here they were sitting in his car outside her Streatham flat. She wasn't too tipsy to realise it was a long drive for him back to Essex or the implications of asking him in.

'Coming up for coffee?' she said. It was hard to make it sound casual.

He looked at her for a long moment.

'Are you a bit pissed, Parker?'

'Well . . . I have been drinking for two.'

He laughed. 'I think you'd better have coffee for two as well. I've got to get back.'

She sobered up a bit. That was the sensible decision.

'But,' he went on, 'if you're up for it, there's plenty more places like that we can go. And we can circulate photos round these clubs. See if our boys are known.'

Right. She got it. They hadn't been on a date, they'd been on undercover surveillance.

Whatever Steve wanted to call it, she couldn't wait to do it again.

Chapter Twelve

Reluctant to look away from the line of horses silhouetted against the sky, Simon reached for the trilling phone in his pocket. He glanced down, saw that it was an owner who'd already called him three times that morning, and shut it off. He would ring back when he had more time.

Simon had come up here not only to assess the condition of the horses in the third lot, most of them recovering from one ailment or another, but to have some time to breathe. Life in the yard was hectic, with the Flat season heading into its autumn climax, and everybody wanting a piece of him. Then there were the dramas that weren't anything to do with his job – the hangover of his uncle's death and its bearing on Alison, the police investigation that never seemed to progress and, most important of all if he could only get the time to focus on it, his once-postponed wedding to Mariana.

He felt guilty about leaving all the planning to Mariana and Alison. The day was still a couple of months off but he knew he shouldn't just push it to the back of his mind. For one thing, he'd vowed he'd buy a new suit for the ceremony. For some people – Jeremy Masterton, say – that wouldn't be a hardship or a matter of any apprehension. For him, however, it was just the opposite. He'd promised Mariana he'd take time out that afternoon to start looking. It was a symbolic gesture of commitment. He'd had the impression that they were losing the intensity of their romance and that it was his fault. He realised he'd been focusing his energy on many people and many issues apart from Mariana and she'd been left to drift. Even her work at the yard, tending to Jennifer Eccles and other animals who responded to her touch, had been solitary.

Despite the fact that they lived alone together it seemed they often didn't have time to talk. They'd eat, make love, sleep – there was time for nothing else. He'd watched her sleeping face one morning in the moments before he'd slipped out of bed and felt an irrational fear. Why was this exotic woman from the other side of the world lying here by his side? Suppose she woke up one day and realised she didn't love him after all? If that happened, there would be nothing to stop her vanishing from his life for good.

His phone rang again. Mariana. This was a call he had no hesitation in taking.

'Don't worry,' he said, 'I'm going clothes shopping at lunch and I won't come back till I've got something.'

But that wasn't why she'd rung. She sounded breathless, excited. 'I've just had a phone call from my sister. You know she said in her email I might see her soon?'

'Yes.' No wonder she sounded excited.

'She's in London. I'm going down to see her today. Do you mind?'

'Of course not. But why doesn't she come here?'

'No, no – it's got to be on neutral ground.'

He'd not yet got to the bottom of Mariana's relationship with her sister, though he knew they'd parted on bad terms. Paula was three or four years younger, so Mariana had been expected to keep an eye on her throughout her childhood. Both girls, for reasons he didn't know, had ended up as the responsibility of the father, their common parent. Even though Mariana had been living in England of recent years she had made regular trips back to Brazil, she'd said, with the aim of keeping in touch with her sister. And, at one point, she'd been paying for the younger girl's education. But that had stopped when they had fallen out a couple of years ago. Or maybe that was why they'd fallen out – he remembered Mariana saying Paula had only just gone to college. Whatever the reason for their quarrel, he could understand that Mariana would want to make peace with her sister before introducing her to her future brother-in-law.

'I'll drive you down,' he said. 'I can go shopping on another day.'

'You won't have another day. Anyway, I'm going on the train. It's quicker.'

It made sense, of course it did. But he didn't like the idea of it. Neither of them had been on a train since that day at Ascot.

She seemed to read his mind. 'I'll be fine, Simon. Really I will. I'm so glad she called me.'

Amen to that, he thought and didn't argue further. Later, though, he would wish he had.

* * *

Gabriel woke in a strange room, not an unfamiliar event in his experience. But this was not a night spent on a student sofa with the remains of last night's excesses littering the floor. He was floating on a sea of crisp sheetage in the middle of a bed the size of a barge. He spotted a towelling robe draped over one of a pair of wicker armchairs and got to his feet.

He explored the bathroom and noted the fancy marble fittings, fluffy white towels and a collection of unopened toiletries. It was like a hotel, an expensive one. The kind his American relatives favoured when they visited London.

But drawing the curtains and stepping out on to the balcony revealed a world that was not like London at all. He looked down on to a paved terrace by a pool which dazzled in the fierce sunshine. To his left and right sloped the earthy greens of olive and scrub and above that soared the ridge of a mountain. Straight ahead, beyond the pool, was just blue sea and blue sky merging somewhere in the glistening distance.

There was a girl in a bikini by the pool – of course there was. She probably came with the villa, a standard fitting. She waved at him and he realised the face hidden behind the sunglasses belonged to Sylvie.

'Are you hungry?' she called. 'Come down.' She pointed to a set of steps that joined the far end of the balcony.

He returned to the room, quickly shaved and pulled on some clothes, conscious that he hadn't packed lounging-by-the-pool wear.

Down on the terrace Sylvie directed him to sit

beneath an umbrella – 'or you'll burn' – and fetched coffee and food from a table in the shade by the house. As she fussed around him he couldn't help admiring the way her lithe caramel limbs glistened in the sunshine. He had a mischievous inclination to ring his uncle's dusty old office in Holborn and tell Clive he was being served breakfast by a half-naked supermodel. He guessed it made up for all those greasy spoons in Acton.

Sylvie was crisply attentive – had he slept well, had he been to Majorca before and would he like more coffee? She lectured him on the historic area and its famous visitors, told him the Spanish name of the sugary pastry he was scoffing.

Finally she said, 'So you have come to talk to Emile about the *putain*.'

The poo . . . ? He didn't get it.

She saw the puzzlement on his face. 'The whore. Mariana.'

He got it then. 'Well, yes, I have come to discuss Mr Lambert's past friendship with Miss Hamilton.'

She laughed, a delicate little peal, and wrinkled her perfect nose. 'You might not be wearing the pinstripe suit but you are very English, Gabriel. Emile will like you.'

'Where is, er, Emile?'

'He will be with us very soon. Would you like another *ensaimada*?'

He gathered she meant the pastry he'd had with his coffee. While he'd been eating it he'd concluded it must be an acquired taste. Now, as he devoured a second, he realised he had suddenly acquired it.

'So who is this client who is curious about Mariana?'

she said suddenly, having decided, it seemed, that she'd spent long enough softening him up.

Caught with his mouth full, at least Gabriel had a moment to consider his reply. 'Of course, I'm not at liberty to name names,' he said – not least because the primary name in his investigation was dead, but that wasn't her concern. 'But Mariana is about to marry into a family of some substance and I'm conducting a background check.'

It seemed to be what she had expected to hear.

'And,' Gabriel continued, 'I'm curious to hear an account of Emile's experience with her.'

She nodded. 'OK. I must be honest with you, Gabriel. Emile is very reluctant to speak about Mariana. She is what I believe you refer to as a sore spot.'

'A sore point.'

'Exactly. I will go and find him for you.'

She got up and walked back into the house. Gabriel watched her go, amazed that a woman in a bikini could exude such a businesslike air.

Mariana couldn't sort out her emotions as she sat on the train heading south. The call had come as she was about to leave for the yard.

'It's Paula,' the voice had said and, though these were about the last words she'd been expecting to hear, somehow she'd known it was her sister on the other end of the line. She'd burst into tears, she hadn't been able to help herself, and Paula had laughed at her silliness but then she'd cried too. All in all it was the best way to bridge the gap of the past couple of years – for the moment at least.

As a result she'd dropped everything, even abandoned Jennifer Eccles whose recovery seemed dependent on her daily treatment, and cadged a ride into Leeds. She could have taken the car but driving would have required more concentration than she felt able to muster. It had not occurred to her till she'd spoken to Simon that the train was to be avoided, though yesterday she would have shuddered at the thought of setting foot on one. To think that the sound of Paula's voice had driven the horror of Geoff Hall's murder from her mind. She hadn't realised how much she had missed her.

Now, as she rattled through the green English countryside, her fellow travellers – off-peak shoppers and solitary business types for the most part – sitting comfortably around her, she realised that her gaze was monitoring every movement along the carriage. She'd found a seat next to the compartment door and would be able to view any threat approaching from the front of the train from a long way off. She could easily hide in the toilet behind her or run further back down the train. Of course, if the killers came from the opposite direction then they would be upon her at once.

She didn't like to think about that but increasingly, as the train bowled along, survival strategy took over her thoughts. She knew the threat, had seen the very worst that could happen on a seemingly innocent journey such as this. She was determined not to let disaster take her by surprise.

As the two silver-haired ladies opposite her eagerly planned their shopping stops along Oxford Street, Mariana tried to picture her sister's face. But her gaze never faltered from the carriage doors.

* * *

A man in his mid-twenties wearing sand-coloured chinos and a faded blue shirt emerged from the villa. He raised a hand in a languid wave and strolled towards Gabriel who jumped to his feet, wiping his sugary fingers. This must be his host.

Up close, Gabriel could appreciate that Emile would be irresistible to some women. Raven-black hair framed a long soulful face whose deep-set eyes seemed bottomless. He held on to Gabriel's hand for longer than was necessary, as if trying to draw strength from his guest.

'*Bonjour*, Monsieur Silver.' His wide chiselled mouth stretched into a smile of welcome though his eyes remained unreadable. He flopped into the chair recently vacated by Sylvie. Gabriel sat down too.

There was an awkward pause which Gabriel filled by complimenting the view and the prettiness of the spot.

'Yes,' said Emile without interest. 'So tell me what that bitch has been up to.'

The vehemence in his tone took Gabriel by surprise.

'As I told Sylvie,' he said, 'I'm conducting some inquiries into Miss Hamilton's past history—'

'Because she's about to make a fool of some other sucker.' Emile finished the sentence. 'Let's not waste much time on this, Monsieur Silver. Discussing Mariana gives me no pleasure and it's not my idea that you are here. Ask me your questions and Sylvie,' he said the name without much affection, 'will drive you back to the airport.'

Now he had had time to study Emile, Gabriel

noticed a tremor in the other man's hand and the dryness of his lips, which he wetted frequently with his tongue. Perhaps he wasn't well, which would explain his urge to get the business over.

It was all the same to Gabriel.

'I'd be grateful to hear about your relationship,' he said. He'd come down armed with a notebook and he flipped it open.

Emile sighed, as if casting his mind back caused him physical pain, and began to speak fast. It was as well his English was good, for Gabriel was aware he didn't intend to say anything twice.

'I met Mariana a couple of years ago at the opera in Paris. She was with another man and I had my own company but, frankly, the moment I saw her I was not interested in anybody else. I was sitting next to her and became aware that, throughout the second half of the opera, she was weeping. She whispered to me that she had never seen *Madame Butterfly* before and she found it overwhelming. I ended up holding her hand to comfort her. Even now I don't think she was pretending. At that stage, she didn't know who I was.'

Emile trained his dark gaze on Gabriel who nodded sympathetically even as he kicked himself for not doing more homework. He'd quickly Googled Emile Lambert and found references to an artist. Though Nadine had been disparaging, it seemed he was represented by a gallery in Paris and another in Palma – which wasn't too dusty, in Gabriel's opinion. The bio on his own page made no reference to the industrialist father but it wasn't hard to believe that family money propped up an indulgent lifestyle. It certainly didn't look like villas and boats could be sustained on the back of the shapeless brown abstracts that were representative of his work.

Gabriel concentrated as the artist continued in a low, fast mumble.

'I asked the friend who had brought her to the opera how attached he was to this girl and he made a rather vulgar response. And so I discovered that her company was available to anybody at a price. I suppose I should have bought her for a night or two and had my fill of her. But I'm not like that, Monsieur Silver. My passions are not merely physical.

'After that evening I tried to put her out of my mind but I couldn't. I was intrigued by the way she had been so moved by music from a culture that was not hers and I wondered if she might share the things that moved me too. So I made a date through her agency and spent the weekend in London with her. Where we – where I, at least – fell in love.

'She resigned from Chrysalis Girls. I think I paid them some money to get her out of a contract – I can't remember the details. They were too sordid. For me, she was just an intelligent young woman trying to make her way in the world using what assets she had. And what she had to sell was her beauty.

'None of this mattered to me at the time. Her past was her own affair – a colourful adventure. I was interested only in our future. Of course, we had to win over my father if we were to make a success of that. My father is used to getting his own way. We worked hard on how best to persuade him that we should get married. Mariana had racing connections in Brazil, her father had worked for several important and wealthy people. It was possible to concoct a biography that would please Papa. In the event, he was so captivated by her that I don't think half our fiction was necessary.'

He stopped talking and produced a bottle of water from his pocket, his tongue flick-flicking at his parched lips.

Gabriel was fascinated by the story. 'So what went wrong?'

Emile drank deeply, then set the bottle on the table. 'I've thought about it a lot, as you can imagine. I believed she loved me as much as I loved her. We had an idyllic time here. Sailing trips and parties. All my friends adored her. Her sister came to stay with us and we all got on so well. But it turned out to be a mirage. I was just a short-term good time to her and when the summer was over she cashed me in.'

'How?'

'She went to my father and showed him photographs of us all having fun. There were people swimming naked in the pool – this pool – nothing obscene, just enjoying ourselves. But my father did not find it amusing and he could see how these pictures could be used to damage him.'

'Really?'

'There were photos of me taking drugs. You know how it is, just snorting one tiny line of coke with a girl bathing topless can be made to seem like the last days of Sodom and Gomorrah.'

'And she cashed you in by . . . ?'

'By threatening to take her story and the photos to the scandal sheets. Apart from business, my father has a career in politics – it's where he intends to make his mark. This would have damaged him.' Emile stared steadily at Gabriel. 'So he paid Mariana off, on the condition that she disappeared from my life forever. I think she was happy with the deal.'

Gabriel nodded. The tremor in Emile's hand had spread down the left side of his body, his foot now twitching out of control against the leg of the table. He sympathised with Emile but, looking around at the sun-dappled mountains and the distant sea, how bad could life be, living here?

'Thank you,' he said. 'I appreciate you telling me this. And I'm sorry.'

Emile got to his feet. 'Don't be sorry. Just stop the little bitch ruining someone else's life.'

From behind Emile the door to the house opened and Sylvie stepped out. She'd slipped a shirt over her shoulders and now wore a pair of tiny white shorts. She stood framed in the doorway, looking at them.

Emile caught the direction of Gabriel's gaze.

'Right on cue,' he said.

Gabriel was tempted to say that Sylvie's presence must be some compensation for a broken heart but he didn't need to. Emile read his mind.

'Don't get the wrong idea,' he said. 'This may be a beautiful place but it's still a prison. And she's in charge.'

Gabriel had not considered Sylvie in the role of gaoler but as she walked briskly towards them, car keys in hand, it made a kind of sense.

'So,' Sylvie said as she drove Gabriel back to Palma airport, 'was what Emile told you useful?'

'Yes indeed. He still seems very upset by the whole thing.'

'Sure.' She was driving more sedately than the night before, blending into the tourist traffic. She'd told him there was plenty of time before his flight. 'Emile is very sensitive.' She said the word with a little sneer.

'You think he should have got over Mariana by now?'

'Don't you? Men can screw as many prostitutes as they like, I don't see much harm in it. But it takes a man like Emile to fall in love with one.'

'What kind of man is that?'

'A weak-willed, over-indulged and self-obsessed mummy's boy. Don't get me started on Emile. Poor little rich kid. I don't understand how his father could have produced such a specimen.'

Gabriel shifted uncomfortably in his seat. For all her seductive exterior – and her gleaming sun-bronzed legs were distracting in those little shorts in the close quarters of the car – Sylvie had a core of tempered steel. And now Emile had had his say, she was eager to deliver her twopennyworth.

'Emile's father,' she continued, 'was the sixth child of dirt-poor pig farmers but he is now worth billions and is one of the most powerful politicians in France. Le Pen can't go on for ever – the right need dynamic new blood. Look out for the name François Lambert in the future.'

'You are one of his political supporters?'

'Absolutely. I pledged myself to François after the last presidential election. I told him I would do anything to establish his cause and he promised me a special assignment.' She turned to glare at Gabriel, more animated in this conversation than he had seen her so far.

'What was that?' he asked nervously.

To his relief her gaze returned to the road ahead. 'My assignment was babysitting his son,' she said tersely. 'That is why I am wasting my time here doling out pocket money, keeping the spongers and the dope-dealers away, only letting hand-picked women within touching distance. If I could find Emile a safe, sensible wife then I'd be off the hook – and I've tried. But so far none of them compare in his eyes to a *putain* from Brazil cunning enough to sob all over him at the opera.'

Silence descended for a moment and Gabriel noted with relief the airport road signs. He'd be happy to be on the plane home trying to make sense of what he'd discovered. But not all his curiosity had been satisfied. A remark of Emile's intruded on his thoughts.

'Emile said it wasn't his idea to invite me out here. I assume it was yours.'

She nodded. 'Of course. When you mentioned Mariana on the phone he threw one of his tantrums. But it was necessary for us to find out why you were interested in her. To be frank, I was hoping she had perpetrated some fresh scandal or done something criminal which would help Emile get over her. In any case, we had to know if you were about to involve her in legal proceedings. François wouldn't want his name or Emile's to be dragged into a court. But that does not appear to be the case.'

'Absolutely not. We're just looking to defend our client's interests.'

'And now you have discovered that she not only prostitutes her body but blackmails her clients. Any family which opened its arms to her or her sister would be inviting disaster, as you can see.'

'Emile mentioned the sister. So she's in on it too?'

Sylvie laughed. 'The sister's the worst one. Tell your client to steer clear of the pair of them.'

They were at the airport now and Gabriel was saying his farewells. To his surprise, she asked him for his address and number.

'I come to London sometimes,' she said. 'You can buy me coffee.'

'Sure thing.' He scribbled his personal details on the back of a business card, surprised he'd made that much of an impact and secretly hoping he'd never hear from her.

'Thank you, Gabriel.'

As he opened the car door, a slim but steely hand closed on his arm, halting his exit. 'One last thing. Your conversation with Emile was in confidence, understood?'

'Indeed. We won't make any illegitimate use of it, I can assure you.'

'Good. Because if any of those scuzzy magazine reporters suddenly start rummaging around linking François Lambert's son to drugs and prostitutes, I will tell him you are to blame. I can guarantee François will not be pleased.' She held up the card that Gabriel had just given her. 'And we know where to find you.' Then she laughed.

Gabriel grabbed his bag and headed for the airport building. Fast.

Sitting in the back of the car as it nosed through the London traffic, Mariana felt light-headed with relief and happiness. Next to her on the back seat, clutching her hand in both of hers, was her sister, the infuriating, frustrating but ever-delightful Paula.

There had been a moment of anxiety waiting at King's Cross. Mariana had survived the journey, sitting stiff with tension throughout the entire two hours and twenty minutes, alert to every hiss of the compartment doors behind her and movement of her fellow passengers ahead. She'd got off the train almost dizzy from the strain but proud that she'd survived the ordeal while around her off-peak travellers jostled happily, unaware that they had ever been in danger.

But when she'd passed into the station concourse, busy with its usual whirl of people in transit, she'd not spotted Paula. She'd waited nervously by the barrier, as arranged – at least, as she'd thought they'd arranged. Stupidly she'd not got a contact number – the call that morning had been so much of a shock she'd hardly been able to organise her dash to catch the train.

Then she was grabbed from behind and there was an excited squeal of welcome in her ear. She turned to see her sister's face, split open in a melon-sized smile and they'd hugged and grabbed and jumped up and down in excitement. The fact that their last parting, two years ago, had been so angry and bitter seemed to fuel the reunion with special energy.

'Quick!' Paula said, grabbing her hand and rushing her towards the exit. 'The car's on a yellow line.'

So Mariana had run in the direction she was prodded in a rush to get out of the station and into a car being driven by a man to whom she was not introduced – a minicab driver, she assumed. Now she was being taken to have lunch, so Paula had said, though Mariana didn't much care where they were going. It was important just to be here with her only other living relative, the sister who she'd promised her father she'd always care for. No matter that Paula had cheated and abused her in the past. Who said families were ever easy? And to hug that wiry little body again and laugh along with that smile under those familiar bouncing black curls gave her a feeling that no one else in the world could supply.

She surveyed Paula thoughtfully. She'd seen recent photos, of course, but a photograph was a flat, immovable thing that could conceal as much as it revealed. Here, in the flesh, this was the same girl she had always known but the face was thinner, the cheeks were no longer pinchably chubby and there were shadows under the eyes. Her body had changed too. It was less boyish, fuller in the chest and hips. In her youthful bitchy moments, Paula had declared she was glad Mariana lived a continent away because being a celebrated looker's cute kid sister was a pain in the ass. 'How am I supposed to keep a boyfriend,' she'd complained, 'when I know what he really wants to do is screw you?' Not that it had ever stopped the little devil from attracting men.

But now she looked properly grown, a small curvy beauty with an arresting gaze that, when the smiles had gone, brought a new seriousness to her face. It seemed to Mariana that Paula wasn't anybody's little sister any more.

That was the biggest relief of all.

* * *

251

Lunch passed in a blur for Mariana. She found herself sitting in the back room of a Greek restaurant in, as far as she could tell from their meandering drive, Camden Town or Chalk Farm, though her knowledge of this part of London was not good. Not that she cared, anyway.

The table was laid for three but the driver, not a minicab man it seemed, sat at the bar in the next room. Mariana gave no thought to the empty place as food arrived without them having ordered. She picked at bread and olives and sipped Coke. The food was not important.

She tried to quiz Paula about her college studies but somehow the conversation skidded off in more interesting directions, like her new life at Willowdale, and the preparations for the wedding – Paula was definitely coming – and Simon himself.

'So,' Paula assessed her carefully, 'you really like this guy, huh?'

'Of course, I do. I'm going to marry him, aren't I?'

'Sure, but it's nice it's a love match too.'

Mariana could have taken offence at that, thinking of Emile and the marriage that had never taken place. She'd been in love then too, though in retrospect – and if she could overlook the circumstances – maybe it was as well the wedding had never taken place. Emile had been sweet and so lovely to her, rescuing her from a life she was growing to despise. But he lived in his father's shadow. Simon was twice the man Emile was.

'Guess what?' Paula covered her hand in hers. 'I've got a guy too.'

This was not a surprise. Though Paula was now a

hard-working student, Mariana would never have expected her to devote her life to study. She laughed.

'So, what's new? You've always got a guy.'

'But this one is the best. I could really care about him.'

'Could?'

Paula ducked her head and pulled a face that revealed a trace of embarrassment. She wasn't a woman known to blush. So, maybe she really had fallen for someone.

'His name is Nico.'

'Don't tell me, he's tall and slim, with long black hair and snaky hips on the dance floor.'

Paula grinned in delight. 'Wrong. He's not much taller than me with short hair but he's got muscles and he's built – you know.'

'So your taste has matured.'

'You bet. He's a real man, very strong. He works out at a gym.'

'A tough guy.'

Paula laughed. 'Well, he's not the kind of guy you want to upset. I'm going to be very good to him.'

'Does he go to your college?'

'Oh no, he lives here in London. But I met him back home in the summer when he came home to see his family. He works here in a shop but all he really wants to do is play his guitar. And play with me, of course.'

Of course.

'You'll meet him soon,' Paula said. 'He promised to join us.'

So that solved the mystery of the other place at the table.

* * *

Mariana peered at her face in the smudgy mirror of the restaurant toilet. She didn't, in her opinion, look her ravishing best but she'd fled from home in a hurry and felt a bit travel-stained. She was well aware how lucky she was – she knew she didn't have to spend ages putting on a face to make an impact. Not that she would have gone to much trouble for Paula's latest conquest. Where men and her little sister were concerned she felt like the mother neither of them had. This Nico sounded like all the other arrogant, sexy wastrels Paula had ever fallen for. As far as she could tell, this new guy was over an hour late. It didn't look like Paula's taste had improved in the two years that had passed since she had last been involved in her life.

Had Paula really changed? she wondered. The girl who'd been laughing and boasting and wise-cracking upstairs had been the familiar Paula of old. She'd made no reference to the email she'd sent which had painted a picture of a new, contrite, studious young woman determined to work hard and make something of her life. Mariana rebuked herself for her suspicions but it would be wrong not to acknowledge they were there.

Her face seemed to blur as she stared at her reflection and she forced herself to get her features back into focus. It was odd and she couldn't account for it. Maybe the tension and excitement of her flight to London was having some physical effect. And she'd hardly eaten anything yet, not enough to keep her going anyway.

As she walked back to the table – Paula had been

joined now by the driver fellow – Mariana promised herself she'd eat. But the sight of the congealing kebab on her plate turned her stomach. So what if she felt light-headed? She munched on a piece of cucumber.

The driver turned to her. He had a pleasant doughy-featured face with earrings in both ears, a shading of designer stubble and a receding hairline. He seemed a nice guy and maybe it was a pity he wasn't Paula's new boyfriend. Not that he'd stand a chance, she thought.

'Paula says you are working at a stables,' he said. 'What do you do there?'

Mariana was happy to talk about Willowdale and the animals in the yard. She liked to think – she knew – that Simon valued her for her skill with the horses and the contribution she could make to the yard's success. It was important to her to know she wasn't just tolerated because she was the boss's girlfriend.

She found herself running off at the mouth, as if it were disengaged from the rest of her, and consciously stemmed the torrent of words to force down some bread. She really should eat.

She reached for her bag. 'I've got photos of the horses on my phone,' she said. 'I must show you.'

But she was clumsy in searching and the contents spilled over the table and on to the floor. Her hands wouldn't do as she told them as she tried to pick her things up. The other two watched her.

'Where's my phone?' she said in a voice that sounded far away. 'It must be here somewhere.'

'Are you sure you brought it with you?' said Paula.

'Maybe you left it on the train,' said the driver.

She was on her knees on the grubby floor, but there was no sign of it.

So she'd lost her phone or maybe left it behind. It was a nuisance, nothing more. She'd borrow Paula's and call Simon. He could look for it at home.

She tried to get to her feet but she couldn't. Her legs had no strength in them.

'Help me up,' she called but no sound came out of her mouth.

There were footsteps around the table. She saw a pair of grubby trainers and above that denim legs. There was a new voice in the conversation.

'So it worked?'

'As you can see. It took bloody ages but I don't think we'll have any trouble now. Give me a hand, Nico.'

So the boyfriend had finally arrived.

There were hands under her arms and she was being lifted. She heard the crash of glass as she stumbled against the table and hands caught her. She was held fast.

Paula's face swam in and out of vision, and so did the driver's, but the third remained fixed. A broad face with a large unshaven chin and lips that set into a thin smile. A smile that Mariana had seen before when its owner had leered at her across a train carriage. Just before he had plunged a knife into Geoff Hall.

If Mariana had been capable of making a sound she would have screamed the place down.

Chapter Thirteen

Simon had not enjoyed his afternoon. Shopping – and shopping for clothes – was not his favourite way to pass the time. Especially the kind of clothes-shopping where you had to solicit help from an assistant who, he suspected, was secretly smirking at the notion of clothing a clod-hopping beanpole such as himself. As a result he'd fled several likely-looking shops before he could seriously examine what they had on offer. As he found himself wandering the aisles of Marks & Spencer, well aware that on this occasion his default clothes-buying location would not fit the bill, he realised he needed help. He called Alison.

'You need a proper tailor,' she said at once and promptly named her father's.

'Isn't that a bit old-fashioned? I mean, Uncle Geoff always looked smart but he was nearly thirty years older than me.'

She laughed. 'I think it would be a big mistake for you to try and look trendy, Simon. Mariana hasn't chosen you because you're a fashion plate. Go for a traditional look.'

He supposed that made sense and took her advice.

To his relief, the assistant, a smartly dressed fellow of his own age, seemed to anticipate his worries and needs. They were soon joined by an older man who revealed he was a racing devotee and had known his uncle. They showed him a variety of cloths and cuts, took his measurements and sent him away to talk over his options with his fiancée.

So it was with a feeling of accomplishment that Simon found a café and called Mariana as he waited to be brought a pot of tea. For him, buying a wedding outfit was a more daunting prospect than preparing a runner for Epsom and he felt he'd made a promising start.

To his chagrin, Mariana's phone was turned off. He left an upbeat message on her answering service, hoping that her reunion was going well. It must be if, at this stage of the afternoon – nearly five – she had not thought of getting in touch.

On the way home he took a detour to Alison's place. He found her at the kitchen table with her laptop fired up, working with a notepad and calculator. She looked as if she had been drawing diagrams.

'I'm planning how to do up the old mill cottage,' she said.

'Wasn't Geoff going to turn it into a holiday home?'

'I've got a better idea. I'm considering turning it over to the Jockeys Disability Charity as specialist accommodation.' She went on to explain that she'd been thinking of setting up a sanctuary for retired racehorses but, after talking to Meg, her plans had developed to encompass people too. 'I mean, it makes sense to me to put retired horses and disabled horse people together. Even if you can't walk I've heard that it's possible, sometimes, to get up on a horse and ride.' What did Simon think?

Simon thought it sounded like a fine plan, for all sorts of reasons. Quite apart from being a generous use of Geoff's money, it would give Alison a purpose – and maybe keep her thoughts from dwelling on her father's unsolved murder. Simon did not express this last thought though he enthusiastically relayed the rest of it.

'What do the JDC say? I bet they're thrilled.'

'I wanted to think it through properly on my own before I got in touch with them,' she said. 'Get some idea of what it might all cost before I plunged in. Also, I'm not sure of the best way to approach them. I want this to be done in Dad's name and I'd like him to get proper recognition for it.'

'Why not talk to Jeremy? He's a trustee.'

'I'm aware of that.'

Alison stood up abruptly and fetched a bottle of wine from the fridge. She poured two glasses in silence. Simon knew her well enough to realise that she was mulling over what to say next.

'I know I could take the idea to Jeremy. But I don't see why I should hand him an opportunity to bask in reflected glory.'

He stared at her, taken aback.

'I mean, I don't approve of the way he's treating Meg, do you?' she challenged him suddenly.

'I don't know what you're talking about. What's he done?'

Alison shook her head. 'For somebody who is so sensitive to horses and the way they feel, you are pretty unobservant when it comes to humans. Why do you think Jeremy is always hanging round your yard?'

'He comes to see Aquiline. And to see us, I suppose. He's a friend as much as an owner.'

Alison took a long sip of her wine. 'Well, it's not only you and Mariana he's friendly with. I think you'll find he's become close to one of your stable girls, the one with big eyes and freckles.'

It took Simon a moment. 'You mean Holly? She must be half his age.'

'What's age got to do with it? Meg's older than Jeremy and Holly's younger. He obviously likes them both but I don't think he should be romancing them at the same time.'

Simon quickly assessed Jeremy's recent behaviour – and Holly's. It was true she'd been late on a couple of occasions recently when Jeremy had been around. And she'd had a weekend in London after Sandown. Had she been staying with Jeremy?

'Does Meg know?'

'Possibly, I haven't asked. But everybody else does. Apart from you, of course.'

'You mean Mariana knows about it?'

Alison laughed. 'Of course. She told me.'

Simon felt miffed, though he acknowledged that he wasn't curious about the personal lives of the staff at Willowdale. It wasn't his policy. Unless some drama interfered with their work or someone came to him with a problem, he reckoned it was none of his business. All the same, it was irritating to be the last to hear, especially since Mariana was plainly in the loop.

Alison topped up his glass. 'I imagine she didn't tell

you because she thought Holly might get into trouble.'

'That's ridiculous.' He'd have to put Mariana right about the way he dealt with his staff. He couldn't afford to interfere in their love lives, not if he wanted to keep them. And Holly was doing a pretty good job, in his book.

'All right then,' he said, keen to get off this sticky topic, 'forget Jeremy. Why don't you go straight to the JDC head office? I think it's in London. Go and see the chief exec next time you're down. I mean, your dad has already left them a lot of money, they ought to roll out the red carpet.'

A jangle from his pocket interrupted the conversation – the sound of a text message arriving. He reached for his phone.

'Do you mind? This might be Mariana.'

The message was indeed from her, at least it had been sent from her phone. But the content was not what he could ever have anticipated and it drove all thoughts of charity gifts and Jeremy Masterton right out of his head.

'Hmm.' Clive Silver steepled his hands together under his chin. Gabriel watched the points of his fingers sink into the abundant flesh of his uncle's throat. It had amused him ever since he used to observe Clive in his thinking pose when he was a small boy. These days, however, there were more chins to displace.

'I don't think there's any way round it,' said Clive. 'We're going to have to tell Simon Waterford.'

Gabriel wasn't surprised by this announcement. He had just finished debriefing Clive on his trip to Majorca and his encounter with Emile and Sylvie.

He'd had plenty of time to reflect during the journey back and he'd come to the conclusion that the unfortunate pair probably deserved their fate. 'I don't think they can stand one another and yet they're chained together,' he'd told Clive. 'Prisoners in paradise.'

Clive had rolled his eyes in exasperation but he'd been amused, all the same, as Gabriel well knew. Clive lived vicariously, passing his waking hours at his desk in the office and his desk at home in Hampstead Garden Suburb, with only trips to *schul* and his season ticket to White Hart Lane to get him out into the world. As a result he took pleasure in hearing details – the racier the better – of life as it was experienced beyond his four walls. Gabriel had laid it on heavily about the mountains and *ensaimadas* and Sylvie's sun-tanned legs.

'It's awkward,' Clive continued. 'There's a chance we're simply raking over old coals, in which case we will look over-zealous.'

'You mean, because Geoff's dead and we acted on our own initiative.'

'In a most sensitive matter. And, of course, because technically Simon Waterford is not even our client. I was his father's executor and acted for his uncle but Simon has never instructed me.'

Gabriel shrugged. 'We can hardly keep quiet about something like this. If I was him I don't know that I'd be too bothered about Mariana's adventures in the escort trade, not if I loved her – it's just buying and selling, isn't it? But extortion and blackmail is a different matter. We can't let him marry a crook.'

Clive's great head nodded. 'Indeed. I owe it to his

family to make sure he has all the facts about his fiancée. Then he can proceed as he thinks fit.'

'I suppose you'd like me to put it all in writing.' Gabriel stood up. 'I'll have it on your desk first thing.' And then he could wash his hands of the whole matter. The thought was pleasing.

Clive lumbered to his feet and held out his hand. 'Good job, young man. I shan't be lying when I tell your parents how much I appreciate your efforts.'

Gabriel took the offered handshake – compliments didn't often come his way from Uncle Clive.

'And,' said Clive as he continued to press the flesh, 'I shall expect you to be on hand when I get Simon Waterford into the office.'

'Why?'

Clive was grinning. 'I expect he might want to meet the man who has unearthed his fiancée's secret history. To look him in the eye and judge if he's telling the truth.'

The sly old sod, thought Gabriel, he wants me to take the blame.

'Sure thing,' he said and strolled casually to the door, wondering how on earth he could get out of it.

'What is it, Simon?' Alison was staring at him with concern. 'Are you all right?'

He'd been staring at the message on his phone, trying to make sense of it. But there was no sense to be made – unless it was a joke.

He handed the phone to Alison. 'Tell me what you think,' he said, surprised how calm he sounded.

He watched her read the short text message. It said: 'This is a kidnap demand. Mariana is in our hands. It will cost you one million pounds to see her alive again. Watch your email and you will be told how to deliver it. Tell the police and she will die.'

Alison's face reflected the blank incomprehension he felt. 'It's probably a hoax,' she said.

That's what he thought, too. Someone had got hold of her phone and was having a laugh at his expense. He knew that there had been trouble between Mariana and her sister in the past. Was this an example of her mischief-making?

He took the phone back. 'I tried calling her earlier but she had it switched off.'

But before he could even speed-dial her number, the phone sounded again. He had been sent an image. He pressed View.

The photo was tight-cropped on Mariana, showing her from the waist up, wearing the startling royal-blue sweater that he'd noticed hanging on the back of the dressing-table chair that morning as he'd crept out. She was staring straight into the camera, her head tipped forward slightly, as if it were too heavy for her neck. Her face was without expression and her eyes vacant. A piece of card had been propped against her chest which read: HELP ME SIMON.

He held it out to Alison, aware of a pulse beating in his ear.

She gasped at the sight of the tiny image and grasped Simon's hand. 'Call the police now,' she ordered.

'No, wait a moment.'

He could feel unfamiliar emotions uncoiling within him, urging him to action, but he didn't know what that should be. Keep calm, he told himself.

This time he made the call to Mariana's number. He was switched to her answering service, as before. 'Call me right now,' he barked. 'It's not funny, Mariana.'

'You think it's a joke?' Alison said.

'No – yes. It could be, couldn't it?' He was clutching at straws.

'If this is a joke, it's sick,' she said.

He stared at the phone, willing it to come to life, but there was nothing more.

'I can't get a million pounds,' he said. 'I mean, I can. I can mortgage the yard, I suppose. But it will take time.'

'I've got the money,' she said. 'I can get it quicker than you can. But we're a long way off that. You must talk to the police.'

He knew she was right, talking to the police was the sensible thing to do.

'But the message said she would die if we called the police.'

'Don't kidnap messages always say that? Anyway, how are they going to know?'

He shrugged. 'How did they know Mariana was going to London? Maybe we're all bugged and they're listening to everything we say right now.'

Alison looked around her kitchen in amazement. 'What – here?'

'Well . . .' he knew that didn't make much sense.

'Look,' she continued, 'call the police. They've got experience of kidnap cases and specialist officers who know what they're doing.'

'Oh yeah?' He found himself laughing. It was inappropriate but it helped.

She looked at him in disbelief.

'Sorry,' he said, 'but I'm just surprised at your touching faith.'

'It's true. They have experts.'

'Experts like DCI Henderson, you mean. Him and his specialist murder team talked a good game after your dad was killed. "Don't worry, we'll have those scum in a couple of days." It's been a long couple of days, hasn't it?'

She said nothing but he could see his words had had their effect.

'So what are we going to do?'

He didn't know. Except he wasn't going to sit here when he knew Mariana had gone to London. He jumped to his feet.

'I'm going after her.'

'Don't be stupid, Simon. Are you intending to walk the streets and look for her?'

'I can't just stay here.'

'OK.' She stood up too. 'Give me five minutes to pack a bag.'

'No, Alison. You don't have to come.'

She shot him a look that plainly told him to save his breath.

The telephone in the hall at Willowdale House rang just as Simon was heading for the door. He'd not wanted to stop off but Alison had persuaded him. 'Just grab a few clothes and a toothbrush,' she'd said. 'It might save time later.'

He snatched up the receiver – could this be the kidnappers?

'Yes?' he snapped.

But it was Clive Silver, the solicitor, trying to set up a meeting.

'Not now. I can't.'

'This is rather important, Simon. I need to talk to you urgently about Miss Hamilton.'

Simon froze. How did Clive know about Mariana? Had the kidnappers been in touch with him? Was he acting as a go-between?

He forced himself to take a deep breath. 'Have they told you where she is?'

'I'm sorry, Simon, I don't follow. Who's "they"?'

'The bastards who have taken her. I think she's been kidnapped.'

The whole story tumbled out of him in a few seconds. Simon never considered whether or not it was wise to tell it. Clive had been his father's solicitor for as long as Simon could remember. He'd acted for Uncle Geoff as well. It felt right to tell him.

'Have you called the police?' was Clive's first question.

'No. They say they'll kill her if I do.'

'Oh dear. Look, it's probably an empty threat and you may have to talk to the police later. But for the moment I suggest you get down here as quickly as you can. Come straight to my office – do you have the address?'

'Alison's with me, she knows.'

'Good. I'm glad you're not on your own. Promise me you'll drive carefully.'

'I will.'

Simon replaced the phone feeling, if that were possible, marginally better. Clive's paternal concern was comforting and it was reassuring to think there was at least one wise old head on his side.

Then he thought of that pathetic picture on his phone – of the woman he loved rendered glassy-eyed and incapable, silently begging for his help.

As he rushed for the car, he swore to himself he would not fail her.

Gabriel was almost out of the door and free when he heard his uncle's bellow from the far side of the office. Bloody hell, hadn't he put in enough Silver & Co. graft recently? He returned to find Clive standing by the window staring out at the evening commuter rush of High Holborn. That in itself was unusual. His uncle spent almost the entire day behind his desk, allowing the chair to support his substantial weight.

He turned round when Gabriel announced himself. 'Looks like things are kicking off with our friend,' he said.

Gabriel didn't precisely follow this remark so he said nothing.

'I've just been speaking to Simon Waterford. He's coming in to see us, so bang goes your evening, I'm afraid. No cocktail parties or candlelit suppers for you tonight, the ladies will have to forgo your company.'

Uncle Clive liked to lay on the heavy-handed witticisms, a habit he shared with Gabriel's dad. Gabriel hoped to hell he didn't inherit the trait.

'Simon's coming in here now?'

'Yes. He's driving down from Yorkshire at some speed so let us pray he gets here in one piece. All the same, it's going be half nine or so before he shows up. I'll buy you a steak-and-kidney pie round the corner – best I can do.'

Gabriel wasn't concerned about supper. 'You must have put the wind up him good and proper if he's haring down here now. What did you say?'

'Very little. The mention of Mariana's name was enough. It seems she has disappeared and he has received a ransom demand for her safe return.'

Gabriel might have thought Clive was joking, except that his humorous uncle never joked about business affairs.

'Apparently Mariana came to London this morning to meet her sister and he has not heard from her since. However, he received a text demanding money sent from her phone and a photo of her appearing to be drugged, so he said.'

'Bloody hell.' Gabriel was both appalled and thrilled. He couldn't deny that this, like his meeting with the doomed Charlie Talbot and his sudden trip to Majorca, was exciting. Then of course there had been the adventure of his trip to the delivery room at St Catherine's. Appearances to the contrary, he couldn't say working for his uncle was boring.

Clive was looking at him curiously. 'You find Simon's predicament amusing?'

'No, Uncle.'

'Good, because I don't think he's in an enviable position, though I suspect it's not the matter of life or death that he imagines.'

What did he mean by that? 'So you don't think Mariana's been kidnapped?'

'Do you? Knowing what you do about the way that young lady treated her last fiancé?'

Gabriel reflected for a moment. 'You're saying the kidnap's a put-up job and she's in on it?'

'I'd say it was too early to tell.' Clive took his jacket from the hook on the back of the door. 'But I doubt I shall be advising him to raise the ransom money just yet. Supper? Or is steak-and-kidney pie not to your cosmopolitan taste?'

Gabriel couldn't care less but cheerfully followed his uncle's bulk down the stairs, wondering how Simon Waterford was going to cope with what they had to tell him.

The drive down to London had seemed never-ending, with every traffic black spot and stretch of roadworks designed to increase Simon's frustration. At first he and Alison had talked, rehashing the situation from every angle. She had been relieved to hear that they were heading directly for Clive's office for a conference; it was the only positive element in their current situation. But as night had fallen and the journey had stretched on, both of them had lapsed into silence and the misery of their own thoughts. And throughout it all Simon's phone had remained obstinately silent.

It was past ten o'clock by the time they reached their destination. Simon supposed the solicitor must have kept the office open on his account and mumbled a thank you which the big man waved away as he ushered them into a meeting room dominated by a solid dark wood table and chairs. There were cups and saucers on a side table and some packets of sandwiches. A young fellow, some kind of office junior, Simon assumed, bustled around fetching coffee from the kitchen next door. 'Best we could do,' said Clive, indicating the food. 'Help yourself, you must be hungry.'

Food was the last thing on Simon's mind and, though he appreciated Clive's concern, he could have done without this time-wasting. Alison caught his eye and pushed a plate in his direction. He took a sandwich to keep her happy.

To Simon's surprise, the office junior did not leave the room once he'd finished his table-waiting duties. Instead, he booted up a laptop, closed the door and took a seat at the table next to Clive, opposite the visitors. But Simon's biggest surprise was reserved for the direction of the conversation that followed.

Once the circumstances of Mariana's disappearance had been restated and Simon had checked on the computer that nothing new had been heard from the kidnappers, Clive said to him, 'Did Miss Hall's late father ever speak to you about Mariana?'

It took a moment for Simon to adjust to the change of tack. 'Sure. I talked to Uncle Geoff about everything.'

'I mean, did he ever raise specific objections to your intended marriage?'

'He asked me if I thought I knew what I was doing, if that's what you mean.' Simon was irritated, he couldn't see the point of the question. 'He was concerned about me rushing into marriage with a girl I'd only known for a few weeks. I told him I was absolutely certain I wanted Mariana to be my wife, and I still am.'

'In that case,' Clive looked gravely apologetic, 'I must ask you to listen carefully to what I have to tell you. I regret to say you may find it upsetting but it does have a bearing – a significant bearing, in my opinion – on the current situation.'

Simon couldn't see how he could feel more upset than he was already. But he simply nodded. 'OK. Go ahead.'

'Before he was murdered Geoff asked me to look into Mariana's background. He was worried that so little was known about her. And he felt it was his duty, in the absence of your parents, to look out for your welfare. As a result I asked one of my colleagues to make some inquiries.'

'You put a spy on her?' Simon was livid. 'That's outrageous.'

Clive held up a large hand to pacify him. 'A report was compiled and given to Geoff about a week or so before he died. It contained information which in my estimation would have concerned any prospective marriage partner, though of course that person might choose to disregard it. I take it that he did not share the information with you?'

'Clive, I don't know what on earth you are talking about.'

The solicitor inclined his head towards the young fellow next to him. 'Gabriel wrote the report. So he knows the contents better than I do.'

Simon glared at the lad, fighting hard to prevent his anger erupting. He was known for keeping his cool in a crisis but this situation was different. For once it was tempting to give in to his emotions, to reach across the polished table and smack the youthful confidence out of the fellow who had been sent to snoop into the life of the woman he loved.

By his side, Alison laid a hand on his arm. She would know how he felt. He glanced at her quickly and nodded. He was OK. Whatever indignity was in front of him he would face it without letting himself down.

Curly-haired and fresh-faced, Gabriel didn't look much of an investigator. But he spoke clearly and, Simon had to admit, with some sensitivity for his subject.

Mariana, it seemed, was not the daughter of a famous horse trainer, though her father was half English as she had said. He had worked as an itinerant stable hand in Brazil before dying of liver cirrhosis at the age of fifty-one. After leaving school, Mariana had also worked with horses and had come to England looking for a job in a stables, without any luck. She'd been spotted on a London street by a man claiming to be a model agent, who was in reality looking for attractive girls to attend rich men's parties.

So what? Simon wanted to scream. So what if her father was a drunk and she was picked up because she was pretty? But he kept his mouth shut and forced himself to listen.

Gabriel was describing the business of an agency called Chrysalis Girls who provided good-looking young women to escort men who were willing to pay for their services. He produced some sheets of paper, printed off the internet. He pushed them across the tabletop so Simon could take a closer look and pointed to a thumbnail portrait, one of half a dozen, of a dark-haired girl in a dress with a plunging neckline. She was called Fabiana but, despite the wig and excessive make-up, Simon had no problem recognising her.

Simon read the blurb beneath the agency byline. It

seemed the girls were all personally selected for their intelligence and their outward-going personalities and were deemed suitable companions for all social occasions. He pointed this out to Alison. What was wrong with a pretty young woman hiring herself out as a social companion?

'Simon,' she said in a weary tone and indicated the next sheet in the pile. The girls decorating the page, including Fabiana, wore no dresses at all and the copy comprised a list of eye-watering prices for their time: 'incall', 'outcall' and 'overnight'.

Simon turned the pages face over on the table. 'That's enough,' he said, staring in defiance at Clive and Gabriel. So Mariana had worked as a whore. He couldn't deny it was a blow, though how much of one was too early to tell. He'd have to look into her eyes and hear the story from her own lips before he could judge, that much he knew. In the meantime, he wanted to spare himself and Alison the indignity of thumbing through the results of this boy's grubby sleuthing.

Gabriel met his gaze. 'That is the substance of the report I prepared for Mr Hall.'

'He never spoke to me about it. He obviously didn't think it was important.'

No one contradicted him in the silence that followed.

'So that's it then, is it?' Simon said.

Gabriel hesitated and Simon's stomach lurched. So there *was* more. He didn't want to hear it but he had no choice.

'Miss Hamilton stopped working for Chrysalis Girls more than two years ago when she met Emile

Lambert, the son of François Lambert the French industrialist and politician. She went to live with him in Majorca and they were planning to get married. But the engagement was broken off with some bad feeling, on the gentleman's side anyway. Mariana threatened to publish photographs of Emile taking drugs unless his father paid her a significant sum of money.'

Alison said, 'She blackmailed him?'

'The photos were never published but money changed hands.' Gabriel looked contrite, as if he were to blame. 'Yes, she blackmailed him. I'm sorry.'

'Who says so?' Simon cried.

'I spoke to Emile and to his personal assistant who is employed by his father. François Lambert paid her off.'

'But that's only one side of the story,' Simon said. 'I want to hear it from Mariana. I'm not interested in picking over the bones of her past, I want to know how we're going to set her free.'

The others all stared at him. Clive looked as if he were about to speak but Alison beat him to it.

'But don't you see, Simon, this changes everything. Mariana went to London of her own volition and now you've got a text from her phone demanding a million pounds. Given what we've just heard, who's to say she's even been kidnapped at all?'

The air seemed to rush from Simon's lungs. This was a strike he could not dodge. He sat motionless, in denial no longer.

Mariana looked around her without moving her head. Her head was too heavy to try to move it. She could see she was lying propped up on a bed, a blanket covering her legs. She was fully clothed, and for that she was relieved.

She did not recognise the room around her. It was small and shabby with one small window on the wall to her left above a sink. The curtains were drawn and the room was lit by an old standard lamp with a tasselled shade in the far corner. She could see a stained two-seater sofa positioned next to it, facing an old-fashioned box television with an indoor aerial which stood on a chest of drawers. On the screen a man in a leather jacket was threatening a woman with a gun. She could hear no sound – had she gone deaf? No, if she listened carefully there were noises in the distance. Traffic, muffled voices, doors opening.

She knew she wasn't well but this wasn't a hospital nor any place she recognised. Why wasn't she in a ward with nurses and doctors? Or lying in bed at home with Simon by her side?

Did Simon even know she was here? She had to call him. It must be night-time and he would want to know where she was. Where was her phone? She couldn't see her bag but maybe her mobile was in her pocket.

She found she could move her hands. It was a big effort but she was able to will them into life. That was good. She felt in the front pocket of her jeans, then – painfully slowly – wormed her fingers beneath her hips to explore her back pockets. There was no phone.

Then she remembered. She'd been looking for her phone when she'd fallen ill. She'd been in a restaurant on her hands and knees, searching for it. So she could call Simon. But it had been lost. Paula had been with her.

She felt an enormous sense of relief. Paula must be looking after her. She'd come to London to see her sister and been taken ill and Paula had put her in this room and would be back any moment to see how she was feeling. Then she'd be able to borrow Paula's phone and call Simon. And Simon would come and take her home.

Thank God. She was going to be all right.

A rattling sounded close by and the unsticking of wood. A door was being opened to her right, behind her head, which she still could not move.

'Paula?' That was her own voice, scratchy and feeble, but she could speak. 'Is that you?'

'Mariana baby!' Her sister came into vision, bending over the bed to look with concern into her face. 'You poor thing, how do you feel?'

'Odd. I can hardly move.'

'You're weak. You didn't eat anything at lunch and then you fainted.' Paula's face descended until it filled Mariana's vision. 'Don't worry, I'm going to nurse you till you're better.'

'Have you got my phone?'

'You lost it, don't you remember?'

'I must call Simon.'

'Don't worry. He knows what happened. I talked to him myself.'

'You spoke to him? Please get me a phone, I've got to call him.'

'Sure thing. But first you've got to eat something. Simon says you must rest and build up your strength.'

Mariana thought about that. Simon would be sick with worry. She had to get better for him.

Paula's face had now retreated and she was standing

277

by the bed. 'I've brought you some bread and soup.
You eat up while I go and fetch my phone.'

She turned towards the door and a tray slid into
Mariana's vision. Someone else had been standing
there all along.

At first Mariana couldn't see who it was but she
noticed the large hands that gripped the tray and the
silver bracelet that encircled the left wrist.

Then it all came back to her.

Chapter Fourteen

Simon walked the night-time city street, barely aware of the rushing traffic and the closed business premises around him. Even the muggy town air was a relief from the claustrophobia of Clive Silver's meeting room where the other three were waiting for him at this moment. He'd shaken off Alison's attempt to accompany him. Right now, he couldn't bear anybody's company, even hers.

So when it came down to it Uncle Geoff had been right about Mariana. He'd been sceptical about her from the start but Simon had thought he'd overcome Geoff's objections. That is, he thought Mariana herself had dispelled the doubts from his uncle's mind. He'd taken her for lunch one day and Mariana had said afterwards that they'd chatted for hours about her father and horses. But obviously Geoff had decided to dig a little deeper.

The thought of that kid Gabriel snooping after Mariana stuck in his guts. How could Geoff have even considered it? And yet there was no denying his uncle's instincts had been right. Mariana was not exactly who she had claimed to be.

Simon wasn't a fool. He'd always known there would be some sort of price to be paid for welcoming a woman as glamorous as Mariana into his tough, hard-working world. He imagined there would have been a history of men in her past, men more powerful, more sophisticated and, undoubtedly, more handsome than he was. At first he'd suspected that she was simply using him and Willowdale as a refuge from some heartache and as a means of getting in touch with her childhood love of horses. He'd accepted that one day she might fly his nest and go back to whatever complicated life she had been living before. But she'd stayed and made herself indispensable in every way. And he couldn't believe that when he'd looked into the deep brown pools of her eyes and she'd agreed to be his wife that she hadn't meant it. He still believed it.

But she'd worked as a fancy London prostitute – could he live with that knowledge? And, if he could, what about everyone else? The lads in the yard, his drinking mates in the pub, his friends in the village – the gossip grapevine would be on overtime. And what about his owners? The respectable, staid ones like Ellen Conville, the stodgy old boys like Reg Hartley – would they be so scandalised they'd walk away from Willowdale?

Well, that was a possibility. But until he had Mariana in front of him to tell him her own side of the story, he wasn't prepared to abandon her. He might be soft in the head for her, like this Emile Lambert, but he couldn't turn his back on her without a fair hearing. And he was painfully aware she was not available to give it.

Whatever she had done in the past and whatever she may or may not do in the future, he had to see her once more and hear the truth from her lips. He had to see for himself that she was safe. Then he could decide.

He turned back towards the office. He'd promised he'd only be gone five minutes and it had been twenty already. He quickened his step.

Alison remained seated at the gleaming grand table, alone in the room. She could hear Gabriel in the kitchen next door and Clive had disappeared into the dark bowels of the office. She was worried about Simon, out there walking the city streets on his own, but she hadn't had the energy to protest when he'd stopped her following him. She stared at her reflection in the windowpane across the room. There were dark shadows in her face and her hair was an unruly mop. She looked as weary and washed out as she felt.

Gabriel returned with a tray. He'd made a fresh pot of coffee and he poured her a cup, adding a dash of milk, which was how she'd taken it earlier. He must have remembered.

'Thank you,' she said.

'No problem. Would you like a biscuit?'

'I meant, thank you for telling us about Mariana. It couldn't have been easy.'

He shrugged. 'I think Clive rather dumped me in it. I thought I was along as a back-up rather than the messenger-in-chief. Mr Waterford looked like he'd happily have shot me.'

She raised a smile. 'Yes, he did.'

'Which is why Clive got me to deliver the bad news, I suppose. He's a cunning old bugger.' Gabriel didn't seem too perturbed.

'Can I ask you . . . ?' she hesitated, aware it might sound like a strange question. 'That report you prepared for my father, what did it look like?'

'There wasn't much to it. Just a few pages in a folder. A blue one, I think.'

She considered this information. She thought she'd been through all her father's papers but she'd certainly never come across any incriminating information about Mariana, or a blue folder. What would Dad have done with it?

The most likely place was surely the safe back home in Yorkshire but she'd inspected the contents, more than once, and not come across any blue folder. Similarly, she'd made a thorough examination of all the documents he'd left in the studies in both his homes.

She supposed it was possible her father had destroyed it. It was sensitive material and hardly to be left hanging around. In which case, after reading it, maybe he'd had no further use for it. Was that likely?

'Gabriel,' she said, 'am I right in thinking that your report did not contain any mention of Mariana's affair with Emile?'

He nodded. 'Correct. I didn't know about Emile until recently. I've only just come back from meeting him in Majorca.'

In that case, her father would not have known about the blackmail. Would he have concluded that Mariana's past as an escort was not sufficiently incriminating to bring to Simon's attention? In

Alison's opinion, her father had been reasonably broad-minded though he'd possessed an ascetic streak and he certainly took his responsibilities seriously as head of the family. When Clive had said her dad had been acting on behalf of Simon's dead parents in investigating Mariana, it had made absolute sense. And Uncle Phil, she was certain, would have had a fit if he'd discovered his son was about to marry a former prostitute. For that fact alone, her father would surely have kept the report until he had shown it to Simon – which he hadn't done. So where was it?

From down the hall she heard voices – Clive hailing the returning Simon. She felt dog-tired and part of her longed for the bed that awaited her in the still-unsold flat in Notting Hill. But bed was a way off yet and she put all such selfish thoughts from her mind as the others once more took their seats at the table.

Gabriel scratched idly on the pad in front of him as Clive and Simon returned to the room. The Yorkshireman's expression was grim, the skin stretched tight over the bones of his face.

'First thing tomorrow,' Simon announced, staring defiantly across the table, 'I'm going to start raising the money. I hear what you say about Mariana but I refuse to judge her while she's not here to defend herself. Maybe she *is* taking me for a ride but I won't turn against her, not while I believe her life is in danger.'

What was it about this Mariana, Gabriel wondered, that ensnared men so thoroughly? On first impressions you couldn't get two more different characters than Emile and Simon, yet both of them had been in thrall to her, and evidently Simon still was.

Clive was arguing for caution. There was nothing wrong with making preparations to get the money – a million pounds, in cash presumably, would not be easy to arrange. But now Simon and Alison were in full possession of the facts, maybe they should consider talking to the police. And, before that, perhaps it would be a good idea to run through the sequence of events that had led up to Mariana's disappearance.

Gabriel listened and made notes on his pad as the discussion continued. Simon described the phone conversation he'd had with Mariana that morning. She'd told him she'd just had a phone call from her sister and was rushing to London to meet her. Gabriel hadn't heard that detail before. He wrote down 'sister' and underlined it.

'Have you met Mariana's sister?' he asked.

'No. I was hoping she would come up to Willowdale but Mariana wanted to see her on her own first. On neutral territory, she said.'

'Why did she say that?'

'Because they'd fallen out over something years ago and Mariana had only just got back in touch. I should have driven her down to London then this wouldn't have happened. I could have kept an eye on her.'

There was an awkward silence.

'Unless,' said Clive, 'she didn't want you to keep an eye on her.'

Simon's cheeks flushed pink. 'You've decided she's behind this, haven't you?'

Clive inclined his head gently, as if accepting a

keen debating point. 'I just think we should be aware of all possibilities.'

'It could be a joke,' Alison said. 'That's still a possibility, isn't it?'

Gabriel admired her optimism.

Simon produced an envelope and some photographs which, he explained, were of Mariana's sister, Paula.

Gabriel examined them with interest. It looked like butter wouldn't melt in the girl's mouth.

'How did Mariana get back in touch with Paula?' he asked.

'She had lunch with some friend of hers from London She gave her Paula's address and these photographs. She wanted to mend the quarrel between them – I thought that was kind of her.'

Maybe, thought Gabriel. Or maybe not. 'What was the friend's name?' he asked.

'Carla.'

'Is that all?'

'Just Carla. And I don't have a number or address for her. I looked in Mariana's stuff before I left but all I could find were these photos. Dammit.'

Gabriel caught the glance of concern that Alison shot Simon. Both of them looked completely washed out.

Clive didn't miss the signs of fatigue either. 'I suggest,' he said, 'that you get a few hours' rest and return here first thing in the morning. Then we can contact the police if Mariana hasn't returned. And in the meantime, of course, you should keep checking your email account.'

Simon nodded and stood up. Though he looked the

worse for wear, Gabriel had no doubt he'd be spending the night in front of a computer. He hoped the Brazilian beauty would prove worth it.

It was one in the morning, hardly worth going home, and Gabriel was wondering whether he could get away with bunking down in the office. He still had his travel bag with him as he'd arrived straight from the airport.

Clive appeared in the doorway and seemed to read his mind. 'You're coming with me,' he said. 'The bed's made up in the spare room and you can say hello to your aunt over breakfast. And,' he added as he ushered Gabriel down the hall, 'you can tell me what you think on the way.'

Gabriel would have preferred to nod off in the soft leather seat of his uncle's Bentley as they travelled north out of central London but there were a couple of things that he thought he should mention.

'Simon said that Mariana's friend was called Carla,' he said to Clive. 'That's the same name as the woman who runs Chrysalis Girls.'

'That's interesting. Well spotted.'

'And, Uncle, I reckon I ought to come clean to the coppers about my meeting with Charlie Talbot.'

Clive shot him a shrewd look. 'Why?'

'Because it's going to come out now, isn't it? If you and Simon go to them about this kidnap – if that's what it is – you've got to give them the whole picture, tell them how Mariana is a shady lady with a history of extortion and so on. She was also a witness to the murder of the one person in Simon's family who knew she wasn't exactly who she claimed to be. And he knew it because I'd given him a report which said so. And, funnily enough, when Charlie Talbot tried to buy that report off me, he didn't last the day.

'So either two murders and this kidnap-cum-blackmail are entirely coincidental events or else they are connected. And one of the things that connects them is the report that I wrote and which, on your advice, I carefully did not mention when I spoke to the Ilford police like a good citizen and told them about my meeting with Charlie just before he was killed.'

Gabriel came to a halt, the speech having tumbled out of him seemingly of its own volition. He stared at Clive. Help me, Uncle. I've scared myself witless. Tell me I'm not wrapped up in the middle of two murders and a blackmail plot.

The Bentley drew away from the traffic lights by the Lord's roundabout, the purr of the engine the only sound in the interior of the car.

At last Clive spoke. 'It's true that you do appear to be rather up to your neck in it.'

And whose fault is that? Gabriel was tempted to say but kept his mouth shut.

'I've decided to recommend that Simon talks to Henderson about Mariana's disappearance. I know Simon and Alison are critical of him because he stupidly gave them the impression he was going to catch Geoff's killers in a couple of days. But obviously, as you were implying just now, Geoff's murder is not some random youth crime. I think we have a duty to give Henderson all the facts at our disposal. If he thinks it necessary to call in a specialist kidnap team then it's up to him.

'Meanwhile, I suggest you visit your friends at Ilford and tell them the real reason why Charlie Talbot wanted to meet you on the day he died. Otherwise, sooner or later, they'll come looking for you.'

Tell me something I haven't worked out for myself, thought Gabriel. Or, better still, tell me how to explain why I never mentioned Mariana and the report in the first place.

He caught his uncle giving him a sideways glance.

'Don't worry,' Clive said. 'You'll think of something.'

Alison woke from a deep sleep, instantly alert, sweating as if she had been exercising vigorously. The room was black and hot, for there were no windows in this box room the size of a cupboard next to the utility room in the Notting Hill flat. She slept in here out of habit, in preference to the proper guest room with its king-sized bed which she had been happy to cede to Simon. She could, of course, have taken over her father's bedroom but that did not appeal, for all sorts of reasons. She had grown to like this snug little space – she could, sometimes, slip off to sleep in here believing that the world was as it used to be and her father was lying peacefully just across the hall.

Now she was wide awake. It wasn't just the heat, of course. She sat up in bed and turned on the light. How could she sleep with Simon in turmoil in the next room? She could hear him through the wall, shifting in his chair, clearing his throat. She ought to go through and sit with him but she wasn't sure she could bring herself to say the soothing things that she had repeated over and over on their way back from

Clive's office. Yes, I agree the most important thing is Mariana's safety. Don't worry, I will help you with the money. And, most difficult of all, I'm sure everything will be all right.

The truth was she was uncertain about all of these statements. Of course, Mariana's safety was paramount. The Mariana she knew, that is, the trustworthy companion with the magic fingers and sing-along disposition. But the woman who Gabriel Silver had uncovered, the devious and self-serving party girl, was a stranger – why should she, or Simon, care what happened to her?

She had promised to help with the ransom money when she believed her friend was genuinely in danger. But things were different now. She could easily end up giving away the funds she had earmarked for her charity scheme. How foolish she would feel if she allowed herself to be cheated of her plans now she had heard how Mariana had swindled that poor Frenchman.

And as for everything turning out all right, how could it? Mariana had deceived them all. Except her father, who had died knowing the truth about her. Trying, Alison was sure, to mend the situation somehow. What had he done with that report? The question nagged at her.

She pulled on her jeans and a thin cotton top and padded softly across the hall. It was almost as stuffy in her father's room and it smelt musty and stale. She should fling open the window and give it a good airing but she knew she wouldn't. For in that mustiness was still the scent of her dad's presence, faint notes of his soap and aftershave, and the thought of losing these final reminders of him was unbearable. She remembered Mariana urging her to spruce the room up and Alison had agreed, though she'd never done it.

Now, however, she had a purpose. This room, surely, was the last place her father could possibly have left that folder. It was four in the morning, hours before they were due back at the solicitor's office, and she knew she'd never get back to sleep. Time for her to search.

She went through the desk drawers and the bedside cabinet, looked inside the wardrobe and searched beneath the clothes folded in the chest of drawers. The presence of her father became more tangible the deeper she delved. With her arms full of her father's shirts and sweaters, smoothing her hands over the cloth of his jackets as she pushed aside the garments that hung in the wardrobe, it was as if she were trying to recapture the essence of him – and coming up empty-handed.

There was no blue folder. If it had ever been here, it had gone now.

In the bedside table there were letters she had written her father as a girl when she was living with her mother in South Africa. She sat on the bed and flicked through her clumsy scrawls of long ago. They seemed banal and trite – and shameful. There was a potent subtext to her bright assertions that she'd had a lovely day at the beach with Mummy and Uncle Theo and how he'd promised to buy her a new pony. She'd hated Uncle Theo and had only mentioned him because she thought it would make her dad jealous – and serve him right for abandoning her to her silly selfish mother.

But he hadn't abandoned her. He'd rescued her. And he'd kept her manipulative adolescent scrawls for the rest of his life. She put them back in the drawer.

There were other letters there too, some from her mother, but only one of interest to her at this moment. On notepaper headed Jockeys Disability Charity, it read:

Dear Geoff,
It is with palpable pleasure that I write on behalf of the JDC to acknowledge the cheque you gave me for the sum of £100,000. I have no hesitation in saying that this is one of the most magnificant bequests I have ever received as a trustee of the charity and I cannot begin to describe to you how much it is appreciated by all of us here. Naturally, all donations are received with gratitude but there is no denying that generosity on this scale will enable us to achieve a very great deal on behalf of those whom we support. I shall respect your request to keep this gift private. Please believe me when I say that your philanthropy is matched only by your modesty and is thus cherished all the more.
    Yours very truly,
        Jeremy Masterton

Alison remembered the entry she'd found in her father's chequebook. That stub must refer to this money. Evidently he'd wanted to keep the whole thing quiet. How typical of him. Reading this confirmation of her father's generosity, she was filled with determination to bring her own plans to fruition. But this time she would make sure Geoff Hall received the credit he was due.

With these thoughts in mind – she'd get in touch with the charity head office today if events permitted – she finished off her search of the room. She stood on a chair to look on top of the wardrobe and lifted the rug by the window.

But this was stupid, why would her father hide the folder? Putting it away safely was one thing but concealing it, as if it might be stolen, was quite another. Who would want to steal it anyway?

The moment the question popped into her head, so did the answer. Mariana, that's who. And Mariana had been in here. She'd been surprised to discover the Brazilian girl in her father's bedroom on their trip to London a few weeks ago.

So, if her father had left it in here, then Mariana could have taken it. And Mariana had helped clear up the Yorkshire house too. If she'd known about the damaging evidence against her, she could have kept an eye open for it in both places. And destroyed it.

But did she know about it?

Alison sat down heavily on the bed. Her head was foggy with the sleep she'd been denied but she was determined to think this through. Her father had received the folder over a week before he died and he didn't appear to have acted on it. That is, he hadn't told Simon of its contents. But suppose he'd gone to Mariana?

She could imagine her father, a man of scrupulous fairness, wishing to hear Mariana's side of the story before he laid evidence against her. Possibly he had urged her to come clean to Simon herself – which she plainly hadn't done.

Instead, her father had died and the incriminating report had disappeared.

Alison was not a judgemental woman by nature but she could feel her heart hardening as she considered the nature of the Brazilian girl she had thought of as a close friend. Mariana with her beauty and skill and selflessness had seemed too good to be true. And untrue was exactly what she appeared to be.

'Parker, listen up.' Steve's voice, normally so laidback, was bursting with excitement.

Claire, who had news of her own to impart, pushed the phone close to her ear to shut out the sounds of the busy office around her. Things were hotting up this morning. 'Fire away,' she said.

'You remember that bloke Gabriel Silver? The character who had a meeting with Talbot just before he got killed? He's suddenly decided to tell us what Charlie wanted from him.'

'I thought Charlie was just sounding him out for a possible job. And that Silver didn't know what was behind it.'

Steve's laugh came down the line, a contemptuous bark. 'He knew all right. He claims he wasn't at liberty to tell us because it would have meant revealing information of a sensitive nature relating to a third party or some such guff. He might look wet behind the ears but he's a slippery sod. After all, he works for a solicitor.'

Claire was well aware of who Gabriel worked for after recent developments. The uncle of this Gabriel represented Alison Hall and Simon Waterford. She was kicking herself for not making the connection before – she knew the name Silver had rung a bell.

'What he says now,' Steve said, 'is that he had carried out an investigation into a woman to see if she was suitable marriage material. Talbot had got wind of it and was offering to buy his findings. You'll never guess who this woman is.'

'Mariana Hamilton.'

There was a short silence before Steve said, 'How the bloody hell do you know that?'

Claire knew it because she had spent a fascinating two hours in the offices of Silver & Co. earlier that morning in the company of DCI Henderson. Her boss was on his best behaviour as he listened first to Clive Silver, then Simon, with supporting remarks from Alison. Mariana, it seemed, had disappeared on a visit to London and a threatening message had been sent from her phone, demanding money for her safe return.

At the same time, there was controversy about the nature of Mariana's involvement. It turned out she was an ex-hooker – not a flicker on Henderson's face at this revelation – who had also extorted money from a French politician. On the face of it, it seemed likely that she was the one who was asking Simon for money. That was the conclusion Claire herself had immediately drawn and she could see it was even shared by Alison, though she was doing her best to provide support for her distraught cousin. There was no need even to scrutinise Henderson's face – assuming guilt was his natural reflex.

Only Simon was maintaining any faith in Mariana.

He'd already begun steps to raise money. It was at this point Claire had sensed a resistance in Alison to her cousin's belief that Mariana was genuinely in danger. But Simon's impassioned demand that Mariana be found and allowed to defend her reputation had overridden everything else. For that was the point on which they all agreed. Villain or victim, the only way to get to the truth was to produce the girl, preferably in one piece.

But Claire didn't have time to go into this in detail with Steve because Henderson was banging on the partition, summoning her into his office. 'Got to go,' she murmured into the phone and scuttled next door.

'OK,' Henderson said, pointing to a screen on his desk, 'we've got the CCTV of Mariana arriving at King's Cross.'

'That was quick.'

'It helped that we knew pretty much which train she was on.'

The picture showed the familiar station interior and figures milling around in front of the departure boards. Henderson pointed out a tall blonde girl in the top corner of the frame but Claire had noticed her already – Mariana stood out wherever she went.

'She hangs around for a couple of minutes, like she's waiting for someone and, bingo, there she is.'

A smaller dark-haired girl burst into the picture and grabbed the blonde from behind. The pair of them embraced with great enthusiasm.

'It doesn't look like a put-up job,' Claire said.

'No. At least we know Mariana actually travelled to London. Unfortunately, we haven't yet got a handle on where she went next. We lose her on the CCTV when she goes out of the station.'

'What about the underground?'

'No sign of her there or in the taxi queue. But there's a lot of footage of the streets around the station which we're still going through. And we're waiting to hear from the phone company.'

Claire nodded. Tracing the signal from Mariana's mobile should give them a good clue to her whereabouts.

'Right then,' said Henderson, picking a folder from his in-tray and holding it out. 'Here are some stills of the girl Mariana met at King's Cross. I want you to hotfoot it over to Simon Waterford and get an ID on her. I'm assuming it's the sister but we need to know for sure. OK?'

Alison had slipped away to make a phone call. Clive had directed her to a tiny cubbyhole barely large enough for a desk and chair. He apologised for its poky nature. It seemed the desk belonged to Gabriel who, so far that day, had not made an appearance.

In Alison's opinion Clive had no need to apologise for anything. Considering that this was a busy office, and not over large, he had been more than generous, insisting that she and Simon should remain on the premises during the crisis. Simon had been installed in the meeting room they had used last night, with a computer and a phone available for his use. Since the police had departed he had spent most of his time on the phone to Ken at Willowdale, trying to manage from long distance. Alison wasn't sure how successful he was being but at least it kept his mind off the computer screen where his email inbox remained insultingly empty.

She called the head office of the Jockeys Disability Charity and asked to speak to the chief executive. She was placed on hold and then asked a second time for her name – it evidently meant nothing (but why should it? she thought) – before she was informed that Sir Malcolm Gorringe was unavailable, would she like to speak to the deputy chief executive?

Then things took a turn for the better as a friendly and vaguely familiar voice came down the line. 'Hello, Alison, it's Freddy Fordham here. My lad's been riding your horse.'

It took her a moment to realise that this was her jockey, Neil's, father. She'd met him not long ago at Jennifer Eccles' last outing. She didn't recall learning that he was involved with the JDC, or maybe she had forgotten in the hurly-burly of the moment.

'I've not been in the job that long,' he explained. 'Anyhow, it's a pleasure to hear from you. How can I help?'

She explained that she was considering making a donation to the charity from her father's estate and she'd like to explore the possibility of fixing up some specially equipped accommodation on the land she had inherited. It was the kind of thing her father would approve of, she said, because he had always admired the work of the JDC.

'I knew your father reasonably well,' Freddy said, 'but I never realised he was such a strong supporter of ours.'

'He preferred not to publicise it,' Alison said, 'but I'd like him to get some credit if we go ahead with the cottages. He gave you a hundred thousand pounds last autumn and yet even I didn't know about it.'

'Really?' Freddy was surprised. 'I was running through a list of our major donors with Malcolm the other day and your father's name came up in connection with the money he donated in his will. Malcolm said how surprised he was because that was the first time your father had made a bequest.'

'That's not the case. I know he gave you money last autumn because I've been going through my father's accounts. I've seen the cheque stub. And I've got a letter of receipt here from Jeremy Masterton. Though it does say that Dad had specifically asked for the gift to be kept quiet.'

'That might explain it, I suppose. What's the date on Jeremy's letter, as a matter of interest?'

She told him and, a few minutes later, he rang her back.

'Alison, this is embarrassing but we haven't got a record of that hundred thousand payment. I thought it was odd because, requests for privacy or not, Malcolm's going to know if anyone kicks in that kind of money. It is possible your father thought the better of it and the cheque was never put through?'

Alison absorbed this information. 'Let me make a few inquiries,' she said and hung up.

It was easy to track Jeremy down though she had to make a call she didn't enjoy. She got Holly, the stable girl at Willowdale, on the line just before she left for her lunch break. 'Where's Jeremy today?' she demanded.

'Jeremy?'

'Don't be coy, Holly. I'm not out to make trouble for

you, just give me all the numbers you've got for him and I'll take it from there.'

After that it was easy. It turned out Jeremy was at his London flat. How convenient.

He sounded pleased to hear from Alison – at first.

'Alison, how delightful. What's the weather like up north?'

'I haven't a clue, Jeremy. I'm here in London and anxious to speak to you about a cheque my father entrusted to you last autumn.'

'Are you sure? I can't say I can recall your father giving me cheques, not off the top of my head anyway.'

'Just one cheque, Jeremy, and you'll recall this one all right. It was for one hundred thousand pounds and made out to the Jockeys Disability Charity, of which you are a trustee, are you not?'

'Yes, but it's still not ringing any bells. Why don't I go through my records and get back to you?'

At that moment Alison heard Simon hailing her from across the office. It sounded urgent.

'All right, Jeremy. I'm at my solicitor's at the moment, then I'll be back at the Notting Hill flat with Simon.' She gave him Clive's number. 'I shall expect to hear from you very soon.'

She put the phone down with some satisfaction. She felt as if she'd been on the receiving end of a succession of blows and it felt good to turn the tables.

She found Simon in the meeting room. He had been joined by Claire Parker who was spreading some large colour printouts across the tabletop. Simon seemed excited.

'Look, it's Mariana at King's Cross yesterday. From the CCTV.'

Alison could see that for herself. She also noted the second woman in some of the other pictures. 'Is that—?'

'Yes, it is. It must be.' Simon produced the photographs of Mariana's sister and placed them side by side.

The three of them peered at the images closely. In only one of the CCTV stills was the girl's face fully visible, but that was enough.

Claire was already talking to Henderson on her mobile. 'It looks like Paula, the sister. I'm ninety per cent positive.'

A hundred per cent, thought Alison.

At that moment, the laptop next to them chimed. Simon at last had the email he had been waiting so anxiously for.

Headed 'Mariana' it was short: 'You've got 24 hours to get the money. Or else she returns in pieces. Don't waste a minute.'

That was it.

Alison still didn't know what to believe.

Chapter Fifteen

Mariana had been in a few awkward situations in her life but not one like this. Even when meeting unknown men in hotel rooms someone had always known where she was. There had been pre-arranged phone calls and code words she could utter to get herself extricated from trouble. Here in this room she was on her own. All she had was her wits.

She practised her smile. It had to be good enough to fool Paula and she only had the little mirror she kept in her bag which, thank the Lord, Paula had given back to her. Without her phone, of course.

The smile had to say – I'm happy, I feel no pain, I do not wish to put your eyes out with my fingernails, you evil little bitch.

She'd had a stroke of luck the night before, when they'd brought her the tray of food and she'd once more seen the man who lived in her nightmares. The sight of him had sobered her as suddenly as a wave of ice water. So the vision she'd had of him earlier – in the restaurant when the world was spinning round her head and she didn't know what was real and what was her own sickness inside – that had been true. Her sister was friendly with, involved with, *sleeping with* one of the killers on the train.

She'd picked at the food in a daze, trying to think it through. In her terrified state, trying to think at all was difficult. That wide unshaven face, that thin smile and the memory of Geoff Hall's blood soaking her to the skin turned her stomach, finally propelling her from the bed. That's when she found they'd locked her in. Her own sister was keeping her a prisoner.

She'd screamed and banged on the door and Paula had appeared to lead her to the toilet down the hall where she'd vomited up everything she'd eaten. She'd allowed herself to be led back to bed and feigned extreme fatigue, barely responding to Paula's questions. She hadn't even complained of her treatment or asked again for the phone she'd been promised. She'd even refused the tea Paula brought her, though her mouth was as dry as the desert. And when she'd been left on her own – locked in once more! – she'd slipped silently from the bed and drank directly from the tap over the basin. The water tasted stale and warm but at least it wouldn't put her body to sleep and her brain into limbo.

And now, after an endless night, during which the drugs they'd fed her had slowly loosened their grip on her system, she lay trying to make sense of her predicament. She was being held a prisoner and it didn't take a genius to conclude that, if Paula was involved, the reason would be money. Her sister was only ever truly motivated by greed – as had been demonstrated in her behaviour over poor Emile. Mariana felt such a fool. She'd vowed never to let Paula under her guard again and all it had taken were a few demure photographs and a sentimental email.

So how were Paula and her new friends intending to profit out of keeping her captive? There was an obvious answer to that question. They would be asking Simon for money for her safe return. The thought was stomach-turning. She hoped to God he told them to go to hell.

At least that's what she said to herself. Tell them to go to hell, Simon, and they'll soon get fed up with holding me here. If it were just a question of seeing off Paula and a few of her mischievous friends, she'd have every confidence of getting out of her prison in short order. The next time Paula showed her face around the door Mariana would take pleasure in smacking it – hard. Memories of taking her little sister in hand were not that distant. In fact she'd relish the opportunity.

But behind her sister stood a man who had killed in cold blood. Who with his accomplice had laid Geoff and Simon low in the blink of an eye. He was no juvenile chancing his arm, he was a professional assassin. Mariana knew she was dead if she went up against him.

Maybe she was dead anyway, if Simon didn't pay the money they asked him for. That's what happened when kidnappers didn't get their ransom, wasn't it? Though surely Paula wouldn't allow anything too terrible to happen to her own sister. Correction – her half-sister, and Paula had always been irrationally jealous of her. The answer, Mariana feared, might depend on how much Paula stood to gain. And how angry she would be if she didn't get paid.

These thoughts churned around inside Mariana's

head, petrifying her. What could she do to save herself?

She had to pretend – pretend to eat what they gave her, pretend that her thoughts were still at sea and her body enfeebled and, sickening though it was, pretend to smile.

She heard footsteps on the stair and, as a key was inserted in the lock, she hurriedly tucked the mirror into her bag.

Time to put her smile into practice.

'OK then.' Henderson was looking pretty pleased with himself, Claire thought, as he presided over the meeting. The group of detectives around the table included Steve Gill though she had made sure she was sitting two places away from him. They were on the job here and behaviour was strictly professional. Besides, there was no call to give Henderson any ammunition for his unsubtle innuendoes.

On the screen in front of them rolled a sequence of traffic. 'The street cameras around King's Cross have picked up the car that looks like our target.' Henderson froze the shot and pointed to a silver saloon in the middle lane. 'Note the woman in the back seat – long curly blond hair and a bright blue sweater. There's a good chance that's Mariana.'

The images moved on. 'Unfortunately we lose the motor here but we've now got some info out of the phone company. Mariana's mobile was pinged near Camden Town between half one and three. And,' a new photo flashed up, a small parade of restaurants and fast-food joints, 'we reckon she was in the Greekie with the blue frontage. If you look along a few parking places you'll see the silver car. We've got partials on the number plate and they check out.'

'It's a five-year-old Ford Focus,' a voice piped up.

There was a petrol head in any group of coppers, Claire had long ago concluded. This guy could probably tell them the optimum tyre pressure, given the chance.

Henderson ignored the interruption. 'So we reckon that confirms the sighting of the blonde as our girl.'

The screen changed again to show more traffic on the move. Claire picked out the Focus before Henderson stopped the picture. 'Here we have it at around three thirty in Maida Vale. We can't see the passengers unfortunately, though it looks like there's a different guy driving.'

Claire had noticed that. In the King's Cross pictures the driver's long-sleeved white shirt had been visible. In the Maida Vale shot, he was wearing a lemon-coloured T-shirt.

'We lose the car after that but the good news is we've found the vehicle abandoned overnight in Colindale. From where, incidentally, the text message and image of Mariana was sent on her phone. Since then the phone's been dead. But, looking at the map,' a diagram of north-west London appeared on the screen, 'we can see that there's a pretty straight route up the A5 across the north circular to Colindale. It's a reasonable assumption that the car passengers alighted during the course of that journey.'

He looked around with some satisfaction. 'Narrows it down a bit, wouldn't you say?'

Unless Mariana left the restaurant in an entirely different vehicle, thought Claire. But she wasn't going to pour cold water on her boss's optimistic assessment. After all, they had to start somewhere.

'What about the email?' a voice asked. 'Have we got a location for that?'

'Indeed we have.' Henderson sounded positively jovial. Maybe because all the information he'd requested had turned up in double-quick time, which was a bit of a miracle. 'It was sent from an internet café in Southwark.'

'Southwark?' the voice was incredulous. 'That's the other side of the bleeding river.'

'Correct.' Henderson's smile tightened. 'It is also a mere twenty-odd minutes on the Jubilee Line from Kilburn which is slap in the middle of our target area. If I was sending a ransom demand by email I would make sure I did it well away from my home patch.'

The point was generally acknowledged though Claire had a good idea what they were all thinking. The woman could as easily be in the south of the city as the north and, frankly, they'd be lucky if she was even in London at all.

The meeting broke up as particular tasks were allocated. Claire noted Henderson detailing two officers to track down Carla, the woman who ran the escort agency which once represented Mariana.

Steve tugged her sleeve surreptitiously. He directed her attention to pictures of the Focus captured from the camera on Maida Vale. 'Do you see what I see?' He manipulated the screen to enlarge the area of the driver's window.

Then her heart did a little flip of excitement as she saw it too.

Beneath the short sleeve of the driver's T-shirt,

across the swell of his bicep, was a tattoo of familiar shape.

Steve was grinning, as was she as she waited for Henderson to finish briefing her colleagues. This should make his day.

Mariana was ready when they came to take away the tray. She'd done her best to make it look as if she'd eaten her fill. The soup bowl was wiped clean and the plate was empty but for sandwich crusts. She'd poured the soup down the sink and the crustless sandwiches were curling out of sight beneath the chest of drawers. Luckily they had brought her an unopened can of Coke and she'd guzzled that in the belief that it would not be tainted.

Paula never came into the room on her own; one of the train killers always appeared at her side – Nico, the short barrel-chested one, or the tall dark-haired man who had butted Simon in the face. He was called Spider. Both men terrified Mariana and she tried not to look them in the eye.

'How are you feeling, baby? Oh look, Nico, she's eaten everything up. There's a good girl.'

Mariana could tell Paula got a real kick out of this little act – a masterpiece of role reversal. Paula had always resented her seniority. Mariana raised a feeble smile for her sister, trying hard to wipe all subversive thoughts from her mind. If she had to act docile, it was easier if she believed the act.

The food tray was whisked away and Paula bent over the bed. It took all of Mariana's self-control not to flinch as her sister reached out to run a hand through her hair.

'Ooh, this is getting pretty tangled. Your hair really needs some attention, baby.'

Then Mariana saw the scissors in Nico's hand. They were big, like dressmaker's shears.

'Listen, Mariana, I'm going to make your hair more manageable,' Paula said. 'Just give it a little trim. OK?'

Mariana forced herself to nod. She didn't trust herself to speak.

'Oh, that's fantastic.' Paula seemed genuinely pleased at Mariana's response. As she should be.

The girl took the shears and selected a generous hank of blond hair. Mariana willed herself not to shriek as the jaws closed with a crisp snap. She imagined she could hear a faint crunch as the blond lock came away from her head.

Paula put the hair in a plastic bag that Nico was holding for that purpose. Amidst the hysteria that was mounting inside her, Mariana pondered the purpose of this humiliation.

Snip, snip, snip. Paula was working more confidently now, butchering with precision.

'That's enough,' said Nico.

'Hang on a moment.' Paula had produced another pair of scissors, a smaller sharp-pointed precision instrument. First the meat cleaver and now the scalpel, thought Mariana. Paula leaned forward to snip some ends that evidently displeased her.

'Get on with it,' growled Nico. 'It's not a bloody fashion shoot.'

Mariana didn't know what he meant but she didn't like it. And she couldn't hold herself in any longer. As Paula pulled away, she shoved her sister backwards as hard as she could. Taken completely by surprise,

Paula hit the floor, the scissors spilling from her hand. Mariana sprang from the bed and flew at her, with every intention of smacking her treacherous head into the middle of next week. But Paula raised her arms and they grappled on the floor for a moment until a pair of hands seized Mariana and pulled her away as if she were feather light.

'You mad bitch,' said a male voice and she was thrown back on the bed. A blow landed on the side of her head – it was like being hit with a steam iron.

In a daze Mariana covered her head with her arms, waiting for the next hammer blow to fall. To her surprise she heard Nico laughing.

'What's so funny?' shrieked her sister.

'You two. You're both a pair of crazy witches.'

Mariana's arms were yanked away from her face and held, immovably, behind her back. Paula stood in front of her, glaring with malevolent intent. Mariana was sure her sister was going to strike her. She glared back.

'Come on, Paula,' commanded Nico. 'Take the picture and let's go.'

So that's what this was about, they wanted a photograph of her. But why cut her hair?

Paula pulled a small digital camera from her pocket. 'I hope your fiancé still wants you. I wouldn't pay five dollars for you looking like that.'

The camera flashed in the small room. Mariana could feel the left side of her face tingling and swelling from the blow she had taken.

'Why are you doing this to me?' she said. 'I could have got you money.'

'Why do you always think it's money?

'Because it always is.'

'Not this time.' Paula lowered the camera. 'Sure, the money will be nice but I get special pleasure out of putting you in your place. You're not Daddy's number one any longer, are you?'

'That's not fair, Paula. He loved us both the same.'

'Let's go,' said Nico.

Paula considered the image she had captured then thrust the camera in Mariana's face. 'See,' she smirked. 'You look like shit.'

Mariana stared at it. With her massacred hair, she looked like the victim in some low-grade horror movie.

Maybe that was the point.

As the door closed behind her tormentors, she lay back on the pillow, now strewn with hair clippings, and allowed herself to wallow in the despair of the moment. Her entire head was reverberating like a drum from Nico's punch. What had she been thinking, throwing herself on Paula? If he wanted to, he could easily have killed her.

But, whatever they were up to, she wouldn't be much use to them dead, would she?

And there had been some method to her mad behaviour. She had gambled and somehow come up with a minor victory as, when she had regained her strength, she was able to verify.

She climbed painfully out of bed and bent down to look beneath the chest of drawers. There, nestling against her pile of uneaten bread and cheese, was the small pair of scissors, exactly where she had kicked them as she had flown at Paula.

She might not get out of here alive but now there was a chance she wouldn't be the only one.

* * *

Gabriel reckoned he'd done pretty well in surviving the grilling by DS Gill of the Ilford police, who had been nowhere near as friendly as on the occasion of their first meeting. Not that he blamed Gill personally.

Now Gabriel had returned to his uncle's office to make himself useful in Simon Waterford's cause. Despite the antagonism Simon had displayed towards him, Gabriel felt sorry for the poor sod. He wouldn't fancy being in his shoes.

The others were in the meeting room when he arrived and he headed for his cubbyhole. There was one call he could make which might help.

He found a half-drunk cup of coffee on his desk, still tepid. So someone had been borrowing his space. As he took his seat and lifted the phone he caught a faint whiff of scent – a woman then, probably Alison. That was OK by him.

First he tried the number of the villa in Majorca. The phone rang for a long time before a recorded voice cut in. He spoke no Spanish but he could imagine the sense of the message. He hung up and consulted the address book on his mobile – he had made a note of Sylvie's number. It was probably best to try her directly anyway as he had no particular desire to talk to Emile.

Just when he thought he was out of luck, the call was picked up. '*Allo?*' She sounded in a hurry. There was the snarl of traffic in the background.

'Sylvie, it's Gabriel. You know, the solicitor from England—'

'I know who you are, *idiot*. My memory is not so bad I forget someone I met two days ago.'

'Oh, sorry. Look, er, I need to ask you some more questions. Do you have a moment?'

'No. I am in Paris trying to get to the airport. And it's because of you.'

What?

'Because of me? I don't understand.'

'*Pff.*' She made a French-sounding noise that conveyed clearly that his lack of comprehension was no surprise. 'Your conversation with Emile freaked him out. All that talk of Mariana. He took an overdose of pills yesterday and I had to get him to the hospital to have his stomach pumped.'

Jesus.

'Is he all right?'

'He'll live. It's not the first time, though. He's not what you might call – robust is the word, isn't it?' She repeated it, pleased with herself. 'Robust.' It came out as *roe-boost*.

'Look, I am really sorry.'

'Is that the only word you know, Gabriel? There's no need to be sorry on my account because Emile is going to a home in Switzerland till he feels better and I have been conferring with his father here in Paris.'

'Sylvie, listen, before you go, I must ask you something.'

'You may ask me in person, Gabriel, because I am catching a flight to London. Come to my hotel this evening.'

It took a moment for the words to sink in. 'Oh, right. OK. Sure.'

She gave him the address and rang off. As he noted it on a pad he wondered if he'd survive the encounter.

* * *

Claire followed Steve out of the Pineapple Samba Studio in a leafy road in Maida Vale back to their car.

'OK. Where next?' he asked as he slid into the driver's seat.

'We must be mad, doing this,' murmured Claire, rearranging the map and phone book on her lap.

'Probably.' He didn't seem that bothered. 'Your boss was happy enough to let us get on with it.'

That was because Henderson had no more of a clue than they did, Claire thought. It was one thing checking out music joints and musicians on nights off, especially since it was part of her and Steve's agenda, but to waste their time when some poor girl was being kept prisoner on pain of her life seemed somehow frivolous. But then, the girl could as easily be the brains behind the whole business, laughing up her sleeve at the lot of them. In which case, what did it matter?

She issued a correction to herself. It mattered to find the two men who had knifed Geoff Hall to death and, very probably, Charlie Talbot as well. On the slenderest evidence – mostly the observation and hunches of a grown man who knitted sweaters in public – they had concluded these men were acoustic guitarists or mixed up with small-beer music performance in some way. Which, even in a city the size of London, was a not a large constituency. But large enough, it seemed. The manager of the Samba Studio, a room above the Pineapple pub which held weekend events and occasional daytime dance lessons, had not recognised the photos they had shown him. 'But if you can leave me some copies, I'll ask around,' he'd said, which was good of him.

It was better than nothing.

Jeremy was well aware some people thought him smug, as Meg liked to put it. He acknowledged to himself that his style was inclined to the breezily self-confident but other people never knew how aware he was of his own shortcomings. In his dark and private moments he was capable of acknowledging that he was one of life's chancers, seizing whatever opportunities came his way. Like Geoff Hall's cheque.

Years ago, when he'd set up his wine business, he'd been rather pleased with the name. Jeremy's Drinks Company said it all, in his opinion – simple and to the point, does what it says on the tin and all that. In those days, the Jockeys Disability Charity had hardly even been on his radar and it was some time before he'd even realised that they shared the same initials. It was pure coincidence. Later, when he'd observed the social advantages of being seen to do good, he'd become involved with the jockeys' charity as a trustee. It had tickled him being associated with two JDCs, as if it were some private joke.

When people started handing him cheques by way of charity donations made out to 'JDC', he'd never considered the possibility that he might put them through his business account. Of course he'd soon realised, after a genuine mistake with a £50 cheque, that it was possible. But he'd rectified that error promptly and promised himself he would never do such a thing in earnest. It would be quite against the grain. Besides, what on earth would be the point of risking his reputation for a piddling fifty quid?

He wished now, fervently, that he'd stuck to his principles. But, the way he looked at it, men only stuck to principles they could afford. It you trusted a millionaire to look after a thousand for you, what would be the point of him trousering it? But if you asked a starving beggar to put your pound in the church collection, he'd have to be a saint not to buy himself a loaf of bread instead. The millionaire was probably no more honest a man than the beggar, it was simply that he could afford to be.

And Jeremy couldn't always afford to be an honest man. The night of the charity gala last October when Geoff Hall, in a gesture he had no trouble affording, had written a cheque made out to 'JDC' for one hundred thousand smackers had been such an occasion. It had been a time of straitened circumstances for Jeremy, when creditors – one bookmaker in particular – had been threatening to go public. In addition, there had been the inspirational notion that, if he put the cheque into his business account, once his debts were cleared he would still have half the money left to spend on a decent horse. The kind of horse he'd always wanted but had never been able to afford. And, if it all worked out, the money would simply be a loan. The fact that he'd lent Geoff his own pen to write the cheque somehow seemed to set the seal of approval on the entire proceeding.

Now, as he stood in reception at the offices of Silver & Co., an opulent bunch of yellow roses in one hand and a bottle of vintage Louis Roederer in the other, he rehearsed what he would say to Alison. The flowers and the champagne were just a gesture, of course, but such gestures counted where women were concerned. Alison – a lovely girl, he'd known her since she was a spotty teen – would still be thanking him as he launched into his speech of apology. He would be mortified and embarrassed (that's what he'd say anyway) as he described how he'd spent the morning haranguing his accountant and racking his brains to get to the root of the mystery – which he'd now solved!

'You'll never believe it, my dear,' he said to her, letting his well-rehearsed enthusiasm fizz out of him.

'Can you keep your voice down please,' she said, halting him in mid-flow. 'There are people here trying to work.'

Jeremy smiled apologetically and turned the volume down. This wasn't going the way he had hoped. He'd been brought upstairs through a set of office rooms and ushered into one dominated by a large mahogany table. The space smelt of stale coffee and man hours spent toiling over some tedious legal issue. It was, frankly, a surprise to encounter Alison in here. A pretty fresh-faced young woman like her belonged on a terrace overlooking a well-tended garden or in an elegant town drawing room. He'd have been more confident of winning her round in such surroundings where, maybe, the flowers could have been arranged in a vase and the champagne broached. As it was, his gifts – barely acknowledged – had been dumped on the table next to a humming computer.

'It turns out – I've spent an hour on the phone with my accountant – that your father's cheque became muddled up with my wine business receipts. The charity and the company share the same initials, you see. It's never happened before. I'm most awfully sorry. Mortified and embarrassed actually. I—'

'So the cheque was paid into your company account.'

'Yes. I can't tell you how sorry I am.'

'Then please don't try, Jeremy. Just tell me when you intend to reimburse the charity.'

At least she seemed to have accepted that he had made an innocent mistake. She was making him feel about three foot tall but he felt inexpressibly grateful to her.

'I shall be doing that absolutely as soon as I possibly can.'

'And when will that be?'

'Well,' and this was his get-out-of jail card, 'as soon as I can sell Aquiline. I've had a good offer for him which I'm pretty sure will still be on the table.'

'So your company owns the horse?'

'Actually, no, but there's not enough liquidity in the business account at the moment so I'll make up the shortfall personally, but don't worry about it. I shall ensure the charity is reimbursed in full and, in recognition of my error, I shall match your father's generosity and pay the charity another hundred thousand off my own bat.' He smiled broadly at her – that should put her in a better mood.

'OK, then.' She didn't look all that thrilled, however. More like a school teacher who can see the extent of a fellow's crime but who chooses, on this occasion, not to press charges to the full. 'You do that, Jeremy. I shall be in touch with Freddy Fordham at the JDC to ensure that you do.'

'Alison, please. It was a genuine mistake.'

'I don't care. I only care that you put this right. And,' she stepped closer, her forget-me-not blue eyes unexpectedly fierce, 'that you stop sleeping with Holly behind Meg's back. Or I might tell the police about your mistakes.'

Jeremy's words had suddenly dried up.

She appraised him coolly, waiting.

'I promise,' he said. 'I'll sort everything out. Honestly.'

She stared at him for a moment longer then turned away. 'I suppose you're wondering what's going on here.'

Actually, it hadn't occurred to him to seek a reason for her presence in these offices, he'd been wriggling so hard on her hook.

She turned back to face him. 'Mariana has disappeared. Simon has received a demand for a million pounds for her safe return.'

'Mariana's been kidnapped?'

'Possibly. We can't be sure Mariana hasn't arranged her own disappearance. It turns out she's not the woman we all thought she was.'

'Really?' He kept a straight face. He couldn't afford to admit what he knew about Mariana's naughty past, he was on thin enough ice already.

'She used to work as an escort girl. And she swindled some young Frenchman out of money. It's possible she's attempting to do the same thing with Simon.'

'Good Lord.' He was genuinely surprised. He knew Mariana the former party girl, of course. But Mariana the swindler?

He looked at the disarray on the table – so this 'kidnap' was the cause.

'Who's that?' he asked, pointing to a full-faced photograph of a dark-complexioned girl with black hair and a broad smile.

'Mariana's sister. She met her off the train yesterday at King's Cross and that's from the station CCTV.'

'Good Lord,' he repeated, short of words for once. 'Is there anything I can do?'

She turned those judgemental eyes on him once again.

'Only what you've already promised, Jeremy.' There was a weariness in her voice, as if she were already preparing herself for disappointment.

He left the room determined to redeem himself in her eyes – and in his own.

Simon thought he saw a familiar figure disappearing into the distance as he returned to the office but he paid the sighting no mind. Any more than he did a bunch of roses and a bottle of champagne in the meeting room. He even tried to ignore the look of disapproval on Alison's face as he sat at the laptop and brought up his email screen.

'There's nothing new,' she said. 'I've been keeping an eye on it.'

All the same, he scanned his inbox. She was right.

'Did it go OK?' Her voice was neutral.

'Sure.' He had no criteria to judge his hours at the bank. He'd never asked for a million pounds in cash before and it had not been easy. Luckily, his association with the family bank in Leeds had smoothed the way to the right contact at the head office here in London. It had taken a while and he'd had to promise the earth but the money was being prepared for collection. 'I put up the yard as surety.'

'Oh, Simon.'

'What choice did I have?' He didn't mean to sound reproachful but couldn't help it.

'You mean, because I went back on my word to help you?'

'I understand why, Alison. You made your position quite clear.'

She'd found him in the early hours of the morning and told him she'd lost her faith in Mariana's innocence. She'd said it wasn't because Mariana had worked as an escort – she could understand why a girl making her way in a foreign country might resort to such a way of life, especially if she looked like Mariana.

'So it's the Emile business?' he'd said.

'Partly, though like you I'd like to hear her side of it. But I'm pretty sure she stole something from me.'

Then she'd told him about the missing folder and finding Mariana in Geoff's bedroom. Simon had argued against her – the folder could have been lost anywhere and, even if she had taken it, surely it was permissible to take a dossier of her personal details? You could argue that the information in the folder was really hers to dispose of as she saw fit.

But Alison hadn't seen it that way. It was as if the thought of Mariana searching her dead father's room had turned Alison against her. She'd told him that, in the circumstances, she could not raise money from Geoff's estate to line Mariana's pocket. And that's how things had stood when they entered the offices of Silver & Co. that morning.

Simon felt Alison's disapproval acutely. He'd been counting on his cousin – she'd never backed away from him on any issue before. But now he was on his own. And though he was no less determined to try and reclaim Mariana, to save her from harm and hear the truth from her own lips, he did wonder if he wasn't making the biggest mistake of his life.

Their uneasy silence was interrupted by the arrival of Clive who barged through the door with unusual speed. In his hand he held a large brown package.

He didn't know how exactly – some sixth sense alerted him maybe – but Gabriel became aware that something significant had taken place in the office. Voices were not raised and alarm bells did not ring, but all the same there was something approaching a collective intake of breath from down the corridor, followed by a general scampering of footsteps and urgent scurrying around. He overheard some kind of inquest being held with the lad in charge of the post room.

He slipped into the meeting room, where Simon, Alison and Clive were grouped around the table. They were standing, as if in shock, staring at the tabletop and obscuring what was on it from his view. He stepped up to have a look.

Amidst notepads, pens and coffee cups was a Jiffy bag from which spilled a bundle of golden hair.

'It's Mariana's,' said Alison in response to his unspoken question, though he had already worked that out for himself.

In all his time digging into the Brazilian girl's history, talking to friends and clients, examining photographs, he had never seen Mariana in the flesh. This mound of beautiful hair was the closest he had come to the real woman. He wanted to reach out and fill his hands with the soft weight of it – except that would be ghoulish. Like playing with a relic of the dead.

'It arrived about five minutes ago,' said Clive.

The door opened and Clive's secretary stepped into the room. 'Apparently it was left in the corridor outside the post room,' she said. 'They don't know exactly when but it couldn't have been long ago because people come in and out of the building all the time and it would have been noticed. They sent it straight up.'

Gabriel could see the label on the bag. 'Simon Waterford c/o Silver & Co. – Very Urgent' written in black felt tip. The letters were big and round, deliberately not joined up.

'How did they know where to send it?' he asked.

'Simon's yard has instructions to contact him here,' said Clive. 'Someone must have called them.' He pointed with a pencil to a sheet of paper lying next to the hair. 'This came with it. Don't touch. The police are sending a forensics bod over.'

The warning was unnecessary, Gabriel knew better than to handle anything that might crop up as evidence. But it didn't matter, the sheet of paper was clear enough. It was a colour print of Mariana's head and shoulders, her hair ragged and shorn and a suspicious red weal running down one side of her face. Unlike the last image of her, the eyes were alive and focused – and desperate.

Beneath the photo was a caption, also in black script. 'Pay up unless you want to see her lose more than her hair.'

'Jesus,' he said. 'There are some sick bastards in this world.'

Simon spoke for the first time. 'You see, Alison, not everyone is as cynical as you are.'

Gabriel suddenly realised that not all the tension in the room was generated by the exhibits on the table.

'I'm not cynical,' she said softly. 'I just think that there are many people who would sacrifice their hair for a million pounds.'

Gabriel looked again at the picture. She had a point. Arresting though the image was, it could easily be a fake.

Chapter Sixteen

Jeremy had given up smoking twenty years ago but after leaving Silver & Co. he marched straight into a newsagent and bought a packet of his once-favourite brand. On the pavement outside, he lit up his old friend and waited for the magic to envelop him.

He'd always imagined that, if he should lapse, that first drag would be like nectar to the soul. But the smoke curdled in his throat and gripped his chest in a band of steel. He pulled on the cigarette again. Coughed. The packet in his hand, once a reassuring companion and badge of youthful sophistication, now displayed a picture of a diseased lung. This was not how it was meant to be.

The meeting with Alison had shaken him. He was used to admiration from women or, at the very least, acknowledgement of his standing in the world. He was a sophisticated man of business, who knew his way up and down the social ladder. A fellow whose favour was sought and, in turn, graciously bestowed. A man not short of companions at the dinner table and in the bedroom. In the not-too-distant future, if things went well with his charity connections, he could envisage himself featuring on an honours list. Young Holly had seen that in him straightaway – once, in a moment of pre-coital humour, urging him to 'Arise, Sir Jeremy'.

But Alison had treated him with contempt.

She'd seen through his pretence of innocence, had dismissed his integrity with a flash of those icy blue eyes and, furthermore, threatened him over the conduct of his affair with Meg. He wasn't used to such treatment.

He'd read somewhere that, at the age of forty-seven, a man looks in the mirror and sees both the boy he once was and the old man he is destined to become. He'd scoffed at the notion at the time but it had stuck in his head. He would be forty-seven next month and the shadow of the first look in the mirror on that morning was already upon him.

There had been a lot of women in his life, most of them good-fun companions, but a couple had been of significance. How had he let them slip away? One had been a barrister, clever and resourceful. He'd lived with her for six years until, feeling broody, she'd lost patience with him and gone off with someone truly boring. She'd been married for eighteen years now and, boring or not, the marriage had produced three children. Jeremy was godfather to the eldest and took him to an England international at Twickenham every year – it was the closest he was ever going to come to being a parent.

And the other woman, a journalist of wit and passion, had been married when he'd fallen for her, though the marriage was already doomed. There'd been a window of six months when she'd been devoted to him and he could maybe have marched her up the aisle. But he'd dithered – marriage was such an irrevocable step! – and she'd thrown herself at someone unattainable in typical fashion. She was dead now. Lung cancer. Would pictures on cigarette packets have saved her? The thought was laughable.

But he was alive. There was still time for him to shoulder his responsibilities and grow up. Better late than never. Maybe he should drop his delusions of youth – after all, communication with Holly was of a limited nature – and face up to the future that was heading towards him with the speed of an express train.

He could redeem himself with Alison by making good on the money, as he had promised. If he cashed in his chips on Aquiline it would solve his problems at a stroke. And he was pretty sure there was a way of making it up to good old Meg. He might not ever be a parent but there was still time for him to be a husband.

But before any of this, there was a task he had to perform. If he pulled it off it would go a long way to repairing his reputation – in his own estimation if no one else's.

He must help find Mariana. He had a good idea where to start.

He chucked his fag end in a rubbish bin and the cigarette packet along with it.

Late afternoon in Hughie's wine bar and customers were thin on the ground. Jeremy could remember other summers when this place had been humming at all hours. Perhaps the Hampstead locals had learnt sobriety, though he doubted it. More likely they were ducking Hughie's prices and getting cranked at home for half the price.

He ordered a glass of Viognier at the bar to chase away the foul taste of that cigarette. So he really was an ex-smoker. Now to become an ex-rogue and philanderer and turn himself into a stand-up fellow. He looked around impatiently. Hughie was always here at this hour. In fact, Hughie was always here.

Eventually the proprietor emerged from the back room. He raised a hand in greeting but headed for the door.

Jeremy dashed to intercept him. 'Got a moment?'

'Not really, mate. Busy day today.'

'This won't take a second. I'm trying to trace a girl I saw in here the night before last.'

Hughie's face broke into a broad beam. 'Why am I not surprised?'

'A small dark girl – Latino type – quite cute.'

'Jeremy, there are dozens of cute girls in here all the time. You know that.'

'But you were talking to her for ages. She was wearing a top with glitter on it and a pink skirt.'

Hughie's pliable face screwed into a frown as he thought. 'Oh, her. She was just a kid blowing through. Haven't seen her since.'

'Well, I think she's Mariana's sister.'

Hughie's eyes widened. 'What, Mariana the Brazilian tart up in Yorkshire?'

'Yes. Only she's not in Yorkshire any more. She's gone missing. She came to meet her sister in London and disappeared. And Simon's got a ransom demand for her return.'

'Bloody hell.' After a moment Hughie's face broke

into a smile. 'Are you sure it's not a joke? She's probably had enough of all that fresh air and horseshit and just walked out.'

'They're demanding a million pounds for her safe return.'

Hughie shrugged. 'So? Anyone can send a ransom note. You can't blame her for trying to make a bit of money out of it.'

Jeremy could see he wasn't going to convince him. And, of course, it was quite possible he was making sense.

Hughie put his hand on Jeremy's elbow and turned him towards the bar. 'Look, I'm tied up just at the moment but I'll be back and in the meantime I'll have a think, see if there's a way of tracking down the girl you're after. Susie here will bring you a bottle of Chablis from my new consignment – my treat.' He spoke these last words to the barista by way of an order. He indicated a seat at the counter with a flourish. 'Back in a tick.'

Jeremy sat down, somewhat deflated. He thought he'd been on to something when he'd recognised the girl in the photo in the solicitor's office. He'd hoped to be able to nip in here and find how to contact her before revealing his discovery. It was hard to believe Hughie didn't have her number tucked away somewhere, he'd certainly been paying her plenty of attention. Maybe Hughie was worried he was trying to horn in on the girl himself. He pondered how to convince Hughie it wasn't like that.

As he turned the matter over in his head, Susie brought the wine and poured a sample for him to taste.

'The girl's called Paula,' she murmured as she waited for his reaction, 'and she's going out with Nico.'

He looked at her with surprise.

'Nico works in Hughie's music shop in Kilburn,' she continued. 'The Sound Store. What do you think of the wine?'

'Very nice,' he said. He'd barely registered the taste.

She arranged the bottle in a wine cooler. 'Just don't tell him you heard it from me.'

As she walked away he took his phone from his pocket. Time to start reclaiming his good name.

Simon was close to despair as he sat in the office staring at the unchanging laptop screen. This was the lowest point of the crisis so far and the chances were things could only get worse. He was on his own in the room. It was as if the force field of gloom around him had dispelled everyone else. Even Alison had disappeared – maybe out of respect for his feelings. Or possibly because she didn't want to continue their row about Mariana.

It was a relief when his phone rang and he snatched it up. Could it be instructions on how to deliver the money tomorrow?

He was surprised to hear Jeremy Masterton.

'Listen, Simon, I think I've got a handle on Mariana's disappearance.'

What?

'I noticed the photo of her sister when I was talking to Alison a couple of hours ago.'

So it was Jeremy who he'd seen disappearing down the street. It made no sense to Simon why Jeremy

329

should be involved in any of this but he listened intently.

'The thing is, I saw that same girl in a wine bar in Hampstead the night before last. That's where I'm ringing from now. I've discovered she's going out with a guy called Nico who works in a music shop in Kilburn called the Sound Store.'

'This is incredible news, Jeremy. I don't know what to say.'

'Let's not waste time. I'm going to head over to Kilburn now and see if I can find her. I'll keep in touch.'

And he rang off before Simon could even thank him.

He was frozen on the spot for a moment, taking in this unexpected twist of circumstance. The Jeremy connection did not compute but so what? Any news of Mariana, no matter how unlikely, was better than no news at all.

His fingers rattled on the laptop keyboard, bringing up the address of the shop in Kilburn. It only took a few seconds and then he was out of the door.

'Simon, where are you going?' Alison had emerged from Gabriel's cubbyhole and was calling after him.

He explained quickly.

She looked shocked, obviously as amazed as he had been on learning that Jeremy had knowledge of Mariana's sister.

'He saw the photograph when he was here but he didn't say he recognised her,' she said.

But that was neither here nor there.

'He says he's going over to this shop and so am I,' said Simon.

'What about the police? Have you told them?'

He gripped her arm fiercely. 'They said they'd kill Mariana if I told the police.'

'But you've already told them—'

'The kidnappers don't know that. But they will if I turn up with a load of cops. So you mustn't say anything, Alison. Sit tight and I'll call you soon.' And he dashed for the door.

Jeremy stood on the pavement outside Hughie's. In his experience it was a reasonable spot to catch a cab, though it might take a minute or two.

'Don't tell me you've polished off my booze already.' Hughie was back. 'Good wine should be savoured, you know.'

'Sorry, Hughie. I haven't got time to hang around. I've got an angle on that girl now.'

'You must be keen.'

'Not in the way you think. Anyway, it turns out she's got a boyfriend. That guy Nico who works in your shop in Kilburn.'

'Really? Who told you that?' Hughie's eyes glittered with curiosity.

'One of your customers who's got a better memory than you. The girl's called Paula. If I get a cab up there, the shop will still be open, won't it?'

Hughie glanced at his watch and pulled a face. 'You'll have to hurry. I'll run you up there myself, if you like. I've got the car right here.'

'I thought you were busy.'

Hughie grinned. 'What are friends for, eh? Come on.'

Jeremy followed him happily. He'd not spotted one

taxi in the course of their conversation, so this was a stroke of luck.

Alison listened to Simon's feet crashing down the stairs, her thoughts in turmoil as she tried to get a handle on the turn of events.

Gabriel was watching curiously from down the corridor and she beckoned him into the meeting room. She told him what Simon had said.

'You've got to tell the police,' he said. 'Go and ask Clive, he'll say the same thing.'

'But Simon expressly forbade it. And I've upset him enough already today.'

Gabriel nodded. She'd spent the last twenty minutes in his office, explaining the situation, and he'd turned out to be a good listener.

He grasped her problem. 'You don't think Mariana's really been kidnapped, do you? You're worried that Simon's going to arrive at this music shop and find her with her sister. And if the police turn up and arrest her, he'll blame you.'

She agreed that summed it up.

'But suppose,' he said, 'she really has been kidnapped.'

'Don't, please.'

'Look, Alison, there are things going on that you don't realise.'

They were sitting side by side at the table and he leaned forward, speaking softly. 'Your father commissioned a report on Mariana and was killed before he made proper use of it. A man called Charlie Talbot—'

She sucked in her breath at the mention of the

name, halting his flow of words. She had a premonition of what he was about to say.

'Talbot,' he continued, 'tried to buy that report off me and was murdered by the same people who killed your father – the police at Ilford told me this morning they've got a DNA link between the two crimes. I don't know what bearing these things have on Mariana's disappearance but it can't be coincidence. Somebody went to a lot of trouble to preserve her reputation.'

'So they could demand money for her return, you mean?'

'Yes, I suppose I do.'

'But who would be in a position to do that, or even know about your report?'

'I don't know. But if the people who killed your father and Charlie Talbot are holding Mariana, do you really want Simon charging off to confront them on his own?'

She felt the blood drain from her face.

'You're right. We must call the police. But I don't know where he went. Kilburn he said, that's all.'

Gabriel pointed to the computer screen on the table just a few feet away. It showed the home page of a music shop – the Sound Store in Kilburn.

That had to be it.

Jeremy followed Hughie down a flight of steps and through a door that led to the parking area beneath the block of flats just along the street from the wine bar.

'I rent a spot down here,' Hughie explained. 'Costs a fortune but it's bloody useful.'

He pointed to a black hatchback in the far corner. 'That's mine.'

As he opened the boot he said, 'I've got some stuff in the front. Do you mind helping me stick it in the back? So you can sit down.'

There were boxes of wine in the passenger well and some on the seat. Hughie took a couple and carried them to the back of the car. 'I just fetched these from up the road. I was going to send one of the kids down here to pick them up but I'll give you a ride first.'

'Thanks, Hughie.' Jeremy lifted the remaining boxes and carried them to the rear. He bent to manoeuvre them into the boot which, for a small car, was quite spacious. He would have said so if something hard and heavy hadn't slammed on to the back of his head.

He grunted as the blow fell again, this time smacking his face down on to the wine boxes then showering him with glass and liquid.

Hughie was hitting him with a wine bottle.

He tried to turn. 'Jesus, Hughie, what are you—?'

The words were lost as glass tore into his neck. He raised his hands feebly but he was trapped, twisted and slumped over half inside the boot. A hand gripped his shoulder and then a numbness squeezed his throat. He couldn't speak.

Hughie's face was six inches away, almost unrecognisable in the gloom of the garage. He was holding a broken bottle by the neck, its lethal points wet with wine and blood. He spoke urgently, the words tumbling out in a spit-flecked whisper.

'I tried to be nice to you, mate, but you wouldn't mind your own bloody business. You've served your purpose, I'll say that for you. But now you're just a flaming nuisance.'

And the bottle thrust forward again.

They'd left Mariana alone since they'd cut off her hair. She'd lain on the bed most of the day, her head still ringing from the smack Nico had landed. She'd studied her swollen face in the little mirror and the ruins of her once-beautiful hair and she'd wept. But bruises would fade and hair would grow. They'd not done anything serious to her. Not yet.

She'd retrieved the little scissors and put them in the back pocket of her jeans. If they searched her, they'd find them soon enough but what was the point of keeping her only weapon out of reach? The next time Nico raised his hand to her she promised herself she wouldn't be the only one to suffer.

Looking out of the window she'd calculated the possibilities of escape. They were zero. She was three storeys up. The old sash window itself was warped and sealed with paint so it wouldn't even open. There was no magic exit from this quarter.

She spent a long time surveying the view. Depressing strips of neglected gardens ran along the backs of these houses and, ahead, some fifty yards distant, stood the windowless brick wall of an apartment block. She craned her neck to see treetops lining the road of a cross street but the early autumn foliage was thick and she caught only the barest glimmer of traffic passing beneath. She could signal at this window all she liked but nobody would ever see.

What was she to do? She had no idea but unless she

could get them to open the door there was no chance for her to make a bid for freedom.

She banged on the door and shouted. It seemed nobody heard so she kept it up. Eventually there were footsteps but the door didn't open.

'Shut up.' A man's voice – Spider this time.

'Let me out,' she called. 'I need the toilet.'

Spider laughed. 'Use the sink,' he said through the door and shuffled off.

It might come to that, she thought with distaste.

She was helpless.

Simon was not a stranger to London but he was not familiar with the routes north of the Euston Road. He was entirely reliant on his satnav which was not a situation he enjoyed. In his experience, following a satnav blindly could get you more thoroughly lost than the dodgiest map navigation. Here in the big city, his complaint was that the on-board computer simply plunged him into the heaviest end-of-Friday traffic. If he only knew the back roads like a local he was convinced he could at least avoid a few traffic lights.

Every congested yard he crawled and every minute he fumed before a red light, he thought of Mariana, held prisoner in some squalid room, beaten and brutalised, her unique beauty crushed.

Then he imagined Mariana laughing with her sister, waiting for tomorrow's delivery of a million pounds of his money.

Which was it?

And how was he going to find out?

He didn't have a clue.

At the next traffic light he called Jeremy.

* * *

Claire wrinkled her nose. She was standing in the distinctly unglamorous bowels of the Black Boot Club where, in a few hours' time, she could imagine that a cheerful tipsy crowd and a hot band on the stage might make for a good night out. At the moment, though, the place was empty and stank of stale beer and disinfectant from the nearby Gents. When her phone rang, she dashed up the stairs with relief to get better reception. Steve could finish quizzing the harassed-looking guy behind the bar.

'Parker,' she growled, her habitual response during job time in case it was one of her male colleagues. The effort was wasted. It was Alison Hall.

'Claire, I've got some news.'

Claire couldn't make sense of all of it. She'd not heard of this Jeremy Masterton who claimed to have spotted Mariana's sister and Alison didn't know exactly where he'd seen her – a wine bar in Hampstead two days ago – but the gist of her message was plain: Paula was linked to an address in Kilburn, a music shop called the Sound Store. And Simon had gone dashing off there.

She waved Steve out of the basement.

'I know the Sound Store,' he said. 'Funny old place. You can buy anything from a didgeridoo to a PA system – not the greatest quality, mind. It's a couple of miles up the road just after an all-night chemists.'

Claire stared at him in surprise. 'How do you know that, Essex boy?'

'Because,' he looked momentarily embarrassed, 'my fiancée used to live around here. Her nephew played the saxophone so I've been in with him to buy reeds.'

'What fiancée?' It came out in a higher-pitched tone than she had intended.

'The woman I lived with before she decided that wasting any more of her life with a boring work-obsessed bastard like me would drive her round the bend. She went to live in Godalming with a DJ slash drummer who was trying to blag his way into local radio. The glamorous option, see. You're not the only one with a tortured romantic past, Parker.'

She got in the car and prepared to call Henderson. This could be a wild-goose chase or the breakthrough they were looking for. And the thought of the lovesick Simon Waterford charging around out of control had the potential to screw everything up.

But even as she framed the words to keep her report precise, questions were taking shape unbidden in another part of her head. What was the fiancée's name? How long had they been together? When did they split up?

It was most unprofessional of her.

All around was black and Jeremy was in pain. He lay on his side, doubled up, with hard objects pressing into his back and buttocks. There was a horrible sticky wetness beneath him, and movement, and a familiar smell. He tried to call for help but he could make no sound, it was as if his voice box had been disconnected. His face was on fire but that discomfort was superficial compared to the ache in his chest and the weird numbness in his throat. Something serious had happened to him.

His head cleared a little. He was in a vehicle and the wheels were close, rumbling over the road surface not far beneath his face where the suspicious liquid pooled. The smell was wine and he was lying face down in the boot of a car. Hughie's car. His old mate Hughie who had tried to kill him by stabbing him in the throat with a broken wine bottle. Who was probably still going to kill him. Take him somewhere and finish him off. Dump the corpse. Bye bye, Jeremy. So this was what happened when you decided to turn over a new leaf.

Hughie had said he'd served his purpose – what purpose was that?

He'd always been a good friend to Hughie. He knew things about him that others didn't. Had seen him at the time of the worst disappointment in his life. Had kept in touch with him – Hughie's one link to a world from which he had been excluded. Had thought he was doing the man a good turn.

But Hughie was a vicious little bastard after all, just like Phil Waterford had said when he'd kicked him out of Willowdale all those years ago.

Amidst the bumping of the road below and the shifting and clinking of the bottles in the boxes around him came another sensation. A familiar thrum from happier times. The vibrating of his phone.

Hughie hadn't taken it from him.

So maybe there was still a chance that he might live.

His phone was in his left hip pocket and he was lying on that side. One arm was pinned beneath him and he couldn't move it without shifting his entire body – and that would hurt very much. His other arm was free but to get to the phone he would have to twist his torso. Whichever way he did it, pain was a certainty. He might even rupture some vital part of himself and set the blood flowing again.

But the phone was his only hope.

He reached round with his free arm, tried to push his body up and turn. He'd been wrong – it wasn't pain so much as the awareness that parts of him had been ripped open. As if lying the way he was kept his wound together and turning like this – oh God!

But he had his fingers on the small plastic bar, scrabbling and tugging and finally pulling it clear. It had stopped ringing.

He lifted it to his face in the dark. His fingers were clumsy and stupid but surely he could remember how to work his own phone?

Suddenly it burst into life again and the small screen lit up in the dark. Simon was calling.

He pressed to take the call.

'Jeremy? Hi, can you hear me?'

He could hear him all right. The problem was, when he opened his mouth to reply no sound came out.

He'd forgotten. He couldn't speak.

'Here we are, on the left.' Steve slowed the car and parked on the other side of the road. He jabbed a thumb back down the street which comprised the usual mixture of convenience stores, charity shops and dodgy barbers found in this part of town.

Claire peered at the shop window, through whose murky panes could be seen an array of musical instruments: a row of acoustic and electric guitars racked on the wall and keyboards arranged around a shiny scarlet drum kit.

'Doesn't look like it's changed much,' Steve said. 'I reckon those drums were in the window last time I was in this neck of the woods.'

And when was that exactly? Claire wanted to ask but killed the urge.

She'd checked in with Henderson and they had their instructions. Park up with the shop in vision and intercept Simon Waterford before he could do anything stupid. Apart from that, sit tight until Henderson himself pitched up.

'Looks as dead as a doornail in there,' said Steve. 'Bet you this is a complete waste of time.'

Claire didn't respond. She wasn't in the mood.

Mariana heard banging from the floor below and a man's voice. Spider – he was the one who did all the shouting. She put her ear to the door to catch what he was saying.

'You've got one minute or I'm coming in there to sort the pair of you out. We've got to move *now.*' He sounded hyped up.

Then she heard footsteps on the stairs. He was coming up to her room. She moved rapidly away from the door and sat on the bed. There was the scrape of a key in the lock and the door burst open.

'Shift yourself. We're leaving right now.'

She remained where she was – why should she cooperate with this scum?

'Are you letting me go?' she demanded.

He didn't reply, just took two long strides into the room and grabbed her arm.

'Move, I said.' And he yanked her to her feet and pushed her out on to the landing.

'Where are you taking me?'

Not many men loomed over her but this one did. He lowered his face to hers. 'You want to get out of this alive? The best way is to keep your big mouth shut.' His eyes blazed and she could see in their black depths a desire to hurt. But she also saw something that gave her grounds for cheer. Panic. Something had happened to upset his plans and he didn't like it. Whatever it was, she was glad of it.

He shoved her towards the stairs ahead and she went down. Nico stood on the next landing, eyeing her descent. From the room behind him emerged Paula, buttoning her blouse. She ignored Mariana and demanded, 'What's going on?'

Spider said, 'I've just had a call. We can't stay here any longer.'

Paula looked like she wanted to debate the matter but Spider turned to Nico, 'Get the van,' he commanded and Nico vanished down the stairs without argument.

Mariana heard the sound of a door opening, then banging shut.

Spider was staring at her. He lifted his hand so she could plainly see what he was holding. 'We'll just wait here quietly till Nico gets back.'

Mariana said nothing. She wasn't going to argue with a panicky killer. But she slid her hand into her pocket and gripped the pair of scissors. It was not much of a weapon compared to his lethal-looking knife but it was all she had.

Claire and Steve spotted the man at the same time. He came out of the shop door and headed off briskly down the street in the direction they were facing.

'That's him,' Claire blurted. 'Tattoo man who was driving the car.'

Steve had his door open.

She grabbed his arm. 'What are you doing?'

'I'm not letting that bastard get away.'

'But Henderson said to stay here.'

'I don't work for Henderson. That man's a murder suspect and I'm going after him.'

And he was gone, loping down the street amongst the early evening crowd, staying on the opposite side of the road. She cheered him on even as anxiety chewed at her insides. She prayed that he'd be all right.

When they'd both vanished from sight she turned back to the shop.

Jesus – trust her not to be paying attention when it mattered.

Simon's frustration was boiling over by the time he spotted the Sound Store. There was a space in front of it and he jerked to a halt. The place looked deserted and a Closed sign hung on the door. There was no sign of Jeremy – he'd given up trying to call him. It looked like he was on his own.

He had no idea exactly what he was going to do. He just knew that if Mariana was there he was prepared to knock down walls to get to her.

He rattled the shop door but it held firm. Then kicked it in the hope it might fly open. 'Mariana,' he yelled. 'Are you in there?'

He heard a sound from within – a woman's voice.

Hands tugged at his arm, pulling him backwards. 'Mr Waterford – Simon!'

He turned to face Claire Parker. The sight of her infuriated him – he'd said no police!

'Please back away, Mr Waterford.'

'But Mariana could be in there.'

'If she is, then we will get her out. But the best way to get her out safely is for you to leave it to us.'

He recognised the determination in her face and turned away from her, back to his car.

But he was determined too.

First off, he needed something from the boot.

Spider swore under his breath at the noise from the door downstairs. Someone was banging on it. Then yelling.

Mariana could hardly believe it. She heard her name. It was Simon. She shouted back but Spider gripped her by the throat, cutting off the sound. He rammed her up against the wall, holding the knife high in his other hand so she could see it.

'Shut up,' he hissed. 'Or I'll rip you open.'

He pinned her there while the seconds passed. There was silence from downstairs now.

'He's gone,' Paula said.

Spider spoke to her, his grip on Mariana still firm. 'He won't have gone far. Can you keep her quiet while I go down and sort out that idiot?'

'Sure. No problem. Look.'

In her right hand, Paula was holding a gun.

Spider laughed softly. 'What a bundle of tricks you are. Just remember she's worth nothing dead.'

As he slipped away down the stairs, Mariana stared at her little sister in disbelief.

Paula stared right back, the gun rock steady in her

small fist. 'I don't understand you,' she said. 'You're smart enough to land rich men but not clever enough to make any money out of them.'

'When did you get to be such an evil bitch?'

Paula ignored the question. 'It's always the same with you, isn't it? You have to make a fuss. Just make it easy for us then maybe you'll get your share.'

'And if I don't?'

Paula said nothing, just raised the gun.

'But we're sisters.'

'Half-sisters. It doesn't count.'

Simon started the car and waited for the right moment. The road was four lanes wide and there was plenty of early evening traffic. But a light regulated the flow a block to his rear and he impatiently waited his chance to swing the car out across the empty road as if he were performing a three-point turn. But this turn had only two movements. He put the gear in reverse and slammed his foot on the gas. The car shot backwards across the pavement and smashed through the plate-glass shop front of the Sound Store.

The house beneath them seemed to explode. The stairs shook, glass shattered and the smell of smoke and dust billowed upwards.

Paula staggered and turned.

Mariana took her chance and ran at her.

Simon had calculated that the back of the car would shatter the window and the wheels would be stopped by the metal sill that abutted the pavement. But the vehicle had ridden over the obstacle and his rear end was buried inside the store.

The shock of the impact was singing through his body but he didn't care. He leapt from his seat and crashed into the interior, glass and debris crunching beneath his feet. He kicked something and a weird musical note rang out.

'Mariana!' he screamed.

A tall dark shape appeared out of the murk.

Simon instantly recognised the man who'd assaulted him on the train.

The shape flew at him, knife in hand. But this time Simon was ready.

He hit the man smack on the temple with the jack he had taken from the boot of his car.

The man staggered, dropped the knife, clutched his face and Simon chopped him down with a blow to the knees.

He stood over the man as he moaned and writhed. He raised the jack again. 'Where's Mariana?' he growled.

The man's reply – if he made one – was obliterated by the sound of a gunshot.

Mariana heard the gun go off in the same instant white-hot flame licked the side of her face, closing down all awareness of the world. But though her senses were switched off, her body was in motion. She thudded into the woman who had shot her and the pair of them tumbled down the staircase into the smoky chaos below.

Claire was cursing herself. Everything had gone pear-shaped from the moment Steve had scarpered down the road. She'd failed to intercept Simon Waterford and when she'd got him to back away from the shop he'd done the craziest thing she'd seen since she'd last watched a James Bond movie. Who did he think he was?

She'd called for the medics even as she'd run for the shop and was screaming into her phone as a sharp report obliterated her voice.

There were guns?

She froze in the maw of the shattered window. Ahead, inside the smoky, burnt-rubber-smelling, jangling shop she saw Simon Waterford standing over a figure on the floor, threatening him with a metal implement. But the shot had transfixed him too.

'What the bloody hell has been going on here?' said a grumpy voice from behind her.

She'd never thought she'd be so pleased to hear Henderson's voice.

The man at Simon's feet said, 'She's upstairs.'

Simon dropped the jack and headed for the back of the shop.

There were sirens sounding from the street and a voice yelled at him to stop but he ignored it.

He was a fool. He should have listened to caution, let the police handle it. He'd gone blundering in, playing stupid stunts, and all he'd done was panic the kidnappers into shooting Mariana – he was sure of it.

They might shoot him too. He didn't care.

And he didn't care what Mariana had done. He loved her. He knew that for certain.

He almost tripped over the two girls. They were lying locked together at the foot of the stairs, unmoving. A small handgun lay harmlessly on the floor a few feet away.

He dropped to his knees and brushed away the black hair that obscured the two faces.

A girl he didn't know stared at him. Paula. Her eyes were open but unseeing. A pair of scissors was embedded deep in her throat.

Other people were around him now, trying to pull him away, but he was rolling Mariana on to her back, urgently searching her face for signs of life. Her head flopped and her eyes were closed and there was blood on her face. But she was breathing.

Hughie concentrated on driving within the speed limit as he headed out of London. It wouldn't do to get done for speeding with a corpse in the boot.

He'd never killed anyone before – not directly, that is. What would be the point when he had two efficient assassins working for him already? But he'd wondered what it would be like and now he knew. It was . . . liberating.

His only regret was that silly old Jeremy had been his victim. He would have much preferred it if Simon Waterford had been lying back there in his place. But he'd have the money off Simon instead and that would have to do. Money he'd been owed for years.

After his mother had died, all those years ago, he'd been paid fifty thousand pounds. For a short while it had made him feel better about the way she and her husband had treated him. He'd even felt a fleeting pang of guilt. So she'd considered him after all. Fifty thousand pounds was a decent whack. Not that it made up for giving him away as a baby. A million would not make up for that.

But over time he'd realised that fifty grand was nothing. A drop in the bucket compared to what he could have been left. What he should have had. The family were worth a fortune and he was a blood relative. He'd been cheated.

He'd tried to forget it and get on with his life. After all, what could he do?

As it had turned out, he had done plenty. And he was still doing it.

Claire was anxious. It was bedlam in the shattered ground floor of the shop in Kilburn but gradually some order was being imposed. Ambulances and squad cars had arrived. The wounded were being tended. Scenes-of-crime personnel were starting to do their stuff.

So where was Steve?

She'd let him go off single-handed to face down a killer. If anything happened to him, it would be her fault.

'You've made a right mess of this place,' Steve's familiar voice came out of the blue. His approach had been hidden by the crush of medics and uniformed officers. His nose was encrusted with blood and he had a swollen lower lip. 'What's the score then?'

She stared at him with irritation and profound relief. 'We got Mariana but she's unconscious – looks like she's been shot. The sister's dead. And Simon Waterford demolished the building and half killed the suspect with the long fingernails. What happened to you?'

Steve shot her a lopsided grin. 'No sweat. I followed tattoo guy to his van, waited till he was getting in and grabbed him. Easy-peasy.'

'It doesn't look like it was easy.'

'Well, we rolled around on the pavement for a bit till I managed to give him a decent smack. The van's outside. Our pal's tied up in the back and Henderson's checking him out.' His smile vanished as he studied her closely. 'Are you all right, Claire?'

She nodded. Playing it cool like him. All in a day's work – though there'd never been a day like this one.

Chapter Seventeen

Hughie parked up close to the parapet, the rear of the car just a couple of feet away. All he had to do, he reckoned, was manoeuvre Jeremy out of the boot and pitch him over the small wall. It was a fifteen-foot drop to the water beneath so there would be a fair splash. But it was dark and he'd been driving for hours. He didn't have a better plan. He'd never disposed of a corpse before.

It would be late by the time he got back to town. He hoped to hell the boys had managed to move the girl as instructed but he didn't dare call again. No need to take unnecessary risks.

Jeremy looked a disgusting mess in the internal light from the boot. His face was slack and grey, covered with wine and blood. The thought of touching him made Hughie's skin crawl but now was no time to be squeamish. He grabbed Jeremy's ankles and pulled, intending to straighten the body out. The legs yielded with a leaden, gooey reluctance. So what they said about rigor mortis wasn't true – or maybe he'd not been dead long enough. Hughie didn't care, he was just thankful.

He yanked harder, aiming to pull Jeremy's lower half out of the car. Then, if he grabbed him by the arms, he should be able to tumble him forward and on to the parapet. He could easily shove him over after that.

He struggled to turn the corpse on to its back and then prop it, half sitting, against the boxes of wine. Jesus, it stank. He straightened up to get a breather and something clattered on to the floor.

A mobile phone.

He picked it up. Of course Jeremy had a phone – everyone did. He should have checked his pockets back in London.

But so what? The guy was dead. They might track the phone signal to here but they'd probably have found the body by then anyway. He didn't have anything to weigh it down with – and corpses floated, didn't they?

He didn't care. If he got rid of Jeremy and dumped the phone somewhere else, with luck he'd have enough time to get out of the country. Simon was due to cough up the money tomorrow. He wasn't going to hang around after that.

Time to chuck Jeremy into the water. One last effort. He took a deep breath and looked at Jeremy's lifeless face.

Then Jeremy opened his eyes.

Good God. He wasn't dead.

Hughie stared, paralysed.

Suddenly Jeremy swung his right arm up, burying his fist deep into Hughie's thigh.

Sweet Jesus, that hurt!

Hughie grabbed Jeremy's arm and pulled it free

from his leg. The glass shard glinted in the moon-light.

The bastard's stabbed me, Hughie thought, and the realisation spurred him to heave the now-limp Jeremy to his feet.

A pivot and a push and he was gone over the edge.

There was indeed a hell of a splash.

Hughie sat heavily in the open mouth of the car boot, uncaring of the smelly wetness that grabbed at the denim of his jeans. He managed a smile of relief. If Jeremy hadn't been dead before, he would be now.

He examined his wound. It was hard to see exactly how much damage Jeremy had caused but he could feel warm liquid welling up from the top of his thigh. It must be a nasty cut but he didn't have time to worry about it now. He had to be on his way.

God, he felt knackered. He'd leave in just a moment.

Gabriel had not had time to go home and change. Sylvie was not impressed. She herself wore a black trouser suit over a white blouse with her hair pulled back off her face, giving her a distinctly mannish look.

He stood in the hotel foyer – plush burgundy carpet, mahogany panelling and flunkies in tailcoats – and fell back on boyish charm.

'Sylvie, you look incredible. I didn't know I was meeting a film star.'

Her hazel eyes narrowed. 'And you look like shit.'

The charm didn't always work.

Fortunately he had means of getting in her good books. Alison had asked him – instructed him – to remove the flowers and champagne that were cluttering up the office. 'I don't want them,' she'd said and he'd not looked the gift horse in the mouth.

Neither did Sylvie. 'They are very beautiful,' she said as she accepted the roses. 'And your taste in champagne is not bad for an Englishman.'

Seizing on her improved mood, he suggested adjourning to the bar.

'You think I want to be seen anywhere with a scruffy man like you? No. Come with me.' And she marched to the lift and took him up into a room as palatial in style as the reception hall downstairs. He could have fitted his studio flat inside it twice over.

Once inside the door she kicked off her shoes and, to Gabriel's alarm, shrugged off her jacket and began to unbutton her blouse.

'Well,' she said, 'don't just gawp at me, pour me a drink. You'd better open the champagne that's in the fridge because yours won't be cold enough.' And she stepped out of her trousers, leaving them in a heap on the floor as she headed for a door on the far side of the room. Her retreating figure did not look in the least mannish.

By the time he'd found glasses and opened the wine, she had emerged wearing a long white towelling robe with the hotel crest on the pocket. She tucked her feet beneath her on the sofa, took a hearty sip of champagne and sighed with what sounded like satisfaction.

'I'm sorry about Emile,' Gabriel said. 'Monsieur Lambert must be upset.'

She shrugged. 'Sure but he is always upset by Emile. His mother has gone to Switzerland to take care of him so I am off the case. At last François has given me something worthwhile to do.'

'He's pleased with you then,' he ventured.

'I suspect not but he can hardly fire me considering what I know about Emile. He's sent me here to represent him at meetings with some of your MEPs.' She looked around the suite. 'Thank God I'm out of Majorca.'

He nodded, wondering whether now was the right moment to fish for information.

She appeared to read his mind. 'Order some food from room service then you can ask me your questions.'

He rushed to top up her glass but left his own untouched while he located the menu. It was important – to others, if not to himself – to loosen Sylvie's tongue.

Alison carried the coffee back down the hospital corridor to where Simon sat in a drab alcove. He took the polystyrene cup from her with a nod of thanks.

They had been banished from Mariana's bedside, leaving her to the medics. Another inch to the left, they'd been told, and the bullet that had robbed her of consciousness would have taken her life. All they could do now was wait and hope. It was particularly hard for Simon.

Claire Parker had told Alison what had happened earlier at the shop in Kilburn and described Simon's role in the mayhem. Alison couldn't reconcile this account with the cool and reserved cousin she'd known all her life. Even the notion that Simon would purposely damage his car didn't seem credible, much less that he would deliberately drive it through the window of a shop. And then he'd incapacitated one of the men who'd killed her father.

She lifted her free hand to his face and stroked his cheek. He didn't respond. He seemed out of it, exhausted by events and utterly preoccupied. Her heart went out to him.

Even as a boy he'd looked after her. And she wished she could help him now. It had to be love which had driven him to walk through walls and rescue Mariana. But the Brazilian girl lay in a coma, out of reach. Only she could tell them what had really gone on in that house – and if she had intended to kill her sister. But whether she would tell the truth was another matter.

Saint or sinner? As far as Alison was concerned, the jury was still out.

But it transpired that it wasn't just Mariana's fate that was monopolising Simon's thoughts.

'It was Jeremy who told me about the Kilburn shop,' he said.

'Yes.' He'd already told her that.

'He'd said he was going up there too. I tried calling but I couldn't get through. There was no sign of him at the shop and I forgot about him. But I've just found this on my phone. Look.'

He handed it to her and she read the text message on screen: 'Your brother hughie is to blame i told him everything very sorry the horse must go to jdc the rest to meg tell alison sorry too j'.

She read it twice. 'What does it mean "Your brother Hughie"? You don't have a brother.'

'That's what I thought.'

'But you don't – how could you?'

He took another sip of his coffee, put the cup down on the floor, looked her in the eye. 'When I read that message, something clicked. A memory from the yard when I was little. I just called Ken – he knows everything that went on at Willowdale. He says that back in the eighties, Dad took on a lad who didn't fit in. A long-haired lazy southerner, was how Ken put it. The boy could hardly get out of bed in the morning, didn't care for horses, mucked up every task he was given and was only interested in playing his guitar. And smoking dope. Ken couldn't understand why Dad kept him on, anybody else would have been out on their ear in under a week.

'After a few weeks he asked Dad what was going on because the lad, Trevor Hughes, was upsetting the whole place. You know what yards are like. It's a big machine and every tiny part has to work or else you get a breakdown. Anyway, Dad told Ken it was a family matter. He'd taken Trevor on to please my mum and they'd have to put up with him. The next day, the lad disappeared, taking three grand in cash that the secretary was intending to bank and some jewellery of Mum's from the house. Ken was all for ringing the police but Dad said no. Then he explained that Trevor was Mum's son, born when she was fifteen after she'd hopped into bed with a married man. The man had taken custody of the baby and brought him up down south as part of his own family.'

Alison was speechless. Aunt Rose pregnant at fifteen! Things like that happened in lots of families, and these days some didn't even keep them secret. But not then – and certainly not the Waterfords.

'So,' Simon continued. 'It turns out I have a brother

357

– a half-brother. And I remember him in a vague sort of way. The long hair, the earring – he didn't look like anyone else. I was only five or six. But I called him Hughie – he hated the name Trevor. I remember that.'

Alison was thinking hard. 'Who else would have known about him? Your mum and dad obviously. Mine too, surely – though Dad never said anything to me. We can ask Clive, he'll know.'

'And Jeremy, it seems,' said Simon. 'Jeremy's had a share in horses at Willowdale for years. Maybe that's how he knew about Hughie.' He looked again at the text message. 'This is worrying though. All this apologising. And what's this about leaving things?'

'I know what that means. He wants Aquiline to belong to the Jockeys Disability Charity. And the rest of his belongings to go to Meg.'

Simon stared at her. 'But Jeremy's not dead.'

'Have you tried calling him again?'

'Several times but his phone's turned off.'

Alison wasn't one to anticipate catastrophe but she had a bad feeling about this.

'So,' Sylvie licked her fingers fastidiously and reached for a serviette, 'what was it you were so curious to know? Or was your curiosity limited to my legs?'

She stretched one out towards Gabriel, gleaming and golden, her bare foot long and elegant with coral-painted toes. She was entirely feminine, so how come he could picture that appendage landing with crippling force on a sensitive part of his anatomy?

Sylvie had eaten well. He imagined her journey had given her the appetite to polish off a plate of crab cakes and to tuck into a T-bone steak as big as the plate it was served on. Now she'd finished chewing on the bone and had washed it down with her third – or fourth – glass of wine. She seemed content to wait before assaulting her dessert. If she wasn't in a compliant mood now she never would be.

'When you were driving me to the airport the other day,' he began, 'you said something about Mariana's sister.'

'Paula. What about her?'

'You said she was the worst. What did you mean by that?'

She shrugged and the neck of her robe gaped. Gabriel tried to ignore it. 'Just that, of the two of them, she was the one to really avoid. She might be the younger but she's the hard one.'

'Would you like to tell me exactly how you found that out?'

She hesitated. 'You are not intending to talk to Emile, are you?'

'How could I? I don't even know where he is.'

She nodded. 'True. But if you should run into him in the future, I would be very upset to discover that you had told him what I will reveal to you.' She fixed him with a steely look and, unconsciously maybe, swung her foot to and fro.

'Sylvie, believe me, I would not dare upset you.'

'Good.' She smiled craftily. 'Come and sit next to me then and I will tell you.'

Gabriel did as he was told and took his place beside her on the sofa.

Claire found Steve outside the police station, leaning against the wall. He looked all in.

'Have you heard the latest?' she said, knowing full well he hadn't because Henderson had only just told her. 'They've found this Hughie bloke in Surrey.'

The man Steve had arrested had started talking even before they'd got him in an interview room and, as a result, DS Shepherd and another officer had been despatched to Hampstead to find Hughie.

Claire eagerly relayed the news.

'There was no sign of Hughie at the wine bar. The staff said he'd vanished at about half past five, which was severely out of character. While Shep was interviewing one of the bar staff, the phone went. It was some copper calling from Surrey about a Trevor Hughes. The girl who answered the phone didn't recognise the name but the copper wouldn't be put off. He'd got a body and a car registered to Trevor Hughes at the wine bar address.'

'A body?' Steve perked up.

'Two, it turns out. Hughes is Hughie, of course, and his car was parked overlooking a reservoir. The boot was wide open and he was sitting in it in a pool of blood. The femoral artery in his leg had been severed and he'd bled to death. The other body was in the water, just below the car.'

'And who's that?'

'We don't know for sure but it's probably the fellow who's missing. The one who tipped Simon off about the place in Kilburn.'

Steve pulled a face. 'Jeremy Masterton. Poor sod. He owns a bloody good racehorse, you know.'

'Not any more, he doesn't.'

* * *

Gabriel's phone rang at just the right time. Another five minutes of sitting on the sofa with Sylvie, her robe slithering from her tanned body with every Gallic shrug, and he might have ended up as her dessert instead of the summer pudding on the room-service trolley.

As it was, he made his excuses, with many apologies, profuse thanks and an offer of dinner another night (brusquely turned down) and rushed to answer Alison's summons to the hospital.

He found her down some labyrinthine corridor, sitting with Simon. The pair of them looked drained and shocked – as was he, once they'd told him what had happened at the shop in Kilburn.

So Paula was dead.

'How's Mariana?' he asked.

'She's unconscious,' Alison replied. She'd done all the talking so far. Simon sat as if in a trance, staring straight ahead. 'We're just waiting for news.'

Gabriel nodded. Now was as good a time as any to tell them what he had just found out.

'It wasn't Mariana's idea to blackmail Emile.'

Simon slowly turned his head.

'Paula took the photographs of him doing drugs. She was the one who went to Emile's father and demanded money to keep quiet.'

'But Mariana must have put her up to it.' Alison's voice was cold.

'Not according to Sylvie. François Lambert paid Paula off and Mariana freaked out. She offered to try and get the money back. She disowned her sister and swore she'd never speak to her again.'

'It could have been an act.' Alison was a hard woman to convince.

361

'Sylvie didn't think so and, honestly, if Sylvie believed her, you should too.'

'But you said,' Simon spoke for the first time, 'that Emile thought she'd betrayed him.'

'He did – still does. But that's because his father and Sylvie told him Mariana was the blackmailer. As part of the pitch for money, Paula had pointed out that her sister had been working as an escort. François didn't want his son to have anything to do with either of them. Not good for the political profile and all that.'

'So Mariana didn't try to embezzle money?' Simon almost beseeched him.

'No. According to Sylvie, it was Paula.'

'And so there's no reason to believe she tried to embezzle money from me either.' Simon looked a hundred per cent happier than when Gabriel had arrived.

'She's not exactly Mother Teresa,' Alison said.

Simon turned to her. 'I can live with that,' he said. 'If she comes through.'

A nurse was walking briskly towards them.

'Mr Waterford, she's conscious.'

Simon was on his feet. 'Is she going to be all right?'

'The doctor seems to think so. Why don't you go and see for yourself? She's asking for you.'

But the suggestion was unnecessary. Simon was running down the corridor towards the ward.

Alison watched him go. She was smiling at last, Gabriel noticed. She was really very pretty.

'Shall we go too?' he asked. He was curious to finally see Mariana.

Alison shook her head. 'Not yet. Why don't you just stay here with me?'

That was fine with him.

* * *

Mariana was in a bed hooked up to banks of equipment. Medical staff hovered. There was a dressing on the right side of her head where even more of her hair had been shaved away. Simon ignored it all and focused on the life he saw pulsing in her eyes.

Her hand closed on his and her grip was strong.

'I'm sorry,' she murmured.

'I'm not. You're here and you're alive – that's what matters.'

'Where's Paula?'

So she didn't know? But how could she?

It was up to him to break the news.

'I found you both at the bottom of the stairs. You were unconscious and, I'm sorry, but your sister was dead.'

Mariana closed her eyes. 'How?' she said finally.

'She had a wound in her throat. There were some scissors. Can you remember what happened?'

Her head moved painfully on the pillow in a gesture of denial. 'The scissors were all I had. She had a gun. I only remember her firing at me.'

'She nearly killed you,' he said.

Instead, Mariana had killed Paula as she'd thrust the small blades ahead of her and they had tumbled down the stairs together.

The realisation had dawned on Mariana too. 'I'm such a bad person,' she said.

'No, you're not. She tried to murder you. You acted in self-defence.'

'It's not just that, Simon. There's so much you don't know about me.'

He bent close, till his face was just inches away

363

from hers. 'I think I know everything and it doesn't matter a jot. And you'll have plenty of time to tell me the rest after we get married.'

'But—' she started to protest but he stopped her in the best way possible, with a very tender kiss.

Epilogue

October

Mariana had never been to Newmarket before. She had heard about it all her life from her father, who used to refer to it as 'headquarters'. He'd worked at a yard there when he was starting out, he'd told her, though like a lot of Papa's stories she wasn't entirely sure that a story wasn't all it was.

He had made his experiences in English racing sound very glamorous and it had never occurred to her to question them when she was little. But as she'd grown older and seen her father fall further into the grip of his alcoholism, she'd come to the conclusion that his past in his home country could not have been that successful. If he'd seen glory days at Newmarket and Epsom and Ascot, how come he was scraping a living on second-rate tracks in Brazil?

It seemed disloyal to question her father now. He would have been proud to think of her travelling to Newmarket with a runner who had a chance of landing a Group One race. Aquiline was listed as favourite for the Middle Park Stakes, a contest that was supposed to be an indicator of who might fare well in the first three-year-old Classic of the following season, the 2000 Guineas. And she was the girl entrusted with the task of keeping the temperamental animal in line and delivering him to his jockey in sound enough mind to harness all of his considerable ability.

She had begged Simon to be excused from the task. She didn't want to be seen in such a public arena. She'd barely ventured from Willowdale following her release from hospital – just a trip to the hairdresser to repair the massacre Paula and the doctors had wrought. She was fearful of what people knew about her, what they might say. She had once worked as an escort girl and people had died because of her. It was shameful. And some had good cause to hate her.

Alison, for one. If Mariana had never come to Willowdale, Geoff Hall would still be alive. That had to be reason enough for Alison to loathe the ground she walked on. Yet Alison had apologised to her as she lay in her hospital bed. Apologised for doubting that she had been held captive and for refusing to help Simon raise the money for her release. It seemed Alison did not wish her dead, or gone from her life – she didn't even blame her. Mariana found that hard to understand.

Alison had even asked her if she would help in running the refuge for retired racehorses that she was establishing in the grounds of her home. There was more to it than that, because it was to function alongside specially outfitted accommodation for injured jockeys. Meg and Holly were involved too, both women who had been left bereft by Jeremy's death. They had gone out of their way to be kind to her and she couldn't understand it. Because of her, Jeremy was dead and they had both loved him, in their fashion.

As for her, she was still trying to make sense of the part Jeremy had played in her life. He had introduced her to Simon and for that she was eternally grateful. But he had also told Simon's jealous half-brother all about her and that, so she'd been told, was the reason why men had died and she had been kidnapped.

Alison had once said she was thinking of selling Jennifer Eccles because the horse was bad luck. The truth was, it was Mariana, not the horse, who was jinxed. If she was Simon or Alison or anyone connected with Willowdale she'd have sent herself packing. She'd lied and stolen things – that folder – and she'd trailed murder and bloodshed in her wake. Yet these people still wanted her in their lives. A girl who'd killed her own sister. She had to be the worst luck going.

She tried to say this to Simon but he'd smooth over her fears, then shut her up with a kiss. She supposed she could understand. He'd risked his life and reputation for her. The gauche repressed Yorkshireman had laid everything on the line in her cause. He was blinded by love, that was plain, and the wedding was still planned for November.

Only Ken had heard her out. He'd leaned on the door of the box while she was massaging one of the horses and let her reveal the extent of her self-loathing. And after she'd talked she'd felt better. And all he'd said was, 'The horses like you, girl, so you can't be all bad.'

She guessed that had to be good enough.

* * *

Simon watched Holly lead Aquiline round the parade ring. He'd have liked Mariana to perform that task but knew she'd have hated the public gaze. It was appropriate for Holly to lead the horse that Jeremy had owned. It was still listed as his on the card and had attracted a lot of added publicity on that account. Fortunately the animal himself was unaware that the spotlight was on him as much for the murder of his former owner as for the likelihood of him landing the race.

Freddy Fordham and Alison stood by Simon's side. Freddy was all smiles, as well he should be with the prospect of his son Neil landing a significant victory on an animal that would soon be officially owned by the charity he represented. Though Jeremy's dying wishes had been conveyed by the unorthodox means of a text message, legal opinion deemed that they were valid.

The three of them were the only people who knew the truth of Aquiline's proprietary rights. Considering the circumstances of Jeremy's death, it was only right that his memory should not be sullied by the suggestion that he had stolen a charity donation to buy himself a racehorse. At least, Simon thought, he'd had the nous to buy himself a good one. If Aquiline pulled off this race, Jeremy would have turned Geoff's generous donation into a small fortune and the charity would benefit many times over. In a funny sort of way, Jeremy deserved the glowing obituaries his death had generated.

Simon could see the nerves in those around him. Freddy's smile grew tighter and he was making a lot of bright chit-chat to Alison, who said nothing, chewing nervously on her bottom lip.

He himself felt the tightness in his chest magically dissolve, the way it did before a race when the whole business was about to pass out of his hands.

Thank God for racing, he thought to himself. It had brought him back to sanity since the madness in London. Every time he'd felt himself becoming obsessed by what had happened he had fallen back on the everyday demands of running a big training yard.

The police had told him some of what the two killers in custody had revealed. Hughie – his brother – had been driven by the belief that he'd been cheated of his birthright. Simon wondered why his parents hadn't told him he had a half brother. If he'd known about Hughie, he could have made his peace with him, couldn't he? At least he could have tried.

Mariana had met Hughie – briefly, she said. She'd thought he was a minicab driver. And Jeremy, it turned out, had known him for years. Had been a regular at his wine bar where he'd gossip about Willowdale – according to the girls who worked behind the bar. And that's what had led to murder and kidnap.

Sibling jealousy was a poisonous thing. Mariana had ended up killing her sister. But Simon wasn't going to blame her for that – she blamed herself enough already.

'OK, boss, what's the deal?'

Neil was looking up at him, waiting for his instructions for the race ahead.

They were simple – a six-furlong race along a straight track did not lend itself to complicated tactics.

John Francome

'Just ride him as you find him,' Simon said. Anyone could be a trainer at moments like this.

Claire took the tops off a couple of beers and looked for the nachos in the kitchen cupboard.

'Parker.' The shout came from the living room. 'Hurry up, they're off in a moment.'

She was in a particularly good mood this afternoon – for one thing, it was rare for her and Steve to have the same time off. But the real reason was that she'd finally got to Carla, the chain-smoking boss of the Chrysalis Girls escort agency. At first the woman had not cooperated. But when the two knife-killers in custody had uncovered her relationship with Hughie, Carla had indicated she might reveal more were she to be promised immunity from prosecution. Henderson had not been inclined to show any kind of mercy to a jumped-up old prossie, as he put it, but he'd changed his tune after someone from on high had had a quiet word. It seemed Carla had influential friends.

So a deal had been done and the madam had talked freely of her past association with an escort girl known as Fabiana and her plans for a stable worker called Mariana. The girl had been the unwitting means of fleecing a rich French boy, undone by the intervention of her greedy younger sister. When she'd retired to London to lick her wounds, Carla and her sleeping partner in Chrysalis Girls, Felix Alves, had provided her with a home and a notional role in one of Alves's legitimate companies. The aim had always been to fix her up with another suitable man – purely out of friendship, of course.

At first, Carla had thought that one of Hughie's

370

friends would fit the bill. She'd known Jeremy Masterton as an occasional user of her online service and he appeared to have money. But the appearance was deceptive and, anyway, it turned out he'd once bought an incall with Fabiana. But he agreed – for Mariana's sake – to squire her around his racing circle. Before long she'd caught the eye of the most successful trainer of thoroughbreds in Yorkshire, a man who saddled horses worth millions.

So far, Carla had claimed, her scheming may have been self-serving but it was hardly evil. Matchmaking, after all, whether for the short or long term, was her trade. But she admitted she'd made a mistake in mentioning her plans to Hughie. She wasn't to know of his special interest in the affairs of Simon Waterford or the lengths to which he might go to turn this unlikely romance into an instrument for his own revenge. Through Jeremy, Hughie had got wind of Geoff Hall's suspicions – he'd admitted he'd hired a private detective to investigate Mariana. Carla swore on her mother's life that she'd known nothing of the assassination on the train that Hughie organised. She admitted, however, that she herself had told Hughie about Charlie Talbot threatening to expose Mariana. Just as she'd passed on the information, gleaned from a former Chrysalis Girl who'd had a baby, that an investigator was still at work looking into Mariana's background.

Claire concluded that it was at that point that Hughie and Carla – despite her protests, the old buzzard was plainly culpable – decided to adopt plan B and hold Mariana to ransom. With the wedding months off and the threat of exposure still not extinguished, Paula had been summoned from Brazil by the promise of a decent pay-off and she had lured Mariana to London.

Steve's voice came again. 'For God's sake, Parker, I'm dying of thirst.'

'Yes, your lordship,' she called with maximum sarcasm.

His long legs seemed to take up half the space in front of the television.

She put the beers and eats on the coffee table and he grabbed her round the waist, seating her comfortably on his lap.

On the screen horses were being ushered into the starting stalls.

'This is the life,' he said, gulping from the bottle and fingering the neck of her shirt. 'Horses, beer and loose women. London's intrepid crime-fighters enjoy their day off.'

'Speak for yourself.'

'You're not enjoying yourself?'

'I'm not loose. And you can do my blouse up again. Dad might come back any moment.'

'Your dad won't mind. He thinks I walk on water now I'm going to take you off his hands.'

She didn't contradict him – she had a strict regard for the truth.

'Why won't that horse go in the starting thingy?' she asked.

'Because he's a temperamental bugger. That's Aquiline.'

'The one who's going to win us a honeymoon in the Maldives?'

'Skegness more like, at his price. But that's Simon's

horse, used to belong to poor old Jeremy. The neurotic one Mariana keeps sane. See, he's in now.'

Claire was suddenly interested. The gates flew open and they were off. The animals looked fantastic, all raw power and silky grace. She'd forgotten how much she enjoyed racing. And they could go any time they chose, they had a standing invitation to join the Willowdale team.

'How's he doing?' It was hard to tell one horse from another but two of them were drawing ahead of the rest of the runners.

'Aquiline's out in front with the French horse. They're the two favourites.'

The two animals were neck and neck, the rest appeared to be going backwards.

'Come on, Aquiline,' she shouted. This was exciting. She found herself thoroughly immersed in the thrill of the moment as she bounced up and down on her future husband's lap.

Simon watched the race from the owners' and trainers' stand with Mariana.

'This is close,' he murmured into the shell of her ear, now fully exposed by her radical new haircut. She'd told him she was going to keep it short from now on, if that was all right with him. He'd said she could shave her head bald if that's what she wanted, it would make no difference to how he felt about her.

'Aquiline always does just enough,' she said. 'He is very lazy – I've told him.'

'You're sure he's going to win?'

She said nothing, just nodded, her eyes rapt.

Around them was excitement. The professionals

and their connections were as caught up in the moment as everybody else.

The leading horses were emerging from the Dip, a slight but significant trough in the course which inclined upwards for the final furlong.

The French horse appeared to falter as he looked ahead at ground which rose well beyond the finish line. Aquiline took no notice but sped on. He knew where the winning post was.

The race took just seventy seconds. Standing there next to the girl he loved, with the certainty that the race would be won, Simon wanted to freeze the moment. Life couldn't get better than this.

But as Aquiline crossed the line to win by a length and Mariana leapt into his arms, he realised it just had.

Final Breath

John Francome

Eighteen painful months ago, jockey Danny Clark's fiancée Kirsty was murdered. Now he's found happiness again with her best friend Tara – though it seems strange to move Tara into Kirsty's place in the cottage at Latchmere Park, the training yard run by his mother Christine. But with Tara by his side, Danny can try to forget that Kirsty's killer is still at large.

Tara is on a knife edge. She's focused not on her future with Danny but on the past she's desperate to leave behind. A trainee solicitor from Manchester, Tara knows enough to put her corrupt former employer and his drug-baron client in prison for years. Till the case comes to court she needs sanctuary, and she prays this country refuge is beyond the reach of the inner-city gunmen. It had better be – she has nowhere left to hide.

Acclaim for John Francome's thrillers:

'Thrills to the final furlong' *Daily Express*

'The story races along . . . Realistic enough to excite a confirmed non-racegoer' *Scotsman*

'Teases to the very end' *Country Life*

978 0 7553 5295 1

headline

Dark Horse

John Francome

What kind of person are you? If you caused a fatal accident but there were no witnesses – would you confess? Or would you stay silent?

It's been five years since former jockey Mark Presley kept quiet about the hit-and-run crash that left a beautiful young woman dead. But when his wife is killed in an accident with cruel echoes of that tragedy, it seems that justice has come calling. A broken man, he is driven by grief to clear his conscience.

The truth is about to come out. Or is it? Mark has nothing left to lose. But others have plenty – and by confessing, he will implicate them all. In the world of flat racing everything rides on reputation, and some people will do anything to keep theirs intact. *Anything*. Even murder . . .

Acclaim for John Francome's racing thrillers:

'Thrills to the final furlong' *Daily Express*

'The story races along . . . Realistic enough to excite a confirmed non-racegoer' *Scotsman*

'Teases to the very end' *Country Life*

978 0 7553 3727 9

headline

Free Fall

John Francome

Like all jockeys, Pat Vincent has ambitions to win big races and make himself wealthy. But when Pat realises his career isn't going anywhere he devises a brilliant scam to fulfil his dreams. Though guaranteed to make him rich, it is also certain to land him in prison if he gets caught.

Pat's girlfriend Zoe is an up-and-coming jockey. A talented rider, she has a chance of becoming champion apprentice, if she's not sidetracked by the disaster of her sister Harriet's unhappy marriage.

Along the crumbling cliffs of Somerset, a man walks his dog. Every day Andy Burns – Pat's partner-in-crime, Harriet's tortured husband – wrestles with the demons that haunt his life. But Andy would be better off keeping his thoughts on the ground – it's a long way down to the beach below . . .

Acclaim for John Francome's racing thrillers:

'Francome provides a vivid panorama of the racing world . . . and handles the story's twist deftly' *The Times*

'Curiosity and clever writing will compel you to keep reading this tough and torrid tale . . . a fun read' *Horse & Hound*

'Thrills, twists and turns on and off the racecourse' *Irish Independent*

978 0 7553 2695 2

headline

Now you can buy any of these other bestselling
books by **John Francome** from your bookshop
or *direct from his publisher*.

FREE P&P AND UK DELIVERY
(Overseas and Ireland £3.50 per book)

Final Breath	£6.99
Dark Horse	£6.99
Free Fall	£7.99
Cover Up	£7.99
Back Hander	£7.99
Stalking Horse	£7.99
Inside Track	£7.99
Dead Weight	£6.99
Lifeline	£6.99
Tip Off	£6.99
Safe Bet	£6.99
High Flyer	£6.99
False Start	£6.99
Dead Ringer	£6.99
Break Neck	£6.99
Outsider	£6.99
Stud Poker	£6.99
Stone Cold	£6.99

TO ORDER SIMPLY CALL THIS NUMBER

01235 400 414

or visit our website: www.headline.co.uk

Prices and availability subject to change without notice.